D0650083

THE YEAR OF NEEDY GIRLS

PATRICIA A. SMITH

KAYLIE JONES BOOKS

This is a work of fiction. All names, characters, places, and incidents are a product of the author's imagination. Any resemblance to real events or persons, living or dead, is entirely coincidental.

Published by Akashic Books
©2017 Patricia A. Smith

ISBN: 978-1-61775-487-6
Library of Congress Control Number: 2016935225

First printing

Kaylie Jones Books
www.kayliejonesbooks.com

Akashic Books
Twitter: @AkashicBooks
Facebook: AkashicBooks
E-mail: info@akashicbooks.com
Website: www.akashicbooks.com

ALSO AVAILABLE FROM KAYLIE JONES BOOKS

All Waiting Is Long
by Barbara J. Taylor

Sing in the Morning, Cry at Night
by Barbara J. Taylor

Unmentionables
by Laurie Loewenstein

Foamers
by Justin Kassab

Strays
by Justin Kassab

Starve the Vulture
by Jason Carney

The Love Book
by Nina Solomon

We Are All Crew
by Bill Landauer

Little Beasts
by Matthew McGevna

Some Go Hungry
by J. Patrick Redmond

To all my students

PROLOGUE

AUGUST

The air, electric, buzzes and hums. It's the end of August. One of those humid, still Saturdays, the city empty, or holding its breath.

East of the river, near the abandoned textile mill and the old shoe warehouse, Leo Rivera rides his bicycle, a ten-speed hand-me-down from his brothers. He pays no mind to the heat. Leo stands and pumps past a vacant lot, one of several in his neighborhood, littered with broken glass that sparkles in the sun. Tufts of stiff, burnt grass poke though cracks in the concrete, and red plastic milk crates sit overturned and empty in the lot, waiting for the men who will gather there later to drink beer and listen to the game. Through the opened window of a shingled brown triple-decker, he hears Portuguese, the same radio station his mother listens to, the same one that will broadcast the soccer match this afternoon, Brazil versus Chile.

Leo likes soccer but unlike his brothers, he prefers baseball. Best of all, he likes riding his bike. He pedals hard past the chain-link fence of his school, Most Precious Blood Elementary—MPB they all call it—and the hot tarred blacktop where he will be having recess again in a few short days. He whizzes past Most Precious Blood Church and the white sign that advertises Wednesday-night Bingo in the parish hall next door. His grandmother is a regular. She wins, but not big, not enough to buy him a new bike, which he wants more than anything, which he *covets*. He doesn't covet anyone else's bike, just a Trek he has seen advertised in a magazine, but he knows that wanting things and praying for them is bad. Greed, the MPB Sisters say, is a sin. Not a mortal one, like killing, but a venial one, a misdemeanor. Leo tries to avoid wanting the bike outright because he doesn't like to disappoint the Sisters at MPB, but worst of all, he doesn't like disappointing his mother.

His mother tells him that he is her pride and joy. The One Born in America. Does he know how lucky he is to be living in a country where his father can get decent work and he and his brothers can go to good schools? He must thank God for America, his mother tells him. Every night. He must pray and thank God for sending them all to this good country.

The American boy doesn't know any other country. He hears the stories and he thinks he is the luckiest of all not to know anything but America, this city, this neighborhood where he goes to school and plays baseball, this land of shiny bicycles. At night, when he is saying his prayers, always thanking God for America, Leo slips and tries to make deals about how he will help his mother and how he will do all his homework if he can only get that Trek for his birthday. His birthday isn't for weeks, but he is thinking about it now, riding past the library, past the empty Little League field with the backstop halfway torn down, past the mechanic shop where Mickey, his next-door neighbor, works part-time. Mickey is almost a friend. He's much older, but he helps Leo with his bike, lubes the chain for him or replaces it outright like he did at the beginning of summer. Leo is thinking of his birthday and how much he would like that Trek to ride to school and show his friends. He won't even mind the helmet his mother makes him wear. He won't complain ever about the helmet, he promises God.

So when Leo coasts down the sidewalk toward his grandmother's house, a white triple-decker surrounded by a chain-link fence, and Mickey is waiting, sitting in the passenger seat of a car alongside the curb, engine still running, Leo is only thinking of his Trek, seeing himself on the first day of school, riding to MPB on the shiny bike. He isn't thinking how strange it is that Mickey is here waiting for him. No, he is thinking only of his birthday and the way it will be when his mother leads him to the dining room.

Mickey calls, "Leo!" out the car window and tells him to hop in. In the driver's seat, a man Leo doesn't recognize flicks his cigarette butt onto the sidewalk, where it lands next to Leo's sneaker. Mickey says he's found the bike. He will buy it if it's the one Leo wants. Mickey can't remember if it's a Trek or not—he thinks it is. It'll just take a second—he's seen the bike in a shop downtown and it isn't too expensive. If they go right now, if Leo will just get in the car and . . . it'll just take a minute, his grandmother won't even know he's gone—she doesn't even know he's here yet—then Mickey'll know whether or not it's the bike to buy for Leo's birthday. They'll bring him right back, they promise.

So his grandmother won't worry, they put his Schwinn in the trunk. "If she sees the bike lying in the yard, we don't want her wondering where you are, do we?" Mickey says.

Leo agrees and climbs in the backseat.

Mickey's friend, the driver, smiles in the rearview mirror. "You like bikes, huh?"

This is too good to be true. This is maybe some crazy dream.

PART ONE

SEPTEMBER

CHAPTER ONE

AT SEVEN THIRTY, WITH SJ STILL ASLEEP, Deirdre Murphy left the house for school. She walked side streets shaded by trees in their glory—pale autumn reds, yellows the color of honey. She scuffed through piles of leaves, each whoosh a reminder of every other autumn and every other beginning of the school year, the only way Deirdre knew how to mark time. She kept track of events based on the girls she taught: the drama queens, the freaks, the year they all were brilliant. This year, Deirdre could already tell after a week of classes, was the year of needy girls.

Each house that Deirdre passed, she tried on. These were not houses meant for her, with their mansard roofs, turrets, and gables. They were dream houses only, forever inaccessible. Still, she pictured herself making coffee in that one. Eating breakfast on the porch of this one. Working in the garden, pulling weeds after school. She imagined herself alone in the houses, NPR on the radio while she cooked dinners with ingredients she grew herself. In Deirdre's mind, the interiors of the houses were tidy and looked like the magazine pictures she flipped through in the grocery store check-out line. Artfully draped afghans. Throw pillows just so. Old books piled alongside the fireplace—dust free, all of it. The pictures, so sharp and real they made her ache with longing, became fuzzy if she tried to include SJ. Then the images slipped away and she was back on the outside looking in.

Seventy September degrees. Blue, blue sky. Who could tell that just days before, Hurricane Rita had blown through, canceling school? Or that over in the East End, the Rivera family was mourning their missing child? Outside, the city was moving. Men and women, courier bags slung over their shoulders, hurried toward the train station to catch the commuter rail into Boston. Deirdre could tell if she was running late by the location where she crossed paths with the woman from Hanley's Hardware Store, where she and SJ had just bought their first power drill. Every day this past week, the woman, stout and square with a kerchief tied over her stiff, beauty-parlor hairdo, smiled and waved good morning to Deirdre. A steady stream of familiar cars crawled by on the street, the carpool brigade on its way to Brandywine Academy.

An institution in town, Brandywine was in many ways a typical private school—small with a kind of clubby feel about it, catering to the more prominent families in Bradley, Massachusetts—with girls whose last names were Saltonstall, Hallowell, Conant, Fitzgerald. Except for the fact that it was surrounded by blacktop and a parking lot, Brandywine could be mistaken for another of the larger houses in the neighborhood. But there it was, next door to the Blue Moon Café, the favorite hangout of Brandywine parents, the ones who didn't work or who drove the carpools in the mornings and afternoons. On the front door of the Blue Moon, Leo Rivera's face fluttered from a flier with taped corners. Smiling, in that blue Red Sox cap. Deirdre pushed the door open, breathing in freshly ground coffee, rich, buttery croissants.

Frances Worthington and Evelyn Moore, the mothers of Deirdre's two neediest sophomores, sat huddled at a table off to the side and toward the rear. Frances, with her back to Deirdre, seemed to be doing the talking. Elbows bent at her sides, she twirled manicured hands in the air. Frances was the president of the board at Brandywine and her husband, a child psychologist, enjoyed a successful private practice. He was pretty famous and appeared from time to time on morning talk shows. Around town, word was that he was having an affair—the former babysitter, a girl closer in age to his own daughter—but the talk shows never mentioned that.

Evelyn sat across from Frances, nodding. Her small round face bobbed to the rhythm of Frances's hand motions. Evelyn glanced briefly up toward the door, but Deirdre looked away in time, fumbled in her backpack for the money she already gripped in her other fist.

"May I help you?"

"Um, yes, a decaf latte," Deirdre said. "Skim." She felt her face grow hot as if the counter girl knew what Deirdre was doing, as if she had been caught in a lie. The girl didn't show any emotion even though Deirdre was one of her regular customers, coming in most days before school.

Deirdre moved away from the register to wait for her latte. She looked around at the art hanging on the walls, art that changed with some regularity, most of it modern and urgent-looking, as if the artists heaved it onto the canvases in one violent push. Some of the paintings still looked wet.

"Yoo hoo! Deirdre?" Evelyn Moore half-stood, hovering over her chair, waving with her fingertips.

Hi, Deirdre mouthed, and waved back.

Frances turned and looked over her shoulder, smiled a gracious lipstick smile, the kind she learned how to do as president of the board, the kind the counter help would never attempt. "Deirdre." That smile again. "How nice to see you," Frances said.

Nice. Deirdre glanced at her watch and frowned, the comic strip balloon above her head saying, *Oh, look how late it is. I've got to go.*

Evelyn said, "I was hoping I might run into you this morning."

Uh-oh. That meant kid trouble. "Is everything okay with Lydia?" Deirdre crossed the café to their table.

Evelyn brushed her frosted hair behind her ears and tugged her cheery blue sweater over the tops of her corduroys. "I bet you didn't know you were the topic of conversation at our dinner table," Evelyn said. "Ev-ery night." Evelyn took a sip of her coffee and smiled, lipstick-less, at Deirdre. "You are a big hit."

Frances tapped her manicured nails on the café table, wrapped her other fingers around her coffee cup.

"Oh, thanks," Deirdre said. "I guess." She laughed, glancing first at Evelyn and then at Frances. Frances said nothing, shrugged her eyebrows, and took another sip of coffee.

"It's true," Evelyn said, motioning to Frances. "Tell her. Anna's the same way," she said.

Frances blushed, ever so slightly. Her lips parted and she frowned. Turning back to Deirdre, she said, "The girls *do* like you. There's no doubt about that."

"Well, that's nice to hear," Deirdre said, picking up her latte and readjusting her backpack.

"Finally," Evelyn said, "a teacher who understands our girls. *I* think it's great."

Deirdre took a step away from the table.

"Oh, and Lydia can't wait for Friday," Evelyn said, talking with her hands. "She is so impressed with the way you insist they learn about Africa. *French isn't just spoken in France, Mother,* she says to me. *It's spoken in West Africa and Canada and even Vietnam.*"

At that, Frances rolled her eyes. "Vietnam, honestly," she said. "The next thing, you'll be wanting to take our girls *there*."

Deirdre laughed. "Oh no," she said. "I can't imagine that." She looked at her watch. "I should be going. Lots to do before school starts."

Outside, Deirdre squinted in the sunshine. Brandywine's parking lot was nearly full, and the long line of cars inched their way down the street to the drop-off area. The girls gathered in groups on the blacktop. They wore new outfits, carried shiny backpacks and lunch boxes. It was a scene replicated in schoolyards everywhere, even across town at Most Precious Blood Elementary. But this year amidst all the newness, the haircuts and outfits, the resolutions of a few seniors to *make something of this year*; amidst the freshmen who were officially high schoolers and important members of the upper school; amidst the braces and eye shadow, the ear piercings and growth spurts; and even down amidst the littlest ones with shiny Mary Janes and hopeful expectations about their new teachers, there were reminders that this year, things were different. Because a child was missing. And though Leo Rivera was not one of *theirs*, he was still part of the community.

Deirdre's classroom was covered with photographs she had taken during all her trips to Paris and the south of France, trips that usually included students. Each time she went, she collected more things—train schedules, pages from hotel phone books, menus, copies of her own restaurant bills, maps of Paris—she saved everything. These objects made the language come alive for her students in a way no textbook could. When her students practiced ordering food, they used real menus. When they learned to tell time, they asked questions with train schedules. Deirdre had a prop for any kind of dramatic situation. She was intent on bringing the real world into her classroom.

This morning, Deirdre had to finalize the plans for her Friday field trip to an African art gallery, a new one, just opened in the East End. She'd had to fight for this trip. Since Leo Rivera's disappearance, parents weren't excited to let their daughters venture to the East End, even for a supervised class field trip. The exhibit at the gallery featured the Dogon, a region and people in Mali, known especially for their intricately carved wooden doors. The Dogon were cliff dwellers, still even today, and Deirdre wanted to show her students firsthand examples of their impressive artwork. She'd had to convince Martin Loring that the kids would be strictly supervised and she'd had to convince the girls that nothing awful would happen to them.

Deirdre dumped her backpack and headed to the office to pick up her signed field trip forms.

"Morning, Lil."

Lil worked in the front office. Had been there since the day the school opened. Technically, she was an administrative assistant, but that title didn't do her justice. Lil ran the school. When teachers needed something, they came to Lil. When parents had requests, they called Lil. Martin Loring was the headmaster, but Lil did all the work.

"Lil, I'm looking for those field trip forms? The ones for Friday?"

The phone rang. Lil held up her index finger. "Brandywine Academy," she sang into the phone. On those rare days when Lil was sick, the school didn't run as smoothly. Audiovisual requests went unfilled. Carpool notices didn't make it into the right hands. And Martin Loring went into overdrive, overcompensating for being without Lil to tell him what to do. Now that she was nearing sixty, everyone was afraid that Lil might retire soon, and Brandywine without her didn't seem possible. It remained an unspoken fear that when Lil went, Brandywine would close down.

"Hey," Forest Macomber strolled in, carrying a pile of books over to the photocopy machine. He looked over his shoulder. "Weird they found that kid, huh?"

"What?" Deirdre turned to Lil and mouthed, *I'll be right back.* She followed Forest into the faculty workroom. "When?"

Forest fanned open a copy of *Best American Short Stories* facedown on the machine. "Jeez, where've you been? It was all over the news last night. *And* this morning."

"Where'd they find him?"

Forest punched in the number of copies. A piece of paper emerged looking like a crumpled fan. "Shit. This thing jams every time I need it." He stopped his copies and opened the front of the machine.

"It's bad, isn't it?" Deirdre shifted her weight.

"Yep," he said. "It's bad. Found him at the bottom of the river, in a plastic container."

"Oh God." Deirdre hoped her students hadn't heard yet. They would want to talk about it. All week, every day since school started, somebody brought up Leo Rivera. The newspapers covered it daily on the front page and then in the City section, a kind of lurid human interest story, like a bad soap opera. Each night on the news, there was Leo Rivera's face, a sweet smiling boy in his baseball cap.

Forest pressed the red lever, lifted the top of the photocopying machine, and pulled out the piece of stuck paper. He crumpled it up and threw it in the trash. "I need these first period," he said and looked at the clock. "Shit." He slammed the top down and looked at Deirdre. "I guess he'd been dead awhile," Forest continued. He turned back to the machine and started copying again. "That poor mother. She looked *awful*."

"Well, can you even imagine? Your ten-year-old kid disappears like that without a trace, and they find him in the *river!* In a *container!*"

Forest gathered his collated copies and switched books. He shook his head. "Makes you wonder."

The bell rang and there it was, the chaos of the day erupting. Shrill girl voices and high-pitched squeals. Little bodies running pell-mell toward the first and second grade classrooms.

Forest swore again. "Listen, Deird," he said. Only Forest and her brother Paul could get away with calling her that. "Would you mind . . . ?"

Deirdre waved him away. "Don't worry about it," she said. "I'll keep an eye on the lovelies." With that, she turned and walked back through the office. Little kids crowded around Lil's desk, their pudgy hands holding out crumpled envelopes with money for the Fall Supper or raffle tickets or maybe even tuition payments. It was amazing what parents entrusted their children with. Deirdre tousled the hair on one little girl. Savannah, she thought her name was.

"Hey," the girl said and turned, grinning a toothless grin, cheeks dotted with brownish freckles. Deirdre smiled back.

The others clamored and waved their envelopes at Lil. "Hold, please!" she said into the telephone. "Deirdre?" Lil flashed a stack of papers held together with a paper clip.

Deirdre reached over the little-kid heads and took her field trip forms. She climbed the stairs and thought about Leo Rivera's mother. How do you survive something like that?

In Deirdre's room, the students unloaded backpacks into their lockers.

"Morning, everyone," she said and walked to unlock

and open the door between her room and Forest's. The girls stood huddled around Morgan Abernathy, one of the most popular tenth-graders.

"Hey, girls!" Deirdre yelled over to them from the doorway. "Mr. Macomber is on his way up, okay? Behave yourselves."

The little group broke apart and eight or nine faces turned to look at Deirdre. Morgan emerged from the center. "Did you hear about the Rivera kid?" she asked, walking in long, even strides. Her jeans sat just below her hips, belted. "How they found him?" Morgan's blond hair was cut short, a Charlize Theron look-alike.

"Yes," Deirdre said, taking a deep breath. "I did."

"What?" Lydia Moore walked up behind Deirdre.

"Saw your mom this morning," Deirdre said, turning to Lydia. "In the Blue Moon."

Lydia rolled her eyes and draped herself over Deirdre's shoulder.

"Don't be such a lezzie, Moore-head." Morgan rolled her eyes and crossed her arms.

"What?" Deirdre said. "Morgan, what did you say?"

"Sorry. But I mean—" she gestured to Lydia, who hadn't moved, "it's gross."

Deirdre shook Lydia off her shoulders.

"It isn't *gross*," Lydia responded, rolling her eyes.

"Whatever." Morgan sauntered back across the room. Her long-sleeved T-shirt just reached the top of her jeans and she left behind the clean smell of Tide laundry detergent and a sweet, sharp perfume.

Lydia leaned in closer to Deirdre. "My mother says her mother is a real jerk."

"Lydia!" Deirdre frowned. She should have said something to Morgan. She'd had the perfect teachable moment and she'd let it pass. The girls in Deirdre's homeroom sat grouped on top of the desks or leaning against the lockers. Deirdre glanced around. "Where's Anna?"

"Field hockey meeting. Remember?"

Deirdre didn't but said she did. She watched Lydia skip over to one of the groups and slide up on a desk next to Hilary, lean in, and rest her head on Hilary's shoulder. They were beautiful girls. Lydia, with that long, shiny hair and brown eyes. And Hilary. She had an athlete's body, an effortless beauty. Natural blond curls framed her face. Clear, creamy skin. Even in the dead of winter, Hilary liked to wear sleeveless sweaters. Deirdre had joked with Forest once that it ought to be against the dress code, girls with arms like that wearing sleeveless tops.

Forest, out of breath, cut through Deirdre's room to his, arms full of books and photocopies. "Hey, thanks. I owe you one."

"Yeah, right," Deirdre said. The girls were used to Forest's scatterbrained ways. They adored him. He always managed to train one of his homeroom girls to take attendance.

Deirdre shut the door between the two rooms and turned back to her own class. She watched the girls laugh, talk about their TV shows, their homework. They seemed so comfortable with each other, so at ease in their own bodies, definitely not the way Deirdre felt about herself back when she was fourteen and fifteen. Even now, the girls had a way of making Deirdre feel self-conscious. They had a sense of how to wear their clothes that Deirdre was convinced came only with a private school education. Her students, all of them, had a kind of clear-skinned, Breck Girl confidence that she had always lacked. And no matter how hard they tried, to Deirdre, they still looked like rich kids.

This trip to the gallery would be an eye-opener for them, she thought with satisfaction. Deirdre unclipped the field trip forms and flipped through them. Seventeen, eigh-

teen, nineteen. She counted again. Nineteen. Which one
was missing? She put each form on her desk and read the
names. Hilary. Lydia. Even Morgan. She looked again. They
were all there, all her tenth-graders, except for Anna. Left
stuck on the last form, a yellow Post-it with Martin Loring's
handwriting, doodles from a phone conversation—*D. Murphy*
circled in black pen.

THE GIRLS

The girls acted as if they themselves had known the murdered boy, had babysat for him, though of course none of them had. None of them would have ventured into Leo Rivera's neighborhood; their mothers wouldn't have allowed it, wouldn't have wanted their daughters parking the BMW on the street. The Volvo might have been okay, especially an older model—it wasn't the type anyone wanted to steal, not in that neighborhood—but the girls would still have had to walk alone on darkened streets. For all the mothers knew, their daughters might be alone in houses without security systems, houses that, according to the nightly news, got broken into with some regularity. No, it was certain that none of the girls had babysat for Leo Rivera.

They might have babysat for boys who *looked* like him, ten-year-olds with gangly arms, scarred knees, and sharp elbows. After the news of Leo's murder broke, the girls might have inexplicably teared up the first time they babysat their charges, unconsciously making the connection between the dead boy and this living one, a boy they had previously felt neutral toward but now they couldn't help but hold and kiss on the top of his sweaty head because all they could see when they looked at him was Leo Rivera, his body buried in a container of lime, skin dissolved like an animal carcass.

The girls think of the boys they know—their brothers,

boys in the neighborhood, the ones they babysit—as vulnerable. The way the boys scratch at their mosquito bites and pick at their scabs. The way their pants hang when they don't wear a belt, laces straggling from worn-out sneakers. Even the way the boys swagger onto the baseball field and nonchalantly toss gloves onto the bench makes the girls catch their breath and wonder at the flutter they feel in their chests. They wouldn't know how to name what they're feeling, wouldn't yet understand that now, every boy in town is a stand-in for Leo Rivera. The girls might even worry that what they are feeling isn't normal, some mixture of maternal, big-sisterly affection and longing, some weird form of desire to which, if they were Catholic, they would have to confess.

Except they wouldn't. Even in Confession, the Catholic girls can't admit that what they feel for someone else's brother might be—they can't even whisper it, can't let their minds think it—might be *sexual,* might have the least bit of connection to that *pervert*, that monster who molested and then killed Leo Rivera.

Anna Worthington's mother refused to discuss it. When Sam started wetting the bed, an old problem their mother thought they had conquered, only Anna thought there might be a good reason. Anna could point out that Leo and Sam were on the same Little League team, the Wildcats, and that it was only normal for Sam to wonder if what had happened to Leo could happen to him too. If their mother would only talk to other Wildcats moms, she might find out that their sons had also revived or, in some cases, started questionable behaviors—another couple of bed-wetters and one boy, Eli, a friend of Sam's, had even gone back to needing a nightlight.

CHAPTER TWO

SJ PULLED UP TO THE INTERSECTION in front of the library. A police cruiser, blue light spinning, idled at the curb. SJ had received two tickets for sneaking through yellow lights at this very intersection. She flicked on her left blinker, glanced over at the guilty driver—a black kid (no one she knew)—and took a left-hand turn into the employee parking lot.

"Thank God, thank God!" Like an apparition, Florence emerged from the tall green bushes that lined the perimeter of the stone-faced library and hurried toward SJ's car. Florence waddled a little, like a penguin, in her pumps.

"Florence, were you *hiding*?" SJ laughed, then rolled up her window. She got out of the car and pulled her tote bag from the backseat of the Honda. "What's going on? What are you doing?"

Florence seemed startled. She clutched the brooch at the nape of her neck. Another scrimshaw. For all of SJ's seven years at the library, Florence had been writing a book about the wives of whaling captains. Even during SJ's job interview, Florence had sneaked in several references to her whaling obsession. How, SJ couldn't remember anymore. But half-kidding, SJ had said then, "Maybe in a previous life, you *were* the wife of a whaling captain. Or the captain, even." Florence had seemed to like that. She had offered the job to SJ on the spot.

"You've heard, haven't you?" Florence said now to SJ in the library parking lot, the sun directly overhead and Indian-summer warm.

SJ locked her car. "What?" she asked.

"They found the Rivera boy."

SJ stuffed her keys into the pocket of her black jeans.

"They found him . . ." Florence fiddled with her scrimshaw.

"Dead?" By this time—two full weeks after he'd disappeared—no one really expected to find the boy alive. Of course he was dead. But you still hoped.

Florence held up her hand. "They found him in the river. You didn't hear? It was all they talked about on the news last night. And this morning. It's more horrible than horrible . . ."

"Oh God."

"Yes, terrible." Florence stopped walking. "SJ, the police have been around, asking questions." She slid her brooch back and forth along its pin. She folded her arms.

"And . . . they think, what, that we have a clue? *Do* we have a clue?" SJ put down her tote bag and stood facing Florence. Leo Rivera was a neighborhood kid. He came into the library from time to time. Yes, SJ had seen Leo in the library before, but she didn't know him, not the way she knew some of the other kids, the regulars. She didn't remember the last time she had seen him—probably sometime over the summer, before school started back up again. SJ had told all this to the police officers who'd come around immediately after the boy disappeared.

"SJ, listen. That guy, Mickey . . . ?"

"My student Mickey?"

"Him, yes. I think he might be involved."

"What?" Ever since SJ had suggested to Florence that she might have been a whaling captain in another life—that

she might have *had* another life—Florence swore she had
psychic abilities, that she knew things.

Florence shook her head. "Sara Jane, listen to me. I don't
know. They had questions about him. Who he was, what he
did here at the library. I said *you* knew him, not me. They
came in again this morning, when the library opened. I told
them you didn't come in until the afternoon."

SJ shielded the sun from her eyes.

"I told them he'd be in later today and they seemed to
like that. Now, if there's something to this, we might be in
a whole lot of trouble, letting him hang around the library
like we've been doing."

"Hang around? He's learning to read, for God's sake.
Isn't that what we do here in the library? Help people to
read?"

Kids in this neighborhood got no breaks. You always
heard on TV about things going on in the East End—
break-ins, shootings. ("Jeez, SJ," Deirdre would say, "we
need to find you a new job.") SJ looked at Florence here
in the sunlight, a short, middle-aged white woman whose
colored hair was professionally styled at least every three
weeks, whose husband retired early from a banking career.
Florence, in her Evan Picone suits and crisp Talbots dresses.
Her scrimshaws and pumps.

But this was Florence. Her *friend*. Still, sometimes SJ
didn't think that Florence had a clue about the real world.
Florence ran the library. Had been its director for over seventeen years now. She hadn't left when things got rougher
in this part of town. She never requested a transfer. Florence
began beeping her car secure—something that SJ found
ridiculous and somehow offensive—but Florence didn't
quit her job. She kept working at this library in this bad
part of town. Why couldn't SJ admit that maybe Florence
knew more than she gave her credit for? Why couldn't SJ

consider that Florence might have some words of wisdom about things other than relationships? Or that maybe Florence cared about this neighborhood as much as SJ did?

"So, what do we do?" SJ looked at the ground, pushed gravel around with her foot. "Should I cancel his tutoring sessions? What?"

"Listen to me." Florence took hold of SJ's shoulders. "If those detectives come in looking for him, we will let them. If he . . . that man . . . Mickey . . . is involved in this terrible, terrible murder, we will want him to be caught. Won't we?"

SJ looked at Florence. Those eyes, warm pools of blue-gray, soft and deep. Florence seemed to be reading SJ's face, looking for a way in, a way to make her understand. She gave SJ a little squeeze and removed her hands. In the distance, a siren wailed.

"Let's go," Florence said.

Mickey. Involved in a murder. Do child killers want to learn to read? Do they look awestruck when they manage whole sentences on their own?

"This is crazy." SJ lifted her tote bag onto her shoulder and climbed the steps. At the top, she opened the door and paused, turned back around to Florence. "Does he seem like a killer to you?" She wanted to say, *Do I look like someone who would mistake a murderer for a nice person?*

Florence shrugged. "Come on, SJ. Let's go inside. You're already late."

When Mickey Gilberto had first sauntered into the library the day after Labor Day in a blue mechanic's uniform, SJ recognized him immediately.

"I know you," she had said. "You moved us in."

Mickey looked blank.

"The green house? Lime green, over on the west side?"

"Oh yeah," he smiled. "That house. Christ, I never seen a

house that color before." He laughed. SJ couldn't tell whether or not he was making fun. "It's a great place, though . . . inside," Mickey added. "You own it, right?"

"Yes," SJ said. "We own it."

"You and the other girl . . . you own it together?"

This was one of those questions that took SJ by surprise and that she didn't know how to handle. It struck her as a personal question, crossing some invisible boundary or at least teetering over one. She found herself blushing. "Yes," she said, "we own it together."

"So, you're a couple?"

And now, the result of having answered the first personal question, SJ was in an awkward position. Now SJ was in a place she didn't want to be. Not that her relationship with Deirdre was secret, definitely not. The question wasn't phrased with any particular tone, no edge that SJ could discern, but what was he after? Was he making conversation, or was he fishing? The question—*you're a couple?*—made SJ a little suspicious, unsure of his motives. She didn't know how to answer. She didn't want to seem embarrassed or secretive but you had to be careful. You had to at least *wonder* if this guy was a nut case.

"Hey," Mickey said, taking a couple of steps back from the front desk, hands up, "whatever. That's cool if you are, cool if you aren't. Whatever floats your boat, you know what I'm saying? I got nothing against gays."

SJ fiddled with the pencils in the holder on the front desk and tried not to seem flustered. "I'm afraid I've forgotten your name." She could feel the skin burning on her neck and along her jawbone.

"Mickey," he said, sticking out his hand. "Mickey Gilberto."

Now SJ remembered. She recalled the other mover, the older guy, calling out to Mickey on the sidewalk in gruff, accented English. She remembered Deirdre yelling from the bathroom later that night, her mouth full of toothpaste, "Didn't that Mickey guy weird you out?" and SJ saying truthfully that she hadn't noticed anything strange about him. Here, with Mickey right in front of her, SJ decided that Deirdre had disliked him because of his bad skin and because he looked poor. SJ couldn't admit to herself that maybe she had mistrusted Mickey's motives for the very same reasons. "Yes," SJ said now, "Mickey, that's right. I'm SJ." She shook his hand. "So, you're a mover and a mechanic?" she asked, pointing to his uniform, *Bob's* embroidered in red on his breast pocket.

"Yeah. Extra money, you know—something to keep me out of trouble on weekends." He grinned.

Mickey had a lazy way of talking and when words came out of his mouth, they sounded droopy and thick. SJ caught herself wondering if he was high but pushed the thought out of her mind. He had a lazy stance too, as if his limbs weren't quite attached to the rest of his body. At any minute, it seemed to SJ, his legs might buckle beneath him.

Mickey had come to the library, he said, to learn to read. He hadn't ever learned correctly, he told SJ. Hadn't ever really bothered. "It wasn't like I was the best at school, you know what I'm saying?"

SJ could see him: A scrawny kid, with the kind of face that looked like trouble. A wise guy. She imagined him as a prankster maybe, the kind of kid who spent too much time in detention but who wasn't *bad,* really. Mischievous. An imp.

SJ told Mickey about the adult literacy program the library offered. She pulled out a brochure from her top drawer. "The Wilson Reading System. It's great. Really works. The adult branch offers it," she said. "It's free," she added when he seemed to hesitate.

Mickey said that he would rather work one-on-one with a tutor, that he had never been much of a joiner of groups.

"Can I ask what made you decide now to learn? Are you thinking about going back to school, getting another job . . . ?"

"Nah," Mickey said. "It's hard to explain. I guess I just want to, you know, better myself?" He shifted his weight uncomfortably from one foot to the other.

Maybe this was the reason, without knowing it, that SJ had opted to become a librarian—because she had an unwavering faith in the power of books. She believed that reading could save lives. She knew it had saved her own, growing up with parents who didn't understand her, who didn't *want* her, really. Cold and distant, they had treated her like a detail to be managed, like the other tasks they successfully accomplished in their busy world of law and finance. SJ's parents had hired excellent au pairs and had sent SJ to the best summer camps. They made sure her schools were top-notch. Maybe this was the reason, too, that SJ had such disdain for Deirdre's students at Brandywine—because she knew them all too well. She hadn't liked them back when she was one of them, and she didn't like them now.

"I'm trained," SJ said after a moment. "I could teach you."

Mickey brightened. "Yeah?"

"It's a big commitment. Three times a week minimum."

Mickey nodded. "After work. I can do it. If . . . if that's all right. Can we start tomorrow?"

The next day, Mickey showed up fifteen minutes early. He arrived, clean-shaven, hair wet and combed back off his head. Jeans and an ironed white T-shirt hung on his skinny frame.

SJ glanced at the clock. "You're early. I've got a few things to finish here first." She held up the papers in her hands and peeked over at the children grouped around books at two round tables.

"No biggie," Mickey said, folding and unfolding his arms. "I'll just wait over here." He pulled out one of the tiny chairs made for small children and sat. His body bent in half like a crane's. "Whoa," he said. One of the little boys looked up and laughed.

SJ pointed to the rack on the wall. "There are magazines," she said. "Help yourself. And bigger chairs." She pointed to the tables in the back. "We'll meet back there."

From over the top of her computer, SJ watched him. He was like a giant in the land of little people, loping past the pair of shiny heads—Isabella and Rosie—hunched together over *Where's Waldo?* at one table, and the bodies of little boys who couldn't sit still, their feet and hands in perpetual motion, one with the chair tipped back on its hind legs, the other on his knees, rocking forward in his chair, and the third half-sprawled across the table, all of them reading *Captain Underpants*, their favorite. These were the library regulars and no matter how many times SJ lectured the boys about sitting in the chairs the way they were meant to be sat in, Freddie rocked, Marco sprawled, and Paulo knelt and straddled. All of them were good kids and mostly SJ left them alone. She helped them find new books and gave them ideas for their school projects when they asked. The boys were fourth-graders; Isabella and Rosie were a year younger.

SJ watched Mickey scan the magazines on the wall, pick up a WWF publication, and hunker down in a chair, body bent in half, knees jutting out, back hunched. He flipped a few pages, put the magazine back, picked another. *People*. Mostly, he seemed to be looking at the pictures. SJ hadn't told Mickey that he was her first student. She had recently received her certification, and while she was eager to begin working with a real person, she suddenly had her doubts. Somehow all the practice and the theory seemed like hocus pocus with someone like Mickey. Would he tolerate the tapping out of sounds and syllables? Would he have the patience? SJ watched him move his lips over a piece of text, frown, and stop. He went back again, used his finger to follow along, and mouthed each word. SJ thought she heard him trying to pronounce the words under his breath.

"You've got your work cut out for you," Florence murmured, coming up behind SJ. "He's trying to read *People*. *People*. What's that—a third grade reading level?"

"Just look at him. It's so sad."

"Listen, don't forget, we have that meeting at five thirty. We can't be late."

"Don't worry. Class is an hour, no more."

"One hour?"

"One hour, yes. Okay? Quit looking at me like that."

"You know what you're doing, right? What you're taking on?" Florence put down the stack of books she had been holding and wiggled her scrimshaw back and forth.

"Florence," SJ said, folding her arms, "I can do this. I didn't take a lunch break today, so I'm allowed."

"Allowed, of course you are allowed. That's not what I meant. Don't you think this guy needs more than an hour one-on-one with you? Don't you think he needs a class? *Structure*?"

"I told you, he doesn't like groups . . ."

"I know, I know. He isn't a joiner." Florence picked up her pile of books. "Five thirty," she said over her shoulder. "In the conference room."

SJ didn't want to insult Mickey. She half-wished she had insisted he sign up for the adult literacy course, but in the back of her mind she was also thinking that after working with him one-on-one for a few weeks, she might convince him that a class was what he needed. She would just get him started and up to the next level. SJ pushed the student reader and workbook over to Mickey. "I know this seems like a little kid book." She took a deep breath, tried to summon confidence. "But we have to start here. First, I need to assess your reading level. The program is intended for adults too," she had added, rushing her words together.

"All righty," Mickey had grinned sheepishly, sitting upright in his chair.

Now, SJ waited, uneasy, for Mickey to arrive for his lesson. What had Mickey said about wanting to learn to read? He hadn't really explained, had he? He had given SJ some vague excuse, some plausible reason, but nothing for why *now exactly* he had finally decided to learn to read. She shrugged off her worry and focused instead on the way his face lit up when he read his first two-syllable word and later, a whole sentence. No, she decided. They were wrong about Mickey. But she never thought to ask herself why the police might be interested in Mickey in the first place.

CHAPTER THREE

IF YOU GREW UP IN GLOUCESTER, Massachusetts, if you were Portuguese or Italian, your father fished. Deirdre and Paul's father commuted to Salem to make shoes and, before him, his father had come to Gloucester to work the granite, but when Deirdre and Paul were growing up, most of their neighbors fished. Or built boat parts. Or worked at Cape Pond Ice. Growing up in Gloucester, especially in the West End, you knew everyone's mother best. You knew women who, by and large, raised their children alone, their husbands away for days and sometimes months. Having a fisherman for a father was akin to having a father in the military—you didn't ever know if he was coming home. At Our Lady of Good Voyage, you were always praying for the fishermen along with local politicians and the president, but the fishermen were fathers whose kids you knew, kids in your class at St. Peter's. The kids at St. Peter's were usually of two types—the wild ones who came from families so big their parents never knew what the kids were up to, or the dutiful ones who helped out at home and didn't make their mothers worry.

It was weird, Deirdre had complained to Paul, wasn't it, that they had nothing to do with fish?

"Well, not *nothing*—we eat it," Paul had pointed out. They had been walking along the rocky edge of the beach on one of those early summer mornings when you could feel the heat pulsing behind the thin layer of clouds, the humidity threatening to vacuum-seal the city. From the harbor, the cawing of seagulls, the clanging of halyards, a boat's motor. Deirdre and Paul were taking one of their long walks, a precursor to their runs together, both of them opting for cross-country at Gloucester High. For Deirdre, running became a way to channel all her energy so she wouldn't explode. Even in seasons other than summer, she felt the sky threaten to give way, the town ready to swallow her whole. Boston was only thirty-some miles away, but you wouldn't know it from the way her classmates talked, some of them never venturing into the city at all. Her parents hardly ever made the trip.

At least fishing brought adventure. Who didn't want adventure?

Paul, ever the practical one even though he was younger, reminded Deirdre, "I'd rather have both my parents, wouldn't you?"

Gail Murphy, their mother, was grateful her husband worked in a factory and they never had to go through the drama the others faced. Take the Da Silvas who lived next door. A cod fisherman, Mr. Da Silva was gone more often than he was home, which meant that Maria, the oldest—Deirdre's age—enjoyed new clothes more than other kids, and her mother drove a car that worked.

But it also meant that Mrs. Da Silva drank.

Gail Murphy tried to help out. She brought over tuna noodle casserole, had Maria spend the night. She even watched the littlest ones on a few occasions—Manny, the baby, who lived with one continuous glob of snot hanging from his left nostril, and Gerald, just a year older, smart-mouthed even at three. There were two others in between

Gerald and Maria, a boy and a girl, Frankie and Delores, both of whom ended up getting killed by a drunk driver when they were in high school. Not that their getting killed had anything to do with their father's fishing, but still somehow you wondered if having a father around more often might have prevented some things. Gail thanked the Lord that Ed did factory work.

Everyone in town knew someone who didn't make it back. Sometimes, entire crews disappeared and there were all the funerals and memorials, the flag at the town hall perpetually at half-mast. By the time you were in elementary school, you were used to going to funerals, and on some level you understood that nothing lasts forever. You even knew that sometimes, young ones go first.

Families dealt with the stress in different ways. Mrs. Da Silva drank, and she was not alone. There were several divorces, even among families in St. Peter's and Our Lady of Good Voyage, where this wasn't supposed to be an option. Sometimes the mothers just couldn't take it anymore and hauled the kids away before their fathers even returned. There were affairs. In school, there were fights that the nuns did not condone but understood as the way the kids had to let off steam. The fights did not involve weapons, just fists and faces, black eyes and bloody lips.

It was a life that Deirdre and Paul were witness to but not exactly a part of, mostly because, as Deirdre pointed out, they had nothing to do with fish. Still, they lived in the midst of it, in a neighborhood of small clapboard houses, well-kept mostly, some with peeling paint or a Madonna on the half-shell, some with broken, rusty cars on cinder blocks in the front yard and a smattering of plastic toys strewn about. It was a life Deirdre vowed never to be a part of. She had counted the minutes until she could get away.

Chapter Four

Autumn meant field hockey. Cheering on the side-lines, yelling out the girls' names. You could be passionate about them here, wearing your Brandywine sweatshirt, school spirit on visible display. You could love the girls openly, a kind of parental love and pride that was acceptable.

When you were learning to be a teacher, taking graduate classes in methods, sitting in lectures about differentiation or the plight of the gifted child, no one talked about the most difficult thing—how you were going to love the kids you taught, how you might even love them inappropriately or want them for your own, how you had to learn not to resent the parents. No one facilitated a discussion about the possible disasters waiting to happen if you mistakenly forgot that you were the teacher and the kids were your students—not your children and not, God forbid, your friends. But it was sometimes difficult to remember this.

Deirdre couldn't talk about how she felt to anyone, not even SJ. Especially not SJ, who was already judgmental about the amount of time Deirdre spent at Brandywine, the hours she spent agonizing over the girls' private lives, which, SJ liked to remind her, were private.

"Do you have to go to *every* home game?" SJ often complained. "You do get to take time for yourself, you know."

But if Deirdre missed a game, then she might miss Anna's biggest goal and then she would feel terrible, like she
had let the girl down and missed an important moment in
her young life. She wanted the girls to take her seriously in
the classroom, she tried to explain to SJ, and if she showed
them that their lives mattered to her, they were more likely
to listen in class and learn.

The truth was, Deirdre loved attending the field hockey
games, the long autumn afternoons a kind of symphonic
lull in the middle of the city. The field, located a few miles
from Brandywine, did double duty. Used both for youth
soccer league as well as the Brandywine field hockey games,
it was surrounded by oaks and maples, and made you feel
as though you were not in Bradley with its factories and
triple-deckers but out in another part of the state, in one
of those picturesque New England towns with its own private school, the kind with glossy catalogs and a campus,
the kind of place with big town greens where festivals were
held and rich people retired, the kind of place in which the
West Enders pretended they all lived, forgetting about the
East End that was, in spite of their amnesia, part of Bradley.
Here at the games, Deirdre stood near the cluster of parents, mothers mostly, dressed in smart-looking outfits, all in
inappropriate footwear, heeled boots or cute slip-ons that
did not navigate dampened grass fields effectively. Their
hair, Deirdre noticed, always looked newly cut and styled,
smooth and shiny, not the mess that hers inevitably turned
into after a full day of teaching. Next to the mothers, she
felt unlovely, but she tried to reassure herself that no matter
what, the girls wanted her here and, in some cases, wanted
her here even more than they wanted their own mothers.

Secretly, Deirdre was thrilled when any of the girls
confided in her something they couldn't discuss with their
mothers, though she always encouraged them to bring it up

at home. "Your mother," she would insist to the girl sitting in front of her, wiping away tears, "she needs to know how you feel. You need to tell her." And when the girl would resist, would say something about how her mother just wouldn't understand, about how it was amazing that Ms. Murphy *did* understand, how it was awesome they had a teacher like her, who *got* them, then Deirdre felt the power she wielded and reveled in it, just the tiniest bit.

But here, at the first home field hockey game, Deirdre didn't feel special; she felt disheveled, inconsequential. She felt the way she had back in high school, always on the outside, wanting to be *in*.

"Deirdre?"

She turned.

"Or should I say Ms. Murphy? So nice of you to come cheer on the girls!" Evelyn Moore's smile seemed warm, genuine.

"I love coming to the games," Deirdre said. "Where's Lydia?"

"Rehearsal. They have an early fall concert this year." Evelyn adjusted her sunglasses.

"That's right. September 20? It's on my calendar."

Evelyn nodded. "She hopes they'll be ready." She rolled her eyes. "According to Lydia, the cellos are weak this year after losing those two seniors who were fantastic."

Deirdre agreed. It was rare to have such a strong cello section, in her limited experience with high school orchestras. Rare, too, in such a small school to have the orchestra they did have, a tribute to their teacher and director, Mrs. DeBesse, one of the original teachers. *Joan,* Mrs. DeBesse insisted the other teachers call her, but the younger ones, Deirdre included, couldn't bring themselves to drop *Mrs. DeBesse.*

"See you at the fall supper, I hope?" Evelyn smiled again

and turned to walk toward the group of mothers. Deirdre recognized a few of them, mothers of juniors and seniors she had already taught. They were friendly enough. They waved hello or tried to encourage Deirdre to join the PTSA. The Fall Supper was the big fall fundraiser, but Deirdre had mixed feelings about going. SJ made it clear that she had no interest in Brandywine activities. She didn't feel comfortable, didn't like the way everyone would stare at them, surely the only same-sex couple in attendance.

"But how do you know that's true?" Deirdre tried every time to get SJ to admit that they wouldn't know what it was like unless they attended, at least once.

"Jesus, Deirdre, I *went* to a school like Brandywine, remember? I *lived* that life. No thank you. I do not want to go back there now." And she refused.

Deirdre wanted to say, *Won't you do it for me?* But she was afraid of the answer. She thought about asking Forest, about maybe the two of them going together. She'd check with him tomorrow.

Now, on the field, both teams warmed up, each with their series of stretches and drills, Brandywine in red plaid kilts with white polos, the other team in blue. There was Anna, already one of the best players, even as a sophomore. She was so in control of her body. Her movements looked effortless. Even when she lined up to take a free shot, she hit the ball with a hard whack of precision, graceful. Deirdre couldn't stop watching, following Anna as she ran, those legs, taut and strong. She glanced over to the mothers, wondered if they watched each other's daughters, what they saw, what they imagined.

"Yeah!" Deirdre shouted when Anna flicked the ball past the goalie. She pumped her fist in the air. "Nice one, Anna!"

The girls ran to high-five Anna, plaid kilts flapping. They

grinned through plastic mouth guards, and Anna glanced to the sideline. Mrs. Worthington wasn't among the cluster of mothers. The women clapped. "Good one, Anna!" yelled Evelyn Moore. "That's the way!"

Late-afternoon sun filtered through clouds and shone in slanted rays on the field. Some of the girls put up a hand to see. Deirdre squinted, reminded herself to bring sunglasses next time.

"Hey, Ms. Murphy!" Jennifer, one of the girls on the sidelines, a junior, waved. She leaned on the head of her field hockey stick alongside a few other girls, the other nonstarters, the subs. They grinned and waved. A few of them were pretty good; they just weren't stars. Anna's star status bothered her. Even as a freshman, Anna had played entire games, often scoring multiple goals. But that fall, new to Deirdre's French classes, Anna hadn't yet confided in her. Now she often talked to Deirdre about it.

"You should be proud," Deirdre had told her the last time. After school, Anna had hung around Deirdre's classroom as she often did, wanting to chat.

"But, like, the other girls . . ." And she stopped. She paced the classroom, fidgeted with an elastic band.

"Don't you think the other girls like it when you score? Don't they want to win?"

She nodded. "Yeah, but . . ." She twisted the elastic.

"And don't you think Ms. Jerome knows what she's doing? You're always saying what a good coach she is—no, but seriously," she said, when Anna started to object. "What now, she suddenly doesn't know anything? C'mon, Anna. What girl doesn't *want* to score? Who wouldn't *want* to be in your shoes?" She might have said, *Who wouldn't want to be you*, but she held back; too much, she knew, even if it were true. Deirdre hadn't convinced Anna that day, but now, on the field, the doubt didn't show. Anna played with a kind of fierceness that seemed to say, *I want this*. It troubled Deirdre that Anna couldn't enjoy her abilities. What she would have given to be as talented as Anna athletically, to have had Anna's ease with other kids, her friendships. It hadn't been easy for Deirdre growing up in Gloucester, and looking back, she could see now that she had brought on so much of it herself, feeling different from her classmates but not knowing why, spending so much of her time with her brother Paul, instead of trying to make new friendships; relying on Maria Da Silva next door.

Being a teacher, one the girls loved, offered a kind of redemption, visible proof that things do get better. If pressed, she wouldn't deny that she enjoyed the attention, but most of the time she simply took it as the reward for her hard work and dedication.

CHAPTER FIVE

THROUGH THE OPEN WINDOW, a warm September breeze rustled the paper grocery bags on the kitchen chairs. The air smelled faintly of apples. *You of all people.* In the grocery store, Frances Worthington had emptied her cart at the checkout right next to Deirdre's. What had Frances meant by that? Deirdre unpacked the groceries and began stacking the contents in the cupboards.

When Deirdre had asked Mrs. Worthington why Anna had not yet returned her permission slip for Friday's field trip, Frances replied, "I'm sure you of all people understand that the safety of our children is of utmost concern."

Why, *of all people?* That was the thing with Frances. You just never knew what she was thinking, but everything seemed to have a secret agenda or hidden meaning. It drove Deirdre crazy trying to puzzle it out.

The front door opened and closed.

"Hey, hon." Deirdre stuck the bottle of olive oil on the top shelf.

"Hey yourself," said SJ. She walked into the kitchen, tote bag over her shoulder, jean jacket in her hand. "Have a good day?" She kissed Deirdre on the cheek. "What's for dinner?" SJ peeked around Deirdre to see what was left inside the open paper bags.

"Pasta, how about? I bought some fresh veggies to go

with, and herbs. And wine." Deirdre closed the cabinet.

SJ yawned. "Sounds great." She pulled open the utensils drawer and rummaged around for the corkscrew.

Deirdre started gathering the ingredients for dinner—the farfalle pasta, artichoke hearts, red peppers from the fridge, cremini mushrooms, broccoli, and garlic. "You mind chopping?" She handed SJ a wooden chopping block and chef's knife. "Peppers into slivers. I'll do the broccoli and mushrooms."

Deirdre put on the water to boil, salted and covered it. "You know who I saw at the store? Frances Worthington."

"Oh God. Your favorite." SJ pulled the cork from the bottle of sauvignon blanc and poured two glasses. She settled at the kitchen table, a find at an antique store. They both loved the rich maple hues and the silverware drawer at one end—a country kitchen look but small enough for a city-sized kitchen. SJ plucked a scrunchie from her pocket and pulled her hair into a ponytail. Except for her long hair, SJ had always seemed rather boyish to Deirdre—slim hips, not much of a waist, small chest. She made choosing clothes seem effortless.

"Yeah, and she's so strange." Deirdre shook her head. "She said something—no big deal—but something I just can't figure out." She told SJ about the conversation. "I mean, why me *of all people*? What's she getting at?"

SJ chopped neat slivers of red pepper. "I think you're overanalyzing. I think she just means that as someone who is particularly sensitive to her students' needs, you should be understanding . . ."

"Of her reasons for not letting Anna go on the field trip?"

"She's not letting Anna go?" SJ moved her red pepper slices into a pile.

"She said something about children's safety, that I *of all people* should understand that."

SJ put down the knife. "You're so paranoid sometimes. You're reading way too much into this conversation that, as far as I can tell, was no big deal."

Maybe SJ was right. Since the administration knew about her sexual orientation, it wasn't as if Frances was insinuating something that wasn't public knowledge. Well, for her students it might not be public knowledge, but being gay was not something that would get her in trouble with Martin Loring. Still, Deirdre couldn't shake the feeling that Frances seemed to be getting at something, hinting, insinuating. The water boiled, and Deirdre poured in the pasta and stirred with a wooden spoon.

"But what kind of a message is Frances sending to Anna if she doesn't let her go on the trip?"

SJ swallowed a sip of wine. "Would you let it drop? Can we talk about something else? Anything?"

"You don't think it's wrong?"

SJ did not say anything.

"You think it's fine for the Frances Worthingtons of this world to never cross the line out of their safe little neighborhoods and that I should go along and not challenge that?"

"Listen to yourself, would you?" SJ fiddled with her ponytail. "You, Deirdre Murphy, queen of the I-want-to-live-in-a-nice-neighborhood club . . ."

Deirdre stirred the pasta.

". . . the I-want-to-teach-in-a-private-school club . . ."

Deirdre spun around. "Why *shouldn't* I want to teach in a private school?" She shook the wooden spoon and boiling water dripped onto the kitchen floor.

SJ put down her wineglass and walked over to Deirdre, touched her on the arm. "Let's not fight about this. All I'm saying is that you and Frances Worthington might not be all that different, you know? *You* don't love the East End. You hate that I work there." She rubbed Deirdre's arm, caressed the back of her neck.

"It's dangerous," Deirdre said.

"See?"

"See what? Anyone can tell you that and only crazy people think otherwise. But that doesn't mean we can't go visit an art gallery because it's in a dangerous neighborhood. We're not strolling through the streets, for God's sake. We're going to an art gallery." Deirdre turned away from SJ and laid the wooden spoon on the counter.

People with guns don't go into art galleries. People with guns don't go into schools, either. Little boys don't end up in containers in the river.

"For Anna's sake, you might make less of a big deal about this. She has to live with her mother, remember." SJ hugged Deirdre from behind and sat back down at the kitchen table. She took another long sip of wine.

Deirdre tested the pasta and drained it in a colander, poured olive oil into the sauté pan, and waited for it to heat before adding the vegetables. It didn't occur to Deirdre right then that SJ hadn't apologized. Or for some reason, maybe SJ resented moving into this neighborhood. These things Deirdre would think about much later. What Deirdre focused on now was the notion that she and Frances Worthington were alike. Could it be true? Could SJ really believe that Deirdre was anything like that cold, awful woman? Frances didn't care about her daughter—all she cared about was her image. Her standing in the community. Maybe Deirdre had lobbied hard to live in this part of town—on this very street even—but no, she was nothing like Frances Worthington. No, SJ was dead wrong

Deirdre drank her wine and sautéed the vegetables until they were soft and the room smelled of red pepper and garlic. Woodsy, from the mushrooms with that slightly sour smell of broccoli. She quartered the artichoke hearts and added them to the mix, sprinkling them with bits of fresh oregano she rubbed from the stems. She snipped pieces of basil too, breathing in that sharp, sweet smell that on her fingers smelled like sex.

"So," SJ said, setting the table in the dining room where they liked to eat dinner, "remember that guy who moved us in?"

"The older one or the kid?"

"Mickey."

"Right. The kid."

SJ swallowed. "Yes. Him. So, I'm teaching him to read."

"He can't read?"

"He can sound out words—mostly—but read like an adult or make sense of what he reads? No."

"Wow. That's . . . crazy." Deirdre poured the drained pasta into a huge bowl, and mixed in the vegetables and herbs. She took some cheese from the fridge and grated it on top. "I know there are illiterate adults, of course I *know* that, but . . . I guess I'm a little surprised. Not that he looked like someone who knew how to read!"

"What's that supposed to mean?" SJ stopped what she was doing, left the silverware drawer open.

"He looked like a thug. You didn't think so?"

SJ shut the drawer, two forks, two spoons, and two knives in her first. "No," she said, "I don't."

"He did *not* look like . . ." Deirdre made quotation marks in the air with her fingers, "a fine upstanding young man."

"Because he's a mover?"

Deirdre carried the bowl of pasta to the dining room and placed it in the middle of the table. She pulled her chair out to sit down, but the phone rang. "You start," she said to SJ. "I'll grab this."

"Tell whoever it is that we're eating," SJ said, as she helped herself to some pasta.

"Hello? . . . Anna? What? Slow down. What's going on?"

"Tell her that we're eating, okay?" SJ yelled into the kitchen.

"No, Anna . . . listen . . . I can't hear what you're saying . . ." Deirdre peeked around the corner, receiver to her ear, and mouthed to SJ, *Anna Worthington.*

SJ stabbed at a piece of broccoli. The phone calls had started toward the end of Anna's freshman year. Legitimate homework questions first and then a fight with her mother or some disagreement with one of the other girls. Whatever it was, she always needed to talk it over with Deirdre. And when SJ complained, when she tried to point out the growing frequency of the phone calls, Deirdre accused her of being heartless, of not understanding. But what SJ wanted to tell Deirdre was that she understood all too well.

Even all these years later, she could still hear Mr. Freeman's voice clear as rainwater. Truthfully, they could've been and probably had been talking about calculus, but that voice in SJ's ear was at once silken and throaty. Now, sitting in the dining room with Deirdre on the phone in the kitchen, she remembered the shivery electricity of it, as if via the voice, some part of Mr. Freeman—who through it all she had continued to call Mr. Freeman—had entered her, and even after hanging up, SJ had carried it within, a secret pleasure. For days after that first time, SJ had walked around school in a dreamy state, her body tingling with desire.

Mr. Freeman insisted that his students call him with any homework difficulties. He wanted them to succeed, and if that took getting calls at home, then so be it. SJ had scoffed at first. Who would call a teacher at home? But then after hearing a few kids talk about it at lunch, about how helpful Mr. Freeman had been, how totally open he was, how he genuinely wanted them to understand, and how it was "totally cool" that a teacher would go so far as to give out his number, she thought differently. She called one night after struggling with the chain rule. She remembered the surprise in Mr. Freeman's voice when SJ identified herself, how he had said something about what a treat it was to hear from her, how she always seemed so confident in class, not needing help, how he'd noticed SJ's efforts to work out the problems on her own, how he admired her tenacity.

Noticed. Admired. Tenacity.

Tenacity. Her mother might have said *stubbornness*. But after that first conversation with Mr. Freeman, SJ saw herself differently, as someone willing to figure things out and not give up. It was a positive trait for sure, Mr. Freeman had told her. An excellent attribute for a scholar.

After that, SJ called almost nightly, problems or no. Mr. Freeman didn't seem to mind. He seemed happy to hear from her. Sometimes they talked about things other than math, about SJ's loneliness, about movies they had seen, books. SJ remembered saying something about how it surprised her, a math teacher liking reading so much. And Mr. Freeman had laughed that silken, throaty laugh, the one that made you feel as if you'd rather be nowhere else in the world except right here, that laugh, a gift more precious than anything, more intimate than a touch, more erotic.

"Listen, sweetie . . ."

SJ stopped chewing. She got up and walked to the entranceway to the kitchen, but Deirdre was sitting at the table, hunched over, her back to SJ.

"It'll all work itself out. You've . . . you've got to do what your mother says, I can't help you there . . . I know . . . Yeah, I know, but what can we do? No, listen . . . don't do that . . ." Deirdre pushed her hand through her bangs and over the top of her head. "Anna? I've got to go . . ."

SJ returned to her place at the dining room table. Her pasta was already lukewarm. She got up and retrieved the wine bottle, poured what was left into her glass. She had never told Deirdre about Mr. Freeman. What could she say? What could she admit out loud without making it all too real? How could she explain the phone calls that had turned into after-school visits and then the occasional Saturday afternoon?

"Damnit." Deirdre walked back into the dining room, shaking her head.

"You need to be careful with that girl."

"What?"

"Anna Worthington. You need to be careful."

Deirdre said nothing, then, "She was upset." She pulled out her chair and sat. "I was just calming her down." She picked up her fork, scooped up some pasta and vegetables. "You want yours nuked?" She pointed to SJ's half-eaten dinner.

SJ shook her head. Crossed her arms in front of her stomach.

Deirdre carried her plate into the kitchen. "That Frances Worthington is such a bitch!" Deirdre yelled from above the drone of the microwave. "Forbidding Anna to go on the trip—telling her she doesn't trust *me*, that if another teacher were leading the trip, then maybe Anna could go. Do you believe that?"

SJ did not reply.

"She doesn't trust *me*? Like I'm not going to be careful with those kids? What does she think I'm going to do, lose her daughter?" Deirdre returned, put her plate back on the table, and sat down.

SJ poked at the pieces of broccoli left on her plate. Pushed around the pasta.

Deirdre looked at SJ, waited for a response.

"I don't know. You'll have to ask her."

"Well, I mean, come on, who does that woman think she is? And what kind of support can I expect from her if this is what she tells her daughter—that I'm not to be trusted? Thank God Anna is smart enough to see that her mother is a control freak. I feel bad for the kid but at least she's smart enough to see that her mother is full of it."

SJ didn't want to hear any more. She felt a thickening in her gut.

Deirdre ate a forkful of pasta and vegetables. "You don't have much to say," she added between bites.

"I'm just sick to death of *Anna Worthington this* and *Frances Worthington that* . . . It's all we ever talk about."

"We're talking about my credibility as a teacher!"

"If you're so certain that Frances is full of shit then ignore her, what else can I say?"

Deirdre swallowed her wine. "You could agree with me."

"You *know* I agree with you. This is ridiculous. You're just venting. All I said was you need to be careful with her."

"Okay, okay! Forget it." Deirdre finished her wine. "So, anyway, before . . . you . . . you were saying something about that Mickey guy, the mover?"

SJ pushed back from the table, stretched out her legs. She hesitated.

"Something about him not being able to read?"

"Yes, well, he . . . I'm . . . I've been teaching him. For a week now. He stopped in just after Labor Day."

"Why?"

"Why what?"

"Why are you teaching him?"

"Because I want to."

Deirdre pushed the last of her pasta onto her fork with

her knife. "Aren't there classes for that sort of thing?" She dabbed her finger at the bits of grated cheese on her plate.

"There are, but he . . . I agreed. That's all. I wanted to do it."

"Florence approved?"

"Florence doesn't have any real say in the ma—"

"But she thought it was a good idea?"

"She . . . Yes, she's fine with it." SJ stood and picked up her plate. "Anyway, I just wanted to let you know."

"Kind of a weird coincidence, don't you think?"

"What?" SJ said from the kitchen.

Deirdre got up and carried her plate to the sink. "You know, that first this Mickey guy moves us in and then he shows up in your library to learn how to read?"

SJ ran water over her plate and stuck it in the dishwasher.

"Don't you think?" Deirdre said again. "A coincidence?"

SJ looked blankly at her. "I guess so . . . I didn't really think about it."

"Well," Deirdre said, rinsing her own plate, "I just can't believe you'd want to. He doesn't scare you?"

SJ laughed. "You saw him all of what, a couple of hours, for minutes at a time? You couldn't possibly have any reason to be scared of him."

"He looked scary."

"Looked scary?"

Deirdre closed the dishwasher. "Oh God, here we go. The lecture about the poor. Let me tell you, sweet pea. I know what it means to be poor. You don't." Deirdre tapped SJ on the chest. "So don't go telling me what it means to be poor." She walked out, leaving SJ standing in front of the sink.

How was it, SJ wondered, that Deirdre was the one who ruined dinner and SJ was the one left in the kitchen, feeling like the bad guy? It was Deirdre who made ridiculous assumptions about people because of the way they looked or the job they had, but here was SJ, alone in the doghouse, for what? For defending the underdog? Deirdre would tell you that in the classroom, it was her job to always defend the underdog and make sure all students felt included. She was particularly sensitive to that issue, Deirdre would say, because of her own feelings as an outsider. "Oh, I know what it feels like to be on the outs," Deirdre had said more than once. "All gay people do." She never talked about what it felt like to teach such affluent students, though, to be around people with so much money when she herself grew up without much. Not even with SJ would Deirdre really discuss what it was like to grow up without money.

"I think that guy is bad news," Deirdre called now from the bedroom, "and I don't think you should be alone with him. It's just a feeling I have," she said, coming around the corner to the kitchen's entranceway.

SJ wanted to remain angry with Deirdre but she couldn't. "I'll be careful," is all she said. "And you," she pointed her finger, "you need to be careful with Anna Worthington."

Deirdre did not reply.

THE GIRLS: PART II

The girls were losing any feelings of courage and wonder they had retained through their teenage years. They were aware of how scared they felt, in spite of their forced bravery. They didn't like thinking of the world as a closed and frightening place.

In some cases, their mothers were to blame—mothers who on their own might have been strong and confident, but who in their marriages felt silly or insignificant and so had lost their own sense of awe and wonder and passed on to their daughters a belief in practical matters.

Even before Leo Rivera disappeared, even before their little brothers started wetting their beds and turning on nightlights, before the sight of a small bicycle lying abandoned at the park's entrance might cause the girls to stop breathing and their hearts to pound, they had already started to see the world in terms of hairstyles, outfits, and pedicures. Controllable things.

Now, of course, fear was palpable in the whole town and the world did not seem to hold much wonder at all. The girls minded that they couldn't reassure their brothers. They were too needy for that.

CHAPTER SIX

DEIRDRE BACKED THE BRANDYWINE VAN out of its parking spot alongside the building and pulled in front of the entranceway. She could fit fifteen in the van; the rest would ride in cars driven by Evelyn Moore and Ellie's mom, one of the new mothers, Beth Ann or Sue Ann, Deirdre had already forgotten. She would have to look at the field trip forms again to be certain. Deirdre had been surprised when Ellie, whom she didn't really know yet but thought of as quietly belligerent—*resistant* was the word she used with Martin Loring at the child study meeting about new students—volunteered her mother one morning as a driver and chaperone.

"She don't work," Ellie had said. "She'll do it."

"*Doesn't*, Ellie. She *doesn't* work."

Deirdre had called and sure enough, a quiet, breathy voice said on the other end of the line that she would be delighted to help out. Deirdre told her they would be leaving at eight thirty sharp and would be back to school by four o'clock.

"After pickup, then?"

"We do it all the time," Deirdre had explained on the phone. "We just make sure the parents know they have to get their kids that day."

"That's just fine," Ellie's mom had said, her voice lilting and Southern. "I will be there. I am happy to help." *Thank yew*, she had said, her words stretched out, full of diphthongs and air. *Thank yew.*

Deirdre jerked on the emergency brake and climbed out of the van. The last few cars pulled up and dropped off the younger students who tumbled out, scrambled toward the front door, swinging lunch boxes and handfuls of paper. Anna Worthington rushed in among them, through the gate, out of breath, brown hair flying. Cheerleader hair, Deirdre called it.

"Oh good! I was afraid I was too late!" Anna dropped her backpack with a plunk at Deirdre's feet. "Here," she said, between breaths, handing Deirdre the torn-off section of the field trip permission form with her mother's signature scrawled on the bottom line. "I. Can. Go."

Deirdre looked up from the paper.

"I talked her into it," Anna said. "She knew she was being a jerk." Anna scowled and wiped her bangs off her forehead.

"Well, I'm glad you can go," Deirdre said. "You better sign in at the office, though. You're late." She folded the permission slip in half, stuck it in her pocket, and turned to walk into the school. "Don't forget your backpack."

"Can I ride in the van with you?" Anna asked, hurrying to catch up to Deirdre. "In the front seat? Be a copilot?" Her voice carried that hopeful tone that Deirdre both longed for and dreaded. *You're coming to the field hockey game, right, Ms. Murphy?* You could get used to feeling loved and wanted. But it was a hard thing to admit.

Deirdre stopped just short of the entranceway. She looked at Anna's face, those blue, adoring eyes. "I think you'll have to ride with Ellie's mom," she said.

Anna pouted. "But . . ."

"Let's just be glad you're going at all, right?" Deirdre

held up her hand. "We figured out the rides before we knew you were coming." And when she saw the hurt on Anna's face she added, "You can probably switch with someone for the ride back, okay? Go sign in at the office. I'm heading upstairs to tell the others we're ready. Meet you out here." She patted Anna on the shoulder.

Deirdre was relieved that Frances Worthington had given in and signed the permission slip. And she was grateful that Anna cared enough to fight with her mother. Deirdre ran up the last few steps so she could relieve Forest before it was time for him to teach his first class.

With the morning paper opened in front of him, Forest leaned against the doorway in the middle of the two class-rooms. Deirdre's homeroom students sat clumped on top of desks with their backpacks on the floor surrounding them. "Thanks," Deirdre said. A couple of the girls smiled when she walked in. Lydia waved.

"You all set then?" Forest asked. "Wish *I* was going on a field trip." He folded his paper in half.

Deirdre grinned. "Yeah, well, have fun without us. It should be quieter anyway."

"Great. I get to listen to my kids, *Why don't* we *ever get to go on trips?* They'll whine and moan all through our discussion of *Lord of the Flies.* I can't wait." Forest rolled his eyes.

"And you tell them that next year, when they're in my French class, they *will* go on field trips. Or better yet, *you* take them somewhere. To a play or something."

The bell rang and the morning hubbub began. Voices rose, chairs and desks scraped across the floor, lockers slammed.

"Have fun!"

"See ya!"

"Later!"

From the doorway, Forest saluted with his newspaper

and turned to go into his own room. "Have a good one," he said.

"All right, folks, if you're coming with me, let's get going. We're meeting in the front hallway. Be sure you have your jacket, and don't forget your notebook and something to write with. Lydia, would you get the first aid kit from the office? Okay, we're all set. Let's go!"

They rode to the East End Gallery, Deirdre and the Brandywine van in the lead, Evelyn Moore behind her, and Ellie's mom bringing up the rear. *Beth Ann, Beth Ann,* Deirdre repeated to herself, checking in the rearview mirror to be sure the two cars were still there. They drove through the West End first, past the town green and the Congregational church. Past the public high school, the library's main branch, past the town hall and the flagpole rotary, the flag still at half-mast. They drove down near the old railroad tracks and past a row of triple-deckers.

They stopped at a red light, the abandoned textile mill on the left, the river on the right.

"Where the heck are we?" one girl, Samantha maybe, asked from the back.

"Yeah," another piped up. It sounded like Morgan. "Isn't that where they found that boy? The Rivera kid?"

Murmurs from the back and then another girl: "Is this safe?"

The light turned green; Deirdre accelerated. She wondered if similar conversations were happening in the two cars and how the mothers were handling them. She realized then that although she had given the address to Beth Ann, she hadn't been explicit about the gallery's location. A quick peek in the rearview mirror told her that Beth Ann was still with them. "Hey, listen up . . . shhhh . . . I mean it . . . listen . . . Remember we had this conversation in class? About the fact that what happened to Leo Rivera could have happened in *any* neighborhood?"

Silence. Deirdre looked over at Hilary sitting in the seat next to hers.

"It *is* a little freaky," Hilary said, wrinkling her forehead and twisting her blond curls around her finger. "It's, like, scary." She hugged herself with her bare arms.

"Okay everyone, just relax." Deirdre pulled into the gallery's parking lot. "Anyway, we're going to a gallery, remember? We're not walking the streets."

Deirdre shut off the van and hopped out. She opened the side door and her students emerged in that rough-and-tumble kid way, like a collection of body parts—first arms, then legs, long and gangly. From Evelyn's car, Lydia and a small group of girls laughed and pushed and pulled at each other's bouncing ponytails, and then the last car, Anna and the oddballs—the girls who weren't in any particular group—opened the doors and climbed out without speaking. Anna scuffed and scowled her way over to be with Lydia, but it was as if simply riding in that car with those particular kids had tainted Anna already and you could see Lydia hesitating a bit, wondering about her very best friend in the world, before finally linking arms with Anna and including her in the group.

"Well, we're here!" Evelyn Moore sang out, locking the doors of her BMW with the remote. *Beep beep.* "You didn't lose us, thank God." She put on her leather purse like a backpack and walked toward Deirdre, her clogs clopping on the blacktop.

"Beth Ann, everything okay?" Deirdre shielded the sun from her eyes and waved Ellie's mother over.

"Gosh, you learn a lot chaperoning," Evelyn said. "They couldn't stop talking about what's-his-name, that singer, you know who I mean, and who's seeing who—I had no idea." Evelyn gestured with her hands and Deirdre was struck by the redness of her nails. "Oh, hey, did I see Anna over there?" Evelyn pointed to the group of girls surrounding her daughter.

"Frances gave in at the last minute." Deirdre felt the need to explain.

"Oh good." The girls, holding notebooks and pencils, scuffed the blacktop and toed bits of loose gravel. "Frances is too hard on that girl sometimes," Evelyn mused.

Beth Ann walked quietly up to Deirdre and Evelyn. She was dressed in knit pants and a coordinated sweater set, a pale blue that reminded Deirdre of cream. It struck Deirdre that this was the kind of woman who made her feel *wrong*—made her feel messy and underdressed, lacking in some important way, the way Frances Worthington did, only Beth Ann was of a different style. Beth Ann's blond hair was pulled back from her face with white mother-of-pearl barrettes. Deirdre noticed, too, that Beth Ann's lipstick, a glossy pale pink, matched her fingernails perfectly. Beth Ann smiled at Deirdre and Evelyn, her eyes gray and distant. "I don't believe I have seen this part of town before," she said.

Deirdre laughed. "Wait until you see this gallery, though. We're just going in here." She pointed to the large brick warehouse on the left and the sign over the middle door, *East End Gallery of African Art.*

"It is a strange place for a gallery," Beth Ann said. "How ever did you find it?"

Deirdre stood up a little straighter and shifted her weight. "My . . ." and she hesitated before saying it, pictured Frances Worthington herself and her disapproving frown. "My partner is a librarian in this part of town and we've passed this place a couple times. I finally dragged SJ in with me to check it out." Deirdre laughed a little, felt the blush pulse warmly on her cheeks.

Beth Ann said nothing, simply stared at Deirdre with those gray eyes.

In the gallery, Mario, the owner, led them quickly through the vast collection but focused, as Deirdre had suggested, on the Dogon artifacts. Deirdre was especially taken with the doors—large, imposing wooden structures, intricately carved, each one telling a different story.

"The Dogon people are cliff dwellers, in the northwestern part of Mali," Mario explained. Deirdre stood in the back of the group and looked around to see who was paying attention and whose mind was wandering elsewhere. Lydia smiled up at the gallery owner. Hilary seemed mildly interested but you could never tell. Morgan's blond head stuck up above everyone else's. She nodded at whatever the gallery owner was saying, jotted down things in her notebook. Behind her, the wall was covered with initiation masks from Côte d'Ivoire, from the Dan ethnic group, wooden masks in all sizes with the customary raffia framing the face, some of it thin and brown, most of it black, thick, beardlike.

"But they don't live in cliffs *now,* do they?" Hilary asked. She twisted her curls around her pencil.

Mario seemed to expect that particular question. "Oh, they sure do. Today, the Dogon people of Mali are still cliff dwellers." He looked from student to student, waiting for their reaction.

"But, like, in the cliffs? Like, they live in dirt?" Hilary again. Giggles from a few other girls.

"Are you a moron or what?" Morgan said. "No, they build their mansions up in the cliffs, big houses with swimming pools!" She widened her eyes at Hilary. The other girls laughed. The exaggerated, bugged-out eyes on the masks seemed to mock Hilary too.

"Shut up, Morgan!" Lydia said.

"Hey!" Deirdre intervened, and Evelyn grabbed her daughter's arm at the same time.

"Okay, okay," Mario hushed the group with his hands. He laughed a little. Deirdre shot her fiercest teacher look at Morgan. "This is a hard concept," he continued. "When we think of cliff dwellers we think of who? The Anasazi, right? Mesa Verde?" He looked at each student. Deirdre was grateful for a tour guide who could speak to kids and for the most part hold their interest. "We don't think of people today, in this day and age, living in cliffs." He turned to Hilary. "They actually *don't* carve their dwellings into the cliffs anymore . . ."

Hilary twisted around and stuck her tongue out at Morgan.

"But they build huts high up in the cliffs and these doors," he pointed to two massive wooden doors leaning against the wall next to him, "are what they hang on the front of their huts."

"What's with all the carvings?" another girl asked.

"Each door tells the story of that particular family," Mario responded.

Anna sidled up next to Deirdre, leaned her arm on Deirdre's shoulder, and whispered, "I'm so bored."

Deirdre stepped aside. "Try listening," she said, and walked to the other side of the group. *Bored.* She could never understand that particular complaint. *With all there is to do in this world . . .* she heard her mother's voice in her head and smiled. Most of her students knew better than to admit boredom to Deirdre. She glanced back over to where Anna was standing, arms crossed, a scowl on her face. Deirdre would speak to her during the next break, try to get her to see how all of this was worthwhile and interesting, though it annoyed her that Anna couldn't see it on her own.

"Here," Mario went on, pointing to a set of carvings in

the top part of the door, "these figures represent the ancestors, the spirits of this family who are, I might add, very real and very present to the people living in this hut. See the eyes . . ." and he indicated the bulging lids, the exaggerated facial expressions.

"I wonder," Deirdre said when Mario had finished talking, "what you all would carve in *your* family's door?" She looked at her students. "What might represent your families?"

One by one, they offered some ideas—a shamrock, Star of David, a cross, the usual symbols—and then from somewhere on the fringe of the group, a quiet voice rose up.

"I would carve a weeping willow," Ellie said. Her eyes were closed and she held her hands out delicately at her sides. "One giant weeping willow. It would be enough," her voice grew quieter now, "to cover us all . . ." She fluttered her arms, graceful, like a ballet dancer. "To protect us," she added, opening her eyes, blinking a couple of times, "from the sadness." Nobody said a word, and Deirdre, stunned, looked around for Beth Ann, who stood a couple of feet behind her daughter, hands folded in front of her, those shallow gray eyes, it seemed, shiny and wet.

"Wow," Evelyn said to Beth Ann. "You've got yourself a poet there. Or an actor."

They were taking a snack break. The kids sat in circles on the gallery floor—Ellie with a couple of newfound admirers near the Dogon doors, the others in groups scattered throughout the gallery. Deirdre, Evelyn, and Beth Ann were perched on stools with Mario at a large wooden board stretched across two workhorses. Deirdre noticed Morgan off by herself, sketching the masks.

"Ellie's always been sensitive," Beth Ann said. She smiled a little, but her eyes remained sad.

"Well, I was impressed," Deirdre said, turning back to face the woman. "I've never heard Ellie speak like that in class."

"She loves your class, Ms. Murphy—"

"It's Deirdre, please."

Beth Ann smiled. "She says she just loves French and the way you get everyone to speak. She has never had a teacher take an interest in her before."

Deirdre didn't know what to say. She hadn't taken an interest in Ellie—that was painfully clear the minute Ellie opened her mouth on the gallery floor—Deirdre had been as shocked as everyone else. She made a mental note to talk with Martin Loring and revise her earlier assessment.

Mario stood. "Well, I've been impressed too," he said. "Obviously, you knew just the question to ask." He looked right at Deirdre. "I can see how you get good work from your students. A simple question, but one I had never imagined asking any of the students who pass through the gallery . . . Not that many students even *get* the chance to come see our little gallery!" He laughed. "That in and of itself is impressive."

"Well, I guess I'm always trying to make the material relevant to them," Deirdre said. "That's all." She got up and walked toward the center of the large, airy room. She looked at Ellie talking with two other girls, sitting there in their circle. She had definitely misjudged her. Deirdre had completely missed the sadness in her and had seen only resistance. Odd that Ellie had gone home and told her mother how much she liked the class when she seemed so clearly *not* to like it while she was there. She almost never looked up at Deirdre when she was teaching. Never wanted to answer a question. When Deirdre tried to get Ellie's attention, she wouldn't let her. She looked away. Never returned her gaze. She was an odd duck for sure. Her skinny arms were covered with blond hair, downy.

Where was Anna? Deirdre wanted to talk with her, be sure she was getting something out of this trip. Deirdre was sure she could change the girl's attitude. There, sitting cross-legged next to Lydia, Anna braided Lydia's long red hair. Lydia was regaling the other girls with some story, and they sat rapt, laughing when it was appropriate, their smiles a display of braces and even, white teeth.

"Hey," Deirdre said, squatting down next to Lydia and Anna, "how's it going?"

"Great," Lydia replied. "This is so cool."

The other girls agreed and nodded.

"Yeah? Anna, what do you think?" Deirdre tilted her head to get a better look at the girl's face.

"It's okay," Anna said, the typical scowl marring her brow. She kept braiding Lydia's hair, didn't look up.

"What did you all think of the doors? Pretty wild, huh? The Dogon people live in cone-shaped huts but they take the care to have these beautiful doors put on the outsides . . ." Deirdre remembered reading about how the Dogon people were famous for their hospitality and took pride in their humble living quarters, keeping them tidy and clean.

"Yeah, like, that's weird," Hilary said. "It's a *door*."

"I want to get my mother to buy one," Lydia said.

"Right," Anna laughed. "Where are you going to put that thing in your house? I can see it now." She dropped the braid she was working on and spread her hands wide. "You come into the living room and there's this . . . door . . ." The two of them burst into giggles. When Deirdre tried to smile at Anna, she scowled again and went back to her braiding.

"Well, I'm glad you're enjoying your visit," Deirdre said to all the girls. "We'll be finishing up the tour in a bit, okay? Anna, can I see you for a minute?" She motioned her to follow.

The other girls resumed their storytelling and laughing.

Hilary took up where Anna left off with Lydia's hair. Anna took her time making her way over to Deirdre.

"What's up?" Deirdre asked. She tried to make her voice sound concerned, caring.

Anna shrugged.

"Come on. You're not giving this a chance. You're barely listening to the guide." Deirdre tried to get Anna to look at her. She touched her on the shoulder. "Is something the matter? Do we need to talk?"

Anna looked up. "No," she said, still pouting. "Can I go now?"

Deirdre folded her arms. "Sure," she said. "I just wanted to be sure everything's okay."

"I'm *fine*."

"Well, all right then." Deirdre patted Anna gently on the back and Anna looked right at Deirdre, her eyes clouded. In that instant, Deirdre got it. She understood that Anna was pissed off because Deirdre wasn't paying enough attention to her. That's what this was about. Deirdre took a deep breath. "Anna," she said, and the girl turned around. There it was. The hope. "No, forget it . . . never mind." She waved Anna back to her group. "We'll talk later."

They finished the tour with Morgan asking questions at every section. Deirdre couldn't believe it. Morgan was never that interested. Deirdre made another mental note to talk with her, express appreciation for her enthusiasm during the gallery visit. She had few opportunities to praise Morgan and she wanted to take advantage of every one. So often lately Morgan was driving her crazy, putting down the other girls, making those generalizations that Deirdre did her best to teach them *not* to make.

"Thank you." Deirdre shook Mario's hand. "I think they got a lot out of this visit."

"Thank *you*," Mario said. "They're great. Interested— but I suspect that you have a lot to do with that." He smiled at her with a twinkle in his eyes, as if they shared some little secret.

Deirdre said nothing. She never knew how to respond to praise like this. She honestly didn't know if what she did with her students was out of the ordinary. She often told SJ that in fact she didn't even know what it was she was doing at all, that she ran on instinct. "Then you have the right instincts. Be grateful," SJ always told her. Still, even in her seventh year of teaching, Deirdre wondered. She couldn't help but think there was some hidden skill she was missing, some important knowledge about how to teach that eluded her.

Evelyn interrupted her thoughts. "A great trip," she said. "I enjoyed myself."

"Thanks for helping out," Deirdre said. They walked down the gallery steps, the students in a pack on the blacktop already, alongside the van. Deirdre turned to look for Beth Ann behind them. "Where'd she go?"

"Who?"

"Beth Ann. Do you see her?"

"Down there." Evelyn pointed to the crowd of kids and the blue and blond figure unlocking the white car. "I wonder what her story is."

"Hmmm." Deirdre wanted to find out. "Whatever it is, it's big."

They walked toward the van and Evelyn's car. Anna Worthington stood leaning with her back against the passenger door of the van, arms crossed. Hilary paced in front of her.

"Ms. Murphy," Hilary said, "Anna says she's sitting in the front seat on the way back. She says you promised."

"I said no such thing."

A hurt look from Anna. "You said I could switch . . ."

"I said we'd see. I didn't say you should bully your way onto the van." Deirdre turned to Hilary "You know, it would be a nice thing to switch with Anna for the ride home."

"Ride in that car? I don't know those kids!" A whine.

"C'mon, Hil. I'd do it for you." A plead. Anna. The adoring eyes turned on Hilary. Hands in prayer position.

"You two decide. But do it quick." To the others, "Let's go, folks. Time to get home."

They drove in near silence back to school, Anna in the van's front passenger seat, Hilary sulking in the backseat of Beth Ann's car. "You owe me major," Hilary had said, shaking her finger at Anna as she walked away from the van. "Like, huge."

Anna said little on the ride back, hummed an unrecognizable tune, and stared out the window. Deirdre tried to engage her in conversation, but all she got were one-word answers. So why did it matter if Anna rode with Beth Ann or in the van? Deirdre wondered. Funny kid. Even Morgan was subdued on the ride back. None of her usual wisecracks. Deirdre peeked in her rearview mirror. Morgan sat slouched in the way back, head resting against the vinyl seat. The rest of the girls looked out the window. One or two had their eyes shut.

They passed the turnoff for the library and Deirdre wondered what kind of mood SJ would be in that night. She had been so odd lately—aloof and preoccupied. She'd hardly spoken at Paul and Kris's the other night. Some kind of thing going on at the library—an accreditation, she thought SJ had said. Deirdre decided she'd make an asparagus quiche, one of SJ's favorites. See if the market had fresh flowers. And she'd call Paul, thank him for dinner. She loved spending time with Sophie and Mark. After Sophie was first born, Deirdre used to fantasize that something would happen to Kris and she and SJ would have to help Paul raise the kids. For Paul's sake, Deirdre wouldn't kill Kris in her fantasies but have her run away, decide to abandon Paul and the kids, though of course in real life the chances of that happening were pretty remote. Kris doted on Mark and Sophie. And Paul. It was only Deirdre she didn't seem to like.

"All right," Deirdre said now, turning into the Brandywine parking lot. "We're here." Grunts and groans from the back. Bodies stretching, unbuckling seat belts.

"Hey, there's my mom," Morgan said, banging on the window.

Deirdre jumped out of the van. Some parents, mothers mostly, stood together at the edge of the parking lot, and they approached, smiling at Deirdre, looking for their kids. Deirdre didn't see Frances Worthington. A few other parents emerged from their parked cars, lined alongside the curb. Martin Loring walked out the front door and down the front steps.

"Good trip?" he called to Deirdre, waving a beefy hand.

"A great one!" she answered.

Martin greeted several of the parents and kids. "Glad it went well," he said when he got closer to Deirdre. "They seem happy." He motioned to the group on the blacktop.

"They were terrific," Deirdre said. "In fact, can I stop by Monday? I'd like to talk with you about some things I learned today."

"Sure." He looked around, waved to the parents who pulled out of the parking lineup. "You got this under control? I'm on my way out. Got a board meeting in an hour," he said, looking at his watch.

Deirdre waved her hand. "Go on, I'll wait. I'll be sure they're all taken care of."

A few of the parents approached Deirdre and thanked her for organizing the trip, for taking the time to do something out of the ordinary. She noticed Morgan and her mother, an elegant, tall woman with frosted hair, standing alongside a maroon Mercedes. "Mrs. Abernathy," Deirdre said, hurrying over to them.

"Oh, hello." A friend of Frances Worthington's, no doubt. She gave off no warmth. Offered that familiar icy smile.

"I just wanted to tell you how terrific Morgan was in the gallery today." Deirdre paused and glanced at Morgan, who looked uncertain and clutched her notebook to her chest. "I mean, she was great. Asking all sorts of questions—she was interested . . . by far the most engaged student." Deirdre nodded enthusiastically.

A sort of amused smile twitched at Mrs. Abernathy's lips.

A look from Morgan stopped Deirdre from saying anything else. *Waste of time*, her eyes said.

"Well, she was great. I think she learned a lot."

Mrs. Abernathy beeped her Mercedes unlocked. She opened her door and motioned for Morgan to do the same.

Deirdre surveyed the group. A few kids and parents were getting into their cars. No one else was left waiting. She wouldn't let Morgan's mother get to her. It had been a great day. Ellie had come out of her shell in front of everyone and might have made a couple of new friends. Even Anna seemed to turn around at the end. Anna—Deirdre never saw Frances Worthington and Anna had left without saying goodbye.

Weird.

Deirdre shrugged and opened the van door to drive it around to its parking spot. There, in the passenger seat, sat Anna.

"Anna! What are you doing in here? Where's your mother?" Deirdre remembered then that Martin said there was a board meeting in an hour. She couldn't imagine Frances Worthington making two trips out to Brandywine within an hour. "Anna, were you supposed to ride home with someone else? With Evelyn?"

The girl sat hugging her knees. She smiled at Deirdre. "The thing is," she said, "my mother doesn't know I'm here."

"What?"

"Look, she wasn't going to let me go . . ."

"What's going on?" Deirdre stood holding the van door open. "This isn't funny. What's going on?"

"I forged her signature."

"You did *what?*" Deirdre climbed into the van. "Do you know how much trouble I could be in?" She heard the harshness in her voice.

"You wanted me to go!" Anna let go of her knees, turned to Deirdre. Here was the child—bright-eyed, with cheerleader hair. The little kid. "I did it for *you!*" Tears forming.

"Oh." Deirdre reached over and rubbed Anna's arm. "Of course you know I wanted you to come . . ."

"No, you didn't even care!" A full-fledged tantrum now. "You couldn't have cared less! I should have listened to my mother. I should have stayed home."

"Anna, look at me." Deirdre sat sideways in her seat, tried to grab both of Anna's shoulders, but the girl twisted away. "Anna . . ."

She stayed still with her arms wrapped around her knees, head down.

Deirdre stroked her hair. "Listen," she said, making her voice soft. "Of course I wanted you to come on the trip—I really hoped you'd like it too." She ran her hand the length of Anna's silky, baby-fine hair. "But forging your mother's signature—that's wrong, Anna. We both could be in a lot of trouble."

Anna stopped crying, said nothing.

Deirdre continued to stroke her hair. "I didn't mean for

you to disobey your mother," she said, still using her soft voice. She glanced at the clock on the dashboard. Nearly five o'clock. "Don't you think she's worried about you?"

"I don't care." Muffled, from between her knees.

"Well, here," Deirdre said, taking the school's cell phone from her bag. "I think we should call her, at least let her know you're okay."

"No!" Anna sat up. "I don't . . . It's just . . ." She fidgeted with her rings, twisted them around her fingers, silver on nearly every one.

"Look," the teacher-voice again, "let her know you're safe. She's got to be worried sick!"

"If she was worried, why wasn't she up here looking for me? Huh? Why didn't she call Mr. Loring, wondering where I was? She *acts* like it's all about me, but it's really all about *her*." Anna's voice got excited again and she pulled harder at her rings. "She acts like it's you she hates, but it's me. She hates me." Tears, cascading now.

Deirdre leaned over and put her arms around Anna. "Shhh. She doesn't hate you. She's your *mother*." Deirdre thought of her own mother, and her own mother's disappointment—disapproval—when Deirdre had told her she was gay. How Deirdre had been so naïve, how she thought that a mother's love for her daughter could outweigh anything.

Deirdre hugged Anna close. She held her, whispered that it would be okay, that she was sure her mother loved her, that she would take Anna home and everything would work out.

"Shhh," she said, rocking Anna a little, patting her back. Anna put her head on Deirdre's shoulder and wrapped her arms around her, tight.

"I love you," Anna's little kid voice mumbled.

Deirdre continued patting. "I love you too. Everything's going to be okay."

"No, I mean I really love you." Anna raised her head. And before Deirdre could respond, before her mind could think of what to say, Anna leaned over and kissed her on the lips.

Now Deirdre's mind seemed to stop. Anna's lips on hers. She held one hand, she realized, suspended above Anna's long hair. Her body tense. Frozen. Her other hand still on Anna's shoulder. Stuck there. She removed it, an action that got her mind working again, racing. Deirdre pulled away from Anna, words forming in her brain, a plan, an action. *Trouble,* a voice said inside her head. *Big trouble.*

"Oh shit," said Anna.

There, with one hand on the handle of the driver's-side door, her face contorted in anger, stood Frances Worthington.

CHAPTER SEVEN

DEIRDRE SEARCHED THE BOTTOM SHELF of the refrigerator for a beer. Nothing. She picked up the carton of skim milk, pushed aside the orange juice. No wine either. She slammed the refrigerator shut and glanced up at the wall—six o'clock. No word from SJ. She crossed the kitchen and opened the cupboards, looking for . . . something. She peered behind the arborio rice and the pine nuts. Whole wheat crackers, fig cookies, packages of all-natural macaroni and cheese. There was nothing she wanted. Deirdre paced the kitchen. She thought of calling Paul. Yeah, right. *Hi, Paul—guess what? I just got caught kissing one of my students.* Already, Paul could only go so far in his understanding of Deirdre's "lifestyle" as he called it. In his mind, homosexuality was wrong, but he loved Deirdre. *Deird, what the hell were you doing kissing a student?* Then, in the background, she could imagine Kris telling Paul to hang up, that his sister was a pervert.

Where was SJ? Deirdre picked up the phone and held the receiver. Put it down. Picked it up again. Put it down. She strode over to the dining room hutch, opened the liquor cabinet, and pulled out a bottle of Johnnie Walker Red Label. She didn't bother with ice cubes, just filled a tumbler, one of the crystal ones SJ's mother had given her once as a birthday gift, before she knew Deirdre.

Just holding a full glass of Scotch helped. Deirdre breathed in the burning, sweet smell, swirled the liquid, licked the rim and insides of the glass. What was she going to do? She took one tentative sip. What in God's name could she say to Martin Loring on Monday morning to make everything okay? There was nothing—the anger on Frances's face, in her voice. The look in Anna's eyes, the fear, the terror—what were they going to do?

Forget Monday morning. Martin was certain to call immediately after the board meeting. Deirdre was surprised he hadn't called yet, but then, that was like Frances to maintain protocol and pull Martin aside once the meeting was over. That would be—Deirdre looked back again at the kitchen clock—in another hour, maybe a little more. She brought her glass of Scotch into the kitchen and picked up the phone again. She dialed without having to think of the numbers.

"Bradley Public Library."

"Florence? Hey, it's Deirdre . . ." Trying not to cry, taking a deep breath. "Is SJ . . . Did SJ leave yet?"

"An hour ago. Actually, more than that. She left around four."

Breathing, breathing.

"Deirdre, is everything okay? Are you all right?"

"No . . . yes . . . yeah, I'm fine. Thanks, Florence." Hanging up.

A swig of warm Scotch burned her throat. Deirdre swallowed. She wanted to feel her insides burn. She wanted to purge herself—of what? What had she done that was wrong? What was she guilty of? She needed to calm down.

She lifted the receiver again. Looked up Forest's number in the Brandywine faculty directory. She should have it memorized by now, but she didn't.

"Yeah?"

"That's a nice way to answer the phone . . ."

"Deird?"

"It's me." She finished her Scotch. "Yuk, nothing like warm Scotch . . ." Her throat burned.

"Are you drunk?"

"Forest, I think I just got fired." Tears now. Real tears. "Can you come over? Do you have any beer?"

"You got fired?"

"Well, I will." Pause for nose-blowing. "I need to talk."

"What happened? What . . ." Forest, alert now, his voice sharp and edgy.

"Can you come over?"

"Yeah, sure, I guess so. Give me a couple minutes to put something on. Deird, you got fired?"

"Hey, let's meet at Tony's. Can you meet me at Tony's?"

"The one near the rink?"

Yeah. I'm leaving now, okay? You'll come, right?"

"Be careful, Deird. I'll be right there."

From the outside, Tony's looked seedy, run-down, but inside it was a neighborhood bar. On red leather stools, older men, the same three or four as always, sat grouped around one corner of the bar—retired guys in blue Baracuta jackets, one in a faded blue cap, another one balding, his nose a bulbous red mass. Also at the bar, a couple of women, hair frosted and teased a little too much, cheeks polished, eyes lined in thick black mascara, smoking Pall Malls, their legs crossed, still in nylons and pumps, part of the after-work crowd. A small TV, sound off, flashed scenes from the local news. Deirdre chose a small table alongside the wall behind a youngish couple eating pepperoni pizza, drinking draft beers. Pizza was the only decent thing to eat at Tony's.

"A Guinness," she told the waiter, an oldish white-haired guy.

The waiter placed down a white square napkin with a

flourish and produced a basket of popcorn. Deirdre scooped up a few pieces, chewed on them, tasteless, butterless. She ate a few more. Chewing helped her think. This was all Anna's doing. Deirdre couldn't have known that Anna had forged Frances's signature. In the van, Deirdre had only been comforting Anna—thank God she had suggested Anna call her mother. Didn't that show responsibility? Clear thinking?

The waiter brought over Deirdre's Guinness. She nodded her thanks and took a long sip. But what bothered her the most—what continued to pull at her brain, to flash like a warning—was the thought that she had liked being in that van with Anna. She liked being needed so much. Maybe she had willed all this to happen. She had a vague memory of SJ telling her to be careful. Isn't that what SJ had said the other night, during dinner?

"Hey." Forest shrugged off his jean jacket and pulled out the chair opposite Deirdre. He looked like he'd been sleeping—hair tousled, flannel shirt misbuttoned. Forest motioned to the bartender to bring a Guinness for himself. "So, what's going on?"

Deirdre didn't know where to begin. "I'm in deep shit," she said. And she launched in. About how Anna wasn't going to go on the field trip and then showed up at the last minute with the signed permission slip. How she pleaded with Deirdre to ride in the front seat of the van. "You know how those girls are? The way they all want to be the special one?" Deirdre stopped to eat a handful of popcorn, then pointed at Forest. "Like Kelly and Gretchen? The way they always fight over who gets to take your attendance?"

Forest nodded, ate some popcorn, smiled thinly.

Deirdre described the trip, the way Anna had been sulking, then ignoring Deirdre altogether after Deirdre reprimanded her. "I should've seen it coming, but I didn't."

"Seen what? What happened?"

"She kissed me."

"She—what?"

"Kissed me. On the lips." Pointing.

Forest laughed. "Do you know how many *guys* would kill to kiss Anna Worthington?"

"This isn't funny."

The woman behind Forest got up and pushed her chair into his. "Sorry," she said, and glanced briefly over at Deirdre. The woman was pretty—frail-looking, with dark, dark eyes. Her boyfriend tossed money on the table between the empty pizza plates, and they walked out, the boyfriend with his hand on the woman's shoulder, guiding her, or keeping her steady.

"Wait, do guy teachers think about that stuff? Kissing their girl students?"

The waiter brought Forest's beer. "No—not really. I mean, yeah, sure, but not like we'd *do* it or something. Anna's hot—what guy's not going to think about kissing her?" He took a long sip.

"She's fifteen. She isn't *hot.*"

"Oh, so you never thought about it?" Forest narrowed his eyes and gave Deirdre his cut-the-bullshit look. He wiped the Guinness mustache from his lip. "Thinking about something isn't a crime, you know. We all think about it."

"No, Forest. We don't *all think about it.*" This conversation was not going at all the way Deirdre had hoped. She didn't need to get mad at Forest right now. She needed his help. She picked through the popcorn kernels.

"Anyway," Forest said, "you think Anna's going to tell anybody she kissed you?"

Deirdre looked up. "She doesn't need to tell. Frances saw us." She watched Forest's reaction. "Yeah, now tell me I'm not in big trouble. Frances Worthington, chair of the board at Brandywine Academy, caught me—her least favorite teacher in the first place—kissing her daughter." Deirdre finished off her Guinness and immediately looked around for the waiter.

"Deird, where were you guys? You weren't alone with her, were you?"

"Oh great. Let's just blame the victim here. *Miss Murphy, can you tell the jury why you were wearing a short skirt on the night you were raped?* That's just great, Forest." She wanted to throw the rest of the popcorn kernels at him.

"You think Martin's not going to ask you that? Come on. It's a fair question."

"It's bullshit and you know it." Deirdre fought the tears. "*I* don't think about kissing Anna Worthington, but you do, but you would never be alone with her, is that it? So it would never happen to you?" One of the women with frosted hair kept glancing over her shoulder. Deirdre lowered her voice. "Fuck you." She blew her nose on her damp bar napkin. "I need another."

Forest took his out from underneath his Guinness and handed it to her. "I'm just trying to help here."

"You're not helping at all." She balled up the napkins and shoved them in her pocket. "I'm going to get fired! I'm going to lose my job!"

"Are you sure Frances saw you?"

"She opened the van door—"

"You were in the van? Alone with Anna?"

"We were coming home from the field trip . . ." And Deirdre told him again about Anna forging the permission slip, about Anna wanting Deirdre to take her home and what the girl had said about her mother.

"I should've seen it coming. I mean, somewhere deep down, I knew Anna was gay . . ."

"What?"

"Come on. I mean, I don't think—well, I didn't think she

realized it yet, but she must have and that's what this whole thing is about. And of course, according to Frances it'll be my fault that Anna's gay." She laughed hollowly. "Like, you know, I talked her into it or something. Recruited her for the club!" She laughed harder now, made eye contact with the waiter, motioned for two more beers.

On the small television above the bar, Leo Rivera's face appeared. Still a news item, his killer still at large.

"That poor, poor child," said one of the women with frosted hair. Her friend shook out another cigarette from the Pall Mall pack lying on the bar.

"They ought to fry the guy did that to him," one of the bald men said, not looking away from the TV.

"Sick bastard," said the man in the cap.

Deirdre looked away from Leo's ten-year-old face, smiling, in his gray and blue baseball uniform. "Like I'm going to recruit someone to go through this crap? That's a laugh." She waved the empty popcorn basket at the waiter. "What do people think? That we like being the butt of jokes? If I could help it, do you think I'd choose to be gay?"

Forest looked straight at Deirdre. "I don't know," he said.

The waiter put two more Guinnesses on the table and a full basket of popcorn. "Anything else?" he asked, and removed the empty beer glasses and popcorn basket. Deirdre shook her head.

"Because sometimes—" Forest stopped to clear his throat. "Sometimes I think you *do* like it, you know, being the oppressed one. You *enjoy* being different, the underdog." He twisted his beer glass around between the tips of his fingers.

Silence.

"I cannot believe you just said that."

Forest removed his hands from his glass and gestured

as he spoke. "Come on. Don't tell me it isn't really a choice. Don't tell me that the right guy . . ." Deirdre pushed her chair back from the table, but he grabbed her arm. "Look, I don't give a goddamn, you know that, but hell, you don't even seem . . . gay. So what if you do like being part of the oppressed? What's it to me? I'm just saying that, hell . . . I don't know what I'm saying, but maybe it *is* a choice and maybe you made that choice and maybe you should think about that."

Deirdre watched Forest gulp down his Guinness. Her own was untouched. She sat stuck to her chair, afraid of what might happen if she moved. Anything seemed possible—she might hurl her mug full of beer against the wall, her fingers might fly off, she herself might be propelled into Forest, so great was her rage and her desire to pummel him. She felt like a character in a Stephen King novel, no longer fully human, her body invaded by a foreign demon with a mind and will of its own.

"Fuck you," she said under her breath. And then she got up, dug a few bills from her pocket, threw them on the table, and walked out.

CHAPTER EIGHT

DEIRDRE LEFT TONY'S AND DROVE IN A BLIND RAGE. Scary how much she trusted the car and herself to drive it. Her mind raced. Where the hell was SJ? And what had just happened?

Forest. Her only friend at Brandywine. Friendships were hard enough to come by in the adult world, not like kids who just started playing together, who, because they were climbing the jungle gym side by side, started talking to each other, because they sat next to each other in homeroom became besties, because their parents were friends became friends too. Adult friendships seemed so much more complicated, fraught as they were now, for Deirdre, with possible sexual tension in addition to the regular friendship worries.

Not that those tensions were anything new.

When Deirdre was ten, she had her first memorable crush. Of course, back then, in Sister Theresa's fifth grade room when Deirdre and Lizzie O'Connor teamed up to make their diorama of Popsicle-stick log cabins for the unit on the Westward Movement, Deirdre didn't call it a crush. Instead, she told her mother that fall that she had made a new best friend. Though technically Maria Da Silva was still Deirdre's best friend, they no longer had any of the same classes together. Maria had already started wearing blue eye shadow and talking about boys she thought were cute. So she barely noticed when Deirdre started spending all her time with Lizzie.

When Lizzie's family moved away at the beginning of seventh grade, Deirdre and Lizzie promised each other they would always keep in touch. They would go to college together, share an apartment, be each other's maid of honor, a godmother to each other's children. Deirdre started seventh grade at St. Peter's bereft. She wrote in her diary—long, painful entries about what it felt like to be the only seventh-grader without a best friend. She wrote about missing her Friday walks with Lizzie to Brigham's for chunks of break-up milk chocolate or small vanilla ice cream cones with jimmies, though she easily could have asked Paul or any number of others to go with her—Maria Da Silva, for instance, when she wasn't busy making out with boys behind the Woolworths.

She imagined that Lizzie, listening to her *Best of Bread* album, thought about Deirdre the way Deirdre thought about her, in that longing, almost desperate kind of way. She knew that Lizzie must be sad to be without her, that starting a new school without a best friend was even harder than what Deirdre was going through. It was difficult to picture Lizzie with new friends, so Deirdre imagined instead the way Lizzie might look when she saw her again—the exuberant smile, her brown hair pulled into a bouncing ponytail, how happy they both would be, how exactly right it would feel to be together again.

When Lizzie finally did visit right at the end of seventh grade, Deirdre skipped an end-of-year beach party because it coincided with her friend's arrival.

"You could take Lizzie," Deirdre's mother suggested. "I'm sure she would enjoy meeting your other friends."

But Deirdre didn't want to share Lizzie with anybody. In fact, Deirdre didn't even tell her friends Lizzie was visiting. She and Lizzie stayed up all night the first night in

Deirdre's room talking about books and new albums. They had pushed Deirdre's two twin beds together, moved the nightstand out of the way. There, they painted each other's toenails. Listened to Carole King over and over again. But every time Deirdre tried to get Lizzie to reminisce about the things they had done together, every time she brought up one of their silly private jokes, Lizzie would say, "*Deir*dre," and roll her eyes. Then she would launch into a story about one of her new friends and one of the coolest things she and her new friends had done together and then, finally, about Evan, a cute blond guy who sat in front of her in science class, a guy she had been meaning to write Deirdre about.

"He's wicked cute," Lizzie said, "his hair's kind of long," and she sat up in the twin bed, motioned to her shoulders with her hands.

"Yeah?" Deirdre felt a sickening thunk in her stomach. She lay on her side under the covers, her thighs sweating, and gripped the blanket.

"We're going out, sort of."

"What do you mean, sort of?" Deirdre sucked on the satiny ribbon edge of her blanket.

"He kissed me . . ."

Silence.

"So, I think that means we're going out." Lizzie had flounced back beneath the covers on her own side. And when Deirdre didn't say anything, she continued, "I would've written you right away, but it just happened, I swear." She made an X on her chest with her finger. "I swear. You're the first non–Emerson Junior High person I've told! My parents don't even know."

Deirdre knew she was supposed to feel grateful, but she didn't. She felt sick and miserable and irritated. She didn't have words for why she was feeling this way, and she might have even laughed if anyone had suggested that what she was experiencing was her first major breakup.

After Lizzie, new friendships were hard. And it would be years before Deirdre would figure out why. She spent her teens always half in love, longing for her new girlfriends the way they pined after boys. There were the girls on the cross-country team. And Lois in the drama club. Deirdre's senior year, there had been the young student teacher in her French class, Mademoiselle LaPointe—Agnès. *Ahn-yes*, she told the class, so much more beautiful and elegant than the English version. It was this possibility—that you could be Ahn-yes in French and Agnes in English—that produced in Deirdre the desire to learn French, to see who she might be in another language.

It was Agnès who suggested that Deirdre might think of studying French in college. "You should," Agnès told her in her Parisian accent. "There is great need for Americans to know such a beautiful culture, yes? You will visit me one day in Paris and I will show you my city. There, you will fall in love."

Of course, Deirdre was already in love.

She did major in French in college and worked hard, so that she might impress Agnès the next time she saw her. Deirdre imagined how Agnès would react to seeing her when she arrived for her junior year abroad—how much older and closer in age to Agnès Deirdre seemed now that she was out of high school and almost out of college, how much more sophisticated she had become, how really good her French was. For two years before Deirdre's junior year abroad, she and Agnès kept in touch via postcards and letters, Deirdre reporting about her decision to major in French, and after that with regular updates on her progress. Agnès wrote brief letters back or sent cheerful cards congratulating Deirdre on her studies. One day, Agnès started replying only in French, "because, *ma chère*, your French is now that good."

In Paris, because of Agnès, Deirdre felt at home more

quickly than her fellow exchange students. Agnès helped her find a room to rent in a safe neighborhood. She invited Deirdre to dinner parties in her small apartment, introduced Deirdre to her friends. There were frequent Monday-night films, when movies were half price. And there was the night out at a lesbian bar—a small, dark place tucked away in the third arrondissement—where men and women sat in the front but only women were allowed in the back. Deirdre had been fascinated.

"You have never been to a lesbian bar before?" Agnès asked in French. She motioned for Deirdre to slide in along the banquette covered in cotton cloth, pillows tossed at infrequent intervals. Agnès followed and sat next to Deirdre, offered her a Gitanes.

"No," Deirdre said, and waved away the cigarette.

"I am surprised," Agnès said, flicking on her lighter. "You are lesbian, no?"

"I . . . I . . . don't know," Deirdre replied.

Agnès laughed. "But of course you are. And in any case, it does not matter, no? We are here. We are relaxed. We will have a drink and you will see if you are lesbian or not."

It seemed both exotic and familiar, sitting in the bar with Agnès, drinking a Belgian beer and watching the women—beautiful, long-legged women who looked like models; women in leather pants, in short skirts. Women in stiletto heels and boots. Women in jeans and T-shirts who were unmistakably French, who had that elegance that Deirdre had first noticed in Agnès back when she was Deirdre's student teacher; women who were clearly *not* American, who were Ahn-yes and not Agnes; women who showed Deirdre there were other ways to be than what she knew, ways different from her mother, from her own self. It would take Deirdre a few years to make the connections between her early crushes and the sense of comfort and familiarity she felt in that bar, but she had known immediately that she wanted to be like these women.

Back in the States, Deirdre found college social life confusing. As she became more certain of her sexual orientation, her relationships with women grew more difficult to decipher—which ones were strictly friendships and which ones might be budding romances? Or, more correctly, because many of the women Deirdre met were straight and not interested in a romantic relationship, which of the women did Deirdre truly want to establish friendships with and which one was she secretly in love with, settling instead for a friendship, since that is what was offered? Certainly, Deirdre wasn't attracted to all of them, but there were several instances when she couldn't tell whether or not she was about to embark on a friendship or start a relationship, and she didn't like the confusion.

So when she started teaching at Brandywine, Deirdre had been immediately grateful for Forest's friendship because of its uncomplicated nature. As first-year teachers hired at the same time, they became instant friends and confidantes, and work buddies, helping each other navigate the private school politics, complaining to each other when colleagues seemed resistant to their new ideas—a book club Deirdre tried to organize, or Forest's idea of running mini-courses during activity period—because what they proposed wasn't "the way we do things here," and why change what was working? Deirdre had found it easy to come out to Forest, and though he rarely socialized with Deirdre and SJ, he didn't seem to mind hearing about their squabbles or weekend adventures over beers at Tony's on an occasional Friday night, or coffee at the Blue Moon after school.

Teaching at Brandywine without Forest was unimaginable. But now it seemed that Deirdre had lost her best, and possibly her only, ally.

FIELD HOCKEY

At Brandywine, it was assumed that all the girls would play at least one sport—field hockey, volleyball, lacrosse, or tennis. Sports were required—if not varsity or junior varsity, then intramural.

The best games, the girls all said, were the ones with Ms. Murphy on the sidelines, cheering them on, her voice growing hoarse as she yelled, *Go! Shoot!* And, *Play your position, for God's sake!* If Ms. Murphy yelled Anna's name, then Anna felt every cell in her body vibrate.

On this early September afternoon, a day before the field trip, Anna had sat in the locker room next to Joanie, the goalie, a senior.

"So, I heard Ms. Murphy's got a thing for you," Joanie said. She bumped Anna's shoulder with hers. "You cool with that?"

Anna scowled. "Don't be a jerk."

"No, it's the story around school. You two are tight."

Anna bent over to tie her cleats.

"Ah, Anna-banana, I think you're blushing!" Joanie poked her in the side, then leaned in closer. "I didn't think you played for that team."

Anna felt the heat rise, her skin pulsate. She said nothing, kept fussing with her cleats, knotting and unknotting her laces.

Joanie was one of those girls everyone liked and looked up to. She had an aura—not the popular-girl thing, not exactly, but something cooler, a spirit that said, *I'm above all this*. That spirit is what drew the other girls to her, what made the hairs on Anna's neck shiver when Joanie noticed or talked to her. *Anna-banana*.

The mothers watched the girls play, each of them assessing her own daughter, measuring her up. They kept silent score—Anna, fearless, a gazelle girl who ran effortlessly, her stick an extension of her body; Joanie, fierce and relentless in goal. They were a wonder to watch, and each mother thought: *Why can't my daughter play like that?* The mothers heard Ms. Murphy shouting encouragement. They watched her jump up and down when Anna scored. It was good, wasn't it, that she was such a fan?

CHAPTER NINE

SJ CRUISED DOWN EAST MAIN. Her car doors were locked—force of habit—and the windows rolled up. She drove past the baseball field and Most Precious Blood, all the way down Main, deep into the East End. When she passed the old brick mills and the East End Gallery, she turned left and slowed on 15th, a residential street packed tight with triple-deckers and chain-link fences. Empty lots and asphalt. Lights burned in windows, and some yards were littered with kid stuff: plastic Big Wheels, push toys, a bicycle or two. A skinny man with brown skin sat on a porch, smoking, the sleeves of his T-shirt drooping from his arms. He seemed to be looking directly at SJ, and she gave a little wave and drove on. She turned right onto Q.

Like the houses on the other streets, the windows were barred. Brazilian flags flew from doorways. Here was a house with golden mums growing out front, flowers that softened the concrete and asphalt, made the house look homey. Another triple-decker was freshly painted baby blue, and its front porch sported a couple of metal chairs and a hammock. More than one house had a pumpkin sitting on the stoop. People weren't too cynical to put out pumpkins, even in this neighborhood where they were sure to be smashed well before Halloween—or at least that's what the news would have you believe. SJ was inclined to believe it. If

Leo Rivera could disappear from outside his grandmother's house and end up in the bottom of the river, it was hard to count on much of anything.

She made a left onto 19th. Many of these houses were run-down, with sagging roofs and crumbling steps, badly in need of paint. But even here, curtains hung in front of windows, some simply tied in knots that dangled in the center. A well-tended garden bed bordered the edge of one aluminum-sided triple-decker. Several houses had garden plots, remnants of crops in some—squash, old tomato vines, gourds, sunflowers. Kids gathered on the steps of one house and a few more, boys mostly, spilled out of a white car parked in front, the stereo pulsing, reverberating against the asphalt. These kids were black and brown, Brazilian maybe, it was hard to tell. SJ looked at them, laughing together, their music loud, their bodies loose and at ease. She longed to feel that camaraderie, had never been part of a group, not even in high school, especially not in high school. She had wished for it, but she hadn't known exactly how to make it happen. She had been too serious back then, and maybe even still now.

The odd thing was, until she met Deirdre, SJ could not even imagine herself in a relationship. Blame this on Mr. Freeman maybe, though that hadn't happened until senior year. Sometimes she blamed her inability to see herself as part of a couple on the fact that she was an only child. She was used to living a certain way and she liked things just so. SJ didn't know what it was about Deirdre that had made her feel differently, but she recalled with tremendous clarity the moment when she decided living with Deirdre was a possibility. Early in their romance, they were at dinner at their favorite Mexican restaurant. Drinking margaritas, nibbling on chips and salsa while they waited for burritos, Deirdre had been asking SJ about her family and growing up. She had asked something about being an only child, something about not being able to imagine going through life without another person. Wasn't it hard? Deirdre had asked.

SJ had wanted to tell Deirdre that she yearned for someone to go through life with, at first anyway, when she was young, because she spent so much time alone. Her parents didn't exactly neglect her, but they had their adult pursuits—their cocktail parties, their jobs, their trips abroad—and just as often as not, SJ was left to her own devices. She wanted to tell Deirdre what it was like to really need imaginary playmates because she spent so many hours alone. And at first, there had been the au pairs. The good ones—Mireille and Eva, a French girl and a blonde from Denmark—played with SJ, or at least came up with interesting projects for her to work on. The others—and there had been plenty of others—were useless as far as SJ had been concerned. None of them stole money from her parents or forgot to feed her dinner. They were all competent in their way, but for the most part, they did their household work and interacted with SJ only when necessary.

After the au pairs, there had been classmates, but even then, none who materialized into the longed-for best friend, no one who would sleep over at SJ's and giggle long into the night, no one who passed her notes in school or saved her a seat in the lunchroom. Even by the time she was seven or eight, SJ had the reputation of being a loner. The other kids assumed she liked it that way and though they were all friendly enough, they didn't go overboard in their attempts to include her. The girls in particular. Most of the time that was fine with SJ. She didn't really want to be taken in a limousine to see *The Nutcracker* in downtown Boston or wear a fancy dress and have a tea party, activities the other third grade girls in her private school had organized for their birthdays. (When she admitted this to Deirdre, Deirdre had exclaimed, "Oh, I would have loved that!") SJ might rather have attended the Red Sox games with some of the boys and sat in their fathers' corporate skyboxes at Fenway, but the boys didn't ask her. Not in third grade, or fourth, or fifth. Birthdays then were strictly single-sex affairs, and by the time the parties developed into boy-girl events, SJ wasn't particularly interested in those, either.

In high school, SJ had thrown herself into athletics and clubs. She made the fencing team and edited the literary magazine. And she read. SJ had always been a reader, but in high school she was never without a book. And there had been Mr. Freeman, his presence palpable at this very moment as she sat in the car, though if she were experiencing an actual memory, Mr. Freeman would have been driving, SJ riding shotgun. There had been a time in the car, hadn't there? Yes, a Saturday or maybe it was a Friday, a ride home from school. SJ had stayed after, talking as she often did, and Mr. Freeman had offered a ride. It was dark, winter, the heat on in the car. SJ remembered wearing mittens, remembered a hand, remembered—had she taken her mittens off?—felt again the finger, skin on skin, remembered again that rush, the pleasure, saw her mitten in Mr. Freeman's hand, his finger tracing her knuckles.

SJ stared at her knuckles now, white, gripping the steering wheel. The fact that she thought of him as Mr. Freeman and not Aaron—that said something, didn't it? Deirdre had tried to get SJ to tell stories of high school—"You didn't have any friends?" Incredulous. "Not one?" Though she loved, too, she said, the idea of SJ being a bookish loner, destined to become a librarian, the very epitome of the word librarian. Deirdre loved having a "super-smart" girlfriend, bragged about it to their small circle of friends. Even in the early days, SJ shrugged off the idea that Deirdre loved the idea of SJ more than she loved SJ herself, because at first it was simply nice to be with someone at all. Maybe, she had thought back then, maybe it was enough.

At the end of 19th Street, SJ could only turn right. And there, on the next corner, Mickey's auto body shop. Light shone from the office, though the shop looked closed, the garage door down. SJ pulled up next to the curb and turned her car off and waited.

She glanced at her watch—well past six o'clock. Deirdre would have been home for at least an hour, maybe more. She might well wonder where SJ was, but it wasn't likely that she would worry or call the library looking for her. That wasn't Deirdre. She might fume, she might be angry when SJ got home, but she wasn't a worrier. Maybe if Deirdre worried more SJ might feel more compelled to come home after work. More crazy logic, but it seemed to SJ that she and Deirdre were little more than two people living in the same house these days. They were hardly lovers. Sex between them was infrequent—"Not on a school night, for heaven's sake," Deirdre said if SJ tried, which she'd recently stopped doing. School was the focus of Deirdre's life. She might worry about her students, but worry about SJ?

"Errands to run?" Deirdre had said just the other night when SJ came home well after nine, after drinks with Florence and then a drive through the East End. SJ had driven up and down similar streets, looking at the houses, wondering about the people behind their windows, what their lives were really like. Whether they wished they lived elsewhere. Whether they were happy in this neighborhood. Whether their kids were scared to be out at night. Whether drugs were really a problem.

Now, sitting in front of Mickey's shop, looking at the light on in there, SJ realized too—and this was a hard one to admit—that maybe she wanted out of her relationship with Deirdre. SJ craved passion. She wanted to be somebody's lover, not a housemate. She wanted to be with someone who cared as much for her as for a job. SJ wanted a life, not the semblance of a life she had with Deirdre, a façade, a cover-up, not the real thing.

SJ unlocked her car door and got out. She shivered a little in the September evening and grabbed the hoodie she kept in the backseat, locked up the car, and headed across the street to the garage. She pulled on the hoodie and took a deep breath. She knocked on the office door and peered in; she didn't see anyone. Just a metal desk covered with papers and a heavy-looking cash register, old. Shelves of car products—oil and lubricant, SJ wasn't sure what all was up there. There was a red clock with the Coca-Cola logo painted across the front. A vending machine. Two metal chairs with green leather seats. And in the corner, what looked like a kid's bike. Old and beat-up.

SJ knocked again, harder. She thought she heard something, but wasn't sure. Radio? A voice? "Mickey?" she said and knocked again. "Are you in there?"

The evening breeze blew across the back of her neck. She shivered and zipped the hoodie. Before she could turn to leave, Mickey cracked the door.

"SJ? What are you doing here?" He looked tired.

"I . . . was kind of worried about you when you didn't show up today." She laughed a little and wrapped her arms around herself. "Can I come in? It's cold out here."

Mickey hesitated, then stepped back.

"You didn't call to cancel."

He followed SJ's gaze around the office until it rested on the newspaper clippings.

"Practicing?" SJ said and took a couple steps toward the desk. "That's great!" Several articles were scattered across it. She glanced at the ones on top, both recent articles about the investigation surrounding Leo Rivera's murder, as the police were now calling it. She riffled through a few others in the pile—all about Leo Rivera: when he first disappeared, after he'd been missing a couple of days, and a front-pager from the day his body was found.

"Did you know him?" SJ put down the article with ten-year-old Leo Rivera smiling from beneath his Red Sox cap, the same picture the TV flashed each night during the local news. By now, everyone in town felt as if they knew him.

Mickey didn't say anything.

"He lived near you, right?" SJ replayed her drive through the very same streets where Leo Rivera had disappeared, just a couple of blocks from where she now stood.

Mickey looked up. "Yeah," he said. He rubbed his hands together, cleared his voice. "He, uh . . . We were neighbors, you know? Good kid too, that Leo." He shoved his hands in his pockets and shuffled his feet.

The office felt suddenly hot and cramped and airless.

Mickey stood, his body loose and gangly, hands jammed in his pockets.

SJ wanted to know what he was thinking. She turned away, glanced at the bike leaning against the far wall, red and faded, with black handlebars, then at the articles on the desk, Leo Rivera young and smiling. Dead. SJ looked back at Mickey. "You know, there've been people in the library asking about you."

"People?" He leaned back against the doorframe and folded his arms.

"Detectives, maybe, I'm not sure. Police."

"Yeah? Why's that?"

"They say . . ." SJ took a deep breath. "They say you might have had something to do with Leo Rivera's mur-der." Beyond Mickey, through the doorway, she could see her gray-blue Honda parked alongside the curb on the other side of the street. Such a short, infinite distance.

"Well, they can come and ask me myself, why don't they? Matter of fact, maybe I'll go on down to the station, just tell them I got nothing to hide. Hook me up to a lie detector right now and I'll show them." Mickey, animated, paced the floor in front of SJ, arrogant and cocky.

"Listen, *I* know it's ridiculous to think you might be involved." SJ found herself on more familiar footing, in the role of mentor, comforter.

"Hell yeah. Like killing my own brother, man." He stopped pacing and turned to SJ. "What'd they say about me, those detective people?"

"I didn't talk with them. They spoke with my boss."

"The white-haired lady?"

"Florence."

"Do they think the person who did it is a real sicko? A perv?" He trembled, wiped his brow.

"Don't you? Anybody who would do that to a little kid is sick."

"Do what? Killing the kid? Or . . . the other stuff?"

"All of it. Jesus, Mickey."

Mickey stepped closer to SJ. "What if the boy, you know . . . what if he . . ." He swallowed. "What if the kid, you know, wanted to have sex with the guy?"

SJ stared. "He was ten."

Mickey was quiet for a minute. "Yeah, yeah, okay. I was just wondering, you know, what if? Like maybe the kid wanted to have sex with a man? Like maybe he didn't know other kids his age he could do it with or something?"

"So why'd the guy kill him, then?"

"Freaked. He'd just done it with a kid. He wasn't a friggin' homo, just did it with the kid, but then he freaked cuz maybe now he might be a homo?"

"Is that what you think? Do you think Leo Rivera wanted to have sex with the guy?" SJ asked.

Mickey flopped into one of the metal chairs. "Not Leo. Not that little kid, but I don't know, man. I think the guy must've *thought* he wanted to or something, cuz why else would he pick up a little kid and screw with him? It don't make no sense . . . Sorry about today," he added without looking up. "I should've called."

SJ shifted her weight. "Listen, I'm going to leave." She peered at Mickey slumped in the chair. He looked small himself. So young. SJ stepped in front of him, and Mickey jumped up and grabbed her shoulders, waited just long enough that she could register the grip of his hands and the beery smell of his breath, and he kissed her, hard. For a moment she stood, frozen, accepting his kiss. Finally, she pulled away and walked out without a word.

When SJ pulled into the driveway, the lights in the living room were on. She had been hoping that maybe Deirdre had gone out, Friday night and all. But no such luck. SJ wasn't in any mood to face her questions. She held out her hands; they were still shaking. She took a couple of deep breaths before heading into the house.

"There you are," Deirdre called from her stretched-out position on the couch as SJ opened the door. Deirdre kept her eyes on the TV, watching a sitcom SJ didn't recognize. "Where've you been?"

"Out," SJ said. "Driving around." She closed the door behind her, shrugged off her tote bag, and let it drop on the floor.

"Yeah? Driving around? Great. The one night I need you . . . the one most horrible night of my life and you're out driving around." Deirdre drank from a beer bottle on the floor next to the couch.

"Don't . . . start," SJ said weakly. "I'm not in the mood." She scuffed through the living room, the dining room, and went directly to the bedroom. She pulled off the hoodie without unzipping it, stopping to breathe in the smoky smell of the car shop. She could still taste Mickey's mouth, wet and sour, feel the imprint of his lips on hers.

Had she wanted it, back in high school? She thought she did, but *had* she?

"Oh great!" Deirdre yelled. "You come home *hours* late . . . How did I know you weren't road kill somewhere, and you totally ignore me, like I'm the one who's done something wrong?"

SJ started to reply, "Have I done—" then stopped. What was the point? She walked into the dining room. "You've been lying there on the couch, waiting for me to come home?" She waved her hand at the beer bottle.

"I'm so pathetic, is that what you think? I have no life of my own? What is wrong with you? Why do you not even care that I might have gotten fired today?" Deirdre started to cry.

"What?" SJ hurried into the living room. "What happened?" She sat in the rocking chair opposite Deirdre.

Deirdre blew her nose on a used tissue wadded up and lying on the floor next to her bottle of beer. "It's a long story . . ." She sat up cross-legged on one end of the couch.

"Before you start, can you shut that thing off?" SJ pointed to the clicker. "That's better."

And Deirdre told the story again, of how Anna had come late to school, how she'd forged her mother's signature, how she had ridden in the van on the way home, and then, finally, how Anna had kissed her in the school parking lot and how her mother saw the whole thing. When she was finished, SJ was silent.

"Say something," Deirdre said.

"Like . . . what? What do you want me to say? Not *I told you so*. Not *I told you to be careful*."

"Like, how about, oh, you know, *Deirdre, everything will be okay because you didn't do anything wrong,* or how about that school needs me, maybe, and so there's no way Martin Loring will fire me on Monday morning, you know, something like that?"

SJ didn't say anything.

"And don't give me some shit like I was asking for it, being alone in the van with Anna," Deirdre continued, her voice rising. "I've heard enough of that already from Forest."

"Come on, Deirdre. You're a veteran teacher. You *should* know better than to be alone in the van with one of your googly eyed girls. I've been saying this for years . . ." She had been alone with Mr. Freeman. She had willingly climbed into that car, hadn't she?

"Oh, *years* you've been saying this—right. What kind of crap is that? Since when is it a crime for a female teacher to be alone with a female student?" Deirdre grabbed a pillow from behind her head and hugged it with both arms.

"And if Forest had been alone in the van with Anna, and she kissed *him*?"

"That's different . . ."

"How is that different?" SJ asked quietly. She sat on the edge of the chair.

"For one, because Forest admitted to me tonight that he thinks about kissing students like Anna Worthington, something I don't think about, thank you very much!"

"No?"

"What?"

"Look, as far as Martin Loring is concerned, he's got to treat you like he would a male teacher in the same situation, since as a lesbian, you *are* sexually interested in females . . ."

"Not fifteen-year-old girls!" Deirdre tossed the pillow across the living room, where it landed with a soft thud in front of the TV. "SJ, of all people, you know how seriously

I take this job. You know how dedicated I am, how much being a teacher means to me. You know that."

"I know," SJ said, getting up out of the rocker, "that you spend way more time than is normal worrying about those kids and that you get way too involved with their personal lives, for whatever reason. That's what I know." She reached back and pulled her hair into a ponytail with her hand. "Look, Martin Loring seems like a fair guy. He'll do what's right, but personally?" She let go of her hair and crossed her arms. "Maybe it's good that something like this finally happened so you could wake up and see what is really going on between you and those girls." SJ raised her eyebrows, a what-do-you-think-of-that expression, clicked the TV back on, and turned to walk out of the room.

But instead, she stood frozen in place when the newscaster from the local ten o'clock nightly news announced the lead story—an arrest in the disappearance and murder of Leo Rivera.

"*. . . just moments ago,*" the newscaster said. "*We go live . . .*"

SJ must have turned from where she stood. She must have had some sense of foreboding to stay riveted to that spot on the rug, aware of Deirdre on the couch behind her—painfully aware—while they both stared at the familiar figure of Mickey Gilberto, handcuffed, emerging from his gas station where, "*according to sources,*" he had been living lately, and not in the house he shared with his mother, a house that, ironically, was right next door to Leo Rivera's.

The chief of police spoke before a crowd of reporters, saying how proud he was of the investigative team, that the suspect had been under surveillance for the last few days, saying that they had waited until the right moment to go in and make the arrest, "*until we had all the facts.*" He must have continued talking, because he remained on the TV screen and his mouth was moving, then the program cut back to the live scene at the shop, the very spot SJ had been less than an hour earlier. (Had those same detectives been waiting outside the shop? Had they watched SJ go in, heard the conversation on a wiretap? Watched as Mickey grabbed and kissed her?) In a sickening moment, SJ wondered if maybe *she* had been followed, if she were the one who'd given Mickey's whereabouts away.

"Oh God," she said out loud. *Mickey, what have you done?*

Pleading, wondering, his voice thin and childlike. Not the voice of a murderer. But the things he'd said . . . Not the face of someone who would do that to a kid. *Like killing my own brother, man,* he'd said too, hadn't he?

The mouth with the silk wisp of a mustache kissing hers, pressing her lips, his tongue slippery and dangerous. His grip strong and exciting.

"Oh God," SJ said again.

SJ, the voice played like a broken record. *SJ,* the voice repeated in her head. *SJ,* the voice wondered, *what if he wanted it?*

CHAPTER TEN

DEIRDRE LIKED RUNNING IN THE FALL. For one thing, the weather was cooler, and on weekend mornings she could sleep in before taking her run. This morning she lay in bed awake but unwilling to move, even to make coffee, even to grab a cup after SJ put the coffee on. Even to see where SJ was going as she headed out the door.

They had gone through all of Saturday hardly speaking. Deirdre had spent the day in the yard, cleaning up the garden, pulling weeds, planting mums in the front. She needed to do something physical, dig in the dirt. Partly, she had to get rid of her hangover from Friday night, and partly, she had to do some kind of work with her hands in order to focus on something other than the phone call she knew was certain to come from Martin Loring.

Why he hadn't ever called Friday night was a mystery in itself. Maybe Frances Worthington hadn't said anything yet? Maybe she was going for something more dramatic—saving her announcement for Monday morning, in front of the whole school? In one of their brief conversations on Saturday, before SJ had left the house, SJ suggested that maybe Deirdre should call Martin herself, give him a heads-up about the other phone call he was certain to receive if he hadn't already. Headmasters like that, being tipped off so they weren't on the defensive; hadn't Deirdre said that herself?

"You should call him," SJ had said, arms crossed, standing next to the phone in the kitchen.

But Deirdre couldn't do it. She couldn't see any good way of really explaining how Anna Worthington had ended up kissing her in the van, how it wouldn't at least *sound* like it was Deirdre's fault.

"I'm sure he's going to call," Deirdre had said to SJ. "He must not be around, or else I would have heard from him."

Late morning, the phone had rung and Deirdre froze. SJ was out of the house already, and Deirdre let the machine pick up. Her hand shook until she heard Florence's voice.

"Florence. Hi." A big sigh. "SJ's not here."

"You know when she'll be back? This is pretty important."

"Don't know. But I'll leave her a message."

Some sounds on the other end. Florence's breathing or tapping of some sort. Then, "You see the news last night?"

"The arrest? Yeah, we saw. How freaky is *that* that he was one of our movers . . . ?"

Again, nothing on the other end of the phone except Florence's breathing. Then, "Tell SJ to give me a call as soon as she can, will you? Tell her it's urgent."

After talking with Florence, Deirdre had gone to the garden and tidied up, pulled dead flowers and weeds. She had needed to do *something* while she waited for the phone to ring. She spent the rest of the day outside, came in and washed up, and still no phone call.

When SJ came home—well after six o'clock—Deirdre asked where she had been and SJ had said, "The library—went in to do some work."

"So what was so urgent?"

SJ looked puzzled.

"Florence? She called looking for you, said it was urgent. She didn't tell you?"

After that, neither of them spoke to the other for the rest of the evening.

Now, here it was Sunday morning, SJ gone again and Deirdre didn't know where. The clock ticked lazily past nine and Deirdre didn't move. She had agreed to meet Paul at ten for a run. She stretched her legs and rubbed them against the flannel sheets she had put on the bed in spite of SJ's protests that it was too early in the season. "Putting on the flannel sheets now," she had said, "gives us nothing to look forward to."

Deirdre winced at the unintended omen. Only one week ago, Deirdre and SJ had been arguing over the appropriateness of flannel sheets—and now, *now* they were hardly talking to each other. Now SJ was disappearing for hours, entire afternoons, and lying about it. Now Deirdre was about to lose her job and her entire career. Funny that in a week your entire life could change.

Deirdre threw back the covers and put one pajamaed leg onto the floor. *Get up*, she told herself. She at least wanted to stretch before she had to meet Paul. As soon as she got her second leg out of bed and was standing on the floor, the phone rang.

Deirdre picked it up immediately. "Hello?" she said.

"I'm sorry if I woke you." Martin Loring sounded sad and a little distant.

"No, no, I'm up." Cold all of a sudden, Deirdre looked around for her robe.

"You . . . I'm sure you know why I'm calling . . ." He hesitated.

Deirdre said nothing. Nodded stupidly, as if Martin Loring could see her. Where was her bathrobe?

Martin cleared his throat. "You have to know this is serious. Or I wouldn't be calling you at home on a Sunday." Why hadn't he called immediately on Friday? But Deirdre had the sense that to rush in with her own version of the story was foolish, that it made her look defensive, and guilty. Still, she wanted to say something.

"Martin, I . . ." But what was there to say? *Anna Worthington is in love with me? That's why she kissed me?* "I'd rather talk about this in person," she said. What was she thinking? If she couldn't get the words out with Martin Loring safely on the other end of the phone line and not sitting directly in front of her, how was she going to be able to say anything to him in person? "Could we . . . Would it be possible to meet somewhere? Today, even?"

"I'm sorry," he said. "But I'll need to see you first thing Monday morning. Seven o'clock in my office. Okay?"

"I'll be there," Deirdre said, and she hung up.

As she pulled on her running tights and then a Cool-Max shirt, Deirdre felt an odd sense of relief. Martin hadn't yelled and screamed—not that she imagined he would do that exactly—but had been rather gentle. Still, Deirdre was certain the man was going to fire her on Monday morning.

Paul was stretching his hamstrings when Deirdre pulled up and parallel parked next to the entrance. They always began their run here at the park, halfway between their two houses.

"Deird!" Paul yelled, dark hair bent to his outstretched leg. "You're a little late. Thought I'd have to start without you."

"I'm—what—ten minutes late?"

"Fifteen. You stretched?"

"Some. Here, let me just do a couple of these . . ." Deirdre said as she crossed one leg in front of the other and half–sat back to stretch her glutes.

"Great day for a run." Paul jogged in place, shaking out his hands.

But Deirdre's heart wasn't really in it. After hanging up

with Martin Loring, she wanted nothing more than to sink back beneath the covers. Sleep and sleep and sleep. Total inertia controlled her body, but something convinced her to keep this running date with Paul, some sense—both absurd and real—that being with him was just the thing she needed to keep her sanity.

"All right, let's get this show on the road," Paul said. "You up for fast or slow?"

"Don't know. Feeling kind of sluggy, so could we start off slow?" Deirdre jumped up and down, loosening her muscles.

"I'll do my best, but listen, if I'm on a roll, you'll understand, right? If I get in that groove . . ."

"Just run, would you? Like a normal person? . . . Hey, slow down!" Deirdre ran to catch up with him at the stop sign. "You're already being a show-off. Cut it out."

Paul grinned. "Come on, Deird. You usually kick my butt. What's with you today?"

Deirdre concentrated on her breathing. *Martin Loring. Martin Loring.* She ran beside Paul without talking, without looking at the trees, the colors of their leaves so vibrant they could hurt your stomach with the pain of their beauty and with the knowledge that such beauty was fleeting. Those last days, in early November, when the few remaining leaves clung to bare branches—they were the hardest to endure, and Deirdre sometimes wished for a big wind to blow through and take the leaves all at once, so difficult it was to watch them drop one by one, the stabs of red left dangling. She couldn't bear it. But now, in late September, the leaves were almost at their deepest hues, and normally it was all she could do to run past them without tripping, staring up at them, mesmerized. Yet the hurricane had blown many off early this year. So she ran and breathed. *Martin Loring. Martin Loring.* What was she going to do?

"Hey, slowpoke, you really *are* sluggy today. What's up?" Paul slowed to let Deirdre catch up.

"I've got a lot on my mind."

"Like what? Things okay with SJ?"

Deirdre stopped and stared at Paul's back, waiting for him to realize she wasn't beside him. "Do you realize that's the first time you've ever asked about her?" she said when Paul turned around.

"That's crazy. I like SJ." Paul jogged in place.

"I didn't say you didn't like her—I said you never ask about her. There's a difference."

"So that's it, huh? Something going on with you two?"

Deirdre started running again. "No, that's not it, smart-ass."

"Then what?" Paul asked, jogging beside her.

"I don't want to talk about it." Deirdre ran harder now. She headed up the hill, past her favorite Victorian, painted mauve with white trim. She didn't complain, as she usually did, about the incline, but instead started to sprint, running furiously. She ran up School Street and right on through the intersection to Oak. Past her next-favorite house on the route, the one she always had to point out to Paul if he didn't beat her to it. Mentioning the house turned into a game between them, to see who would say something first, but today, Deirdre ran right by it, Paul behind her, yelling to wait up, to stop. She ran with a fierceness she couldn't control, straight past Sophie and Mark's school—JFK Elementary—past shaded lawns and parked cars. Past another house she had looked at with SJ, a house they could better afford than what they bought and a house SJ preferred to the one they ended up with. Because it was farther from Brandywine, farther from the Brandywine neighborhood, a more "mixed" neighborhood, as SJ would say.

"For Chrissakes, slow down, would you?" yelled Paul from a few yards back.

But Deirdre kept running. She kept running until her chest hurt, until it burned, until her heart pounded. Even then, she did not stop. She slowed to a jog and evened out her breathing, then jogged to the end of the block. She was afraid to stop, unsure of what might happen if she did.

"What the hell?" Paul said when he caught up, huffing, bent over with his hands on his thighs.

Deirdre was breathing hard.

"Sluggy, my ass."

"Paul." Deirdre looked at her brother. "I'm going to get fired."

He didn't look up. "Yeah, right. Ha ha." But when Deirdre didn't say anything else, he raised his head. "You're serious."

Deirdre nodded and started to cry.

"Okay, come on. Let's . . . let's walk back, come on." Paul put an arm around her. "Since we sprinted half of our usual route anyway." He jostled her a little.

"This is serious. I'm in big trouble."

"What happened?"

Deirdre wriggled free. "It's a long story—but basically, Martin Loring thinks I'm involved with a student. And I'm *not*," she added when she saw the look on Paul's face.

He gave a little laugh. "Wow. So, like, what's going on? Did some girl make up a story about you or what? Somebody you flunked in French class?"

They walked and Deirdre felt chilled, the sweat on her skin cooling now. She rubbed behind her neck, at the base of her hairline. Off in the distance, bells at the Episcopal church, maybe, or First Unitarian, rang out cheerfully, marking time for eleven o'clock services.

"It's . . . kind of complicated, but the thing is, I'm not involved with her but I think I'm going to get fired anyway." Deirdre scuffed through dried leaves on the sidewalk, kicked at a pile along the edge of someone's lawn.

"But you're one of their best teachers."

Deirdre gave Paul a smile for that one.

"So why wouldn't the headmaster believe you?" Paul walked with his arms folded across his chest. "Why doesn't he know it's a load of crap?"

Deirdre took a deep breath. "Because . . . because . . . because someone saw us kissing." She glanced quickly up at Paul. He seemed to go rigid, his face stiff and unmoving. "I know it sounds bad, but she kissed *me*. I didn't do anything wrong, I swear."

Paul kept walking slow, deliberate steps. He wouldn't look at her.

"I know you think this whole gay thing is weird, but I'm telling you, I swear to God, I'm not involved with any students. This girl . . . she . . . It's a long story, but her mother hates my guts and the girl is troubled and so Martin Loring is definitely going to fire me." Silence from Paul. "Oh, and her mother is the president of the board, did I mention that?"

"Jesus." Paul shook his head, gave that little laugh again.

"Please don't tell Kris." Deirdre reached over and grabbed his arm.

"I can't promise. You know that." Paul patted Deirdre's hand, then removed it. "We tell each other everything."

"But not this. You can't. You *know* how she'll react— she's not so fond of me as it is." Deirdre tried to make it sound funny, like a private joke they shared, but Paul wasn't laughing. "Please?"

"I'll see," was all he could promise. They walked the next few blocks without saying anything, Deirdre feeling deflated, empty inside. Then, just before they reached the park, Paul looked at her. "How can a kid just *kiss* you?"

"Yeah, that's what Martin Loring's going to ask me." She dragged her toe on the cement. An orange leaf drifted in the air and landed on the ground next to her foot. "I know it sounds bad but I really didn't do anything wrong." She looked up at Paul. "I really didn't."

He nodded but didn't smile. Didn't offer any other words of encouragement.

"Sorry for the sucky run." She punched him in the arm. "Okay. So, talk to you soon?" She stretched on her toes to hug him but gave him a peck on the cheek instead.

Paul untied his key from his sneaker. "Let me know what happens."

"Oh, and Paul? Mom and Dad do not need to know about this."

Paul nodded again and got into his Volvo wagon, the safest car for carting around children, he said.

Deirdre watched him drive past the lavender Victorian to the end of the street where he put on his blinker and took a left. She stood fixed to the spot, the sounds of kids playing basketball on the courts behind her. Leaves rustled and blew, danced across the pavement at her feet.

Chapter Eleven

SIX THIRTY. DEIRDRE STEPPED OUT into the cool morning air and locked the door behind her. Normally, she relished this early-morning time and the quiet walk to Brandywine. These days, whenever she was able to get up ahead of schedule and have the street almost to herself, she reveled in that prewinter chill—the dry, sharp air that would later melt into warm spots on the playground, heating the kids so they tore off jackets and piled them on the edge of the blacktop. Deirdre felt a certain security on those mornings, a kind of knowledge that came with seeing the day start before everyone else. Today, there was no joy in the walk. She felt as if the rustling of the trees and shrubs, the piles of leaves, even the trills of the mourning doves mocked her as she walked past. They all knew it. She was a condemned woman.

Deirdre pulled her jacket tighter and hoisted her backpack up onto her shoulder. Disconnected, that's how she felt passing the familiar houses, seeing the woman from the hardware store approach the opposite side of the intersection. Everything was the same and everything was most certainly not the same. But outwardly, who could tell? Who would know, for instance, if they passed by 47 Hillside Street that inside, all was not as it seemed? That SJ and Deirdre were barely speaking? That SJ had in fact spent the entire weekend away from the house, except for those hours at night when she slept next to Deirdre, sometimes reaching out, but still not talking? It was unsettling, this possibility, that things looked one way and were actually another. That you could walk past houses which gave the appearance of solidity and comfort—the illusion that living in them offered a certain kind of life—but that beyond the front doors what you found was something very different. It was a cruel joke. What kind of security was there in buying a house, then? What did it matter, the neighborhood you chose? How did you know what to think of your neighbors when outwardly, their lives appeared to be one way but unless you could peek into open windows unnoticed, you might never be sure? If you couldn't count on certain truths, what was there? How did you know how to proceed?

In the Brandywine parking lot, Frances Worthington's silver BMW was parked next to Martin Loring's old Volvo. Oh God, was Deirdre going to have to face her this morning? But there were several other cars too—Beth Ann's white Chevrolet among them. Deirdre walked up the steps to the front door and opened it. She heard voices down the hall toward the library. The new-parent coffee. Martin must have forgotten there would be other people around as early as seven that morning. Deirdre certainly had forgotten. Well, she would do what she could to avoid them.

She walked down the hallway past the trophy cases full of championship teams—varsity lacrosse, swim, and tennis— and the framed, formal faces of former heads of the school. Each of them seemed to pass judgment, admonishing Deirdre with their silent stares and half-smiles. *You should know better*, they seemed to be saying. *See what happens when you try to fit in where you don't belong?* When Deirdre had first been hired, she felt uncomfortable each time she walked down this hallway. She had felt the stares of those faces. But later, as she began to feel at home at Brandywine—as she developed her reputation for being a good teacher and one whom parents frequently requested for their daughters— she felt a kinship with those same photos. An alliance. *You see? I can be one of you. We are all in this together.*

"Deirdre, come in." Martin looked up from his desk and motioned to the leather chair when Deirdre peered around the corner into his office. There was Lil's trench coat, hanging on a hook on the wall behind her desk, but no Lil. She must be helping the mothers with the coffee in the library.

Deirdre felt her face flush hot red and sat on her hands to keep them from shaking. She wanted to say something but didn't know what. She wanted to start this awful procedure and she wanted it never to happen. She wanted Martin to look up from whatever it was he was working on and tell her that he was sorry for the terrible misunderstanding, that he knew Deirdre would never do anything to compromise her job or her students' safety. She wanted him to tell her she was so valuable he didn't know what he would do without her and therefore couldn't do what she was pretty sure he was about to do. She wanted him to tell her that in all his years as an administrator, he had never known such dedication.

Deirdre tried to control her breathing. The clock on the wall ticked—a loud, mundane sound that she found oddly reassuring. She heard heavy footsteps outside the office and wondered how much Lil already knew and what she thought.

Heels clicking down the hallway and then that familiar buttercream voice.

"Lil . . ." *Please, dear God, let Martin shut the door to his office before Frances Worthington rounds the corner into the main office.* "Lil, do you know where we might find the larger coffee pot? I have this one . . ."

"Well," Martin Loring cleared his throat. He stood and set his glasses on the pile of papers, shuffled out from be-

hind his desk, his plaid jacket unbuttoned, shirt a little wrin-
kled. Deirdre had always thought of him as a kind man.
A bit disheveled and unorganized—a typical academic—his
love and respect for children evident in the way he knew
each girl's name and favorite activity or pastime, the way
he greeted them one by one in the hallway or kept his office open. The walls of his office were covered with student
artwork, and Deirdre stared now at a framed abstract wa-
tercolor in bright blues and reds.

Martin closed the door. "So," he said.

Deirdre tried to look casual and not terrified. Her face
burned hot.

"This is very difficult." Martin sat in the leather chair
opposite her. "Very difficult. But I'm sure you can see my
position on this thing." He smoothed his tie, navy blue with
thin stripes.

Tick, tick, tick. A ringing phone and then Lil's voice—
"Brandywine Academy." For a moment, this could be any
day beginning in the usual way—Deirdre stopping in to
chat with Martin about any number of things en route to
the classroom, Lil answering the phone as always—but it
wasn't.

"I'm sorry," was all Deirdre managed to squeak out,
and was horrified to feel her eyes fill with tears. "I . . ."

Martin continued: "You can understand that in my position I have to think of what's best for the school." He looked
up at her then, thick brows furrowed, unsmiling. Deirdre
resisted the urge to smooth down the wiry ones that curled
askew. Martin rubbed his hands together, cleared his throat.
"I've had to, ah, consult with our lawyer . . ."

Lawyer! Deirdre couldn't prevent the shock from reg-
istering on her face. "I assure you, I didn't do anything
wrong," she said, her voice rising. She coughed, cleared her
own throat. "I know it looks bad but—"

Martin raised his hands and stopped her. "This thing, it is bad. The fact is that Frances saw you . . . I'm sorry . . . ah, embracing Anna, isn't that right?"

Deirdre nodded, miserable. "Yes, but—"

He held up his hands again. "Then I have no choice." He shook his head. "I have to put you on leave. Immediately."

Deirdre, as much as she had been expecting those very words, was startled to hear them. "But," she sputtered, "can I . . . Do you want to hear my version?" And she launched into the story, the version she had told herself hundreds of times since Friday, about how Anna had forged the permission slip, how Deirdre hadn't known, how when she found Anna in the van, she had tried to console the girl, how Deirdre had insisted she call her mother immediately and how, while Deirdre was doing her best to calm her down, Anna had kissed her.

Martin looked at her, his brown eyes kind and soft. "The situation is this, to be frank: I have little choice here. After consulting with our lawyer—" he rubbed his hands together again and looked away, then back at her, "I have been advised to let you go immediately."

"Like, today?"

Martin nodded. "Yes," he said. "Paid leave," he added after a long second. As if that mattered.

"Today?" Deirdre repeated. "I have to . . . go home?" She felt stupid, as if Martin were using words whose meanings weren't immediately clear. If she couldn't teach today, why hadn't Martin insisted on telling her over the phone?

"I'm afraid so, yes. I have no choice."

"You keep saying that—but what about what really happened in that van? What about my version?" Deirdre stood and began pacing across the office. Her voice sounded shrill in her ears, like a whinny. She felt her body charged by anger, a drug pulsing through her veins. Her hands shook.

"Anna kissed me. I didn't kiss her, for God's sake. She . . . What was I supposed to do?" Now the tears fell and Deirdre crossed her arms. She paced, knew that she was crying but couldn't stop. "How . . . What was I supposed to do? What did I do wrong?" She looked then at Martin before she sank to the leather chair, the tears falling freely now, uncontrollable.

Outside the office, Frances Worthington spoke to Lil. Something about napkins and cookies, about not having enough platters. Deirdre imagined the woman standing in front of Lil's desk in one of her seamless outfits, the kind that you knew cost a fortune, the kind that, no matter what you had on, made you feel poor. Ashamed. Ragged and underdressed.

"I didn't do anything wrong," Deirdre tried to regain control. "Ask Anna," she said after a moment, catching her breath. She sat upright. "Have you spoken with her? Did you ask Anna what happened?"

Martin moved to the edge of his chair, his hands still pressed together. "I'm afraid so." He glanced up at the wall clock.

"Was *she* there?" Deirdre asked in a whisper, thrusting her hand toward the office door, pointing. "Did you get to talk with Anna alone?"

"I can't discuss that." Martin stood. "We can talk more later—I'm sure we'll have more to say as we investigate further, but for now . . . for now, I'm sorry."

He couldn't do it. Martin couldn't even bring himself to ask her to leave. That gave Deirdre some hope. "So, you are investigating? This isn't the end?"

Martin nodded. "Absolutely. Understand, you're not *fired* here. This could be just temporary. We will be in touch, of course. It's just that . . ." And he let his hands fall open then.

Deirdre finished the sentence for him. "You have no choice." She sucked in a big breath. She got up and wiped her nose with the back of her wrist. She took two steps toward the door, then turned back to Martin. "You're saying this is temporary?"

"I'm not promising anything." He sighed and walked toward the door. "But will we investigate? Absolutely. Will you be given a fair shake? Without a doubt." He gripped Deirdre's shoulder and squeezed. "And you're still getting paid," he reminded her. "We're not cutting you off here."

Deirdre tried to smile. "What about . . . my stuff? My room? Can I just go up and see if there's anything I need?"

Martin reached over, grabbed the doorknob, and opened the door. "Lil?" he said, poking his head out. Deirdre peered out from behind Martin's back. No sign of Frances.

A file cabinet slid shut and Lil walked around the corner into the doorway. She didn't say anything to Deirdre nor did she look at her. "Yes?" she said to Martin Loring.

"Could you accompany Ms. Murphy here up to her room? She needs to gather her things."

Deirdre felt her face burning. She was being treated like a criminal, not being allowed to even go up to her room alone. Did they think she might steal something? Deface school property? She gave Lil a weak wave.

Lil motioned for Deirdre to lead the way. "Things get crazy around here real fast."

Deirdre knew Lil meant the morning hours at Brandywine, the chaos. Still, it sounded like a reprimand, as if the craziness were somehow her fault. Deirdre picked up her backpack from the floor and turned to Martin. "I . . . You'll call me, then? You'll let me know what's happening?"

"Absolutely." He shook her hand. To Lil he said, "I'll get the phone. And yes, I'll look in on the ladies."

For ten years, Deirdre and Lil had been colleagues, of

a sort. All those years, Deirdre tried very hard to be on time with administrative forms and requests—her grades especially—because she was aware that being late caused Lil extra work. She made special efforts to bring treats to the front office during those crunch times—little things, cookies or brownies—to perk up Lil's day, to let her know that at least someone realized how much work she did. Now, Deirdre didn't know what to say to Lil as they climbed the stairs to her classroom. She wanted to launch into her side of the story, find out what Lil knew exactly, what she had heard from Martin and from Frances Worthington herself.

Deirdre glanced over her shoulder. "This is pretty weird."

Lil said nothing. Just trudged up the stairs behind her.

"I mean, who'd have thought I'd be in this situation?" She tried to laugh.

Silence.

Deirdre opened the door to her room. She walked over to her desk and Lil stood in the doorway, arms folded across the front of her beige pantsuit. "I hope you don't think—"

"It's of no mind what I think," Lil interrupted.

"My God. Do you honestly think I would hurt one of these kids? Or jeopardize my job?"

Lil remained silent.

Deirdre was stunned. Had she mistaken their good working relationship all these years? Had she misinterpreted Lil's friendliness, read into her morning chattiness? Of course, socially they weren't friends—Deirdre had never invited Lil to her home—but she had been certain that Lil thought well of her and that the two of them were good colleagues.

Deirdre heard footsteps coming up the stairs and there was Forest, arms piled with books. For a moment, she wanted to run, grab him and drag him for a quick coffee at Blue Moon so she could tell him the latest developments, confide in him Martin Loring's "need" to let her go immediately. She played the conversation in her head—*He says he has no choice*. Deirdre, laughing, sipping her latte and Forest, downing an espresso, laughing with her—*Yeah, no choice. Like he ever does something without kowtowing to those parents*. It had always been like that, teachers against administrators, even when you liked them, even when your head of school was someone as basically kind and sweet-natured as Martin Loring. He was still one of "them." And in conflicts between parents and teachers, the administrators always took the side of the parents. "That's the way it is in private schools," SJ had explained when Deirdre first complained. "The parents pay the big bucks and so they have the last word. Who do you think really runs that school?"

Deirdre wanted desperately to have that conversation now with Forest, but there he was at the top of the stairs, at the door to her room, and he didn't even look in. He didn't wave or make any motions to indicate that he wanted to speak with her. He walked with his pile of books directly into his own room, and shut the door.

Deirdre felt as if she'd taken a punch to the gut. Of course she was still mad at Forest too, but she had hoped for an instant that he might feel some remorse for their argument, or at least some pity that she was being let go. Then again, maybe he didn't know. Maybe Martin had not yet announced to the faculty what was going on and so Forest was still stuck in mad mode, couldn't let go of their fight, the way she still couldn't. Maybe she should stick her head in his room and let him know what was happening. She felt pretty certain that once Forest knew that Martin had asked her to leave immediately, he would be back on her side. She listened at the door between their two rooms but couldn't hear anything. If she could just see what he was doing—

"Are you all set?" Lil asked, still in the doorway.

"Just a minute. Let me just check in these drawers." Deirdre couldn't think. What would she need at home? What shouldn't she leave here in her desk? She would feel strange not having her schoolwork with her, or her grade book—her notebook filled with lesson plans. There was no need for that at home and still, Deirdre couldn't leave it behind; it felt too personal. The grade book she supposed the new teacher would need. She looked up. "Who'll be teaching my classes, do you know?"

Lil shifted her weight. "Martin has hired somebody, I know that much. Who it is, he hasn't told me."

She's lying. Martin would tell Lil first thing. "Are they . . . coming today?"

Lil took a couple of steps toward her desk. "Do I think you were a good teacher? You gave that impression, yes. Do I think you did what you are accused of doing? I don't know. I honestly don't. I know that Mrs. Worthington works hard for this school. I know she wouldn't want to hurt Brandywine. And I know I've got to get back to the office soon or chaos will reign." Her voice seemed softer to Deirdre, more sympathetic.

"Let me just . . ." And Deirdre was cut off by the sounds of heels clicking their way up the staircase.

CHAPTER TWELVE

LEO RIVERA'S FACE WAS STILL EVERYWHERE. Smiling in his baseball cap, he looked out from stapled fliers on telephone poles and shop windows. He was plastered to tree trunks. Although no one would say so, or perhaps they were not even quite aware of it themselves, everyone felt there was something sinister about the way the papers flapped in the breeze, corners of the sheets lifting in a kind of careless disregard for the boy. Cats and dogs went missing and that was bad enough—but little boys? Still, people thought, it was absurd to be so surprised—children went missing all the time, their faces stamped on waxy milk cartons—but somehow these fliers stuck to trees and on stop signs seemed less serious. Here a reward for a missing boy, and there, an advertisement for a yard sale.

And, of course, he was no longer missing.

Even though Leo Rivera didn't live in the same neighborhood as the Brandywine families, he did live in Bradley, a town divided in half by the river, on one side asphalt and more asphalt and triple-deckers so close there was no breath between them, and on the other, renovated Victorians with deep blue hydrangeas and sprawling lawns of lush green, cut thick like a boy's crew cut. How was it that people who lived on the Victorian side nevertheless felt connected to Leo Rivera and his family?

It was still September in Massachusetts. And for a great many people, that meant time to pay attention to the Red Sox. Leo Rivera had loved the Red Sox with a ferocious ten-year-old's loyalty. He had never been to a game at Fenway Park, though his father had hoped to surprise him for his birthday. Leo had wanted a bike; his father had wanted an outing to see the Sox in person with his youngest son. It seemed the American thing to do. Just one week after Leo disappeared, the Red Sox swept the Yankees in a three-day series in the Bronx. Normally, a sweep like that in the early fall meant hope for the fans scattered throughout Red Sox Nation, but in Bradley, it was hard to feel anything except a kind of distant longing. Sportscaster after sportscaster reminded viewers how much young Leo Rivera had loved baseball and how, most of all, he would have loved to see his beloved Red Sox win their division and maybe even the World Series. They reminded viewers, too, of how talented Leo was, how he played shortstop for the Wildcats, how it looked like he could have had a future.

When Jason Varitek heard that Leo Rivera's father was going to be in the stadium on what would have been Leo's eleventh birthday, he wanted to meet the man. He lobbied for Mr. Rivera to be the one to throw out the first pitch. Leo's face grinned from the big screen at the start of the game against the Orioles, a somber reminder that you couldn't let your hope grow too big. It was moments like these that made everyone in Bradley—and throughout Massachusetts—feel connected to Leo and his family.

Leo had disappeared at the very end of Little League season, his own team, the Wildcats, headed for the play-offs. The boys attached white ribbons to their uniforms as a reminder and tribute to their dead teammate. Their coach felt a little guilty about using him as a reason to win, but he rationalized it by thinking that winning would help the boys overcome their grief. For most of the kids, though, it wasn't grief they were feeling exactly, but something more akin to confusion. How could a boy they knew disappear from their own neighborhood?

"He lives—lived—four houses down from me," one boy said on the news, the night of the Little League playoffs. *"It makes me real sad."*

"I'm scared," said another, the replacement shortstop.

Frances Worthington's ten-year-old son, Sam, when asked, stared silently at the reporter and said nothing.

At the library Monday morning, all the talk was about Mickey and his arrest. How he had been around children in that very library. How SJ was teaching him to read. One of the young catalogers wanted to know if SJ was nervous knowing how close she'd been to a child murderer.

"And molester," Randall chimed in.

"Innocent until proven guilty," SJ reminded them. She poured herself a cup of coffee, left the staff room, and ran right into Florence.

"You're here," Florence said. "You never returned my call. Didn't Deirdre tell you it was urgent?"

For a minute SJ thought of using Deirdre as her excuse. "Sorry," she said, "I . . . time got away from me." She sipped her coffee.

Florence fiddled with her scrimshaw. "I wanted to pre-pare you. You-know-who has already called."

"You know who?"

"The police. They want to interview you again."

"God. What else can I tell them?" SJ circled her hands around her mug.

"I told them you'd be late—that you'd called in but that I didn't know when you'd be here. Certainly by noon. Anyway, just FYI. Thought you'd want to know."

Florence straightened her blouse and started to walk on.

"Thanks. Hey, Flo?"

Florence turned around.

"I hate to say this, but I need to leave early. I have to . . . I have some errands I need to run before five. I'll make it up, okay? The time. I won't take lunch."

Florence folded her arms. "Today? It *isn't* okay. I have that district-wide meeting at four, remember? You agreed to be in charge? Until six?" Florence slid the scrimshaw back and forth. This one was a horizontal oval shape, with a schooner in black, one of Florence's favorites.

"What about Elliot? Couldn't even one of the kids cover the front desk for an hour or so?"

"It isn't a matter of covering the desk. It's about being in charge. Is it really that important?" Florence pursued.

SJ gulped down more coffee. "I'm . . . I've found an apartment. I need to get to the bank and move some money around."

The expression in Florence's eyes changed. Softened. "Wow," she said.

"Deirdre doesn't know yet."

"She doesn't know?"

SJ looked down into her coffee cup. "I haven't said anything, but I don't think she'll be surprised. We hardly spoke all weekend."

"Did you have a fight? Why didn't you call? Is this why you were late? You didn't even say. You left a message like I was . . . like I was . . . I don't know, your *boss* only and not a friend too."

SJ took a deep breath. "It isn't that. We didn't fight. We just . . . I can't live with her anymore. Come on. Are you surprised? You're the one who told me what a crazy move I was making to buy the house with her in the first place."

"The house. Oh." Florence stopped fiddling with her

scrimshaw. "Is this—are you sure you're making the right decision?"

"You of all people are asking me that!"

"But when did it come to this? I mean, a new apartment. It sounds so drastic!"

"Yes, no. I don't know. I really don't want to talk about it right now. But I'm sure," she added when Florence started to say something else. "I've never been more sure."

As SJ went into the office to take care of orders, she thought first of the new apartment—how small and stingy it seemed. But sufficient, her practical side said. And though it wasn't anything great, it would be all hers. Then she saw the picture of Deirdre she kept on her desk. Taken years ago at the beach, on the Cape somewhere, Provincetown maybe. It had always been her favorite picture of Deirdre. Back when Deirdre had been a new teacher, before the students had begun to consume her. SJ stared at the photo. Deirdre had that look in her eyes that used to make her melt.

And SJ had wanted to be that person for Deirdre. She had been seduced by Deirdre's desire, she realized now, and she thought back again to her initial surprise when Deirdre first suggested they look for a house together. More than once, she had half-admitted to herself that what she had with Deirdre was familiar and comfortable—and that was it. But then they started to look at houses. SJ loved the idea of a house, of being in a relationship and living like a family. But she wondered if maybe her expectations about the relationship—about any relationship—had been too high and that maybe comfortable and familiar was the best you could hope for.

Her parents hadn't really provided a good example. SJ couldn't even tell if they had loved each other. But what could you tell about watching someone else? When you lived with someone for twenty, thirty, or forty years, what did your love look like to the rest of the world? Could it look boring but be something else? When you were in love with your partner, you certainly didn't leave them when they were going through a tough time.

SJ put the picture down. She was not looking forward to telling Deirdre that she was moving out. Just thinking about it made her stomach cramp.

Minutes after twelve, two detectives arrived. A man and woman, both in dark suits, the man wearing a white button-down shirt and a striped tie and the woman more casual, a T-shirt beneath her jacket, pleated pants, both of them looking like they walked right off the set of *Law & Order*. From her office window, SJ watched them show their badges then shake hands with Florence. The man had that preppy look. Blond crew cut. Square shoulders. The woman was attractive. Her jet-black hair was cut short. She was tall, five ten or eleven, SJ guessed, and slim. The kind of woman Deirdre always pointed to when they were out and said, "I wish I could look like that." When the detective put her hands on her hips, SJ thought she saw a gun holster. Florence turned and motioned toward SJ's office, folded her arms, then reached for the scrimshaw, all the while nodding and smiling. SJ could imagine Florence's tone—concerned, maternal—*If there's* anything *I can do, if I can be of* any *help.* SJ looked down and noticed her hand was trembling. She hit *Save* on the computer and stepped out to meet the detectives in her office doorway.

"Detective Mahoney," said the man, shaking SJ's hand and then pointing to the woman. "And you've met Detective Rodriguez?"

SJ shook the woman's hand. "No," she said, "I've only spoken to police officers before. The ones in uniform, I mean. After . . . after Leo was first missing. That's all." She swallowed, suddenly thirsty. The two detectives shared a brief glance.

SJ ushered them into her office and motioned for Detective Rodriguez to sit in the one chair facing her desk. She dragged another from the corner, removed piles of papers, and stacked them on the floor. "Here," she said to Detective Mahoney. She walked back behind her desk, happy that it was between her and them and that it concealed her legs that were starting to shake too.

"You obviously know why we're here," Detective Rodriguez began, glancing at his partner, who looked directly at SJ. Rodriguez's eyes seemed warm and encouraging. SJ relaxed a little and nodded. "Tell us, how well do you know Mickey Gilberto?"

"He comes here to learn to read." SJ sat with her arms folded and willed her legs to be still.

"Since . . . ?" Detective Mahoney asked. Detective Rodriguez sat with her pad of paper unfolded, pencil ready.

"Couple weeks?" SJ said. "He stopped in just after Labor Day . . ." She hesitated. "He was actually one of our movers too, but I didn't know him then."

Detective Mahoney nodded and waited.

"I didn't know him then," SJ repeated, unfolding her arms. "So I guess it was sort of weird that he stopped in here to see if we could teach him how to read. And that I ended up being his teacher. But he lives in the neighborhood, so I guess it wasn't that weird," she added quickly.

"You didn't question the coincidence?" Detective Rodriguez asked. "Didn't wonder if he had planned it that way?"

"Absolutely not," SJ said. She rubbed her palms on her thighs. "I mean, sure, it crossed my mind what a funny coincidence, but not in a strange way. Deirdre—my . . . my partner—she thought it was odd. She made a big deal of it, actually. But I didn't see anything to it. Deirdre thought he was creepy."

Detective Rodriguez jotted notes on the pad. She looked up. "Your partner, Deirdre. What's her last name?"

"Murphy. But why do you need to know? She doesn't know Mickey at all. Like I said, he was one of our movers, but that's it—"

Detective Mahoney interrupted her: "But she thought he was creepy?"

"Yeah, in a poor-guy-from-the-hood kind of way. That's it." SJ chewed on a thumbnail. "Deirdre teaches at Brandywine Academy? So, you know, Mickey doesn't fit that kind of mold. He isn't what she's used to." She chewed again then folded her arms. "You sure he's your guy?"

Both detectives looked up then. Detective Rodriguez frowned a little.

SJ went on: "It's just that . . . people who . . . want to learn to read don't . . . don't molest little boys and then kill them." She was aware of how silly she sounded the minute she had finished speaking.

Detective Mahoney rubbed a hand across his face and coughed, but SJ thought she saw him smirk.

"Of course it might seem that way," Detective Rodriguez said, leaning forward in her chair. "And it probably is that way for most people. But the criminal mind doesn't work like everyone else's." She tapped her eraser tip on the edge of SJ's desk. Her nails were manicured, polished a smooth dark red. "The criminal mind is narcissistic, concerned only with itself . . ."

SJ's mind flashed to the newspaper clippings on Mickey's desk in the garage.

". . . intent on its own delusions of grandeur. Which is hard to imagine unless you've seen a lot of criminals." Detective Rodriguez leaned back in her chair, smiled at SJ, and crossed her legs.

"You say Mr. Gilberto took reading lessons from you?" Detective Mahoney unbuttoned his suit jacket.

"Yes," SJ said. She straightened a stack of papers on her desk.

"What can you tell us about his relationship with his family?" he asked.

Detective Rodriguez sat poised, ready to write again.

"His family? I have no idea."

"He never confided in you?"

"Confided? No, I taught him reading. Look, I'm not sure I can be of much help here. I already told the other policemen everything I know." She folded her hands. Outside the office window, Florence walked past with Randall, and SJ could feel them straining to keep their eyes forward.

"But you do know him . . . personally?" Detective Rodriguez spoke again, looking directly at SJ. Her voice was soft. SJ felt her legs start to shake again. She pushed down on her thighs.

Florence stood at the checkout desk with her back to the office, pointing out things. *You're a doll*, SJ thought. Getting Randall to cover. Twice, Randall turned his head around to peek at what was going on in SJ's office. What could she say, that she didn't know Mickey personally but that he had kissed her when she had driven over to his garage?

His garage.

They *knew*.

"Look," SJ said, "he didn't show up on Friday. So I went looking for him. He comes to his lessons on time. Early even. He's polite and friendly. The things he's accused of doing—I just don't see it. The guy who sits with me sounding out his words, that is not the same guy who . . . who assaulted . . . who raped Leo Rivera and stuffed his body in a plastic box to sink to the bottom of the river. It just isn't." SJ was aware that she was trembling. Her whole body felt tense, worked up. "That monster," she said, pointing at Detective Rodriguez, her voice quivering, "is not the same person who grins when he reads whole sentences on his own, who shows up like an eager puppy dog . . ." *Who kissed me the other night.* "I don't see it. I don't." She wiped her eyes. "I'm sorry."

Detective Rodriguez stood and offered SJ a tissue from the box on the desk. "Sara Jane . . . is it alright if I call you that?"

"SJ," she said and blew her nose. "Everyone calls me SJ."

"SJ," Detective Rodriguez smiled, "you're not in trouble here. You're not. But we have pretty good reason to suspect that Mr. Gilberto is involved in this murder."

"Or we wouldn't be here," Detective Mahoney added, pushing his chair back onto its hind legs.

"That's right. We wouldn't be here. But we are here because we know—we're certain—that Mr. Gilberto is involved."

"Involved?" SJ said, tossing her tissue into the wastebasket. "So you're not sure he actually did it, then?"

Detective Mahoney tipped his chair back down. "Let's just say we've got some strong evidence against him, okay? What we want to know is what he might have told *you*."

"Leo Rivera," Detective Rodriguez said, sitting back down in her chair, "he was in the after-school program here. You knew him?"

SJ shook her head. "Not in the program. But he stopped by sometimes after school."

"Cute kid? Nice, wasn't he? Sweet?"

"I knew him," SJ said. "I knew who he was. He—"

"You'd like to find his killer, wouldn't you? Figure out what kind of a person—what kind of, as you said, monster—would do that to a little kid?" That soft voice. Dark, intense eyes. Bloodred nails on the desk.

SJ was suddenly exhausted. "Absolutely. I'm just saying—"

"Then whatever you can tell us about Mickey Gilberto

would be very helpful." Detective Rodriguez stood back up. "We would appreciate it very much, SJ." She handed SJ her card. "Call us if you think of anything."

Detective Mahoney stood and rebuttoned his suit jacket. He extended his hand to SJ. "Thanks for your time."

The detectives let themselves out, shook hands again with Florence as they passed by the front desk, and headed for the door. Randall peered back once more at SJ then pretended to be looking for something on one of the shelves.

What kind of monster. SJ slumped in her seat. She knew that she'd come across as terribly naïve to the detectives. Silly, even. She just couldn't explain what she meant. How she knew that reading was not the pastime of criminals. Did child murderers go in for self-improvement? But she saw again the metal desk in Mickey's garage, its surface littered with newspaper articles, all about Leo Rivera. And she heard again that voice, *What if he wanted it?*

CHAPTER THIRTEEN

AFTER LEAVING BRANDYWINE, Deirdre walked home. Now that she was here, she didn't know what to do. Her daily schedule revolved around school. Even on the first day of summer vacation, Deirdre always needed to spend at least one entire day doing nothing, flopping onto the couch, wandering about aimlessly, stunned into a kind of inertia without the routine of work to structure her days. She wasn't a soap opera fan, and at her own insistence she and SJ didn't have cable. She didn't feel like taking a run. She tried reaching SJ, but Florence insisted that SJ couldn't be interrupted and promised that she'd call back just as soon as she could.

Deirdre wandered through the rooms downstairs. *Think of this as a day off. Read that book, the one you left by the bed. Take a nap.* Instead, she took inventory of her belongings, as if the knowledge that she owned this painting or that plant could shore her up, give her some confidence, lend some validity to her sense of self. It's true that belongings did say something about a person. Who didn't check out the books on someone's shelves the first time you were invited in? Who didn't immediately reassess the potential value of a budding friendship after discovering the new friend's passion for collecting tiny glass animals or fuzzy velvet paintings of clowns? You looked for those things, those signs that let you know this person might not be someone you really wanted to befriend after all. At least Deirdre looked for those signs, and she assumed everyone else worked the same way. You knew what you liked, what constituted good taste, and the rest, well, the rest you hoped you never had to deal with.

Walking from room to room, Deirdre knew it was silly, but she could almost convince herself everything would be okay. *Breathe. Breathe.* Each room, like the houses on her walk to school, gave the appearance of undisrupted status quo. *This room. This vase. This desk and chair.* And because they were real, solid, unchanged, Deirdre could almost convince herself that nothing else had changed, and that she was the same person she had always been. The Deirdre standing now in the living room was the same woman who'd recently bought her first house, *this* house, a charming cape with built-in china cabinet and an unfinished upstairs. She was the same Deirdre who'd always gotten good grades, who'd read books in the adult library before she was twelve, who'd graduated from college with a 3.9. She was the same woman who so far had been offered every job she had applied for, had convinced the faculty development group to read *Reviving Ophelia,* had suggested Carol Gilligan, books by Theodore Sizer and Parker Palmer. She was not the kind of woman who could ever be guilty of . . . of molestation, if that's what she was being accused of.

Deirdre was a teacher, a competent one, better than that. She was a good teacher with a solid reputation. And the problem that had her wandering aimlessly—besides the fact that it was still early morning (about ten o'clock, she guessed) and normally she would be teaching her fourth-period intro class, the girls who still muddled their greetings when Deirdre met them at the classroom door and offered each one a handshake and a *bonjour*—was that if she suddenly weren't a teacher, she couldn't imagine what else she might be. She couldn't even really think about that very remote possibility, not for very long at least, without her stomach cramping. Nor could she think about the possibility that she might be someone who could be fired.

Fired. Worse, *a child molester*. Some kind of monster.

Deirdre knew how things worked in a school like Brandywine. News traveled faster than fast. By the end of the school day, everyone would know what had happened. If they didn't already. She hadn't discussed with Martin what he would say to the other faculty, but Deirdre knew he would have to say something, explain her absence. She wished she could call Forest to see how the other teachers had reacted.

Christ, if Forest reacted the way he did, what would the rest of the faculty think—the teachers who weren't even her friends, the ones who criticized the time she spent with students, who found her preparation excessive? Forest was the one who was supposed to understand Deirdre, to be on her side. Get her. She paced back and forth in the living room. Maybe she should call and leave a message on his machine. And say what? Deirdre stopped pacing and dropped onto the couch. She had nothing to say to Forest—that was the problem. He needed to apologize to *her*.

She got up and wandered into the kitchen. She pulled down a couple of her favorite cookbooks, and although it was still early, she poured herself a glass of chardonnay. At the table, she flipped through *The Best of Gourmet*. She decided to cook, to make something fancy, something more complicated than what she might fix on a normal weeknight, especially a Monday.

Maybe tonight would be the night she and SJ would patch things up; for whatever reason they needed to be patched up, Deirdre wasn't exactly sure. She knew that SJ was frustrated with the amount of time she spent teaching and organizing projects at school. And of course this thing with Anna Worthington had taken up a lot of time. But in general, Deirdre didn't understand how SJ seemed to dismiss the hard work—and time—teaching required. There were the lessons to plan, those alone required hours of creation, of figuring out the exact right method to engage her students. What nonteachers didn't seem to understand was that you couldn't simply get up there and explain things. Couldn't, for example, just reinterpret the book, if you used one at all. You had to make your subject come alive, had to make it seem real for students, or else they couldn't see the point of learning it. And then, of course, things kept changing, methods improved.

SJ teased her about her pile of professional journals stacked by the bed. She complained that Deirdre hardly read the journals and they took up space, gathered dust. But Deirdre did read them. She was always on the lookout for new ways of thinking about grammar instruction. She had to keep them nearby, ready to be picked up and read again, gleaned for wisdom on those nights when she had trouble sleeping, worried, as she often was, about how to introduce a new concept—for example, the *imparfait*, or the indefinite pronoun *on*.

And, of course, it wasn't just the lessons that required Deirdre's time and attention. There were the students themselves, and their messy lives—their home troubles, some serious: sick parents, absent parents (the occasional one in jail), parents who couldn't care less, and parents who smothered; upcoming divorces; and the parent who hit when drunk. And some less serious: the busy social calendars that kept the girls from studying enough; the parties they were or weren't invited to; the boyfriend woes; the complicated dynamics of girl relationships; best friends and changing cliques; crushes they couldn't always admit to. All of it mattered. And all of it required Deirdre's time and attention.

She was not ready to accept the fact that she might not be a teacher any longer—or no longer a teacher at Brandywine—but if she had to take some time off, she might as well get something out of it. Right? She flipped a few pages and sipped her wine. For starters, she considered making a pâté but realized she had too little time. She wanted more than a salad, even one with warm goat cheese. There were soups—cream of mushroom, cream of broccoli, smoky pumpkin. Here's what she wanted—lobster bisque. She would start with that.

Deirdre grabbed an envelope out of the recycling bin and started to copy down the ingredients. What next? Pasta? Chicken dishes seemed too ordinary. She didn't really feel like eating beef, though she toyed briefly with the idea of Moroccan meatloaf. There were grilled dishes, but not after a lobster bisque. That didn't seem right. She looked through a few more pages. Veal. Scaloppine. Parmesan. Picatta. That was it. Veal picatta. She settled on the idea, too, of serving risotto on the side, and steamed green beans. She already had a pinot grigio. Perfect. For dessert . . . hmmm . . . she didn't know what to make for dessert. Normally, she and SJ didn't have dessert, but Deirdre felt that tonight the occasion might call for one. Something . . . not necessarily elaborate, but substantial. Something chocolate. Yes, a cake, maybe, with a ganache.

Deirdre glanced at the clock. She didn't have much time to get all this done. First she had to shop. Maybe a cake with ganache wasn't the right thing. Maybe she would have to settle for cupcakes. Or a mousse. She'd make her decision in the store. For now, she wrote down the ingredients for all three possibilities.

* * *

Deirdre had the veal in the fridge and all the rest of the ingredients lined up on the counter. She had decided on the mousse and was making that first to give it time to set. In the grocery store, she had even gotten excited about the idea of this meal, of cooking. But back in the kitchen, her mind switched to school again. She wondered if any of her students would suddenly hate her. Or feel betrayed. Would they question her motives, or her behavior? Remember a time when she had touched them, maybe—in all innocence, of course, but now they might misconstrue every gesture. There were some girls who were certain not to care at all, but the ones Deirdre cared about most, they would have an opinion one way or another. She tied her apron behind her back.

Deirdre hoped that at least some students would rally to her side. That's what she liked to imagine. A troupe of them storming Martin Loring's office, demanding to know why he had put Deirdre on leave. Why couldn't he trust her, they would want to know, when she was the best teacher they had ever had? Lydia would lead the charge. But then again, Lydia was Anna Worthington's best friend.

Deirdre beat the egg yolks with a whisk, her hands shaky. Hilary would stand up for her. All those afternoons they had spent last year in Deirdre's classroom, going over irregular verbs. The days they spent drilling disjunctive pronouns, practicing the *passé composé*. At least Hilary knew firsthand how hard Deirdre worked, how much she wanted to help her students succeed. But that was the most insulting thing—couldn't Martin Loring see that? Didn't he know how much effort she put into her teaching? How much love she had for her students? Because if he did, then how could he accuse her of wrongdoing?

Her chest constricted and she had to stop, breathe deeply. What was Martin Loring thinking? Why wasn't he relying on what he knew about Deirdre, not what Frances Worthington was accusing her of, the lies she was spreading? She stopped, sat for a moment, sipped more wine. He would come to his senses. He had to.

Deirdre put the cut-up squares of chocolate into a saucepan and stuck it over another of simmering water. Watching the chocolate melt was always her favorite part of making mousse, swirling the pieces with a wooden spoon around the bottom of the pan until they softened into smooth satiny ribbons.

Light streamed through the open shutters, speckling the red tablecloth, warming the wooden floor in pools of yellow gold. Deirdre tilted the pan and stirred the chocolate pieces. She breathed in the smell, rich and dark, and placed the wooden spoon on the spoon rest, turned off the flame, and wiped her hands on her apron. She clicked the metal bowl onto her standing mixer, the egg whites pooled together, pale and goopy. She hooked up the wire whisk attachment and turned the mixer first onto low and then higher, watching the egg whites increase in volume and froth. If she were—Deirdre glanced at the clock—in fifth period, she would be drilling the *passé composé*: *Today I am reading a book; yesterday I read a book; Right now, I am singing; yesterday, I sang.* She would be cold-calling the girls, starting with Lydia—because Lydia always caught on so quickly. She would start with the easy verbs, the regular ones ending in *er,* and move to the harder ones. Deirdre would go back to Lydia, or Alice or Courtney (if Courtney seemed to have the spark and didn't look too mopey), every time she wanted to change things up, and introduce an irregular verb or shift the order of the questions. The fifth-period girls didn't need too many overt explanations. They were the types of students who would actually read the textbook, study the grammar explanations, and come to class ready to see if they could pick up on Deirdre's questions and model answers. They preferred class that way; they thought of themselves as quick learners, and for the most part, they were.

Deirdre had to smile thinking of Ellie in their midst. She didn't fit in, that was clear, but Deirdre had been proud of the way the other girls allowed her to be herself, and didn't try to force her to be like them. They were good that way. Maybe because each had her own eccentric personality. They cultivated that in each other. Sometimes even for effect, Deirdre was certain.

Thinking of Ellie brought her right back to the field trip, back to the van and Anna. She replayed the scene over and over, her arms around Anna, comforting her, the girl looking up, the kiss sudden and unexpected. How had she responded? And what message had she given Anna that she thought kissing Deirdre might be okay?

Deirdre turned the mixer on low, hands still trembling. She stopped for a minute, then shook some sugar into the revolving bowl and scraped the sides of it with her rubber spatula to keep the sugar from clinging instead of mixing in with the egg whites.

The doorbell rang. She stood, spatula in midair. The doorbell rang again. Should she be very quiet and pretend not to be home? Who would come to her house in the middle of the day? A knock. Female voice: "Hello?"

The voice didn't sound like SJ's—and what would she be doing ringing the bell anyway—but it was hard to hear over the mixer. Deirdre turned it off, put the spatula in the bowl, and wiped her hands on her apron. The voice, a bit louder: "Ms. Murphy?"

Deirdre hurried to the front door and unlocked it. Beth Ann, in another pale sweater set, pearls around her throat, stood pressing her hands against the seam on her pant legs.

"Ms. Murphy. Am I interrupting? Forgive me. You're

cooking," Beth Ann said, her voice soft like tapioca. She motioned to Deirdre's apron.

"It's fine," Deirdre said and opened the door wide. "Come in." She ushered Beth Ann into the living room. "Actually, do you mind coming into the kitchen? I'm making mousse."

"I was . . ." Beth Ann followed Deirdre. "I was at Brandywine this morning. For the coffee." She fingered her pearls. "The new-parents coffee?"

Deirdre turned and nodded.

"And—this is awkward—I normally don't repeat gossip," Beth Ann said, giving a little laugh. "I just hate gossip." She exhaled and smiled.

Deirdre offered her a chair at the kitchen table, and waited for her to continue.

Beth Ann folded and unfolded her hands. "My daddy drilled it into me. *No gossip*, he always said. *Good girls don't*. But it isn't really gossip now, is it, if I tell it to you? I'm only reporting what has been said about you by others. Ms. Murphy—"

"Deirdre, please." She turned down the heat under the chocolate.

"Oh, this is crazy," Beth Ann said. "Why can't I just say what I need to say?" She stood and paced. Fingered her pearls. "I don't care." She turned to face Deirdre after several moments. "I don't believe it, but even so, I don't care. I've seen the way you are with those girls and I don't for one minute think you would do anything to harm them, I know you wouldn't. I'm sorry you've been let go—"

"Beth Ann—"

"It's ignorant." Beth Ann blushed, crossed her arms. "I want to help. In any way I can."

If Deirdre had expected anyone to show up, it was Forest. Or maybe even Evelyn. But here was Beth Ann in her soft pastel colors, pacing in her living room. And of course Deirdre wanted to know exactly what the women were saying—Frances Worthington especially—how they looked when they talked about her, with what kind of sneer or laugh. And if anybody seemed shocked. How many new parents were against her now? And what exactly was Frances telling everybody anyway? She waited for Beth Ann to give the details.

"*You've got your ignorant element, Beth Ann,* my daddy would say, *and such people are not worth your while.*"

"I would've liked your dad." Deirdre stirred the chocolate with a spatula.

"Oh, he was—is—he's still alive. He is a real gem. A Southern gentleman, truly." Beth Ann pulled out a kitchen chair and sat on the edge. "Daddy—well, I didn't come here to talk about my daddy." She ran an index finger beneath her pearls.

"I appreciate you coming over." Deirdre stirred. "I'm just sick about this." She felt tears begin to pool. She swallowed and glanced over at Beth Ann, willed the tears not to fall.

"People will think what they think—"

"That's what your daddy said?"

Beth Ann blushed. "But isn't it the truth?" She shook her head and gave a little laugh. "People can think all they want that Southerners are backward. In the South, you grow up hearing about *Yankee this, Northern that.* When we're little, we find out all the fancy, famous schools are up North too, like y'all are smarter? Now, Northerners might be more liberal, but less ignorant? The South does not have a monopoly on that." She stood again. "Ms. Murphy, if you need anything, you call me, you hear?" She extended her hand.

Deirdre put down the spatula and shook her hand, then walked her to the front door. "Thanks for stopping by," she said. "I really appreciate it."

"Now, I mean it. You call. If you need anything."

"I will," Deirdre told her, and closed the door.

The brief moment of ease she had found while mixing the mousse had disappeared. She supposed Beth Ann was right: people would think what they wanted to think, and there wasn't much she or anyone else could do about that. But it didn't seem fair, that people who didn't even know you might form an opinion based on a rumor—and worse, a rumor that wasn't even true.

Well, there was no sense jumping to conclusions just yet. Deirdre didn't know what people were thinking, and Beth Ann was a perfect example of someone she had never expected to have on her side. Why was it that you automatically thought the worst of people? Still, walking back to the kitchen, the dread turned her stomach sour—the desire to cook, to do anything, was gone. She scooped the egg whites into the melted chocolate, turned over handfuls of stiff egg whites with the spatula, folding each new bit into the chocolate, blending the two so that slowly, what was in the bowl turned a paler shade of brown and grew puffier and lighter. She worked on automatic, the repetitive motions calming the hysteria that was building in her chest. She spooned the mousse into six small ramekins. It would be like Forest to come by when school was over, when he was fairly certain SJ would be working. Deirdre scraped the side of the chocolate pan with a spoon and licked it. She glanced at the clock. School would be out in another half hour. And it had been several hours since she'd phoned SJ at the library. Deirdre put the ramekins into the fridge and dialed the library's number.

"Bradley Public Library."

"Sara Jane Edmonds, please." The light in the kitchen had faded; now everything seemed to have turned a shade of gray. Outside the window, a breeze blew the yellowed leaves of the oak tree. A squirrel scampered across the phone line.

"Hello?"

"Hey." Deirdre twisted the phone cord around her finger.

"Deirdre? I was expecting . . . I didn't think it would be you."

"You didn't get my message?"

"Message? Oh, yeah. Yeah, but it was . . . Things were crazy here today. Listen, don't count on me for dinner. I'm probably going to be late."

"But I'm cooking! I've already started. It was supposed to be a surprise." Before SJ could say anything, Deirdre added, "So officially? I'm on leave."

"God, the meeting with Martin, I forgot. I'm sorry." SJ sounded distracted and Deirdre heard her riffling through papers.

"Are you listening?"

SJ sighed.

"Forget it. Just come home, would you? We can eat dinner late," Deirdre said. "Nine o'clock if you want." She hung up.

So much for patching things up. SJ wasn't even home yet and Deirdre was already mad at her. And vice versa, it sounded like. For the first time, she imagined the scenario through SJ's eyes. How humiliating. Could you be the spouse of a child molester? How did those wives of embezzlers do it, appear on TV as if nothing their husbands had done was wrong? In private, did those women still love their husbands, or was it all for show only? Deirdre didn't see how anyone could fake it like that—either you were still in love and supportive of your partner, or you weren't. And maybe in their heart of hearts, those women believed in their husbands, believed that they hadn't cheated at all and had been falsely accused, as Deirdre had been. How important it was for the husbands, Deirdre realized, to have *someone* who still believed in them. She rubbed at a spot of chocolate on the counter. No, she corrected herself, it wasn't having someone; it was having a spouse.

Deirdre took the veal from the refrigerator. Damn SJ. She could have at least asked about the meeting with Martin Loring. She could have at least pretended that she wanted to know what had happened—her partner, for God's sake. Deirdre wanted to be furious with SJ, but she wanted more to get things back to normal, to the way they were just before they moved into the new house. Already that seemed like ages ago, when in truth it had only been weeks. Deirdre didn't even want to think about how they would afford the new house if she did get fired and no longer earned a paycheck. Maybe finances were part of the reason SJ was so mad and distant, but Deirdre doubted it. SJ never worried about finances.

It was actually one of the things she appreciated about SJ. Because SJ came from money, had always had enough growing up, and would, frankly, have enough for the rest of her life, she didn't need to worry. Deirdre never knew that feeling. In her house, money had always been an issue. Her parents discussed it constantly. She loved the kind of easy confidence SJ had about money and brought to their life as a couple. She didn't feel like she was entitled to any of SJ's money, it wasn't that, but just the air SJ had about finances not being an issue helped calm Deirdre's own worries.

By now, the sun had moved almost completely to the front of the house. Deirdre poured herself another glass of chardonnay. What day was it? Monday. Nothing after school except sports practice. Forest might be working late, getting organized with lesson plans. Every fall, both he and Deirdre resolved to be better organized, and they always started out eager and committed, their good efforts lasting until October, if they were lucky. Then, the usual overload got the best of them. They could never figure out how it happened—a special assembly, a field trip, a request by another teacher for additional class time, an all-grade project—any one of these was enough by itself to throw the schedule into disarray, and when the schedule was crazy, everybody felt it. Deirdre never understood how a simple rearranging of classes could have such an adverse impact on everybody, on their moods, their ability to be organized, their productivity, but there you had it: one glitch in the schedule and they all flipped.

Deirdre sipped her wine and stepped out onto the front porch. The sun was warm out here still. Two boys shot baskets across the street, both of them in T-shirts and shorts. Deirdre liked picking out the girls in her classes who would wear shorts if they could (not at school, of course) right up until Columbus Day, as if avoiding long pants could keep winter at bay. Fat chance of that happening in New England. In fact, winter came faster each year, it seemed, with intermittent Indian summers, those glorious October days of warm, bright sun and crisp blue skies and even occasionally a warm day or two in November. Still, one or two girls would refuse to wear socks right up until the first snow; their way, Deirdre supposed, of hanging onto the feel of summer. And pushing the dress code a bit too.

A horn honked, and Deirdre looked to see her neighbor Susan parallel parking by the curb in front of her house. She backed in the end of her black Saab and turned off the car.

"Hi there," Susan called over, stepping from her car.

Deirdre waved, too late to duck into the house and pretend she hadn't seen her.

"Let me put this stuff in the house and I'll be right there. I want to talk to you about something."

Deirdre nodded. "Okay." She wished suddenly that she hadn't encouraged Susan to join the board at Brandywine.

She looked at the other houses on the street. Three of the four had some relationship to Brandywine, either a current child attended, or a past child, or the parents had some other connection.

Susan walked over holding a glass of white wine. "Thought I'd join you," she said. "How are you?"

"Okay. I mean . . ." Deirdre shrugged, aware that the wine was making her light-headed.

"So, we had an emergency board meeting this afternoon." Susan sipped her wine. "I'm sorry."

Deirdre felt her face growing hot. A board meeting already? She looked to see how Susan was reacting but she couldn't get a sense.

"I guess Martin thought it necessary to hire a new person right away." Susan looked away as she said this, over toward the park.

"For how long, did he say? I'm only on leave." Deirdre tried to keep her voice even, not panicked.

"Martin didn't want to leave your classes in the hands of a sub." Susan sipped more wine.

"Who'd he hire?"

"A Mrs. Delambre? Actually, *Madame* Delambre is what he said." Susan raised her eyebrows and brought a hand to her heart. "Do you know her?"

"She's legendary! She taught for years at St. Michael's. She wrote one of the books we use, the beginning one. Great, this is all I need. Madame Delambre teaching my kids." All Deirdre needed was for the legendary Madame Delambre to say something to Martin Loring about how her students were far behind where they should be and how their teacher obviously hadn't taught them much of anything. Plus, wouldn't Madame Delambre have to know why she had been hired? Even if Martin didn't tell her outright, by now she would know the reason for Deirdre's absence—

and that meant everyone at St. Michael's would now know too.

Susan looked right at Deirdre. "Frances Worthington is one powerful lady."

"Don't I know it." She didn't know how much to confide in Susan about Frances or Anna. "You said you wanted to talk about something?"

"I just wanted to see how you were doing. I imagine this has been a tough day for you."

"Martin, he's a good man. He's fair." Deirdre crossed her arms.

"Let's just say that Frances Worthington has a single-minded pursuit right now."

"But why can't Martin see this for what it is?" Deirdre blurted out. "Why can't he see that Frances Worthington is nothing more than a power-hungry woman? She's been out to get me ever since Anna started the upper school. She hates that I'm gay, and what's worse, I think Anna's gay and Frances is taking that out on me. God forbid Frances Worthington might have a gay daughter." Instantly, Deirdre regretted saying as much as she had. She had no idea really what Susan's relationship was like with either Frances or Martin Loring. Well, too late.

"Have you spoken with a lawyer?"

"A lawyer? God no! That's—Martin wouldn't take it that far . . . He . . . for God's sake, he told me this morning that we'd work it out."

"He may have no choice," Susan frowned. "If I were you, I'd find a good lawyer. Murray and I have one if you'd like. He's pricey but he's good."

Deirdre couldn't believe what she was hearing. Things were already getting out of hand. "When Martin investigates—and he promised me he would—he'll find out that there is nothing going on here. I know he'll do the right thing."

"He will—but will Frances Worthington? She's the one you need to worry about."

"I don't think Anna will let it get that far." Deirdre finished her wine. "Sure, I know that Frances has a lot of power—over Anna too—but you make it sound like there's a lynch mob out there."

Susan didn't say anything.

"Was the meeting that bad?"

"It was pretty bad," Susan said after a moment. She swirled the last bit of wine in her glass. "Ugly. The real problem is that Leo Rivera is still very much on everyone's mind. Now that they've arrested that guy—who, by the way, Murray swears was one of your movers?"

"Oh God, people don't think he's some friend of ours or something, do they?"

"No, no." Susan waved her hand. "But you know, the boy was sexually molested before he was killed and . . ."

Where is she going with this? "And what?" Deirdre put her hands on her hips.

"Well, people—and I'm sure you can understand—get nervous when something like this happens—"

"Of course they get nervous! A little boy is murdered by his next-door neighbor and gets dumped in the river! Who wouldn't get nervous?"

"But he was raped. And so people . . . feel that . . . having homosexuals around children is too risky. You can see how people might think that."

Deirdre was stunned into silence. "So what you're saying is that because Leo Rivera was raped by some crazy man, I might not get my job back?" Her breathing quickened and she could feel her heart racing.

"You've got to understand—"

"God, this is crazy. This is too crazy." Deirdre ran her fingers through her hair.

"I'm just afraid—and I'm sorry to say this," Susan spoke softly and put a hand on Deirdre's shoulder, "that Martin Loring will be under a lot of pressure to let you go." She gave Deirdre's shoulder a little squeeze.

"Because he's already under a lot of pressure, you mean," Deirdre said quietly, tears brimming.

"I'm sorry." Susan removed her hand. "Any other time, you could explain your side of things. But the way people feel right now, I'm not sure it matters."

"Guilty before proven innocent. This is just . . . awful."

Susan took a couple of steps down from the porch. "Remember, the lawyer. If you want his number, give us a call."

Deirdre watched Susan walk back to her house. What was she supposed to do now? She wondered about Beth Ann. If people were as riled up as Susan suggested, Beth Ann would surely have a hard time defending her, particularly in public—which is where, it was beginning to seem, Deirdre was going to need some serious defending.

CHAPTER FOURTEEN

AT FOUR, SJ LEFT THE LIBRARY and drove to First National Bank. She needed to transfer money from savings to checking and drop off the deposit check to the realtor. But Deirdre had whipped up some kind of special dinner—God knows what she was thinking—and either SJ had to tell her about the new apartment or she had to go through the motions of dinner. She didn't relish either option.

What else to do except play it by ear? If it seemed reasonable, then SJ would bring up the new apartment and suggest, maybe, the idea of a separation. The problem was, of course, when was it ever reasonable to talk about separating? And what kind of person would break up with her girlfriend on the same day that the girlfriend was let go from her job? For that matter, what kind of person would go through all the work of buying and moving into a new house and then leave less than a month later? SJ knew people did such things all the time, you heard about them from friends, you read about them in *Redbook* and *Ladies' Home Journal* in the dentist's waiting room. It's just that SJ didn't see herself as one of those people. When she heard the stories, it was always a man who left an unsuspecting wife, a man you could get angry with for being so insensitive, so selfish that he would leave the relationship that quickly and, the articles always suggested, with so little thought and consideration for the other person. Now, SJ wanted to reread the stories, knowing there was a much bigger part they were probably leaving out.

But she didn't know how much longer she could continue to live with Deirdre and pretend things were fine.

Not that she was doing such a good job of pretending. This past weekend, SJ hadn't been around much, and then when she was, things had been tense. She knew that tonight's dinner would be Deirdre's peace offering. Deirdre would have spent hours making some kind of fancy dish— or several, and they all would be delicious—and Deirdre would try to apologize for something she wasn't even sure she'd done. This last part infuriated SJ. Why, instead of trying to get back into SJ's good graces, couldn't Deirdre confront her about what was going on? SJ admitted that, a few times over the years, she had deliberately provoked Deirdre to make her angry, to just get her to react, but each time Deirdre responded with puzzlement, first about where the argument had come from, followed by immediately acquiescing, admitting that if SJ were mad, then she, Deirdre, must have done something to provoke her. Each apology came with a lovely dinner. The tendency was to smooth things over and not to deal with them. Of course, tonight's situation was much worse. The stakes were higher, for one thing. Now, SJ wasn't simply provoking Deirdre. Now, SJ really wanted out, and her timing was absolutely lousy.

At the bank, she pulled up behind a blue Dodge Caravan in line for the ATM. She fished her bank card from her wallet and watched as a skinny boy walked down the sidewalk, clutching his droopy pants. For a moment, she wished Deirdre were with her. They would turn, raise eyebrows, and without a word, each would know what the other was thinking. And in that moment, SJ understood why so many bad marriages continued even after it was clear to everyone except the couple that it was better off over. Because the world was made for couples. How much easier it was to have another person ready to attend events with you, help you with all the chores of running a household, to eat dinner with. Florence had pointed out on several occasions that you could have all those things with a roommate or good friend, you didn't need to enter into a relationship in order to have companionship, but SJ thought there was a big difference. Having a lover, SJ thought it was too obvious to admit, meant having a sort of intimacy with another person that seemed necessary now that she had it. Even when SJ thought of leaving the relationship, even when she admitted that she probably wasn't in love with Deirdre anymore, that maybe she really never had been. Even then she still hung onto the fact that there was one other person in this world who knew her, really knew her. Losing that felt like giving up too much. Now, taking her receipt from the ATM, SJ reasoned that breaking up wouldn't necessarily mean you were giving up that intimacy, not altogether, but you were severing a tie with the one person who knew you best. Just thinking about that possibility gave her the beginnings of a headache.

SJ could smell the dinner as soon as she walked in but couldn't identify right off what Deirdre had cooked. She heard the radio, NPR, in the kitchen, Deirdre humming some tune.

"Hey," SJ said, dropping her black courier bag on the couch. "I'm home."

Deirdre turned and smiled. "Hey. So you are."

Deirdre always looked cutest when she was cooking, and SJ half-wanted to hug her, wrap her arms around Deirdre from behind, but that wouldn't give her the courage she would need to say what she knew she had to say.

"You've cooked up a storm, looks like."

"Veal piccatta and risotto. Chocolate mousse for dessert. There's wine there if you want. Open on the table."

SJ turned and saw the bottle of chardonnay and poured herself a glass. "So, this dinner," SJ said. "You have some particular reason?"

Why SJ asked the question, she wasn't certain. She knew why Deirdre had cooked the dinner. Okay, so she was stalling for time. Or maybe she wanted to hear Deirdre's take on things, what the last few days had been like from Deirdre's point of view.

Deirdre turned down the flame and wiped her hands on her apron. "We've hardly seen each other lately," she said. "I know you're frustrated with me—" She put her hands up when SJ started to protest. "Okay, really? Because what else was I going to do with my time, home all day? I couldn't just sit on the couch. I would've cried. I would've been one pathetic mess when you got home!" Deirdre wiped at the corners of her eyes. "I need a hug."

SJ hesitated for a second, then put her glass down and opened her arms. "Come here," she said. And when Deirdre walked into her embrace, SJ went into automatic. She pulled Deirdre in tight, and held her against her chest. Breathed in the familiar citrus smell of Deirdre's hair, the warm sweetness of the skin on her neck, felt Deirdre's arms holding her, the most secure feeling SJ knew. She ran her fingers through Deirdre's hair and was conscious of the thought: *I won't be able to do this anymore.* How odd to know a body this well, the feel of the muscles in the arms, each freckle and mole. The way the hair felt, coarse and thick, the exact point of the shoulder blades, the ribs, the way the spinal cord protruded like braille down the length of the back, the way the back sloped into the buttocks. SJ held her breath for a minute as if she could keep the essence of Deirdre within her.

Deirdre looked up, expectant. Kissing was harder, demanded more. But SJ tried to smile and act like there was nothing she would rather do than lean in and kiss Deirdre.

"Mmmm. I've missed you," Deirdre said, and kissed SJ again on the cheek.

SJ patted Deirdre on the back. "I'm hungry," she said.

"Good. There's a lot of food!" Deirdre laughed. She let go of SJ and walked back to the stove, grinning. "Table's already set but can you put out the salad?"

SJ lifted the wooden bowl from the refrigerator and felt her stomach knot up. She wasn't hungry at all. But she had the absurd thought that she didn't want the food to go to waste. She didn't want Deirdre to think she'd made it all for nothing. She poured them both fresh glasses of wine. "So," SJ began, "Martin wasn't too understanding?" More stalling. How could she do this? She sat at the kitchen table.

Deirdre stirred the risotto. "He kept saying he had no choice. He said he'll investigate thoroughly and . . . But you know what? Here's the funny thing." Deirdre turned toward SJ, her face so wide and open and innocent it hurt to look at her. "So I'm home, and I don't know what to do, and I decide I'll make this meal, so I'm cooking and it's beautiful in here, the light I mean, and I'm sort of—well, not exactly happy but I'm okay. And I realize—what? What's wrong?" Deirdre frowned.

SJ shook her head. "Nothing. Go on." She tried to appear interested, which she was, or would have been two days ago. Was that true? Two days ago she would have cared about what happened with Deirdre's job and now she didn't? Could that be possible? SJ didn't think human beings were wired that way, but how was it that she could barely keep focused on what Deirdre was telling her?

"So, I'm thinking how funny that I'm okay. I mean really, I've almost just been fired, I should be miserable."

She stirred hard with a wooden spoon and squeezed a bit of lemon into the pan.

"Yeah," SJ said. "Yeah." She played with the salt and pepper shakers, an Eiffel Tower and Arc de Triomphe that she had given Deirdre for Christmas, one of their first.

Deirdre went on: "I just . . . I don't know . . . I think I realized something. I think I figured out that in a strange way, is this at all a good thing?" She looked back to gauge SJ's reaction, but SJ wouldn't look up. She couldn't bear it. They were headed for a train wreck. Deirdre spooned the risotto into a bowl. "I'm thinking that, you know, on the bright side, maybe now we get to have more time together, focus on us?"

Crash. SJ took a deep breath. She spread both hands out in front of her.

"I know it doesn't mean that everything will be fine right away, I know that," Deirdre hurried on. "You've got every right to be mad at me."

SJ started to speak, but Deirdre interrupted: "I know we have a lot of work to do, but the thing is, I want to do it. I'm excited about this . . . What?" Deirdre pulled out a chair.

"Just . . . stop talking, will you?" SJ put her head in her hands.

"What's wrong? What—"

"Please, really. Stop. Talking." The clock on the wall ticked away the seconds. The smell of sautéed garlic and onion. The pounding of her own blood against her temples. "I rented an apartment today," SJ said without looking up.

"What?" Deirdre sounded confused, not angry.

Please don't make me say it again.

"SJ, look at me."

"I rented an apartment today." SJ said it clearly. Lifted her head.

"Why?" Deirdre frowned, scrunched her eyes. "I don't get—"

"To live in." SJ stood and paced.

"To live—?"

SJ continued to pace, afraid that if she stopped, she might break apart into pieces.

Deirdre sat facing the window. SJ thought she could see Deirdre's back moving with each measured breath.

"SJ, what are you saying?"

So this was how these things really went. You were made to spell it out, say every little thing. No wonder so many people stayed in bad marriages. Who could bear to go through this? You wanted to say: *Just beat me. Go ahead and whip me now.* Because that's what it was like. You were saying the hardest words anyone would ever have to say and the person you were saying them to was the person you used to love but didn't any longer. But how does love disappear? That person was making you be explicit, forcing you to admit what you couldn't, even to yourself. What you wanted was innuendo. What you wanted was to say, *I'm sorry.* What they made you say was: *I don't love you anymore.* And SJ couldn't do it.

"I think we need time apart. I need time apart." She wanted to bolt right then and not have to face Deirdre anymore. But she also wanted Deirdre to see things her way, to see how this decision might be best.

"You're breaking up with me?"

SJ could hear the disbelief in Deirdre's voice. The—and SJ almost laughed at the absurdity of having the word pop into her head—incredulity. Yes, she wanted to say: *This is incredible, I know; but yes, I suppose it's true.* "I know it's a bad time—"

"A bad time! Could there be a worse time? This is unbelievable." Deirdre folded her arms.

The risotto congealed in the bowl. The veal dried in the pan.

"I just think we need to figure some things out, and it'll be better if we're apart when we do it. For me," SJ said. "For me, it'll be better. I'm sorry." Deirdre wouldn't look at her. "I'm sorry," SJ repeated. "I really am. But I don't know, I just couldn't keep on like this. You must have felt it too?"

Deirdre turned around then. "But I was willing to do something about it! I didn't decide that because things were hard, I would leave. Don't think I haven't thought about leaving, because I have. Christ, SJ, who doesn't? Don't you think most couples go through hard times? Do they split up? No, they work it out!" Deirdre stood now too, and marched over to the stove. One by one, she picked up the veal cutlets from the pan and tossed them into the trash. "So much for that." She grabbed the bowl of risotto from off the counter and scraped the whole mess on top of the veal. She threw away the butter too, and the herbs still sitting out on the counter.

"Listen . . ."

"No, you listen. I can't believe what you're saying. I can't believe you're actually doing this. You've rented an apartment? Already? Was Florence behind this?" Deirdre picked up a wooden spoon and tapped it against her palm.

"Florence had nothing to do with this. She thinks I'm crazy—"

"Which you are."

"She thinks—well, it doesn't matter what Florence thinks. What matters is that I'm not happy and if you're honest, you're not either."

"And you don't want to work on it?" Deirdre stopped tapping the spoon. "Because we can, you know."

SJ sat back at the table. "I don't know," she said. "I don't know."

"God." Deirdre put the spoon down and sat too. She shook her head and then started to cry. Big fat tears. Unstoppable.

"I'm sorry," SJ said. What else was there to say? She *was* sorry. But she couldn't help how she felt. And she knew Deirdre well enough to know that she wouldn't—couldn't—change. That teaching would always be her priority and the relationship second. So Deirdre needed to be with someone who didn't mind that arrangement. SJ was sure there were women like that; but she wasn't one of them. And, Deirdre needed to be with someone who loved her, who truly loved her. They both did.

"You'd think," Deirdre said through sniffles, "that being an only child, you'd like how things are with us—you know, lots of independence and stuff."

"You'd think," SJ said. She drank her wine.

"But damnit," Deirdre pounded her fist on the table, "couldn't you have figured this out a bit sooner? Why in hell did we buy this house? What were you thinking?"

SJ remained silent. She wanted to reach out and touch Deirdre's arm, but Deirdre seemed to read her mind.

"Don't touch me." She shook her finger at SJ. "You're having an affair!"

"No—"

"You are. I can tell."

"Don't be ridiculous."

"Ridiculous? Me? You're the one who walks in the door of our very new house—the one we just bought together less than a month ago—and tells me you're moving out. Right? Isn't that what you said?"

SJ stood.

"Don't you dare leave! No way. You cannot just come in here and lay something like that on me and then leave."

SJ sat back down.

"Admit it. You're seeing someone else."

"I'm not."

Deirdre started crying again. "At this point, you can admit it." She wiped her face and pushed her chair back from the table. She stood and walked into the living room.

SJ heard Deirdre flop onto the couch. She poured more wine into her glass and took a gulp. It would have been easier if she had left on Friday, when Deirdre first confessed about Anna Worthington. She'd been angry, especially that Deirdre had put herself in such a stupid position, but angry too because she wasn't at all certain that Deirdre didn't really kiss Anna. SJ might have felt stronger then about her decision to leave. But now she just felt tired.

PART TWO

OCTOBER

October 1

To the Editor, *Bradley Register:*

How many of us can imagine those last horrific hours of little Leo Rivera's life? ("Suspect Arrested in Leo Rivera Case," Sept. 27). I don't think that many of us could—or would want to. And no parent can begin to imagine what Mr. and Mrs. Rivera must be going through right now.

One can only hope that the person convicted of these horrible crimes will be sentenced to death. Any fair-minded citizen would agree that the death penalty is certainly warranted in a case such as this one—a senseless, premeditated murder of a young, innocent boy. There is no argument to be made to justify such an awful crime.

Concerned Citizen
Bradley, MA

CHAPTER ONE

DEIRDRE PUT DOWN THE NEWSPAPER. She always read the Sunday Styles section of the *New York Times* first, the human interest stories about people she didn't know, people with lives so unlike hers she sometimes had a hard time imagining they were real. People who spent weekends renting cute cottages in places like Montauk or Fire Island, so remote to Deirdre that they might as well have been in Europe, people who casually hopped on trains to leave Manhattan with baskets full of foods that Deirdre couldn't yet find in any of her local supermarkets. Crème fraîche. Tapenade. Cans of roasted oysters. What would these Manhattanites think right now if they could peek into *her* crazy life that seemed so topsy-turvy, someone's idea of a bad novel?

There wasn't much to see, frankly. Deirdre, curled on the couch, wearing her striped pajamas, drinking coffee, reading the *New York Times*. And SJ flung in the upholstered chair opposite the couch, one leg dangling over the arm, chewing the pencil eraser, a week's worth of *New York Times* crosswords piled on her lap.

Deirdre sipped her coffee. She folded the section of the newspaper to look at the weddings, normally her favorite part of the Sunday paper. Today was disappointing, with only one full-page spread of announcements, and only half of those with pictures. Why didn't more people get married in the fall? What was it about spring and weddings? All teachers knew that fall was really the beginning of the year and not January. Fall and not spring was the season of newness, the bright crimsons and oranges a sign of change and possibility. Anything could happen in the fall. But the spring—to Deirdre, the spring meant the end, a death of sorts, and certainly not a time to start a new relationship. Spring signaled that it was time to look back and assess the year that was finished. She sighed.

"What?" SJ put down her pencil.

Deirdre flashed the paper. "Hardly any weddings," she said. "I hate that."

"I'll never understand why you read those anyway." SJ picked up a crossword. "Five-letter word for *make amends.*"

Deirdre scanned the page before her. She liked to predict which couples would stay together and which were destined to break up. She could tell from the photos, the way the couple held their heads together, or the way they looked at the camera, their eyes a mirror for what was going on inside their heads. There were the ones who posed stiffly. Then there were the ones who just looked wrong, like they had come from two completely different worlds and, no matter what, would just not go together. Deirdre loved the stories of long-lost love, of people who had known each other in their youth, lost contact, and somehow had found a way to be together years after they'd assumed their love was over. Those stories were the most inspirational and sometimes even made Deirdre tear up. SJ thought she was ridiculous, though SJ was hardly a romantic, Deirdre reminded herself, glancing now at SJ erasing one of her words.

"I wonder what our picture would look like?" Deirdre said aloud, then immediately regretted it.

SJ held her pencil aloft. She started to speak, then stopped.

Deirdre snorted. "Oh—*atone*. That's the word you're looking for."

SJ turned back to her crossword. She counted the number of squares she needed to fill for the next word.

Deirdre didn't know any gay people who'd had weddings. She had heard of some of course, but she had yet to attend one. SJ thought the very idea was silly, but Deirdre loved it. She had to admit that partly she just wanted the chance to be center stage, to have a big fuss made over her. She definitely saw herself as the bride, and though she didn't see SJ as a groom necessarily, mentally she assigned SJ a minor role, put her in the background of her wedding scenario. Deirdre wanted an excuse to wear something outrageous that she'd never have the courage to buy otherwise, and a reason to throw a fancy, lavish party. Their circle of friends was smallish, so the wedding would never be a big affair, but Deirdre saw herself inviting Agnès from France, a few colleagues, Paul and Kris, and her parents. She'd want Forest there, in an ideal world. Sophie and Mark. And years afterward, she and SJ would have the pictures to look back on as a kind of proof that their relationship had meant enough for their friends to come together from their various lives and had been important enough for a ceremony to be given in their honor.

SJ counted more crossword spaces. She glanced up at Deirdre. "What?"

"Nothing." Deirdre went back to the weddings. "Just looking," she said.

SJ put down the crossword. "Hungry?" Before Deirdre could say anything, SJ strolled into the kitchen. Deirdre started to answer and then SJ yelled, "Leftovers?" from behind the refrigerator door. "You want any?"

Deirdre swallowed. "Sure," she called back.

SJ was really making an effort. For the past few days

and nights, Deirdre felt like she had been holding her breath. Yet she still couldn't relax, couldn't let herself believe that maybe she and SJ would be okay. Of course it was still so tentative. Deirdre didn't want to fool herself into thinking that things were fine—far from it—but in the past week, she and SJ had seemed to settle into a kind of workable routine that so far felt almost normal. The biggest indication that things weren't normal was that SJ hadn't touched Deirdre—not a hug, not a pat on the arm, nothing. At night, though SJ hadn't gone as far as sleeping on the couch, she kept to her own side of the bed. There were no good-night kisses and no snuggling. Deirdre hadn't slept much in the past few nights and woke to watch SJ, wanting with a heavy ache to reach over and touch her, wrap her arms around her, but she held back. She didn't want to start up anything, didn't want to give SJ the ammunition she needed to remind Deirdre what a bad idea it was for her to stay.

Truthfully, it had been SJ's idea. That horrible night of the ruined veal piccata, they had exhausted themselves with all the accusations they could throw at each other. They had said mean, horrible things. *I don't love you anymore. I haven't loved you for a long time.* Deirdre had insisted that SJ was having an affair; SJ insisted she wasn't. Finally, they had fallen into bed, fully clothed, and slept, drained. The next morning, Deirdre woke with the deepest, most profound sense of sadness she had ever experienced, sadness that gave way to panic when she remembered that SJ had actually already rented an apartment.

"But why didn't you tell me you were so unhappy?" Deirdre kept saying, the tears starting anew. "You're telling me now but it's too late."

SJ had looked defeated and Deirdre almost felt sorry for her. They decided to take a walk around the pond at the far end of their neighborhood. Outside, everything looked dif-

ferent, tinged with this new feeling of sadness and despera-
tion, the trees their normal shades of deep reds and rusts
and gold, but Deirdre had only sensed that she and SJ were
walking through a beautiful fall palette. Her surroundings
felt staged, a prop that had nothing to do with them.

"You're really moving out?" Deirdre said finally, after
they had walked for a half hour in silence.

SJ kicked at the gravel. "I don't know. Maybe I was too
hasty."

Deirdre felt a blossoming of hope. She knew she had
to choose her words carefully. "You must have been feeling bad for a while," she said, "for you to take such a . . .
big step." She swallowed. "I'm sorry. For thinking you were
having an affair. For accusing you of that."

SJ walked with her hands in her pockets. She looked at
Deirdre then with such a sweet, sad face. "It's okay," she had
said. "What else could you think?"

And then they had cried. They had held each other, there
on the footpath along the pond, the trees in symphonic autumn glory, for several long minutes.

"I don't know," SJ said finally. "I guess I could call the
realtor . . . If it's okay. If you don't think it's too late."

Maybe Deirdre should have been angrier. Maybe she
should have told SJ it was too late, that you couldn't jerk a
person around like that—but she had been so grateful that
SJ wanted to stay and work things out. She couldn't manage
to get through losing her job and SJ at the same time.

And so now here they were, reading the Sunday paper,
doing crosswords, eating leftovers from last night's takeout.
Deirdre hadn't felt like cooking, not since *that night*, as they
referred to it. They were being careful with each other and
each night Deirdre looked over to the back of SJ's T-shirt and
longed to run her hand beneath the cotton, feel SJ's cool skin,
kiss her good night, and tell her everything she felt in her heart.

C HAPTER TWO

SJ WAS AFRAID IT MIGHT COME TO THIS. She dropped the *Register* on her office desk, pushed back in her chair. People were so quick to judge. They didn't know all the facts, only what other people told them and what they read in the paper. Even that, SJ knew, was too often skewed. Made to look worse than it was. No one took time to find out the real truth.

Her own parents had been like that. All news was suspect unless confirmed by someone else at the club. *Dick Merriwether says*—her father began almost every counterargument to whatever she brought up, and SJ wondered where Dick Merriwether got *his* information, and why he was the measure of accurate news. Her parents' inability to ever really listen to her—to see things from her point of view—had been the very reason she hadn't ever called them much even when they were both still alive.

SJ looked down again at the paper. *Concerned Citizen.* Whoever wrote the letter couldn't even sign his name. Coward. You could call for the death penalty, but you couldn't admit it publicly. The paper shouldn't even print that crap. SJ tapped her pencil, made flower doodles on a yellow Post-it.

"Hey." Florence knocked on SJ's door, "got a minute?" She stepped in, pulled the door closed behind her.

SJ tapped the newspaper with the pencil's eraser. "You read it this morning?"

Florence shook her head. "Listen, we've got a situation."
SJ motioned to the empty chair.

"The investigation," Florence said. "They—the detectives—
want to know . . . They think we have some information
that can help." She fidgeted with her pearls. SJ noted that
Florence was not wearing her scrimshaws so often now, not
since Elliot had mentioned that they reminded him of his
grandmother.

SJ drew in a breath. She recalled the detectives' last visit,
the way her own palms sweated and her legs trembled the entire time. She hated the way they made her feel like the guilty
one. "They're not looking for another visit with me, are they?"

Florence shifted her weight, one hand still fingering the
pearls. She sighed and said, "Actually, they want to know
what, if anything, Mickey checked out—"

"That's way out of line!" SJ cut in. "That's—"

Florence held up her hand. "Well, wait a minute. He's
a suspect in a murder. It could be that we have evidence—"

SJ stood. She waved the paper at Florence. "You know
they're calling for the reinstatement of the death penalty?"

"Can you blame them? Leo Rivera was a kid." Florence
crossed her arms. "It's understandable that people are angry."

"They don't know Mickey. They don't know the first
thing about him."

"And you do?" After a pause, she continued: "Honestly,
what do you *know* about this man? What do you know
beyond the fact that he has come to you for a few weeks of
literacy classes?"

And SJ saw again those moments of triumph when
Mickey read aloud sentences, when he managed what he
claimed were "tough words," when he grinned, his whole
face lit up, proud. She saw him in his pressed T-shirt and
jeans, arriving early for each lesson.

SJ shook her head and paced behind her desk. "No. It's

not right. What, because a person wants to read murder mysteries, that makes him a killer?"

Florence said nothing.

"I mean, where do we draw the line?" SJ tried to ignore the picture in her head—the newspaper clippings strewn on Mickey's desk, headlines of Leo's disappearance, updates on the investigation into his whereabouts. "You know what I tried to get him to read? *Cars & Parts*."

"Let's just think about it. That's all I'm saying." Florence unfolded her arms and looked as if she were going to make a point, but stopped. "Let's just think about it," she said again.

"What, will we tell everyone on the front desk to put a black mark next to anyone's name who . . . who, I don't know, takes out a book with sex in it?"

"You're being ridiculous." Florence had one hand on the doorknob.

"No, listen to what you're saying. You're talking about censorship. You're talking about monitoring someone's reading habits."

Florence laughed a little, shook her head. "I'm not talking about anything of the kind. I'm talking about a murder investigation. A little boy was murdered. And if we have evidence, I think it's our duty to hand it over. That's all."

"Innocent until proven guilty, have you forgotten that? Or freedom of information? Our duty to protect everyone's right to privacy? The ALA code of ethics?" SJ stood behind her desk, arms folded, legs planted. She thought she noticed Florence waver, hesitate.

"We'll see. We may have no choice."

"My mind is made up."

"Frankly," Florence said, opening SJ's door, "this isn't your decision." She hesitated, then walked out.

SJ slumped into her chair. She could see it at the next

conference: they'd be shunned if news of this got out. All the librarians SJ knew—and she really only knew them from the conferences, plus a few acquaintances from library school—were vehement supporters of the code of ethics. SJ remembered being impressed when she was still in library school, learning about it, the pledge to offer unrestricted access to any information a patron might request—books about gay sexuality, books on making explosives, books and materials about conservative Christian beliefs. You couldn't monitor what people read, what information they wanted access to.

She heard the voice of her favorite professor, Mr. Pollen: "The code of ethics, my friends, the code of ethics." She could hear his Boston Brahmin voice, rising as he made his point. The students would grin and sit forward. They knew his speech by heart. They knew when to expect it, when to be ready for the standard lecture on "your sacred duty to uphold the First and Fourth Amendments." Mr. Pollen's finger poking in the air, head upturned and away from the students. SJ couldn't look at Mr. Pollen without thinking of Nantucket or Martha's Vineyard and she always wondered what types of subversive literature the patrons there requested, how hard it was for those librarians to uphold their "sacred duty."

"It's no joke," Mr. Pollen would say to them then. "Oh no, it's quite, quite serious." And then there would be the debates, the hypothetical situations, all drawn, Mr. Pollen insisted, from real life—the patron who, not finding a certain type of material in his public library, requests it. "Material you might find offensive but to this patron is perfectly acceptable. What do you do? What do you do?" he'd say, pointing to one of them. "Maybe the work denigrates a person's race. Maybe the rhetoric rallies against the government. Maybe a young patron wants a novel that promotes drug use, a novel full of profanity . . ."

Then, one of the rowdier students—there were rowdy students in library school—would shout from the back of the room, "I'd buy it for them!"

Mr. Pollen never paused. This was his time in the spotlight, what he was known for. His reputation was all about the code of ethics. "Libraries," he would always end his speeches, "are one of democracy's greatest allies and achievements. Libraries are among the very institutions that make democracy work!" And though they sometimes wondered together in groups if Mr. Pollen was for real—if he actually believed that "democracy stuff" he spouted—the students would leave his class feeling important, believing in the sacred duty of every librarian to uphold her part in democracy.

What would Mr. Pollen do in this situation? SJ wondered. Here she was, in a real-life scenario right out of his class, and she felt unprepared. The old guy had retired after SJ's class graduated, or else she might have called him up and asked his advice. She wondered whom else she might call from library school. Who taught the class now on the code of ethics? She could ask one of the library school interns, but that would take time. She needed to do something *now*.

SJ logged onto the Internet. She searched for the ACLU website and scrolled through their pages. She wasn't sure what she was looking for, not exactly. She knew Florence was right—that if the court ordered a subpoena, they really would have no choice. She'd told Florence the truth—that she'd tried to get Mickey to read *Cars & Parts*—but what she didn't tell her was that he'd wanted to read the newspaper. He'd wanted, SJ realized after the fact, to read about Leo Rivera's disappearance, see what was being said about it, possibly about him. Is that all the reading lessons were, then—a way for Mickey to find out what the public thought of him? A way to discern how close he was to being caught?

It was hard for SJ to imagine. She couldn't reconcile this guy who came eagerly to reading classes—who smelled of spicy aftershave, whose clothes were pressed and smelled of Tide—with the person who had stuffed a little boy into a container weighed down with concrete and dropped him in the river. Was her judgment that off?

After work, SJ drove to the city jail. She didn't know what to expect, whether or not she would be able to visit Mickey, but she decided to try her luck. She couldn't even explain why she was visiting him—except she couldn't shake the feeling that he was innocent. It just didn't seem possible, with his passive demeanor and childish understanding of the world, that he could have been the mastermind behind the child's kidnapping.

The jail was an old structure, redbrick with vines creeping across one side. If you didn't know better, you might think it was an old school building, except for the metal fence surrounding the perimeter and the wires strung along the top. Otherwise, the jail looked almost quaint here at the end of Main Street, an old oak spreading across the front lawn. A paved walkway led to the entrance. Two vans sat parked alongside the curb—Channel 8 and the local cable station, 56, a Fox affiliate.

Here we go. Let the circus begin. SJ grabbed her jacket and climbed out of the car. October sunshine filtered through gray clouds. The trees, many of them bare already, looked like skinny men, tired and mournful. SJ shivered walking to the entrance. She tried to tell herself that she was just visiting Mickey, but this didn't calm her. She took a deep breath. Behind her, voices—a reporter urgent and insistent—"Mr. Blankenship!" SJ turned. She recognized Mickey's lawyer from the television reports. He was known for taking on high-profile cases. This was certainly turning out to be one.

Metal detectors always made SJ feel guilty, even in airports. Here in the jail she found herself starting to sweat as soon as she walked through the door and tried to wiggle out of her jacket, one arm refusing to shake loose. She smiled at the security guard. "Sorry."

The guard didn't smile back. "Your pockets too," she said. She sounded bored.

SJ handed her jacket to the guard. She stuck her hands in her pockets and shrugged to show she had nothing. Maybe these guards, the ones out here, were resentful that they weren't inside, doing the real work of the jail, though this one looked like maybe she could. The large, beefy woman whose dark-brown skin shone a little in the bright lights looked like she meant business, like she would have no problem knocking you down. She had what Deirdre would call a "fresh face," someone who might have had a tough life of her own, who had been, in her parents' words, "around the block once or twice."

The guard motioned SJ through the metal detector. She turned the jacket inside out, felt the pockets, and handed it back to SJ. "Information desk is through there." She pointed to the doors.

"Thank you." SJ approached a windowed area surrounded by glass. Another guard, this one a young white man, stood in the corner, feet apart, arms crossed. A bundle of keys hung from his belt. She noticed he also had a gun.

SJ cleared her throat. "I'm here . . ." she started to say to the older man behind the window. She cleared her throat again. "I'm hoping to visit someone?"

The man looked mildly amused. He glanced toward the guard. "Lawyer?" SJ thought she detected a snicker. "Do you have an appointment?"

"I'm not a lawyer," SJ said.

"You on the list?"

"List?"

"Visitors list. No visitors who aren't on the list." The man looked back down to a pile of papers in front of him.

SJ didn't know anything about a visitors list. "Can I leave a message?"

The man looked back up. "No," he said. "Sorry. No messages for inmates." He moved to slide the window shut.

SJ leaned forward. "Wait. I need to get in touch with Mickey Gilberto. How can I get in touch with him?"

"I'm sorry, " the man said. "Excuse me." He turned and buzzed open the door next to the information desk. A blond woman entered carrying a clipboard and wearing a white plastic *VISITOR ID* around her neck. She smiled at SJ. "Thanks, Earl." She handed the ID to the man behind the window. "See you tomorrow."

"Alright," he said, smiling. He moved a few papers around and lifted the receiver, started punching in numbers, then looked up and stopped, cradling the receiver between his chin and neck. "Is there anything else?" he asked SJ.

The front door opened. A man and woman, both white, both in suits, entered and flashed IDs at Earl. He buzzed open the door that led to the inside of the jail.

"So, there's no way to get a message to anyone in here? No way to let a prisoner know I'd like to see him?"

"Nope," Earl shook his head. "No visitors who aren't on the list. No messages for inmates. No exceptions." He slid the glass window shut.

The guard in the corner jingled the keys on his belt and glanced over at SJ. There was nothing to do but leave.

October 3

To the Editor, *Bradley Register*:

I am writing in reference to the letter dated October 1 by "Concerned Citizen." I, too, cannot imagine the horror that the Rivera family must face each day, knowing how their little boy met his end.

But it seems to me barbaric to already condemn the man in custody, before we know the extent of his involvement. I am urging my fellow citizens to remain calm and let the legal system work as it is supposed to.

Beth Ann Farraday
Bradley, MA

CHAPTER THREE

IN THE PARK, MOST OF THE LEAVES had fallen now and drifted into piles in the grass and on the walkway, the late-morning sky pulsing with seventy October degrees. SJ looked over her shoulder. She kicked at the dry leaves and pushed up the sleeves of her sweatshirt.

She hated seeing Deirdre so unhappy. At night when Deirdre slept—she claimed she wasn't sleeping at all these days but SJ was the witness—SJ looked at her face, quiet and unguarded, and remembered their first nights together, the wonder and terror of sleeping with another person. SJ always thought that aside from the possibility of pregnancy, teenage sex wasn't the huge issue people made it out to be. No, it was the euphemism for sex—sleeping with someone—that was the bigger issue. Sex in cars, on beaches—furtive, groping sex—that wasn't intimate at all. Too often it was embarrassing. But sleeping. Sharing a bed while you slept, while you dreamed, while you were at your most unguarded and vulnerable, that was the most intimate thing imaginable.

Did Deirdre sleep gratefully, able only then to ignore what was happening in her waking life? SJ's greatest adult fear—one that she might not be able to admit out loud, one that she could hardly admit to herself in those private, dark moments—was that someone might find her incompetent.

Now, with hindsight, she understood that her . . . thing with Mr. Freeman had happened in the first place because he had seen SJ as smart and dedicated. For SJ, that was everything. So it threw her off to have the police questioning her at the library. She thought it made her colleagues wonder about her and so they might gossip and tell stories and question her professional judgment too. Librarian circles were tight, and SJ hated to think that her association with Mickey was now the preferred topic of conversation.

Deirdre, on the other hand, seemed so unconcerned about what people thought. *How can you do it?* SJ wanted to know. *How can you get up in the morning, go for a run, buy groceries, while being that person other people don't want?* She thought about it now, walking through the park, looking left and right, conscious that she might bump into Deirdre on her run. When you weren't a teacher, an attorney, a librarian, or stockbroker anymore, how would you know who to be? How to act? What your place was in the world?

An ambulance screeched past. Two women pushed small children on swings. One yelled, "Higher, Mommy, higher!" The other squealed. It bothered SJ that Deirdre couldn't admit her own responsibility in what had happened at Brandywine. Deirdre couldn't see that she'd crossed boundaries way too often, much more than was advisable for anyone working with young people. SJ wondered whether teacher training programs should spend more time on helping new teachers develop that distance they needed to establish between themselves and their students—though whether or not teacher training programs spent any time on that topic, SJ had no idea. Besides, Deirdre hadn't received any formal training. She had her degrees in French—BA and MA—and that's it. All the teacher training had occurred on the job. Maybe that's why she couldn't see her own role; she didn't realize she'd played any role whatsoever. But it was so clear to SJ.

She kicked at the dried leaves. It had been about a year ago that her colleague Paula had been fired outright from the library. SJ remembered coming in that morning and hearing the news, the reference librarians gathered around the front desk, gossiping. SJ looked at Paula differently from then on. She couldn't help it; Paula who had been fired just wasn't the same person in her eyes as Paula who headed up Technical Services. And when Florence suggested they meet Paula for drinks the following week, "to perk her up," SJ wouldn't go. She didn't want to hear Paula's version of what happened. She didn't want to commiserate and rally against the library administration (didn't Florence feel funny about that too?); nor did she want to feel like a traitor, which is exactly how she'd end up feeling. Paula would go on about how she'd been treated unfairly, about how it was overly critical for the library to expect her to be on time every day, and so what if her lunch breaks were longer than usual? SJ would want to say: *So the rules, then. They don't apply to you?* And SJ would feel bad for liking her job, for feeling that the administration was right in letting Paula go, and that Tech Services would be better off with someone who toed the line.

On the far end of the park, on the track, a runner sprinted, slowed to a jog, and then sprinted again. SJ couldn't understand how anyone could make themselves run like that, force themselves to sprint when there wasn't anything at stake. Deirdre said you got a high from going fast, from beating your own best time, but SJ couldn't imagine it. At a glance, the woman on the track looked like Deirdre. Her hair was about the same length. Narrow shoulders. But the hips were too wide, too rounded, and the gait, too halting. Deirdre ran in long, steady strides, fluid, the same way she spoke French, the way she tried to cajole her students to speak, her accent so perfect she was often mistaken for a native speaker.

A bird chirped—SJ couldn't identify what kind—high-pitched and urgent. She sat on the bench nearest the park's Maple Street entrance, overlooking the empty basketball court, and laid her head against the top of the bench, closed her eyes, and absorbed the sun, felt it penetrate deep into her scalp and the cells of her skin. Would Deirdre notice her on the bench when she ran past—if she wasn't already long gone, well beyond the park by now, maybe past the school? Would she even be looking? Of course, today Deirdre might have taken a different route altogether.

The sun warmed SJ's skin. How she wished this warmth could work some kind of magic, make things better between her and Deirdre. She didn't know how much longer she could talk about the situation at school. Each time they got into a conversation about it, SJ was flooded with . . . was it shame? She could only describe it as a heaviness, a dread, a longing to scream out to Deirdre that the way she was with those girls was wrong; didn't she see that? You couldn't blame Anna for falling in love with her. Why couldn't she see that at least?

In the twelve years since high school, SJ had thought of Mr. Freeman occasionally, but the minute her mind conjured a memory, she brushed it aside. It was almost possible to convince herself that she'd imagined the whole thing. At graduation, Mr. Freeman had slipped her a congratulatory card, given her the requisite teacher hug. SJ tried, now, to recall what she had felt then, at the end of things. Nothing. Was that possible?

Relief?

She couldn't remember. But sitting here in the park,

THE YEAR OF NEEDY GIRLS

the sun like goodness on her face—it was difficult to feel anything but a kind of happiness, contentment in spite of everything.

It was the kind of day that fooled you into thinking nothing bad could happen. By now SJ should have known better. Like last Tuesday. She remembered because it was Tuesday she and Deirdre had made love for the first time in a long while—a surprise for both of them—and SJ had been late to work. She'd spilled coffee on her favorite tan sweater on the way to the library and there, when she pushed through the front door, gathered in a circle in front of the main desk were the reference librarians, Margo and Elliot, heads tilted toward each other, and Florence's boss, the head librarian, Sam.

All of them had turned at once as she entered. The clock had ticked, there was no erasing all the minutes, and Sam, his red bow tie crisp, nodded at SJ.

The rest of the day had been a blur of all other workdays—cataloging, ordering, checking on OCLC updates. And then, waiting like a bad birthday surprise when she returned from grabbing an afternoon coffee, the official reprimand. A written copy for her to sign. It mentioned other, lesser infractions too that SJ thought were petty and punitive. She had waited until she was sure Sam was gone and slipped the signed paper beneath his office door.

Two boys appeared on the basketball court. SJ heard them first, their slang loud and jarring. She opened her eyes. The boys looked misplaced, their pants droopy, belted around the tops of their thighs. These two weren't exactly the athletic type, either. They bounced the basketball back and forth; loud, hard bounces that reverberated on the asphalt, their laughter and words echoing harshly. The boys couldn't have been more than fourteen or fifteen. Old enough to look menacing; young enough to look like kids. The boy holding his pants up threw the ball in an easy arc and it hit the backboard, dropped through the metal net.

"Momm-ee!" From behind SJ, the high-pitched voices singsongy, like faraway recess sounds. The women stood apart from the swings now, paying attention only to each other while the little ones, a boy and a girl, jumped from the swings, chased each other onto the grass.

"Get me!" one of them yelled. They ran in that little-kid way, oblivious and free. SJ smiled watching them. She wished she could remember feeling like that, though she doubted that she'd ever really been that type of child. Even back then, she'd been cautious, an observer. She'd been a perfectionist, her parents praising only the most exceptional accomplishments. The rest had been expected. Ordinary. So SJ grew up with the feeling that she had to excel—and if she wasn't ready to excel or wasn't sure she could, she didn't try. She watched.

Her feeling about childhood was that it was a time of nervousness and challenges. She envied these boys, not athletes, not even physically fit, out here shooting baskets, laughing, obviously not caring what anyone thought, or if anyone saw. She could never do that, not even now. That's why she avoided parties. Deirdre thought it was because she was so judgmental of other people—but it wasn't that. It was because of her fear that she herself would come up short.

SJ got up from the bench and tugged at her sleeves. The runner was stretching now on the track, bending over, her body pliable. She bent to one leg then the other. The basketball players watched her, one of them nudging the other. They laughed loudly. SJ turned and walked out of the park, passing the stately Victorians and the houses converted to condos. Round, fat pumpkins sat on stone steps, some carved into scary faces, most of them full and orange. Other

houses had potted mums, plum and maroon and gold, ar-
ranged on porches. Here was a hanging mobile of black
cats, some fake cobwebs, a bit early still for Halloween,
but people these days merged one holiday season into the
next. A tabby cat rolled on the sidewalk, stretched its paws
long into the sunshine. SJ felt a little guilty for calling in
sick but she just couldn't handle Florence and her questions
right now, or the way the student workers and colleagues
whispered and then stopped when SJ appeared. She knew
they were all dying to ask about Mickey, and that Florence
had probably told them not to. SJ didn't know if the police
had questioned anyone else besides herself and Florence, or
what any of the others might say about Mickey.

In any event, Florence probably thought she was in
turmoil over the state of things with Deirdre, which was
partly true. But mostly, SJ just didn't feel like seeing anybody today. And she really, really didn't want to talk with
Florence about Deirdre. Florence had seemed relieved when
she found out that SJ had decided not to move. "Oh good,"
she'd said. "That makes much more sense."

And SJ had reminded Florence how much she had been
against SJ's moving in with Deirdre in the first place.

"True," Florence acknowledged, "but now that you've
done it, I think you should stick it out. Make it work. Relationships aren't easy, you know."

How irritating. SJ had wanted Florence to revel with
her in the decision to leave Deirdre, to admit finally what
a silly move it had been in the first place. She had expected
Florence to say something like, *It's about time!* But instead,
Florence seemed to be rooting for the relationship. SJ accused her of "flip-flopping."

What SJ couldn't tell Florence, and what she certainly
couldn't admit to Deirdre, was that she had decided not to
give up the apartment after all. She wasn't going to move

into it—not yet. She really did want to help Deirdre through this thing, but somehow the idea of the apartment was comforting. She jiggled the key in her jeans pocket. It was almost like having a lover but not, though if Deirdre knew, she would definitely feel as threatened as she would be by another person. SJ couldn't really explain why she had decided to keep the apartment, not even to herself. She knew how right it had felt when she looked at it and when she signed the lease. Certainly she could have gotten out of the lease, even if she'd had to pay a month's rent in advance, but the more she thought about it, the more she decided it was right to hang on to it. She wasn't yet certain how she would use it, if at all, but just the knowledge that her own private place existed provided her with a sense of comfort and a secret thrill.

She turned onto one of the quiet side streets. Funny how empty and lonely a neighborhood could feel. SJ thought about the street where she had rented the new apartment; the two neighborhoods couldn't be more different, except for the one thing most places in Bradley had in common: a lack of parking spaces.

SJ headed away from the park and her neighborhood and in the general direction of the East End. She fingered the apartment key. In their house, it was difficult to be alone, especially now that Deirdre was there all the time. And SJ needed time to think and figure out what she was going to do. It was hard to turn away from five years together, hard to know the exact right thing to do, for both of them. For now, it seemed best to stay and help Deirdre get through this tough time. No matter how much SJ felt the relationship was over, she could not up and leave right now. It just wasn't possible.

SJ passed the main branch of the public library, such a stately building, all brick and important looking. And up ahead, the town hall. If all you saw of Bradley were this green and the brick New England buildings, the white Unitarian church, you would think: *Charming.* You would think you were in small-town America. You would expect lobster and clam bakes; you would expect town meetings, and you wouldn't be entirely wrong. But you would only get half the picture. In order to really know the town, you had to continue on, the way SJ was headed, over the river and into the East End, where the triple-deckers weren't converted into condominiums, where you heard Brazilian music, smelled grilled beef and onions, and where dried bouquets still stuck in the metal fence surrounding Most Precious Blood Elementary.

SJ could hear the voices of kids at recess. How did they cope with Leo Rivera's death? Were they afraid all the time now? she wondered. How strange that in the early days of September all anyone heard about was Leo Rivera. You saw his face on the evening news and then, once Mickey was arrested, that was it. Tragedies were like that. They occupied the collective imagination for a while, and then everyone went on to something else. It didn't seem possible that right here in Leo and Mickey's neighborhood, though, people could forget that quickly. The people most affected lived here still. Mickey Gilberto's mother, right next door to the Rivera family, and a street away from Leo's grandmother.

SJ knew little about Brazilian culture, but she knew that Mondays were important and devoted to the souls of the dead, which might be why, as she came upon Most Precious Blood, she saw devotional candles, their flames flickering, just outside the schoolyard fence. The kids didn't seem to notice, or at least they didn't pay any particular attention to the candles grouped there beneath a picture of Leo, smiling as always in that Red Sox cap. SJ crossed the street to get a closer look at the picture. What a sweet face on that poor child. How hard to imagine anyone hurting him—how really hard to imagine it might be Mickey. She wasn't so naïve to think that it wasn't possible, but given what she'd seen of Mickey in their few classes together, she could not imagine it. Mickey had seemed genuinely upset by the murder too, called Leo the little brother he'd never had. Well, just as it was possible Mickey had been involved in the murder, it was equally possible that the police had arrested the wrong person.

The TV vans were no longer a constant presence outside the school, though SJ noticed a police cruiser idling alongside one edge of the fenced-in blacktop and she wondered if there was often a police presence at the school or if the cops were here for something else. She pressed up against the chain-link fence. A nun wearing an old-fashioned habit opened the heavy front door and stood at the top of the steps, ringing a little bell. The kids stopped what they were doing and merged into a couple of ragged lines to head back inside. They giggled and whispered with each other. The nun motioned for the children to hurry along, called out a name or two to keep them moving: "Felipe!" "Marie Elena!"

"SJ!"

She was startled to hear her name and for a moment thought the nun knew her somehow and had called out to her.

"SJ," the voice said again. "On lunch break?" It was Detective Rodriguez. She smiled but didn't offer a hand.

"Yes," SJ replied. "No—I mean, I took the day off." She shrugged as if to say, *How could I pass on a day like this?*

"What brings you here?" Detective Rodriguez raised her eyebrows just slightly.

SJ had the strange feeling that she had been caught doing something she wasn't supposed to be doing. "I was . . . just out walking," she said.

Detective Rodriguez folded her arms. SJ could see the holster just beneath her suit jacket.

"I . . . I just wandered farther than I meant to, I guess." She did not want to mention her apartment, although it would certainly provide her with a good reason for walking in this neighborhood; something told SJ to keep the apartment a secret from the police too.

Detective Rodriguez's face didn't register any emotion. "You seemed pretty deliberate just now." She nodded to the picture of Leo Rivera and the little shrine of devotional candles. "Were you looking for something in particular? Someone?"

"Me? No, God no. I . . . I don't know, I was out walking and saw the picture and . . ." She realized how defensive she sounded. "I was just out walking. I'm not sure why I came over here."

"You can understand why the school is leery of having strangers hanging around the schoolyard?"

"Yes, absolutely," SJ blushed. "I'm s-sorry," she stammered. "I didn't mean to cause worry."

Detective Rodriguez nodded.

"Did someone . . . say something? Complain?" SJ looked up to where the last of the kids were entering the school and the nun was closing the door behind them.

"When my partner comes out, why don't you let us give you a lift home?" Detective Rodriguez motioned to the police cruiser.

"It's fine," SJ said. "I'm okay. I can walk. I like walking."

A uniformed policeman stepped out from the school's main door. Detective Rodriguez raised a hand and waved, those manicured nails flashing bright red. She looked at SJ. "It would be no problem. Come on. I think it would be better if you let us give you a ride."

And SJ felt like she had no choice. What a scene it would

be if she pulled up in front of the house in a police car. Not to mention the deeper fear that Detective Rodriguez wanted her for reasons more serious than simply giving her a ride home. The offer didn't exactly seem like a friendly gesture. Detective Rodriguez held her arm aloft as if to say, *This way*, and SJ walked toward the car.

"Detective Mahoney is working another angle on the case," Detective Rodriguez said while they walked. "I'm with Officer Deluca today." Her tone suggested that SJ knew who that was. She felt conspicuous walking alongside Rodriguez. Each car that passed seemed to slow down to see what was going on. But, of course, that was silly. Rodriguez wasn't even wearing a uniform. Still, with the cruiser parked nearby, SJ felt marked and humiliated.

When they got closer to the car SJ recognized Officer Deluca as one of the uniformed policemen who had come by the library in the days just following Leo Rivera's disappearance. "Hello," she said.

Rodriguez motioned to the other officer. "I believe you've met Officer Deluca. Ms. Edmonds."

Deluca nodded. "Ms. Edmonds," he said curtly.

"I thought we might give Ms. Edmonds a ride home." Rodriguez opened the back door. "She's a long way from home, and along the way, I thought we might have a conversation."

Officer Deluca nodded.

"Everything go okay in there?" She motioned back toward the school building and held the back door open for SJ.

"Fine," he said. "Not much new."

SJ climbed in the backseat and felt immediately uneasy, like she had crossed over into enemy territory. *Get out now,* a small voice said. *You're not safe.* But she had a clear conscience—except that she'd let Mickey Gilberto kiss her on the very night of his arrest. And she'd rented an apartment in his neighborhood. And she hadn't mentioned any of it to Deirdre. But other than that, she hadn't done anything wrong. None of that was against the law, certainly.

The police radio crackled and a voice interrupted. SJ heard the word "victim" and heard "Maple Street."

"That's my neighborhood," she said. She sat forward and gripped the back of the front seat.

"I'm sorry." Detective Rodriguez stepped out, and re-opened the back door to let SJ out. "We need to respond. We'll have that chat later."

Officer Deluca called in on his radio. They set the blue lights flashing and off they sped.

Maple Street. The park. SJ's mind immediately flashed to the two boys playing basketball. She remembered the runner on the track and the way the boys had leered at her. She felt strangely lucky, first because she'd left the park be-fore anything happened—assuming, of course, that what she'd heard on the police radio had actually occurred at the park—and second, because she did not have to be es-corted home by the police. And yet, she still felt implicated in something bad. She stepped off the curb and didn't notice a cyclist flying around the corner.

"Get out of the way!"

SJ turned in time to see the guy, his face contorted in panic beneath a shiny blue helmet. He waved one hand wildly. SJ felt like a squirrel, stuck there, undecided about which way to run. The cyclist swerved to miss hitting her, but instead turned his bike right into the curb. The bike went down and, with his feet clipped into his pedals, so did he.

SJ hurried over. "Are you okay?" A stupid question, but what else could she say? He didn't look hurt, but he was lying there awkwardly in his cyclist's getup, matching shirt and Lycra shorts.

"What's the matter with you?" the guy asked.

"I'm sorry," SJ said. "Can I help you up?"

"I'm fine," he said. He shook his head. "Actually, you can help me get out of these." He pointed to his feet, still attached to his pedals.

SJ grabbed one of his feet and pulled.

"No!" he yelled. "Just undo the shoe—here." He pointed to the strap she had to unclip. "Thanks," he said when she had removed them both.

"Are you okay?" SJ asked again.

The cyclist stood. His arm was scratched and bleeding a little. His elbow looked bruised, maybe even swollen.

"Your leg's bleeding."

"Yeah, it's okay, though," he said. "Makes for good stories, you know?" His tone softened.

SJ smiled a little, grateful. "I'm so sorry," she said. "I'm not usually so clueless. Do you think your bike is okay?" She lifted it from where it lay against the curb.

"It's not the first time I've gone down. It'll be fine." He took the bike from SJ and looked it over, checked the brakes, the gears, spun both wheels to see if they turned freely. "Bent water bottle holder, that's no big deal," he said.

"I feel terrible though," SJ said. "Can I—should I give you my phone number or something?"

The cyclist grinned. "This your way of getting dates? There are easier ways, you know."

"No—" SJ blushed. "No, I mean, I don't know, if you find out later something is damaged or something, I'd want to pay."

"Ah." He was still smiling. "I'm Leif, by the way." He removed a biking glove and extended his hand.

"SJ." She shook his hand. She pointed to the intersection beyond Most Precious Blood. "I work down there," she said. "At the library. If you need to find me—"

"If something's damaged," he interrupted, still grinning. "I appreciate that." He put his biking glove back on. "Be careful now. Don't forget to look both ways before you cross."

SJ felt herself blush again. "Yeah," she said and lifted one finger in a sort of wave. She watched Leif as he climbed back onto his bike, heard the clip of shoes attaching to pedals. He started off, raised one arm but didn't turn around, and kept pedaling. SJ watched until he was a blur down the road.

SOPHOMORE SEMIFORMAL

As the sophomore semiformal neared, the girls became more and more distracted—only this year, of course, things were a bit different. The venue, for one.

This year, the Brandywine board agreed that, given the circumstances, the dance would be held at the school itself. There was a general consensus that the girls needed calming, centering, that all the happenings of the fall had riled them up and they needed to be rechanneled. The board members thought that keeping the fall activities at school might help the girls recharge, a kind of circling the wagons.

The girls took the decision without much grumbling. As sophomores, they were still new to the world of fancy dresses and limos, still excited for the opportunity to get their hair done, have a mani-pedi, stay out well past curfew. They were enchanted with the decorated gymnasium, the wooden dance floor laid down to protect what was underneath; the purple mums brought in from La Belle Fleur, Bradley's best florist; the tablecloths and glassware. They could forget the locker room around the corner, the classrooms down the hall and upstairs, and they could pretend they were at one of Jay Gatsby's parties, if they knew about him, if they had read ahead in the American literature reading list or had an older sister who might have shared her love for Fitzgerald, who might have told her younger sister, *Here, you've got to read this. It's the best ever.*

The girls went to the semiformal together or in small groups. Some of them had dates, boys from St. Andrew's or friends from the neighborhood. The St. Andrew's boys were invited anyway, and they would all be there in suits and ties and shiny shoes.

Of course, Ms. Murphy always chaperoned the semiformal, and this year her absence would be noticed. Even Anna found herself wondering what Ms. Murphy would think of her sparkly dress, low-cut and daring, but then realized with a sharp stab that she wouldn't be present. This year, Anna's mother was chaperoning along with several others. Their daughters tolerated their presence as the price they had to pay in order to have the dance at all, but once inside the darkened gymnasium, the deejay spinning the latest music, the girls forgot about their mothers and left them gathered together at the back wall near the punch bowl. Anna was relieved to see her mother and Mrs. Moore off to the side, deep into their own conversation and not paying attention when she and Lydia danced or tried to talk with the cute boys.

For the most part, the semiformal worked to take the girls' minds off the terrible incidents of that fall. For one magical October night, they felt free to enjoy and lose themselves in the party spirit, to be the beautiful girls they imagined themselves to be.

CHAPTER FOUR

DEIRDRE HUNG UP THE RECEIVER. Finally she had gathered the courage to call Susan and Murray and ask about their lawyer. They weren't home, thankfully, and she started to leave a casual message—*Oh, that lawyer you mentioned? I'd be interested in getting the name and number*—but a car pulled up in front of the house, a dark blue sedan. Deirdre peered from behind the living room curtains. From out of the car stepped a man and woman, definitely police detectives, she was sure of it. The woman had cropped dark hair stylishly cut. She looked, as Deirdre's father would say, like "a tall drink of water," lean and leggy in black pants and a cream-colored top. From the car, she pulled out a black jacket and put it on, covering the gun holstered at her hip. The man looked Irish, ruddy-complexioned, and wore his hair in a short crew cut. They didn't speak but walked directly to Deirdre's front door.

She stood frozen at the front window. She felt her heart pound in her chest. The doorbell rang and she walked, wooden, to answer it. She looked down and realized her hands were shaking. She swallowed and opened the door.

"Hello?" she said and forced a smile. "Come in," she said when they presented their badges.

"You're expecting us?" the woman asked.

"Well, to be honest, I never thought it would get this far,

but let's put it this way, I'm not surprised to see you." She motioned for them to come into the living room and have a seat.

"Detective Mahoney," the man said, "and this is Detective Rodriguez. So, Sara Jane has mentioned our visit?"

"SJ? You've already spoken with SJ?" Deirdre perched on the edge of the armchair. The two detectives sat on the couch. Deirdre smoothed her hair and tugged on the hem of her flannel shirt, hoped her jeans didn't look overly sloppy.

The detectives looked at each other. Detective Rodriguez spoke up, smiling directly at Deirdre: "A couple of times. She didn't seem to think we needed to talk with you, but we felt it might be important to get your take—"

"She seemed to think you had pretty strong feelings about Mickey Gilberto," Detective Mahoney interrupted, "based on what you saw the day he moved you in." He looked expectantly at Deirdre and flipped open a small spiral notebook. "Can you tell us about that?"

"Mickey Gilberto?" Her head felt fuzzy. "Mickey . . . I'm sorry, I'm not—can you tell me again what this is about? I think there's been a misunderstanding."

Detective Mahoney spoke curtly: "You are Deirdre Murphy, is that right?"

"Yes—but . . ."

"Sara Jane Edmonds is your partner?" he continued. Deirdre nodded.

"You moved into this house on the first of September, the month previous, yes?" He sounded impatient, almost mocking. "Mickey Gilberto was one of your movers?"

"Yes, that's right, but I'm sorry, I don't know why . . . I'm sorry." She shook her head. "I—well, it doesn't matter. But I'm afraid I don't have much to say about Mickey Gilberto, except what everyone knows who has seen the news."

PATRICIA A. SMITH

She looked first at Detective Rodriguez, then at Detective Mahoney. "You're here to discuss Mickey Gilberto?"

Detective Mahoney tapped his pencil on the notebook. "What *were* your impressions of him on the day you moved in?"

Deirdre shifted in her chair. She sat back and crossed her legs. "Well, it's true that I thought he was . . ." She searched for the right word. "I don't know . . . gross?"

Detective Rodriguez laughed. "Gross how? Did he do or say anything that made you uncomfortable?" She looked at Deirdre in a way that encouraged her to speak.

"He just gave me the creeps. I wish I could say more, but really that's it." She gave a little laugh herself.

Mahoney didn't change his expression but Rodriguez leaned forward, waited a few seconds, and then spoke: "Deirdre—is it okay if I call you Deirdre? Do you have any idea why SJ would be hanging around Most Precious Blood Elementary? Why she would have been there yesterday in the middle of the day?"

Deirdre uncrossed her legs, frowned. "She works near there."

"She didn't tell you that she took the day off yesterday?" Rodriguez asked, her tone a bit more challenging now. "Is that unusual for the two of you?"

Deirdre was conscious now of Mahoney looking directly at her, listening, waiting. His face offered no emotion, no sense of what he was thinking. He sat poised with that pencil. Ludicrous thoughts ran through her head: *I hope you're single. You'd make a lousy partner.* Rodriguez's gaze offered more warmth, but without thinking, Deirdre pulled her flannel sleeves over her hands in a gesture that mimicked her students when they came in to talk with her about their grades or some problem they were having.

"I'm sorry," Deirdre said. "Do you mean is it unusual

for SJ to take the day off?" She knew the number of days SJ had taken off without being sick in the seven years they had been together—exactly two, both early on, after her parents' Cessna went down, before Deirdre ever had a chance to meet them.

"I mean," Detective Rodriguez smiled and said softly, "is it unusual for her not to tell you?"

Deirdre didn't like the question. She leaned back in the chair and crossed her arms. "I guess so, yeah, but it isn't like we tell each other *everything*. Maybe it's a little unusual but it certainly isn't a big deal," she lied. Her left temple started to throb.

Detective Mahoney opened his mouth and started to say something, but Detective Rodriguez put up her hand and cut him off. "So, you don't know why SJ would be hanging around Most Precious Blood if she took the day off? Can you think of any reason she would be over in that neighborhood, what business she might have had there?"

Deirdre heard the accusation in the question, in the tone of voice. She didn't much like Detective Mahoney and now, this woman who had seemed warm and inviting was starting to irritate her. "I don't know," she said. "Like I told you, she works over there, she might've been meeting someone for lunch. We don't tell each other about every move we make."

"You knew your partner was tutoring Mickey Gilberto?" Detective Mahoney said. "You knew that?"

"Of course I knew that!" Deirdre spat back. Not exactly a lie, but Deirdre had assumed SJ had taken her advice and passed him on to someone else.

"And you thought nothing of it?"

"I didn't like it, but SJ is a grown-up and she can make her own decisions." Deirdre felt the blood rushing to her face. Her temple was still throbbing.

"Why didn't you like it?" Detective Mahoney pressed on.

"Because I thought he was bad news. I had a bad feeling about him."

Now Mahoney smiled. He closed his little notebook and glanced over at Rodriguez, raised his eyebrows as if to ask, *Are we done?*

"Listen," Rodriguez said as she started to stand. "Here's my card. If you can think of anything that might be helpful, if you remember anything else about Mickey Gilberto, anything at all that might help us, give me a call." She handed Deirdre her card.

Deirdre nodded and didn't speak. She stood, smoothed her shirt, and followed the two detectives to the door. She watched at the window as they climbed into their car, Mahoney at the wheel. Rodriguez leaned forward to remove her jacket and then tossed it in the backseat. They each pulled seat belts across their chests, looked toward each other—talking, Deirdre could tell—and then they pulled away. Deirdre stayed rooted to the same spot for a full two minutes. She massaged her temple, felt it throb. What was SJ thinking? And why *was* SJ hanging around Most Precious Blood Elementary? More troubling, why had she taken the day off without saying anything about it to Deirdre? God, what was she up to? Deirdre started to get that panicky feeling again, her stomach tightening and twisting.

She grabbed a jacket from the hook in the hall, felt in the pocket for her keys, and stormed out the door. Gone were the immediate worries about Anna and Frances Worthington, Deirdre's job, finding a lawyer. What the hell was going on with SJ? The police couldn't have been interested in their impressions of Mickey Gilberto only because he was their mover; there had to be much more behind their questions, and Deirdre needed to find out what.

Outside, the afternoon air was chilly despite the bright sun. Deirdre tried buttoning her jacket and noticed her hands were still shaking. She struggled to unlock the Honda and took a deep breath. She wanted to cry and scream at the same time. If SJ were here, Deirdre might very well throttle her. She unlocked the car and climbed in. What exactly did she think she was going to do? Barge into the library and demand to see SJ immediately? Deirdre bit her lip. What if she didn't really want to hear what SJ had to say? Just days before, SJ had come home to announce she was moving out, had even found an apartment. But then for a couple of days now, Deirdre had felt a kind of reprieve, a growing sense of calm. She had even started to go as far as to imagine how things between her and SJ might be even better than they ever had been. How stupid. She started the engine, checked the rearview mirror, and pulled out from her parking spot.

At the intersection in front of the town hall, Deirdre made a left and headed east. She passed Most Precious Blood Elementary and felt her heart pound at the sight of all those flowers, most of them yellowed and browned, stuck in the metal fence. The blacktop was empty now. Deirdre glanced at the clock on her dashboard; school would have let out awhile ago.

There were signs of Leo Rivera everywhere, including the store window here on 17th, an old flier with Leo's face still stuck there, promising a reward for his safe return. At Leo's grandmother's, Deirdre knew from the scenes on the TV news, there had been more flowers and teddy bears and notes covering the chain-link fence. It was hard to look back and know what you were missing; Deirdre understood that. It was harder still to say goodbye to something you weren't ready to leave behind.

Deirdre passed the closed-up factories and turned into

the neighborhood of triple-deckers. She could see now how her students had felt back when they had driven through the East End for the field trip. Already that trip felt like it had happened years ago, in another lifetime. Funny to think that she had been so excited to bring her students to the gallery, show them examples of Dogon art. Why would they care? Why did it matter, ultimately? They all would have been better off if Deirdre had been content to work more diligently on drilling the conditional tense or direct and indirect pronouns instead of bringing them to the East End.

The afternoon sun shone through the driver's-side window. Deirdre unbuttoned her jacket and cracked the window. Dry leaves were piled everywhere, heaped alongside the street in the gutters. It hadn't rained in weeks. Maybe she had been too hard on her students back then. She glanced out the window and with her students' eyes she saw the peeling paint, the clutter (the *trash*) piled on porches and in the spaces between houses. She saw the blinds hanging unevenly, haphazardly, neglected. Now, at a traffic light, Deirdre noticed in the house to her left that there weren't curtains in the windows at all but what looked to be towels hanging there, upstairs.

Deirdre didn't get how people could live like that. Couldn't people see how messy their houses looked from the outside? If they could, they might understand how messy their entire lives seemed, how judgment was a normal reaction. It was the same thing with her students. In her early days of teaching, before her reputation preceded her and the girls arrived in her classes knowing that neatness mattered, Deirdre often had to give them "the talk."

"I can't follow you home. I can't see how much time you spend on your homework. All I can see is what you hand in. If it's a mess, if the paper is torn or the handwriting smudged, or if there are cross-outs or misspellings, what else am I to think? What else am I to assume except that you don't care about your work? I can only judge your effort by what I see."

And so it was with the way people lived. If there were broken bed frames stacked on the porch, if there were no curtains in the windows, only blinds hanging crooked or blankets stuck there to block the view, if there were weeds and crabgrass and sagging porches, what were people supposed to think? That you cared about your neighborhood?

Deirdre turned on Q and made a right on 21st. She drove the length of the street, to the intersection with the fire station and on to the East End branch of the public library. She took a left into the parking lot and drove around the building. Florence's Mercedes was there, but not SJ's Volkswagen. Deirdre pulled into an empty spot along the shaded side of the building and turned off the ignition.

She leaned back and closed her eyes. When you were a kid and you pictured yourself living an adult life, it never included things like getting fired from your job, or having the police at your house because they think your partner is somehow involved with a murderer. You didn't necessarily think of yourself in that old American Dream sort of way, but you thought of yourself as successful. You saw yourself with friends and throwing parties. You thought of rushed goodbyes in airports, late nights with a fire and good books, some music, maybe jazz, in the background. You thought of Sunday brunches. Drinks on the patio and weekend morning jogs.

Deirdre had never gotten as far as the imaginary married life. Or having children. Being gay changed that scenario for her. But she never imagined having to deal with anything like this. She had been half-kidding but she also meant it when she'd told Paul there ought to be a course on how to grow up and survive disaster.

"No one tells you about it," she'd said on their last run, a week earlier. "Seriously. Did you feel prepared for being a parent?"

Paul had laughed. "There's no way you can teach anybody that," he'd said and run ahead.

You didn't ever get prepared for the hard things. She remembered thinking that no one taught you how to *leave* college. They did all kinds of things to get you settled upon arrival, freshmen orientation programs that included, these days, outdoor adventure games, group exercises, and trust-building scenarios. They organized an entire week or more with the newly arrived student, but when you were a senior, where was that same attention? Who was there to tell you what it was going to be like when you left college and no longer lived surrounded by hundreds of people your age, people who, for the most part, were happy to meet you and interested in similar things? Who told you what to do when you had to live *out there*, when you had to find a job and meet new friends? When you were struggling as a new teacher and weren't sure about the boundaries? And those weren't even the hardest things. You knew the term "ivory tower" but you didn't think it applied so much to you, because you were of the "real world," with blue-collar parents who had blue-collar aspirations for their kids. You weren't deceived into thinking the world owed you anything, and yet, even *you* were surprised by the disappointments. Imagine what people like the Riveras thought.

Deirdre opened her eyes and took a deep breath. From the corner of her eye, she caught a glimpse of a girl who looked an awful lot like Anna Worthington skipping down the library steps. Deirdre sat frozen. The long blond hair. The shoulders and hips.

"Anna!" Deirdre yelled and climbed out of the car. She let the car door shut and watched as the girl spun around, then noticed who was calling her name. "Anna, wait!"

Anna stood glued to the stone step. You could see the way she wanted to turn back and hurry inside, the way she was searching for what to do. She clutched the book to her chest and looked at Deirdre once, then away.

"Anna." Deirdre hurried over and caught her breath. "I . . . How are you?"

Anna looked over her shoulder up at the library entrance.

Deirdre followed her glance. "Your mother—she's not on her way out, is she?"

Anna shook her head and blushed a little. "I'm on my own," she said.

"Look, can I talk with you for a minute?"

"I don't think that's a good idea." Anna peered out toward the street and glanced quickly at Deirdre, then away.

"It's kind of chilly in the shade," Deirdre said and buttoned her jacket. She was suddenly conscious of how unkempt she looked—unwashed hair, no makeup, old flannel shirt, worn jeans. "I'm a bit of a mess today," she said. She didn't know how to start this conversation. "How are you doing?"

Anna toed the gravel, shrugged.

"I've wanted to know how things are going for you, but I can't call, didn't know how to get in touch." Deirdre rocked on her heels. "Is everything okay?"

Anna tried to keep her face looking neutral, disinterested even, but Deirdre could tell that the girl wasn't unhappy to see her. All those years of working with adolescents and Deirdre knew when to push, when to hold back. "Are they pressuring you?"

A piece of Anna's hair fell in front her eyes. "What do you mean?" she said.

"Your mother? Mr. Loring? Are they putting pressure on you?" Deirdre tried to keep her voice soft and reassuring, but her stomach was still in knots. She was afraid her voice sounded shaky.

"I'm not sure what you mean," Anna said.

Deirdre looked at Anna standing there, her sixteen-year-old athlete's body, curved and lean. She inhabited that body with grace. Even now, caught in an uncomfortable situation, Anna could be posing for the camera, mouth pouting, neck pale and gorgeous, stomach flat and exposed where her long-sleeved T barely reached the top of her jeans, those long, long legs.

Deirdre cleared her throat. "I . . . I guess I'm wondering what's going on, you know? I mean, you've told your mother it wasn't me, right? That *I* wasn't the one who kissed *you*?" There, she had said it out loud.

A red maple leaf swirled in the air and dropped next to Anna's sneakered feet. She clutched the book against her chest.

"You've got to know I'm in a lot of trouble here." She thought of Detective Mahoney, his unfriendly stare and accusations.

A dark-haired woman approached the steps, holding a little girl's hand. She glanced at Anna, at Deirdre. The girl had wild curly hair—a rat's nest, Deirdre's mother would have called it, though secretly Deirdre had always wished for hair like that. The girl climbed the steps, two at a time. "One, two, three," she counted.

"*You're* in a lot of trouble?" Anna said fiercely. The little girl peeked over her shoulder before her mother hurried her into the library. "I'm, like, basically *grounded*. I can't do anything without my mother's permission. Coming here—" she pointed to the library's entrance, "is a major deal." She tucked her hair behind her ears, shifted her weight.

"Come to think of it, why *are* you here?"

Anna flaunted the book. "Duh," she said.

"No, I mean *here*. Why not the main branch?"

"Oh," Anna said. "They, like, didn't have this book? My mother called? It's for my little brother's report?" She rolled her eyes. She went on to say that her mother had a full schedule, that Anna had pleaded with her to let her ride her bike over to the branch library, that Anna was desperate to get out of the house, out from under her mother's watch. "So, like, I pretty much begged her to let me ride over here?"

Deirdre hated it when the girls spoke in that questioning tone, as if they were perpetually unsure of themselves. In class, she had always insisted on the correct French intonation, hoping it might carry over to English. But Deirdre knew better than anyone how you became a different person when you spoke another language. In French class, the girls were transformed into *Ah-na* and *So-fee*, *Bay-a-treece* and *Ee-lair*. They were different girls than the ones who hung out at the mall on weekends and complained about their mothers not allowing pierced navels. The French girls were smart. They were brainy. They relished plays-on-words. Rolled their *R*s like they were the real thing. Deirdre longed to take them to Paris and show them off—see if the Parisians themselves could tell that these girls were typical American teenagers and not the *jeunes filles sophistiquées* their French suggested.

"I'm surprised she let you ride your bike over here," Deirdre said.

Anna kicked at the gravel, jammed her toe into the bottom step. Again. And again. She was trying, Deirdre realized, to keep from crying.

"How're things at school?"

"That place—" Anna kicked hard at the step, "totally sucks. If my mom weren't the stupid head of the board, I'd be like out of there so fast . . ." She let her voice drop off, kept kicking at the step.

"Talk to me," Deirdre said. "Tell me what's going on." She was heading to that familiar place. She could feel it in her body, the way it stood poised, like an animal, ready to protect its young.

"They've all . . . I'm, you know, *lesbo*, *lezzie*." Anna waved her arm around. One tear spilled, then another.

"Even Hilary? Doesn't she stand up for you?"

"She doesn't, like, call me names or anything, but she's . . . We're not friends anymore." Anna grimaced, wiping the tears from her face.

Deirdre couldn't believe it. For the past two years—for as long as she had known them—where there was Hilary, there was Anna. And vice versa. "I can't imagine you not being friends with Hilary." Deirdre didn't know what to say, how to make things better. She reached out to touch Anna's shoulder but the girl flinched. "You'll make up with Hilary. You're best friends." Deirdre folded her arms.

Anna blinked back tears, kicked at the gravel again. "Lydia's still cool, but Hilary says it's my fault you got fired." She shook her head, let fall a lock of hair in front of her face.

At least *someone* was taking Deirdre's side.

"She is *so* on my case about it," Anna went on, her head down. "Well, she was. Until she stopped talking to me at all."

The sun moved out from behind a cloud and Deirdre unbuttoned her jacket.

Anna looked up, shaking her hair into place. "You know what I think?" she said, her tone a challenge. *Go on. Ask me.*

"Look, you guys will work it out—"

But Anna cut her off: "I think *she's* in love with you." She smiled.

"Anna!"

"It's *totally* what's going on." Anna was into it now, playing the role with complete confidence. "I mean, Hilary's always like, *Ms. Murphy this, Ms. Murphy that.* Every other sentence is, *Ms. Murphy, Ms. Murphy,* she mimicked, over-dramatizing Hilary's voice.

Deirdre was stunned into silence. She stared at Anna, unable to speak or move. There might have been a crowd gathering, a storm about to break. There might have been any number of things going on around them and Deirdre wouldn't have noticed.

"*You're* the one who wanted to be friends with us. *You're* the one who always told us how nice we looked, how much it meant to you when we did good in your class, stuff like that." Anna's tone was angry now; her face hardened. "You ruined everything!"

Deirdre looked around the parking lot and noticed a car pulling up, heard another engine shut off. "Come on," she said. "Calm down."

"Everything is totally your fault!" Anna snapped, tears welling, spilling, body tensed, skin flushed. "It's true. Me and Hilary, we would still be friends. Everything would be okay if you hadn't . . . if you hadn't . . ." She wiped her face. "Everyone says so. My mother says it's all your fault, my father says so, even the stupid lawyer agrees . . ."

Deirdre's throat suddenly went dry. "Lawyer?" Deirdre could see that as soon as she'd said it, Anna realized she'd gone too far. She'd said too much.

"I've got to go." Anna turned, hugged the book to her chest again, and walked quickly away.

"Wait!"

Without turning around, Anna said loudly, "My mother says you're supposed to stay away from me. If you'd have stayed away from me in the first place, then none of this would've happened." She hurried on.

Deirdre stood and watched Anna unlock the old ten-speed from the bike rack at the end of the parking lot. She watched the girl toss the book in the rear pannier, hop onto the bike, and pedal off, hair flying, helmetless. Deirdre stood there until Anna passed through the intersection and took a left, away from the East End library.

October 8

To the Editor, *Bradley Register*:

It is sadly typical that the *Register* is printing the same sort of liberal crap that we're all too familiar with these days. Innocent until proven guilty is one thing, but let's not dance around with words. Has anyone forgotten that a child has been murdered? Has anyone forgotten that Leo Rivera is the victim here, not the man in custody? Our sympathies should lie with the Rivera family, period. No amount of psychobabble can change the fact that an innocent child has been murdered. The fact remains: if Mickey Gilberto hadn't come in contact with Leo Rivera, little Leo might still be alive. Isn't that reason enough to be thankful this guy is off the streets?

Frank McDougal
Bradley, MA

CHAPTER FIVE

FROM THE BOTTOM STEP IN FRONT of the library, Deirdre sat and watched the afternoon light shift. Somber-hued trees, leaves dipped in gold. Shadows lengthening across the lawn. The sun shone brightly, ducked behind white cumulus clouds. The days were getting shorter and soon daylight savings time would cut afternoons in half, lob off hours of sunlight, or so it seemed. Maple leaves, even in this waning light, pierced the brightest. Sharp, sharp red.

This is New England in the fall. New England at its best. Picture-postcard New England. Deirdre wanted to caption the scene: *You, too, can be fooled.*

Finally she got up and went inside.

Deirdre walked past the front desk. She didn't recognize any of the new student workers but through the window into the main office, she saw Sam, SJ's "big boss." He didn't look up.

Deirdre walked downstairs to the children's section. Elliot sat at the desk, checking out books. "Hey, Deirdre. You just missed SJ."

"Is Florence in?"

Elliot pointed to the hallway beyond the water fountain. "Back there," he said. "It's fine." He waved her back.

Deirdre walked around the corner and found Florence

logging in new arrivals, a job Deirdre thought one of the assistants should be doing.

"Florence?"

The woman jumped. "Oh, Deirdre, hello." She rose from the computer. "Sorry. You startled me a bit."

"Elliot let me back here," Deirdre said. "Sorry. Is it—can I talk with you for a minute?"

"Oh . . . sure." She reached to touch her scrimshaw before she realized she wasn't wearing one. "SJ—" she started to say.

"Isn't here, I know." Deirdre sat in one of the empty chairs and let out a big sigh. She was afraid she might cry and she didn't want that to happen. Not here. Not in front of Florence, who, Deirdre knew, wasn't one of her biggest fans, at least not in terms of the role she played in SJ's life. "Okay, this is weird, but I'm worried."

Florence knitted her brows and sat back down in her computer chair.

Deirdre took another big breath. "The police came by today . . ." She noticed Florence's interest deepen. "And they were asking questions about SJ, connecting her with Mickey Gilberto—"

"Yes, yes," Florence jumped in. "They've been here several times too. You know that SJ was his tutor?"

She nodded. And she told Florence how she'd had a bad feeling about Mickey and how she told SJ she didn't really think it was a good idea that she tutor him. She said how she thought it was a strange coincidence that Mickey showed up first as their mover and then here, to have SJ as his literacy tutor. "But I didn't mention that to the police," she said, swallowing. "It seemed all conspiracy theory, you know? But now, there are all sorts of things that don't make any sense."

Florence sat leaning forward, hands clasped. She was frowning. "Like what?"

"Did you know that yesterday SJ was hanging around Most Precious Blood Elementary? The police saw her there. They wanted to know what business she might have there, especially if she wasn't working." Deirdre took a deep breath. She didn't tell Florence that SJ never mentioned taking the day off.

Florence nodded as she listened.

"Isn't that a little weird?" Deirdre asked.

"Mmm."

"So, really, I got in the car and came to talk with SJ, but she's not here . . ." She let her voice drift off. "But I'm so worried." Her lip trembled and she felt her throat closing, tears threatening. She blew out air. "I mean, I know it sounds ridiculous, but do you think there *is* something going on with SJ and Mickey Gilberto?" She wiped quickly at the corner of one eye.

"You know Sara Jane better than that!" Florence sat up straight. "I've had my concerns about that character too, to be sure, and the police are putting pressure on us to hand over his library records, but do I think SJ is involved with him? I certainly do not. Are you serious?"

"Look at me, I'm a wreck!" And a few tears escaped. Deirdre held out her hands to show Florence they were shaking. "I don't know what to believe anymore! Seriously." She sat quiet for a minute and wiped her eyes. "I don't mean to pry or anything, but did SJ tell you why she took the day off yesterday?"

Florence seemed a bit startled by the question. "Don't you know?"

"No. I was wondering if you could tell me."

Florence fiddled with her pearls. "Honestly, she said she wasn't feeling well. I didn't push it. I know things . . . things have been a bit difficult for you both lately . . ."

Deirdre blushed. Florence smiled and continued, "And I

thought, well, I thought maybe she was staying home to be with you—not that I had reason to doubt she wasn't feeling well."

"I just don't get it. I just don't know why she'd be over at that school. Or even walking around there. I could see it if she had been at work—that's what I told the police—if she had been on her lunch break, walking around, that makes sense. Otherwise, I just don't know."

"I think you're making too much of this. The visit from the police has you all worked up. Understandably," Florence added. "But if what has you upset is the fact that SJ was walking near Most Precious Blood, that doesn't seem like much now, does it?"

Deirdre had to agree, but inside she still felt as though something was seriously wrong. She couldn't explain it to Florence. "I guess you're right," she said, and got up to leave.

Florence rose too, and straightened her brown linen suit. "SJ is probably at home right now, wondering where you are."

"Wasn't she . . . Isn't tonight supposed to be her late night?" Deirdre stopped and turned from the doorway to the back office.

"She took comp time she had coming." Florence had already turned back to her computer. She looked over her shoulder. "I needed to stay late anyway. I told her it was fine." She smiled at Deirdre. "Go," she said, shooing her away. "She'll be home waiting for you."

But Deirdre didn't drive home. She got on the highway and headed out of town, without a particular destination. She kept the driver's-side window down, let the cool air blow her hair, rush against her face. She drove through Boston, construction cranes and trucks on both sides of the highway. Deirdre loved the drive out of the city, the water off to her left, a reminder of how things had started in this part of the country, the arrival by boat, the exploration of the coast for habitable land, and the buildings behind her, the neighborhood landscapes changing on her right, warehouses to triple-deckers and then, much later, suburban houses, and the train tracks running alongside.

Deirdre drove in the left lane, eager to go fast but not wanting a ticket. She'd had enough of the police for one day. She turned on the radio, listened for a traffic report, which, just shy of rush hour, didn't seem too bad yet. *At least there's that,* she thought. She had three-quarters of a tank of gas. She turned up the music and kept going. She passed the painted gas tanks. SJ would always point to the blue swirl of paint that looked like the face of an elderly Chinese man in profile—though the story was that the face was Ho Chi Minh, and so Vietnamese and not Chinese.

Damnit, SJ, what are you doing? What crazy stunt are you pulling?

But the more Deirdre drove, the more easily she breathed. She felt the tension in her stomach ease. On the expressway just outside of the city, you couldn't really smell the salt air, but it was a kind of relief to know it was there. Seeing the water, the few sailboats still bobbing on their moorings at the small neighborhood yacht club, offered Deirdre a soothing balm, a glimmer of hope. The ocean and the salt air brought her right back to the happiest of her childhood memories, to those carefree days in Gloucester.

She wanted to get to the place where she *could* smell the salt air, watch the scrub pines rush past her window. She wanted that feeling of anticipation, of knowing that you were almost there, close enough to the ocean that you could feel it. The air was always cooler too, a welcome relief in her childhood days when cars didn't have air-conditioning—at least their car didn't, not the sensible Fords that her father always drove. Deirdre recalled sitting in the backseat with Paul, her legs sticking to the vinyl, a cooler jammed in between the two of them. She'd be hot and on the verge of whining about it when the miracle breeze would blow through the opened windows.

"Here we are," her father would say then. "Almost to the beach!"

And every time, Paul and Deirdre would look at each other and smile. *Dad is so predictable.* But they loved it. Deirdre would put her face up to the window and breathe in the salty goodness of that air. Even in Gloucester you could feel the difference, driving from one side of town to the other.

This time, she wasn't headed toward Gloucester. She drove south. And she was getting closer to the seashore. She could tell by the change in the trees and the place where the road narrowed to two lanes, scrub pines on both sides. She felt giddy and rolled her window all the way down, the evening air cool and satisfying. It was nearly dark and she'd put on her headlights. The traffic this far from the city was light, although in a couple of days that wouldn't be the case, the start of a long weekend, Columbus Day. At Brandywine, they had Friday off too, a real October break. This made her wince a little; she didn't want to think of Brandywine or her job right now. She didn't really want to think about SJ either, or that horrible Mickey Gilberto. No, she wanted to enjoy her little escape; that's all.

Deirdre wondered why Paul didn't rent a cottage for Sophie and Mark and Kris. He could definitely afford it. Deirdre would ask him about this on their next run. In fact, she was going to suggest that they go in on one together. SJ would love it. Hadn't their best vacations together been on the Cape?

The Cape! That's it. Deirdre would keep driving, as far

as a person could drive in Massachusetts. She would go all the way to the tip of the state, to Provincetown. Why not? The drive would take another couple of hours at least, and Deirdre didn't have any fixed plan about what to do once she got there, but the destination gave her a reason to keep going. She had enough gas. She'd eat when she got there, fried clams or a lobster roll or some typical touristy food. She felt happier than she had in days.

When Deirdre got to the end of Route 6, she could turn left and head into town or turn right and go out to Race Point, past Herring Cove Beach and the dunes. She chose to drive out to Race Point first, to dig her toes into the sand and look out at the ocean, maybe even stick her feet in the water if she wasn't too cold. At Race Point, she buttoned up her jean jacket, the wind blowing hard as she undid her sneakers. She skipped onto the beach, the soft, cold sand squeezing between her toes. Her hair was wild and windblown; the wind stung her face and made her eyes water, but oh how glorious to be here! She approached the edge of the water. The waves crashed loudly. The beach was empty except for a lone figure farther down tossing something for a dog to fetch. Deirdre closed her eyes and breathed deeply. She pushed her hair out of her face and looked out over the dark water, waves rising, swelling, crashing loudly at her feet. She stuck one toe into the water—freezing! Deirdre laughed at herself. The water on Cape Cod was *never* cold; how her father would make fun of her for saying Cape water was freezing, though here on the ocean side, it was colder than on the bay. Her stomach rumbled.

She got back in the car, pulled on her sneakers, and drove down Commercial Street. She was surprised to see so many bars and shops open this late into the fall. She parked in front of the West End Gallery, and as luck would have it, the Clam Shack was still open. Deirdre ordered a fried clam roll and a Budweiser. She sat at one of the picnic tables overlooking the bay. On both sides, she heard dance music, the unmistakable sounds of disco/techno beats. Down the beach on the left, the women's bar the Marquee was all lit up, and Deirdre could see women gathered in groups on the deck. From the other direction, the Boatslip seemed to be lively too, music pulsing both from inside and beneath the tent erected over its large deck. A Wednesday in October? How strange. She finished her clam roll and drank down her beer. She thought she would check out first the Boatslip and then the Marquee.

Welcome to Women's Week! read the purple banner strung across the front of the Boatslip. Of course! How many times had she and SJ spoken of wanting to attend Women's Week in Provincetown, but knew they never could because of Deirdre's teaching schedule? And now here she was. She looked at her watch. It was nearly eight o'clock. She thought about finding a pay phone and calling SJ, but an attractive older woman called to her from the doorway. She looked like an older version of Detective Rodriguez, that same short stylish haircut, manicured nails, fit in her jeans and tailored shirt.

"Come on in, honey," the woman said. She beckoned Deirdre forward. "Happy Women's Week!"

"Happy Women's Week." Deirdre grinned. "Is there a cover charge?"

"Just your luck," the woman said. "Redheads get in free." She smiled. "Pretty good deal, huh?"

"Can't beat that." Deirdre stepped into the darkened bar, conscious suddenly of the way she looked—her wild hair that she hadn't washed that morning, her jeans and flannel shirt, old sneakers. She certainly wasn't dressed to go out dancing.

"Thanks," she said to the dark-haired woman on her way out. "Guess I'm not much up for dancing, really." She motioned to her clothes.

"Another time, then." The woman smiled.

Deirdre wasn't ready to climb back into the car and drive home, though if she left now, she would be back around eleven, and already that was pretty late. SJ would definitely be wondering where she was. *Well good,* Deirdre thought, *let her wonder.* She headed down Commercial Street, away from the Boatslip toward the Marquee. The street was lively. Women walked in pairs holding hands, or in groups, in both directions. They laughed with each other. It could almost be summer, the way the storefronts were lit up and Commercial Street was crowded. Except there were few men. Deirdre loved looking at all the women, a young-ish crowd primarily but there were certainly older women too, all dressed for a night out.

If you came to Provincetown in the summertime, you had the obligatory stroll up and down Commercial Street. Sure, it was the main drag, but it was also like a runway for people to show off their bodies, their new clothes and haircuts, a place to scope out the scene. In the summer, Commercial Street was practically undrivable; there were far too many people. This was much more pleasant, Deirdre thought, plenty of room for everyone to walk, for cars, (though there weren't too many) to get past. She loved looking at the houses, the cottages and Capes, many of them with white picket fences and eye-popping gardens in the summer. Now, too, the gardens were appealing, fall versions of their summer selves. Lots of mums and tall reedy plants Deirdre didn't know the name of. Dried stalks, and here and there a vegetable garden with a few squash still on the vines, and purple skunk cabbage.

She came to the part of Commercial Street where there

were few houses, only stores and restaurants. The street was a bit quieter than the part down toward the Boatslip, but she could see a crowd gathered in front of the big white town hall. Often people gathered here—the town hall had public restrooms inside and benches outside—but this group of people looked different. They were holding candles—a vigil of some sort. As Deirdre got closer, she could sense that most of the people in this group were not visitors to Provincetown, but residents. She noticed old weathered faces, men and women both. Some young people too—a few teenagers—but mostly older people. They held candles and some held pictures of Leo Rivera.

Even here in Provincetown, even during Women's Week, Deirdre couldn't escape Leo Rivera and Mickey Gilberto. She felt annoyed and then guilty for feeling annoyed. But why a vigil for Leo Rivera here and why now? She eased up to the edge of the crowd. An older man looked like he was going to address the group, and Deirdre wanted to hear what he had to say.

But he spoke in Portuguese. The others murmured along with him. Their voices carried the intonation of prayer, and the older man seemed to be a priest. She wanted to nudge someone and ask why they were holding a vigil for Leo Rivera, but she didn't dare. She knew the Portuguese community was tight-knit. Part of the awful fallout of Leo's murder was the fact that another member of their own community was accused of the crime. Mickey Gilberto's potential involvement was a real heartbreak for everyone, and particularly for Mickey's family, deeply embedded in the Brazilian-Portuguese community, and next-door neighbors to the Riveras. As Deirdre listened to the prayer, she heard the priest say Mickey's name. The group murmured their response. The tone changed; were they blessing him? Cursing him? She couldn't tell, but she saw the way a few of the people glared at two women walking down Commercial Street holding hands. The feeling was definitely hostile.

She sneaked away and headed in the other direction down Commercial Street, back toward her car. She passed the Marquee, and something about it invited her in. Where the Boatslip had seemed so . . . what was it? She couldn't put her finger on it—like a *scene*. The Marquee felt more like a neighborhood bar.

She found a seat at the bar and ordered a beer. The place was about half full, women dancing on the small dance floor under rotating colored lights. A deejay spun records that sounded vaguely familiar, but Deirdre couldn't spot her. In another corner, two women were shooting pool and a few others clustered around watching. The small round tables were covered with tall beer bottles and plastic cups of mixed drinks. Women sat leaning together, laughing and drinking.

"Here you go," the bartender said, placing a tall bottle of Budweiser in front of Deirdre.

She put a five on the bar, then took a long swallow. Mickey Gilberto. What were the odds that he would have been first their mover, and second one of SJ's literacy students? Deirdre wished she knew what exactly had been going on back there at the vigil, what everyone had been whispering and saying about Mickey Gilberto. And why was there a vigil now? Leo had been buried already; Mickey had been arrested, though not sentenced, as far as Deirdre knew. The day seemed random.

"Do you mind if I sit here?" A young woman motioned to the stool next to Deirdre. She had short blond, wispy hair that framed her face in an appealing way. Made her look younger than she probably was. Her blue eyes twinkled.

"Sure, help yourself." Deirdre smiled.

The woman slid easily onto the stool. She wore pressed

jeans and a purple V-neck T-shirt. Revealing, but not overly so. When she crossed her ankles, Deirdre noticed she was wearing black cowboy boots.

"You looked so serious sitting there," the woman said. "I wasn't sure if you wanted company."

"Cute boots." Deirdre pointed. She swallowed more beer.

The woman laughed. "You didn't answer my question."

"If I want company? Sure, that's fine," Deirdre said. "I'm not staying long, though. One beer and I need to get going."

The woman nodded to the beat of the music.

"I'm Deirdre." She stuck out her hand.

The woman glanced over. "Hello, Deirdre-I'm-not-staying-long." She offered a flirtatious grin, shook Deirdre's hand, and finished her beer. "I was going to offer to buy you a drink, but since you're leaving . . ." The woman swiveled to face the bar.

"I . . . could be convinced, I guess," Deirdre said. "One more, why not?"

"Hmmm, don't let me talk you into anything." The woman motioned for the bartender, then turned to face Deirdre, eyes sparkling.

Deirdre felt the other woman's presence more than she noticed her physical beauty. The woman oozed self-confidence. She was cute too, Deirdre had to admit, but it was more the easy way she inhabited her body that was appealing. The way she sat on the stool. Leaned her arm on the bar. Reached up and ran her hand through her hair.

"I'd like that, thanks," Deirdre said. "I can stay a bit longer."

"I'm Jamie, by the way." She handed Deirdre another beer and raised her own in a toast. "Here's to Women's Week."

Deirdre touched her bottle to Jamie's.

"Not many women come alone to Women's Week," Jamie said.

Deirdre didn't hear any judgment in what she said. "I didn't mean to come for Women's Week . . ."

Jamie raised her eyebrows.

"I drove here kind of last minute. I live in Bradley, just north of Boston. I got in the car and drove and ended up here." She realized how crazy it sounded. "It's a long story." She took a breath. "And, yeah, well, it's a long story." She heard the clack of pool balls; the dance music pulsed.

Jamie sat with her legs crossed, arms leaning back against the bar. She waved to someone across the room. "Must be a good long story for you to drive all the way to P-town."

Deirdre searched the woman's face for signs of amusement or boredom but saw none.

"You going back tonight?"

"The was the plan, yeah." Deirdre sipped her beer. She was starting to feel the effects of the two previous beers. "'Course, soon, I won't be in any shape to drive." She laughed.

"Come on. You better dance it off." Jamie hopped off the stool and held out a hand. "Come on," she said again.

Deirdre didn't recognize the song but it was catchy enough. How long since she'd been dancing? "Okay," she said, and took Jamie's hand.

They danced. And danced again. And again. After six or seven songs—she lost count—Deirdre wiped the sweat from her forehead. "I need a rest," she said. But the music changed and a slow one came on. Jamie held her arms open and Deirdre walked in easily.

Was it that first slow dance that marked the line of no return? The way Jamie held her, the feel of her hand at the base of Deirdre's spine? Or the second slow dance, when Jamie leaned in and nuzzled her neck, sending one long shiver right through to her toes? If she were honest about it, Deirdre would have to say that she had crossed the line as soon as Jamie sat on the barstool next to her, but she liked to think that it had taken some doing and that she had been seduced.

Now in Jamie's house, in her bedroom, she reminded herself that SJ had thought about leaving the relationship and had gone as far as renting an apartment. She told herself that she was only having an adventure, and after everything that had happened, didn't she deserve some fun?

"You've gone quiet on me," Jamie said, running her hand the length of Deirdre's arm.

Deirdre shook her head. "It's okay, I'm here."

Jamie leaned in and they kissed. The line now was gone altogether, wiped away by their kisses, their touching, their skin, which felt electric, hands and thighs and shoulders and soft bellies, nipple touching nipple, tongue to breast, fingers and hair, earlobes and breath on skin.

Deirdre moaned. To be touched. To be desired. To want and crave to be wanted.

"God, you're beautiful," Jamie said.

And when they came, they came together and rocked each other and held on, and only after Jamie fell asleep with her arm wrapped around her did Deirdre start to cry.

October 9

To the Editor, *Bradley Register:*

    I am writing out of great concern for the children of this town. We have all waited anxiously, though certainly none more anxiously than the parents of that poor child Leo Rivera, while the police have labored to solve his horrible murder. We should be proud of the excellent work of our fine police department, because not only have they apparently solved the crime, but they have also brought to light a very real and hidden threat to all our children. How many of us are aware, that when we drop off our sons and daughters at schools, libraries, after-school programs, that we might be leaving our precious children in the care of predators? There is a clear need for more extensive background checks for all personnel involved in direct work with children. As much as we can't control who might become our neighbors, we *can* have more stringent control over the people we hire to work with and take care of our sons and daughters.

Frances Worthington, Chair, Board of Trustees
Brandywine Academy
Bradley, MA

CHAPTER SIX

THE MESSAGE SAID FOR DEIRDRE to report to the police station. *Surrender yourself* were the words the officer used. Deirdre played the message over and over again. *Surrender yourself.* It sounded so ominous. And oddly dreamlike. *Deirdre Murphy,* the voice on the machine said. Had SJ heard it, saved it as if she hadn't?

Before falling asleep, Deirdre had called SJ. She didn't want her to worry that something terrible had happened.

"I'm in P-town," Deirdre had said on the phone. She glanced at the clock—eleven thirty. "I . . . ended up driving here, I don't know why," she laughed. "I just felt like driving and I drove all the way to P-town. I found a room and I'll be back tomorrow."

"You drove to P-town?"

Jamie slept, arms and shoulders exposed. Sleeping like that, she looked both inviting and vulnerable. Deirdre still didn't know how old she was or much else about her. She lowered her voice. "Yeah, it's weird I know, but here I am. Anyway, I'm staying. I've had a few beers and didn't want to drive."

"You waited awhile to call," SJ said, her tone even.

"I know, sorry. I . . . wasn't sure if I was going to stay or not, you know? I won't be late tomorrow." She hated lying to SJ, was surprised the lie came so easily.

And now, here she was, back home and needing SJ. *Please be at the library*, Deirdre thought as she dialed. "SJ! Thank God!"

A brief silence. "You're home?" SJ said, voice cold, flat.

"I don't know what to do . . . I have a message. Did you listen to the messages?"

"Yesterday? There weren't any."

Deirdre swallowed. "I . . . there's a message . . . I . . . I have to . . . they said to surrender myself!" She felt the tears coming, the hysteria building inside.

More silence. A deep breath. Then, "I'm coming home. Wait for me, okay? I'm coming."

Deirdre wiped her nose and hung up the phone. She knew the two incidents had nothing to do with each other, but it was hard not to see this message as a kind of payback for the previous night. And here was SJ, coming home to be with her, to help her out.

Mechanically, Deirdre moved through the routine of showering: soaping up, rinsing, shampooing, then applying conditioner. She felt a need to be particularly clean, a thought process that went something like: *If I am clean, I'll be okay. If I'm clean, I can't be in trouble.* Some part of her knew the wishful thinking was ridiculous, but she couldn't help it. She opened her closet and scanned the clothes. She didn't want to seem too vulnerable or like someone who could be taken advantage of. She wanted to look like a slightly better version of herself.

The front door rattled and Deirdre heard it shut tight. She yanked a cable-knit turtleneck over her wet hair. "In here!" she yelled. She pulled on her best jeans and struggled to zip them, hands shaking.

"Hey." SJ stood framed in the doorway of the bedroom. She shifted her weight.

Deirdre felt the tears pooling, the panic rising. She fluffed her hair. "What's going to happen?" She swallowed hard, forced down the lump, readjusted the neck of her sweater.

SJ took a few steps into the room and dropped her bag on the floor. "What did the message say?"

"I mean, they can't arrest me—can they?" Deirdre paced.

"What did it say?"

Deirdre stopped pacing and faced the bureau. "They said to surrender myself." She shrugged. "Surrender myself," she repeated. "It sounds so . . . awful. Like I'm a criminal or something." She pulled a pair of blue socks from the top drawer.

"And . . ." SJ looked cautious, sounded tentative. "Did you call the lawyer?"

Up until now, Deirdre hadn't wanted to admit that she really needed a lawyer. Susan had tried to convince her, but she couldn't quite let herself believe that she was in serious trouble. Sure, Martin Loring had sent her home immediately and that action surprised her, but most of the time Deirdre felt like these days weren't her real life at all, just some sort of temporary bad dream that would end, once everyone realized the truth.

The truth.

What was the truth? How had she crossed the line with Anna Worthington? Well, obviously she knew that kissing Anna was beyond crossing the line. But had she given Anna encouragement, a signal that it was okay to kiss her? How had Anna summoned the courage to kiss her teacher? Unless Deirdre had somehow suggested it first? She knew this was what SJ was thinking too, though SJ had never come right out and said so. Deirdre could see it in her eyes, could hear it in the words SJ didn't say, the silences that might as well have been an outright accusation. *You brought this on yourself.* But now, here was SJ looking nervous and concerned.

Deirdre pulled on the socks. "I haven't called him yet."

"I don't think you should go to the police without a lawyer."

Deirdre cuffed and uncuffed her sweater.

"Don't you think? I mean—I don't know, but it sounds pretty serious."

Deirdre tugged at her sleeves some more. "I don't even have his number yet. When I called Susan—" But she couldn't continue because what she would have to say was that when she called Susan to get the lawyer's name, the police had shown up at the door wanting to question her about SJ and Mickey Gilberto, and then they would need to have the discussion about SJ not going to work and not telling Deirdre about it, and she didn't want to go down that path right now. She shook her head. "I don't have it," she said again. She pulled her clogs out from underneath the bed and slipped them on.

"Let's call Susan and see if we can't get him now." SJ picked up the phone by the bed. She dialed and held the phone out to Deirdre. "It's ringing."

Deirdre wrung her hands. "What'll I say?"

"She knows what's going on. The whole board does, I'm sure. Just tell her the truth."

Deirdre heard the phone ringing on the other end. She felt her hands shake again. But the machine came on and she hung up. "I couldn't just leave a message . . ." She stopped. "You really think they can arrest me?" She played with the phone cord. "Jesus."

SJ sat next to her on the edge of the bed. "Did they give you a time frame? Do you have until the end of the day? Do we have to go immediately?"

Deirdre shook her head. "I don't know. But I don't want them to show up here, that would be awful. I think . . . I don't know . . . I think we should probably go soon?" It was a question, because she wanted SJ to take over. She wanted SJ to tell her what to do, how to make this better. Because somewhere, if only on the surface, Deirdre still imagined that they could make it better. Her gut told her that things were much more serious than she had first thought, but she could not let herself go so far as to imagine the very real possibility that she might be arrested, and if she were arrested, that she might have to go to jail.

SJ drove them to the police station. Deirdre couldn't bring herself to look at SJ. Instead, she watched the houses pass by, felt as though she were looking at them for the very first time, as if she were a foreigner. In French, the word *étranger* meant both *foreigner* and *stranger*. Deirdre didn't usually see the two words as necessarily related. What was foreign, she had explained to her students, doesn't have to be strange. But here she was, driving through her own town, her own neighborhood, and these houses, the people in them, suddenly felt both strange and foreign. Deirdre could not even begin to imagine what lives her neighbors led. She could not even begin to imagine how her own life might play out. Wasn't that the irony? You thought you knew; you thought you were in a relationship that would last the rest of your life; you thought you could envision how your life might unfold, but it was all an illusion. And it always had been, but you were just realizing it for the first time. What kind of mean trick was that? Or did other people get it all along and Deirdre was suddenly waking up?

"You okay?" SJ glanced at her. She took one hand from the steering wheel and reached to pat Deirdre's thigh.

Deirdre gave a small smile. "This is just so . . . surreal, you know?"

SJ pulled over to the side of the road in front of a brown-shingled Victorian and turned off the car.

"What are we doing?" Deirdre looked around.

SJ tucked the loose hairs behind her ears and shifted in her seat to face Deirdre. "Don't you think we should really talk about what might happen? About the fact that you might . . . I'm sorry, but I think we have to admit it . . . you might be arrested?"

The word hit her like a sharp arrow. "But I don't have a record. Doesn't that mean they'll let me go home . . . What's that called?"

"*Personal recognizance.* But Deird, we don't know. It could happen. I just think we should be prepared."

Deirdre threw her hands in the air. "Be prepared? How, exactly?"

"Mentally. I just think we should discuss this first."

What was there to discuss? Deirdre didn't always share SJ's point of view that talking helped everything. She would have liked to believe that, but she just didn't. What good would it do to talk? She laughed. "Getting arrested would suck."

"C'mon. I'm serious!"

"Me too! It *would* suck." She looked directly at SJ. "I just . . ." But she couldn't even begin to say it, to think the words, because there again were the tears, pooling, spilling over, ruining her mascara.

SJ looked sincere, her voice soft and serious. "If that does happen, I'll track down the lawyer. You don't have a record and you've not even ever gotten a parking ticket."

Deirdre wiped her tears, nodded.

"So I'm sure we'll work something out. But I just thought we should admit that it might happen." SJ sat with one arm draped behind Deirdre.

"I guess you're right, but my God, this just seems crazy!

How could . . ." and the tears started again, they wouldn't stop. "I'm sorry, I just can't help it!"

SJ put her arms around Deirdre and held her. "It's okay," she said. "It's terrifying!"

Deirdre waited until the tears were finished and wiped her face. "Jail," she said. She was a teacher, for God's sake. And if she found herself in jail, then she was certain first of all that Martin Loring would never take her back, and that second of all, she might never teach again. "So what, they read me my rights and I'm arrested? Is that it?"

SJ let go of Deirdre and shook her head. "I have no idea," she said, her voice quiet.

On TV even the unlikely suspects were grilled mercilessly by the cops and made to feel guilty. Deirdre twisted in her seat, pulled the seat belt away. "It means the world that you're behind me. I couldn't do this without you." She fiddled with the seat belt. "I don't think I could survive."

SJ glanced out the window. "Don't say that. You'd survive." She rubbed her hands on the steering wheel. "It's going to be okay."

Deirdre nodded. But she wanted SJ to say something more effusive, more staunchly supportive, about how it was ridiculous, this reporting, *surrendering* to the police, how absurd it was to even think she might be guilty of a crime. Deirdre watched SJ take in the street, glance nervously to the dashboard and up to the rearview mirror. She couldn't remember when she had stopped yearning for SJ in that desperate way she had felt in those early days when they'd first started seeing each other. SJ had seemed so remote, which for some reason had been a turn-on. She'd wanted to see if she could get SJ's attention, make this independent woman want her. Winning over SJ had felt like an accomplishment, and in the early days, Deirdre had felt such desire she thought she might explode. It had scared her at first, the intensity, but now, she couldn't remember that it had lasted long or when the feeling had died. Maybe as soon as SJ didn't seem so remote, when she suddenly seemed accessible to Deirdre, the longing had vanished.

SJ started up the car.

Attraction was so mysterious, and even now, at almost thirty, Deirdre didn't really understand the role it played in forming relationships. She glanced over at SJ, watched her hands on the steering wheel, the way she sat slouched in the driver's seat, leather jacket worn and fitted to her form. This was the woman she'd assumed she would spend the rest of her life with. What was going to happen now, to both of them?

"I'm serious, SJ. It means the world that you're with me. I really don't know what I'd do if I were alone."

SJ kept her eyes on the road. "You'd do what you have to do. You'd get through it."

"Maybe. But I'm just saying, I'm glad you're with me." Deirdre reached over and gave SJ's knee a squeeze.

Inside the police station, fluorescent lights glared. Deirdre felt a bit woozy, as if she'd had too much to drink. SJ stood next to her while they waited for an officer to "process" Deirdre. That was the word the heavyset man behind the information desk used.

"What does that mean?" Deirdre felt hysteria rising inside, filling up first her stomach cavity then her chest, the mass of it threatening to spill its mess over and out onto everyone in close range.

"Someone will be with you shortly. You can wait over there." The officer pointed to a row of hard plastic chairs.

"But I'm . . . do I need a lawyer?" She felt her voice rise of its own accord, her arms beginning to flap.

"C'mon." SJ patted her shoulder.

Deirdre let herself be led to the seats. She had to sit on her hands to keep them from flying off. She bounced her knees. "What does that mean, *processed?* It sounds bad, doesn't it?"

SJ looked straight ahead, her face pale and mouth drawn in a straight line. Every now and then she scanned the room.

"*Processed,*" Deirdre repeated. "That means I'm staying here. That means . . . right? I'm being arrested!" There was the hysteria again, filling her up like a helium balloon. What she wouldn't give to be able to float away now, to rise above this room and drift off. The moment had a strange quality to it, made Deirdre feel that she were looking in on a life that wasn't hers. She had the sudden urge to write everything down, to record the moment in a notebook: *Friday, October 8. Waiting to be arrested. Feeling scared and nervous. SJ here with me.* And then in her mind, she revised the entry: *Waiting to be processed.* Processing, she told herself, could mean anything. It could mean a form to fill out. A fine to pay. It could even mean a court date to be determined. It could mean bad things, the kind that stayed with you, went on your permanent record; in short, everything except being arrested, which seemed the worst kind of bad thing on your permanent record. The hysteria subsided a bit, the plastic seat felt a bit less hard. She removed her hands from beneath her thighs, folded them on her lap. She kept her legs still. *Processed.* Like an animal, a chicken or cow, waiting to be slaughtered. Really, they needed some help with their language skills. The officer at the information desk—Deirdre turned to look at him—had gotten up; she spotted him chatting with the security guard by the door. He hadn't seemed at all concerned with the effects of his words. In fact, no one seemed the least concerned with either Deirdre or SJ. They had been sitting, waiting for what felt like half an hour but what was, Deirdre realized, barely five minutes. Still, no one even shot them a look. No one asked if they were okay. No one seemed inclined to think that sitting in the midst of a busy, loud, fluorescent police station might have any effect at all on these two women who, anyone could see, hardly belonged in a police station.

I'm a teacher! Deirdre wanted to shout. *I deserve better treatment than this. I don't deserve to be processed!* She wondered what might happen if she stood and walked out the door. Would an alarm go off? Would an officer try to stop her? Would she have a gun pulled on her? Would anyone even care?

"Ms. Murphy?" A female police officer stood in front of her. She looked young, like a slightly older version of Deirdre's students. *Former* students, she reminded herself.

"That's me." Deirdre stood. Her knees shook. SJ stood too.

"Could you come with me, please?"

"Okay, will I . . . ? Should I bring my jacket with me?" She wanted to ask if she would be leaving or staying. She wanted to ask what was going to happen to her, but somehow the unspoken rule was to not ask questions. Is this where she said goodbye to SJ?

The officer turned to SJ. "We need to speak with Ms. Murphy. It may take awhile. You won't need that." She motioned to Deirdre's jacket. Deirdre handed it to SJ.

The woman turned and Deirdre noticed her neatly braided hair in the back, not a stray out of place. Her own hair was wild since she hadn't blown it dry. She looked down at her turtleneck and jeans. She hoped she conveyed the right sense, whatever that was. Respectable and honest. Her hands were shaking again. She stuffed them in her pockets. She couldn't look at SJ; she was certain she would start to cry.

"I'll be here," SJ said and kissed her on the cheek. They were the best words Deirdre had heard in a long time.

October 10

To the Editor, *Bradley Register*:

I read the October 9 letter from Frances Worthington with great concern. Though she does not come out directly and call for the firing of gay and lesbian teachers and librarians (among others), how else are we to take her words? And how else are we to interpret the publication of such a letter except as a kind of support for the witch hunt that Mrs. Worthington is in favor of?

It frightens me enough when obviously well-educated citizens resort to such hateful and regressive tactics, but when newspapers jump on the bandwagon, we all ought to be afraid.

Sara Jane Edmonds, Librarian, East End Branch
Bradley, MA

CHAPTER SEVEN

IT ALL SEEMED SO CLICHÉ, like a scene from a TV show—
You have the right to remain silent—for God's sake, Deirdre
wasn't some common criminal. Even if what happened with
Anna was wrong, it wasn't as if Deirdre were a predator.
*Anything you say or do can and will be held against you
in the court of law.* This was all a mistake. A huge mistake.
Deirdre was certain that Martin Loring never intended for
her to be arrested. What would her students think if they
could see her now? It was ludicrous, except it wasn't. *You
have the right to speak to an attorney. If you cannot afford
an attorney, one will be appointed for you.* Deirdre had no
idea whether or not she could afford an attorney. She imagined she couldn't and she had no idea whether or not SJ
would help her out. Oh God—her parents. Deirdre would
never be able to tell them what happened, but she knew she
would have to. And Paul. And Sophie and Mark. How could
she explain this to them? Mark, bragging at recess—*My
Aunt Deirdre was arrested*—like it was worth cool points;
his eyes lit up, asking questions, wondering if she met any
real criminals. But Sophie—Sophie would be horrified. She
might never look to Deirdre again for advice. Might never
pedal over on her pink bike with the big basket in the front
just to say hi, or to hang out with Deirdre in the kitchen,
wanting to cook with her, learning to make cakes and cook-

ies because Kris wouldn't do it, wouldn't want Sophie to make a mess in her designer kitchen. And—Kris. Deirdre couldn't bear to think of what her relationship would be like with her now—would Kris even deign to speak to her? Would Deirdre be forever tainted by the stain of *the arrest*?

"Do you understand these rights as I have read them to you?" Officer Monroe asked her.

"Yes," she said. But she didn't. Officer Monroe had a kind face, and Deirdre wanted to trust her. Some instincts led Deirdre to talk, wanting to explain her version of the story. *It happened like this,* Deirdre wanted to say. And it would all come tumbling out—how she had wanted to take her students to see African art, how she wanted them to go beyond the rudiments of speaking French to appreciating all the cultures in the French-speaking world, how she wanted to take them to that particular gallery to broaden their horizons, get them out of their safe world, and how Anna's mother was ridiculously protective, how she hadn't wanted Anna to participate but how the girl had forged the permission slip and how then she and Anna ended up being alone in the van together and . . . That's where things got blurry even for Deirdre. Up to that point, the story sounded okay, good even, but everything that happened afterward sounded crazy as she replayed it in her head. The van. Anna's insistence that she ride in the front seat. Her refusal to get out. The tears. Deirdre trying to comfort her. The kiss. It sounded—horrible, Deirdre had to admit it. Like why didn't she simply insist Anna get out of the van, or why didn't she go inside the school and call Frances Worthington herself? When she thought about it, she had to admit that maybe Forest was right. She *had* been asking for it. Still, Anna had kissed *her*.

Officer Monroe asked a few questions that Deirdre judged were safe enough to answer. Was she a teacher at

Brandywine Academy? What subject? For how long? Had parents ever complained about her behavior with students?

"Besides giving too much homework?" Deirdre laughed. "No."

Officer Monroe didn't smile. And had Deirdre taken her students on a field trip to the East End Gallery on September 24? And had she taken Anna Worthington on that trip, in spite of the fact that her parents had not granted their permission? Deirdre squirmed, felt her face grow flushed.

"Anna forged the permission slip. But I didn't know that until after we got back to school."

Had Deirdre indeed been in a van alone with Anna Worthington? Yes. Had she put her arm around Anna? Yes. Had she and Anna Worthington kissed? Yes, but . . . There were a few other questions too, about things she might have said, other people who might have witnessed the two of them. Deirdre's mouth went suddenly dry and cottony. She felt a twisting in her gut. Had she touched Anna? Well, she had put her arm around . . . Had she touched Anna's breasts? She had given Anna a hug. The girl was crying; she wanted to comfort her. Might her hand have touched Anna's breast? Had she inserted her tongue into her mouth? No! But they had kissed? Yes. And in the course of the hug, it was possible Deirdre might have touched other parts of Anna's body?

Officer Monroe excused herself and left Deirdre alone in the room. Deirdre felt as if she were being watched and any gesture would be noticed, remarked upon, a judgment made about her. She didn't know how to be, what to think. *I didn't do anything wrong!* she wanted to scream. Yet even she had to ask herself: wasn't there just the tiniest something she had done to encourage Anna, even a little bit?

They were charging her with indecent assault and battery.

They made it sound as if Deirdre had attacked Anna, as if she were some kind of pervert. She hadn't assaulted Anna, for God's sake. She definitely hadn't hit her or anything close to what Deirdre defined as *battery*.

"Please come with me." Officer Monroe motioned for Deirdre to follow her out of the small room. *Probable cause*, Officer Monroe had said. *Under arrest*. They were placing Deirdre *under arrest*. She needed to be fingerprinted. Deirdre answered the questions automatically—her name, her address, her occupation. She thought the recording officer flinched a little when she replied, *Teacher*. She wanted to elaborate, say how long she had been teaching, how everyone in the school looked up to her, how the girls all thought she was demanding but fair. Those were the exact words one of them had used recently. She wanted to say that being arrested was a fluke. She wanted to blurt it all out because she was sure that everyone she had been in contact with that afternoon was judging her, thinking about the terrible things she must have done to be charged with *indecent assault and battery*. But she said nothing. She followed Officer Monroe from fingerprinting to taking her mug shot. She imagined how hers would look, the terror in her eyes, hair windblown and untidy, the face of a criminal teacher. She wanted to throw up.

"Would you like to contact your attorney?" Officer Monroe asked.

Deirdre didn't know how to respond. She wanted to, yes, but she still didn't have the information. "I . . . Yes . . ." But should she call Susan? Could she go outside to where SJ might still be waiting? She smoothed her jeans. "I think my . . . my partner is still waiting out there." She pointed to the door. "Can I see her for a minute?"

Officer Monroe shook her head. "I'm sorry," she said. "You can use the phone."

"But you'll—someone will tell her what's happening to me? She's waiting—we weren't sure what would happen today." Deirdre realized how stupid she sounded, like a dumb kid caught doing something wrong. "I just want her to know what's going on. She'll have to call the lawyer for me. I don't have the number."

Officer Monroe led Deirdre to the holding cell. "This is where you stay until your arraignment." She looked at her watch. "It's Friday afternoon, and Monday is Columbus Day, so I'm afraid your arraignment won't be until Tuesday. I need to take your belt. And your watch."

Deirdre froze. "I have to stay here until Tuesday?"

Officer Monroe glanced again at her watch. "It's nearly three thirty now. You don't yet have a lawyer. Tuesday at the earliest. Your belt." She pointed. "And your watch, please."

Deirdre undid her belt and removed her watch.

"We'll keep these for you." Officer Monroe pulled the bars closed and locked them. "We'll have dinner for you later."

Deirdre paced. Hysteria competed with numbness. She paced, sat on the edge of a cot, stood, paced, then sat again. She alternately wanted to scream, pound her fists, or lie down and go to sleep. How would she survive three days in jail?

"Excuse me."

Officer Monroe turned.

"I mean—I really can't go home and then come back on Monday? There's no way? I have to stay here?"

Officer Monroe gave her a sad smile. "I'm sorry," she said. "You can't be arraigned until Tuesday morning at the earliest. The holiday weekend." She gave a little shrug and walked away.

So not only was Deirdre being arrested for some terrible, awful-sounding crime, but she was also being held in jail for three days. It didn't seem right. It didn't seem like justice, more like a technicality, like bureaucratic ridiculousness. *Because I turned myself in on a Friday*, she thought, *I have to stay in jail until Tuesday*. Why didn't anyone warn her? She would've waited until Tuesday to turn herself in. But no, she did what she thought was the right thing, only to be punished for it. That's what got her into trouble in the first place, doing what she thought was right. She wished they would let her see SJ. She needed some reassurance that SJ would find the lawyer, maybe bring her a change of clothes. Could she even have visitors? And wasn't she allowed at least one phone call to someone other than a lawyer?

The cell was small, damp-smelling, and cold. Deirdre was glad she had worn a sweater. Two sets of cots, bunk-bed style, lined both walls. A sink protruded from the far wall and a toilet without a seat. She would go crazy in here for three days. What were people supposed to do? If she only had a book, something to write with. She could hear voices, the officers joking about end of the shift, about it being Friday, about upcoming weekend plans. A general din of voices with the occasional yell from another cell—holding a couple of men, one of them detoxing from the sounds and smell of it. How was it that people were expected to stay in cells like this, with no sense of time passing and absolutely nothing to do?

Deirdre must have fallen asleep on the bottom cot in spite of the moldy smell and the yelling. She woke to another voice, someone else being brought into her holding cell.

"Yeah, yeah," the woman muttered, waving off the officer.

Deirdre lifted her head. She hadn't thought about having to share this cell. She didn't relish the idea of having to make small talk or having to discuss her situation with anyone. What she needed to do was see SJ so she could get in touch with the lawyer. She sat up, brushed her hair out of her eyes.

The woman looked to be several years younger than Deirdre. She was dressed in tight black jeans, a tight white T-shirt. Light brown skin and cropped hair, bangle bracelets clinking on both wrists. Nails manicured and dark red.

"I'll need those," the officer said, pointing to the bracelets.

"Jesus," the woman replied, hands on her hips, "this is some shit." She shook her head.

"Jackie, you know the drill," the officer said. "Come on. Let's have them."

"Like what, I'm going to hurt myself with my bracelets?" She let out a deep, throaty laugh.

Deirdre felt like she had in school when one of the troublemakers, usually one of the more popular kids, made a joke at the teacher's expense and looked to everyone else for approval. Deirdre hadn't wanted to laugh then and really didn't want to laugh now. She looked up at the cop—it wasn't Officer Monroe—and hoped she saw that Deirdre was on her side.

Jackie slipped off the bangles and handed them over, then rolled her eyes at Deirdre. "Yeah, yeah," she said to the officer. "Take 'em. But I want 'em all back." She strolled over to the cot across from Deirdre and sat. "It is *cold* in here." She wrapped her arms around herself and shivered.

Deirdre nodded.

The officer locked the cell and Deirdre watched her walk back toward the main booking room. She wished she had pretended to be asleep when Jackie was brought in, but it was too late now. There they were, the two of them. Deirdre didn't know the protocol in jail—did you introduce yourself? Was it better to keep things anonymous? Or use an alias if the question came up?

Out of habit, Deirdre looked to her wrist, where her watch would have been. Jackie sat hunched over, inspecting her nails. Deirdre coughed. "Do you know what time it is?" she asked. Her own voice sounded strange, childlike, plaintive almost. She still had the impression she was looking in on her own life from afar, that she wasn't really in a jail cell—not her, not now. This was not her life.

Jackie kept looking at the floor and shook her head. She laughed again. "Honey, does it matter?" She sat up, planted her hands on her thighs. "Gonna be a long few days." She tapped her fingers. "And it is *cold*. So this your first time, huh?" She leaned on her knees. "Shit." She spat on the floor. "You look like one of them nice girls."

Deirdre folded her legs beneath her on the cot. She couldn't judge Jackie's motives, but the woman felt threatening. Hostile. Deirdre's stomach balled up. She didn't know how to respond. She didn't detect any hint of sympathy. And she was afraid that if she admitted that this was, indeed, her first time in jail, then Jackie might, somehow, take it out on her. Of course, it wasn't like Deirdre could pretend to have been in jail before; there was no sense in that.

Jackie laid back on the cot, folded her arms beneath her head. "Shit," she said again. "Gonna be a long coupla days."

Jackie was a repeat offender—a prostitute. Deirdre longed to ask her what it was like, how she had ended up like this, was it something she chose? She wanted to say, *Do you enjoy it?* Deirdre couldn't imagine. How could you have sex with someone you didn't know? Deirdre never felt confident in her own sexual abilities. She certainly didn't have the confidence to think someone would pay her for sex. With SJ, Deirdre let her take the lead. If SJ didn't initiate sex, then they didn't have any. Deirdre knew this wasn't fair, but she couldn't bring herself to approach SJ first.

Deirdre tried to imagine what it might be like, the moment when two unfamiliar bodies come together, flesh touching flesh. She shivered. Was there an electricity pulsing through these encounters? An energy? Or simply cold skin meeting cold skin, cells unconnected to each other and so not alive? She wanted to ask Jackie about it, but the questions seemed hopelessly naïve.

Deirdre stared at Jackie. She wasn't all that beautiful. Hair cut short, close to her head. Wide, flat nose. Heavy thighs. Deirdre rubbed her legs. Running kept her muscles toned, strong. Even in her clothes, Jackie looked fleshy to Deirdre. SJ didn't work out, so even though she was thin, she wasn't particularly toned. Deirdre remembered the first time they were together and her surprise at the softness of SJ's legs, how Deirdre almost recoiled when she ran her hand along SJ's thigh expecting taut and hard but getting no resistance, imagining SJ beneath her, flattened, skin falling off bone.

And then Jamie. Deirdre felt the heat rise to her face. What had she been thinking? What craziness. A one-night stand? She hadn't thought herself capable of doing something like that. Deirdre replayed the night—the meeting in the bar, the dancing, the walk back to Jamie's house. She saw again how easily she had been drawn into Jamie's arms, her bed. Hadn't she willed herself there, from the moment the woman sat on the barstool next to her and started talking? It was this willing that made Deirdre worry about Anna Worthington. Had Deirdre somehow willed Anna to kiss her? The thought made it sound preposterous, yet still, somehow, she was afraid it might be true. She heard Forest say: *Thoughts don't make you guilty.* But maybe they did. Maybe the thoughts did make you guilty when they led to actions.

CHAPTER EIGHT

SJ POURED ANOTHER CUP OF COFFEE. She felt as though she had misled Deirdre, believing deep down that the police would never keep her. Back home, SJ had dialed Susan and Murray immediately—"They arrested her? She's in jail?"—and it was all SJ could do to not burst into tears.

SJ had to force out the words, her mouth dry: "I need . . . Can we have . . . Deirdre said you knew a lawyer?"

"Of course."

Arthur Heffernan. A college friend of Murray's. "But he's good?" SJ had asked.

"The best. Call him. Call him right now."

And though SJ had hoped he might get Deirdre out of jail immediately, he was matter-of-fact.

"I'll see her tomorrow," he promised. "There's nothing I can do now." His voice sounded kind; he assured SJ as much as he probably could, and she was grateful that Susan and Murray had been so forthcoming.

Still, SJ hadn't been able to sleep and finally she had given in and gotten up, first trudging around the house, into one room and then the next until she felt too sad and collapsed on the floor in the hallway. All the empty rooms, still new and full of promise. Her chest felt tight, the weight of her sadness pressing onto her heart. She must have sat like that for an hour or more, without moving, just breathing what little air she could, not thinking, immobile.

Now, about ten minutes before seven on Saturday, the sun was rising. SJ caught glimpses of orange light through the kitchen window. She wanted to feel hopeful. She wanted to feel the world was back on track, where she and Deirdre were still a couple, still happily living in their first house in a lovely neighborhood. And although on the surface they were still a couple and they were still living in their new house in a lovely neighborhood, things had irrevocably changed.

SJ sipped more coffee. How had their lives gotten so out of control? She knew it wasn't logical, but somehow she found herself thinking that if only she hadn't rented the apartment. If only she hadn't told Deirdre that she wanted to leave. But she had never said that. Instead, she had fumbled her words, couldn't bring herself to fully admit that she wanted to leave the relationship. What had she said? SJ downed the last bit of coffee in a gulp. She had mumbled something about not being happy. Something about needing time, needing to think things through. And that she had rented an apartment, which now she was paying for. And for which she had a one-year lease.

Outside, the sky brightened. These crisp fall days could make anyone feel hopeful, as though life was about to start anew. Deirdre always said that New Year's should be in the fall. She said all teachers thought like that, saying "last year" for whatever happened in the previous school year, not bothering to count all the way back to January, disregarding the calendar year completely. SJ could see why, on an October morning like this—the way the light shone, clear and bright and everything seemed bathed in golden yellow. The way the red leaves on the maple trees shimmered and burned. The colors could make your insides ache with the wanting. They could make you feel as though everything could be new again: your dreams, your plans, your heart.

She was going to have to call Deirdre's parents. Or at least Paul. Even after five years, SJ didn't feel comfortable talking with Deirdre's parents. She felt judged. She would have better luck talking with Paul and letting him deliver the bad news. Of course, she wondered how Kris would take it. Deirdre was convinced that Kris didn't much like her, or didn't much like the fact that she and SJ were a couple.

"She always acts nice to me," SJ had said one time after they'd come home from a dinner at Paul and Kris's.

"She fools you. She's like one of those popular girls, you know: they smile at you and you think you've got it made? But then, next thing, they're stabbing you in the back, spreading some rumor about you, or laughing at your clothes in the cafeteria with their real friends."

But SJ had never felt that from Kris. She thought maybe Deirdre was wrong on this one, but there was no convincing Deirdre, so she had stopped trying. Still, even SJ had to wonder: now that Deirdre was being charged with a felony, how would Kris deal with that and what it might mean to Sophie and Mark? She looked at the clock and thought about calling Paul now. What was the best time to deliver bad news? The earlier the better. That way, if he was going to help, he would have time to do something about it immediately.

SJ slumped over and rested her head on her arms. The weight of it all pushed heavily at her. The truth was that she wanted to leave Deirdre because she resented her. She resented the way Deirdre let work take precedence over their life together. She resented the fact that Deirdre loved her work so much. SJ even resented the fact that Deirdre liked their life together as much as she did; why wasn't it a struggle for her? Why didn't Deirdre have angst about living life as a couple? Clearly she should have more angst about it because she hadn't even known how unhappy SJ was. SJ pushed herself away from the table and moved around the kitchen, the full morning sunshine pouring in the window and warming the wood floor. Most of all, SJ resented now the way Deirdre had gotten herself into trouble and was somehow forcing SJ to help clean up the mess. She would rather be blissfully off in her new, empty apartment. She let herself think about the apartment for a few minutes, how she thought she might inhabit the space, how she had been looking forward to keeping it stark, how, immediately after she had rented it, she had felt lighter and so knew it had been the right thing to do. And yet here she was, legs leaden, body heavy, the feeling of inertia sinking into her limbs. She had to call Paul. And maybe once she called him, she could let go a little and give over some of the responsibility of taking care of Deirdre. She glanced to the wall. Almost seven thirty. *Soon. Soon. Soon.*

"Hello?"

SJ swallowed. "Kris, hi. Is Paul there?" She heard the hesitation in Kris's voice, her need to know why SJ was calling. But Kris called for Paul anyway. SJ caught part of a whisper, *"Your sister."*

"Deird?"

"Hey, Paul. It's SJ, actually. It's . . . I'm calling about Deirdre." She wished now she were talking to Paul in person. She shifted the receiver into her other hand. "She's okay . . . I mean, well, she's not sick or hurt or anything—"

"What's up?"

SJ imagined Kris hovering there, tapping Paul on the shoulder, wanting all the news immediately. She hoped for his sake that wasn't the case. She heard Sophie in the background, yelling about Pop-Tarts. "Okay, this is weird, but . . . well, she's in jail."

Silence. "Did you say *jail*?"

"Yeah. I know." She gulped air. "I'm sorry to call and just dump this on you, but I had to tell you. She . . . Okay, it's a long story, but they arrested her last night. I should've called then, but I . . . I hoped it was a mistake and she'd come home. Once I called the lawyer, I really did think she'd be able to come home. Dumb, I know. I'm sorry."

"Is this . . . It's about that girl, isn't it? And school." He swore under his breath, "Goddamn."

"You know about it?" Of course Deirdre had confided in Paul. She told him everything. SJ grimaced to herself. "Yes, it's about that girl. Her mother pressed charges. So yesterday, Deirdre got a call to turn herself in and I thought it would be a good idea to go sooner rather than later, but turns out it wasn't. I mean, I don't know, I guess they would've arrested her either way."

"Okay, but you said you've got a lawyer? A good one?"

SJ twirled the phone cord. "A Mr. Heffernan. Arthur Heffernan. We got his name from our neighbors. He seems good."

Silence. Paul's breathing. "Okay, look, we're on our way out the door. Mark's got a soccer game, but I'll call you when we get back, okay? I'll . . . We'll figure out something. Hang tight."

SJ hung up the phone. She didn't know how that had gone. She didn't know how to read Paul's responses. He had seemed more distant than usual. Of course, he wouldn't have liked the fact that Deirdre was being arrested for something connected to being gay—he would've found that unpleasant. SJ had tried to tell Deirdre that it wasn't Kris who didn't much like the fact they were a couple, it was Paul, but Deirdre didn't want to hear that. Not about her brother.

For the rest of the morning and then into the afternoon, SJ moved around in a kind of trance. She didn't get dressed, didn't make a meal, didn't do much of anything beyond shuffle from one room to the other, from the couch to the Queen Anne's chair, to the kitchen table and its circle of light. She tried picking up the crossword, searching for horizontal and vertical clues, but that didn't calm her. She looked at photographs, searched them for answers.

What do I do now? she wanted to ask, wanted to scream. These were the times she wished she had family to call. She wished she could call a brother or a sister, talk to them about her uncertainties with Deirdre, about how to proceed now that this thing had happened. Even as she lay sprawled across the couch, in flannel pajama bottoms and a sweatshirt, lacking even the energy to shower and change, she wished fervently that someone could tell her whether or not what she was feeling for Deirdre was love. And what was it that had propelled her to rent an apartment, decide to leave this relationship? Temporary insanity? Some days she felt crazy and others, completely sane. Saner than she had ever felt. But in all the questions and all the searching and listening, she couldn't find a solid answer.

If this was love, then why did she feel so unhappy?

But if this was love, if this was all she could expect, then she could be okay with it. She just had to know.

The day burned on, Indian summer October. The sun moved from the kitchen into the living room, slanting onto the hardwood floor in bright triangles. From the couch, SJ watched dust motes float in the light and wanted to have the energy to get up and move. She thought about driving over to the apartment, but there wasn't anything there, no furniture, nothing at all. Once again she wondered why she was even keeping it, but somehow she couldn't give it up yet. She rationalized it by saying that the one way she could stay with Deirdre was to have the apartment on the side.

Which reminded her—what was up with Deirdre driving off to P-town? She hadn't confronted Deirdre about it. Part of her felt as though Deirdre deserved something good to happen to her, especially now, at this crazy time. And yes, part of her had been jealous. And relieved. Jealous for the usual reason people get jealous: SJ imagined Deirdre laughing and flirting with another woman. Kissing even. She couldn't let her mind go beyond that, but then again, Deirdre hadn't come home. So something had happened.

And if thinking about it gave SJ an awful stomachache, then wasn't it clear she still loved Deirdre?

The doorbell rang. SJ jumped off the couch and straightened her sweatshirt, smoothed down her unbrushed hair. She looked out the peephole and saw a middle-aged woman, graying hair pulled back into a bun, face without makeup. A black Pontiac sat parked at the curb. SJ opened the door.

"Hello," the woman said, glancing at a folded piece of paper she held in hands that tremored. "I am looking for . . ." She glanced down again. "SJ?" She spoke with an accent, lilting and old world.

"Sara Jane," she said, and offered her hand.

"Maria Gilberto," the woman said.

SJ invited her in, motioned to the easy chair, offered her coffee, something to drink.

"No thank you," Mrs. Gilberto said. "I won't take much time. I'm here . . ." She started to sniffle and pulled a white handkerchief from her purse. "I'm sorry, I told myself I would not do this."

SJ tried to envision Mickey with his mother, how he might speak to her, do things for her.

As if she were listening to SJ's thoughts, Mrs. Gilberto spoke: "Mickey, my son . . ." She cleared her throat. "Mickey asked me to come here. He said you might be able to help him. I am sorry if I am bothering you?"

SJ motioned for her to go on.

"My son, he has always been a good boy. And this, what is happening now, it is crazy." She started to cry fresh tears, dabbed at her eyes with her handkerchief. "That poor boy," she said, and shook her head. SJ wasn't sure whether or not she was referring now to Mickey or to Leo Rivera. "My son," she began again, "he . . . I do not know whether he has done this terrible thing. What mother can think her son is capable of doing such a terrible thing? What mother can imagine it?" She gestured with her hands.

SJ sat in silence. She couldn't imagine it. She couldn't imagine that anyone could do such a terrible thing.

"We would like to ask your help." Mrs. Gilberto straightened herself in the chair, uncrossed her legs.

SJ looked to her then, the smooth polyester pants, the sensible shoes. She had such pity for this woman. She wondered what Mickey had told his mother about her.

Mrs. Gilberto continued: "Can you see my son? He has asked for you. He has no one." She blotted her tears.

"How is he doing?" SJ asked.

Mrs. Gilberto shook her head. "He is alone, in a cell alone. The others would kill him if they could. This crime is so terrible, they would kill him."

SJ nodded. It was true.

"He has asked if you would come to see him. He tells me you are his only good friend." She looked at SJ with such a hopeful face, eyes wide, a tremulous attempt at a smile.

SJ swallowed. "I can see him, sure. He has to put me on the visitors list."

Mrs. Gilberto nodded. She stood, unclasped her pocketbook, and stuffed the handkerchief inside. "Thank you," she whispered. "My son and I thank you."

SJ closed the door behind her. She stood for a moment, leaning against it. How do you survive that? How do you watch your child, accused of a horrible crime, not know-ing whether he committed it or not? You had to believe he was innocent, didn't you? You had to go forward assuming that your own flesh and blood was not capable of heinous crimes. But then, there *were* criminals—awful criminals—who all had mothers. SJ glanced at the hallway mirror. Mrs. Gilberto looked like any middle-aged mother next door. As-suming that was the truth, how could it be possible that Mickey was guilty? How could you ever know the truth?

CHAPTER NINE

VISITING HOURS. Deirdre was both looking forward to and dreading seeing SJ. It would be her first time facing SJ as an arrested felon. Because of the long weekend and the extended stay required before their bond hearing, Deirdre and Jackie had been processed into the jail and out of the holding cell. They were staying with the other women. They had been issued the standard jumpsuits. The transformation had been complete; Deirdre looked and felt like a criminal.

They were led into the visiting room, crammed with tables and two chairs opposite each other. There was a family visiting room too, for those inmates with children. Deirdre didn't know how you could manage being in jail and being a parent. How could you get out of jail and then resume your parenting, as if the jail part had never happened? Didn't the fact of jail somehow negate *parent*? This was a fundamental matter with which Deirdre struggled. When Jackie revealed she had two kids, Deirdre had been floored. When you were growing up, you assumed that all your friends' parents were good people. (SJ would laugh.) You never thought that anyone might have a criminal parent. But now, here she was, in jail herself and Jackie telling her she had two kids at home, being cared for by her sister and sometimes her mother. And Deirdre wondered what Jackie's kids thought, if they minded that their mother was in jail. What did you tell the other kids at school? How did you hold your head up?

The visiting room was already packed, conversations filling the air. At the table nearest Deirdre, she overheard phrases, a lawyer and client. She had met here the previous day with her own lawyer. Thankfully, SJ had been able to get ahold of him. Deirdre didn't know what she had expected, but somehow, she had wanted more of a pep talk from him. She didn't feel reassured. In fact, after the visit Deirdre felt more rattled than ever. She was hoping the visit with SJ might make her feel better. She was hoping that SJ could do what her lawyer couldn't—somehow make her feel as though she were a good person still.

After three days, Deirdre didn't know how people survived years in jail. There were so many people jammed into cells, people who, like Jackie, had lives outside the cinder-blocked walls. Maybe some of them had good lives, who were even innocent, like Deirdre, who were in jail on some technicality. One thing was for sure, though—Deirdre never wanted to be in jail again. There was no other way to say it— you ended up feeling inhuman. You ended up feeling worthless. Deirdre imagined that anyone jailed for any length of time would become another kind of person, someone capable of committing the crime they were accused of, someone who, even if they had been a good, caring person before, would end up becoming . . . hardened. Uncaring. At mealtime, she had been fascinated to watch the women around her and listen to them talk. Many of them, she learned, had been brought in for relatively minor offenses—drug possession, prostitution—and many were repeat offenders. That was the part she didn't understand. How could anyone, in jail once, find themselves behind bars again? She had mentioned this to Jackie.

Jackie laughed. "Three things, love. Food. Heat. Bed."

Deirdre blushed. She felt so stupid. She still could not imagine things being so bad that the only way to get these three basics was to go back to jail. She knew that Jackie found her ridiculously pampered. *You would hate SJ*, she thought, looking now at Jackie stretched out on her cot. *She* was the pampered one, the one who had grown up in privilege. Deirdre always found herself wanting to explain that she had been a working-class kid. But she didn't think there was any moral superiority in being poor. SJ seemed to think that was the case, but Deirdre was sure it was because SJ didn't really know any better. How many times had she told SJ how ridiculous her theory was that poor people somehow lived more authentically? *Here is your authenticity,* she wanted to say. *It's so much better being poor that people want to come back to jail.*

"Hey."

Deirdre was jolted back to her surroundings. SJ stood, hesitating. Deirdre wanted to reach out and grab her hands, but she knew they weren't supposed to touch. Guards hovered. There was no privacy. She would never get used to that. She motioned for SJ to sit.

"I'm so glad to see you." Deirdre smiled. Everything felt stupid, inconsequential. What do you say in fifteen minutes? "I met with Mr. Heffernan yesterday."

SJ inched forward in the chair.

"He . . . I don't know . . . It didn't sound very good to me."

"What did he say? But you'll get out, right?" SJ said nervously.

"Bond hearing is Tuesday. He's sure I'll be able to post bond . . . SJ, it's so awful in here. I can't stand it." She felt hot tears brimming.

"I'm so sorry. I can't stand to see you in there." SJ twisted her rings. "Do you need to contact the school . . . I don't know, it seems like you might have to? Should I call them for you?"

"Mr. Heffernan will, if he hasn't already." Deirdre chuckled. "Martin will love that, won't he? Good publicity for Brandywine. *Come to the school where one of our teachers was arrested!* It'll make for a great admissions tour!" She snorted. Now, Deirdre understood as she said this out loud to SJ, that there was no hope of getting her job back. Up until this very minute, she had still thought it possible. She had still thought *maybe*.

"You can't worry about Brandywine." SJ looked like she hadn't slept in days.

"I miss you. It's only been a few days but it feels like forever. I don't know how people stand it." Deirdre tugged at the sleeves of her orange jumpsuit. "Plus, it's freezing in here."

"When did they make you put that on?" SJ gestured.

"Soon as they knew I'd be here for a few days." Deirdre had been horrified. She told SJ how she and Jackie had been processed. "Like you're meat or fish or something."

"Jackie?"

"My . . . cell mate." Deirdre laughed emptily. "Well, I mean, there are a few of us now, but she was in the holding cell with me."

"I'm sorry," SJ said again. "Listen, what can I do? What do you need me to do for you? I called Paul . . ."

Deirdre flinched. "Oh God. How did that go?"

"I called him in the morning, so we didn't talk long, but he guessed why you were here. He told your parents—at least, he said he would. I've not heard back from him." SJ paused and looked down at her hands, picked at her cuticles. "Paul will always love you no matter what, you know that."

The hot tears spilled over. Deirdre nodded. Did she believe it though? "I can't imagine what my parents think," she sniffled. "I just can't imagine."

"I know. They'll . . . well, they'll get over it too, I suppose."

Deirdre wanted to say, *And what about you? Will you get over it?* But she couldn't bring herself to ask the question. She was too afraid of the answer.

"So on Tuesday, should I be there? Do I go to court too?"

"It'd be nice to have you there. And, I'm hoping . . ." Deirdre hesitated. "You'll post bond for me, won't you?"

"Right." SJ took out a piece of paper from her pocket. "Let me jot that down."

Deirdre bit her thumbnail. "You can do that, right? Post the bond?"

SJ shoved the paper back in her pocket. "Of course," she said.

It wasn't like Deirdre and Paul hadn't known folks who had been sent to jail. More than once, Manny Da Silva had been hauled in by the cops and left to spend the night "drying out." Of course, this was long after Deirdre and Paul had left Gloucester and both settled in Bradley, after Maria Da Silva went to beauty school and started working at Stella's on the corner of Commercial Street, and after Mrs. Da Silva's liver started to wear out and Mr. Da Silva retired from fishing. Their mother kept them posted. In the early days, just after Deirdre had graduated from UMass and first moved into an apartment near Bradley, her mother would remind her that long distance cost money. "You only call for emergencies," she would say. She mailed clippings from the *Gloucester Times*. Then, as long distance got cheaper, she called more often. Filled them in on who in the neighborhood had died, who had babies, who got laid off again, whose babies were growing up and having babies. Deirdre imagined herself now the topic of conversation for other people's phone calls, the gossip at Stella's. She wondered what Maria Da Silva would make of the news.

Deirdre Murphy, in jail.

What Deirdre hadn't been prepared for—what neither she nor SJ had predicted—was the article in the *Bradley Register.*

SJ saw the headline first thing when she picked up the paper the following morning. *"BRANDYWINE TEACHER ACCUSED OF MOLESTING STUDENT."*

It wasn't *molesting,* for God's sake. But they had to make it sensational. They had to lure in readers. Frances Worthington would either be ecstatic or devastated. And of course it wasn't just a teacher. It was a Brandywine teacher. Wouldn't all the public school parents and teachers feel vindicated? *See,* they would say to themselves, *you pay all that money and for what? For a teacher who molests her students.*

And really, SJ wanted to tell them all, teachers and students, it was so much more common than anyone thought. Even Mr. Freeman was still teaching—loved, revered, a teacher-of-the-year award. And as much as SJ felt like she had wanted what had happened between them, she couldn't help but hold a grudge. Back then, she had worn her loneliness like a prized ribbon, an emblem of her specialness. But she knew now how silly that was, how she probably wasn't special at all, how he probably went on every year to another student.

SJ read: *". . . Veteran teacher Deirdre Murphy of 47 Hillside Street was arrested Friday on charges of indecent assault and battery . . ."* The article didn't mention Anna Worthington, probably because she was a minor. It didn't seem fair that the paper could mention anyone before they were convicted, because even though the headline said "accused" and the lede mentioned she was "arrested and charged with," all anyone would remember was Deirdre Murphy "molesting a student." For all intents and purposes, SJ realized, Deirdre's teaching career was over. At least locally. Even if she were found innocent, she was marked. She was ruined.

CHAPTER TEN

THE WEATHER HAD TURNED SOUR, the sky metallic gray with a wind as sharp as knives. New England had a way of doing that. You could have clear blue one moment and then brooding darkness. Even in October, you got snow warnings—moisture that hardened into air too painful to breathe.

The wind blew through Deirdre's jumpsuit. She held her sweater tighter across her chest but she couldn't keep out the cold. She shuffled behind the others and climbed into the van. A field trip to the courthouse, she told herself, and almost giggled, except it wasn't funny and there they were, handcuffed, sitting two to a seat. In the back of the van, behind the cage, a guard, young-faced, like he might be kind but you couldn't be sure. Deirdre was learning here that you couldn't count on much. A kind face meant nothing. A kind face could lash out, spit hard words, and make your life miserable. She had already seen it happen, in just two days.

The skinny guard, for example. The one the other girls called El Magro, who stood there quietly, looking like he felt bad for them all. That was a misread. Darnella, one of the women brought in on a drug bust, had pushed him a little too far at lunch. Deirdre hadn't heard it all—something about mashed potatoes left on her tray, or maybe she moved from her seat without permission, but El Magro said something to her about following the rules, about how Darnella must not think the rules applied to her, isn't that how she landed in here in the first place, and Darnella had smiled sweetly at his young baby face and said something about having vegetables in her fridge older than he was, and he exploded. His sweet doe eyes turned icy black. He marched up to Darnella, the vein in his neck throbbing, one hand gripping the club attached to his belt. "If you ever threaten my authority again," he had said, and the rage in his voice made certain that you wouldn't.

They rode in silence. The city passed by outside, people huddled in their coats, tight and pointed, their faces hidden. Gray buildings against the gray sky. No color, just an old black-and-white movie, reel to reel, in slow motion. Deirdre had been stolen from her real life and forced to take a starring role in someone else's story. She could not predict the ending.

The court building was old and imposing, white stone that looked drab and gray, fortress-like. Deirdre spotted Paul's car in the parking lot, and the Honda. Her knees shook and she took deep breaths. Mr. Heffernan had told her that she would be released on bond, no doubt about it, but she had doubts. She hoped she didn't have to look Paul in the eye. She hoped her lawyer would be in the court already.

"Okay, let's go," the guard from the cage ordered them out. How humiliating to walk in handcuffs. Deirdre wanted to say to the guards: *Do you know what this feels like?* She thought guards should have to know what they were asking of their charges. She thought of the workshop she had taken at a teacher's conference, the leader instructing them on how to make origami paper cranes, a task that for Deirdre was overwhelmingly difficult. She couldn't follow the directions. Frustrated, she'd given up, laying the folded piece of paper on the table.

"That," the workshop leader had said, hustling to Deirdre's side of the table, heels clicking on the floor, "is what your students feel like on a daily basis." She lifted the unfinished paper crane. "We look at their work and we think they're lazy. We think they don't care."

Deirdre had felt herself blush.

"Were you a plant?" the teacher next to Deirdre had whispered.

The workshop leader continued, "Sometimes our students are just feeling confused. They don't get it. The instructions are hard to follow . . ."

Deirdre had stopped following. The point had been made. She had never forgotten that lesson. And now, she wondered if the guards knew what they were asking of the prisoners. She didn't consider that maybe it was best for them not to know, that in some cases you couldn't do your job if you put yourself in someone else's shoes. Somehow, it didn't seem right. None of this felt right.

They were led inside the court building and then the courtroom. Deirdre spotted SJ and Paul sitting together, Paul, hands folded, staring straight ahead, face without expression, and SJ, fingers tapping, knee bouncing, glancing around. Deirdre's eyes locked with SJ's and SJ gave a little smile. A thumbs-up. She nudged Paul who nodded. Deirdre hoped that their being here would be a bonus for her. She couldn't let herself think about how much she was counting on going home after this. Even letting one small thought of jail slip into her brain made her feel heavy and leaden. So she stopped thinking about it and instead focused on the fact that both SJ and Paul were here and that was good.

The bond hearing itself was short, and for that Deirdre was grateful. Five thousand dollars bond, the judge ruled.

Deirdre felt SJ's and Paul's presence behind her as she stood before the judge, her lawyer beside her. Ten minutes was all it took for the judge to issue her decision about bond. Still, it felt like an eternity up there to Deirdre, the judge and court employees looking at her dispassionately, trained, Deirdre imagined, to register no feelings when they spoke, to show no emotion. She had that urge again to scream, *I didn't do anything!* Didn't anyone ever want to hear her side of things? Didn't anyone ever want to know what had really happened on that field trip? Not now, apparently. Just: *State your name, you're charged with this felony, attorneys have agreed on X dollars bond, and that's it, back you go, we'll process your paperwork, we're done with you.*

You had absolutely no power. That was the hardest thing to swallow. For someone who was used to being in charge, losing your voice and any kind of autonomy was really tough.

Deirdre and the other women left the court building still in handcuffs, even those, like herself, who had been freed on bail. There was paperwork to be completed, which Deirdre knew by now took way longer than anyone could possibly imagine. Why in God's name did everything have to be written in triplicate? Especially now that there were computers. But jail, if nothing else, was bureaucracy. In some ways—and the irony was not lost on her—jail felt a bit too familiar, like school. Not terribly different from Gloucester High. Especially when they were eating in the cafeteria, Deirdre felt as if she were fifteen or sixteen years old again, the guards her sour-faced teachers looking in on them, unhappy to be there another day. Once again, she felt grateful to teach at Brandywine.

Brandywine. Her heart lurched. Deirdre knew deep down and with a certainty she could no longer suppress that she wouldn't ever teach at Brandywine again. She had loved it there, the front lobby with its old-fashioned tattered feel like you might get from someone's well-to-do grandmother, a bit worn but still lovely. Being at Brandywine had given her the illusion that she could live a lovely life, be part of something, belong. For a while maybe that had been so. But no longer. She had to let it go.

A camera flash caught Deirdre's eye. She hesitated from climbing into the van, looked to her left, and there, being led by another guard, hands cuffed together and ankles shackled, was Mickey Gilberto. Deirdre felt her breath quicken, her heart beat faster. She climbed into her seat and sat pressed up against the door and window. She hoped Mickey wouldn't notice her, wouldn't say anything. She had to force herself to stay glued to the window, to not turn around when she felt sure he was in the van. She heard him say something to one of the guards and saw him again standing in their dining room, piling moving boxes one on top of the other. She saw his lazy stance, his smile, the way his muscles flexed beneath the short sleeves of his T-shirt. She heard him behind her, felt his presence like that of an ex-lover, or a rival, and she hated the way their lives were intertwined. Somehow, irrevocably, her fate seemed tied to his.

But she hated more than anything that here she was, in the same van, headed to the same destination. Here they were, both in jumpsuits, both headed back to jail, only the color of their jumpsuits and Mickey's shackles distinguishing the severity of their crimes. She felt tainted and dirty. She didn't want to have a single thing in common with that man.

CHAPTER ELEVEN

THE LETTERS TO THE EDITOR DIDN'T STOP. There were more that agreed with Frances Worthington than opposed her, a sad commentary on Bradley, SJ thought. Where was people's common sense? Decency even? It was hard to believe. Worse, though, when she and Deirdre got home from the bond hearing, after waiting for several hours for Deirdre to be released, they found ugly graffiti on the sidewalk outside their house and Susan's husband Murray trying, unsuccessfully, to wash it off with a bucket of water.

"I'm sorry," he said. "I didn't want you to see this."

Deirdre burst into tears and ran inside.

SJ hesitated. She could make out some of the words, what looked like *lezzie rapist* scrawled in black. "Jesus," she said, then glanced around as if she might find whoever had done this hovering there, behind one of the maples or oaks. "Thanks," she said to Murray. "We'll . . . I'll . . . Someone will take care of it."

"What are you two going to do?" Murray put down the bucket and stuck his hands in the pouch pockets of his gray hooded sweatshirt.

"She has a court date in three weeks. Guess we'll wait and see what happens there. It's crazy."

Murray nodded. "I hope Arthur has been of some help to you?"

"Mr. Heffernan? Thanks for that, by the way. He's been fine, yes." SJ glanced to the front door. She couldn't see much past the hallway, couldn't see Deirdre. "So I guess you've been reading the paper?"

"Letters to the editor? Yeah. You've got to ignore them."

SJ scoffed. "Sure, that's easy." She motioned toward the door. "Deirdre doesn't know about them yet."

"Oh boy." Murray resumed scrubbing. "You girls are in for a rough haul."

Inside, Deirdre was collapsed on the couch, newspapers in her fist.

"Oh—I was going . . . I meant to get rid of those." SJ rushed over and sat next to her.

"God, you knew about these? But you didn't say anything to me!" Deirdre's face was tear-streaked.

SJ swallowed. "No. I didn't know how . . . or if I should. It's so mean-spirited." She tried to take the papers away.

Deirdre held on and shook the stack of them. "Frances Worthington—I'm sorry. She is just a horrible person."

"Agreed. She is, and I know this is easier said than done, but you need to try and ignore these, okay?" SJ reached again for the newspapers.

"Ignore? How can I do that? There's hate speech scrawled in front of our house. The neighbors are so mortified they try to clean it off—"

"No, Murray just wanted to help! He was trying to get rid of it before you came home!"

"You know my life is ruined! I won't teach again." The tears poured forth. "I mean, I'm clear on that now. There will be no teaching for me, not anywhere within a hundred-mile radius of this place—Frances will make sure of that!"

SJ sat, hands useless in her lap. "Did you see the letter I wrote?"

"You did? No, how'd I miss that one?" Deirdre's eyes lit up a little. SJ pulled out first her letter to the editor and then Beth Ann's.

"Beth Ann. Wow, what a sweetie." Deirdre wiped her face.

SJ raised her eyebrows and folded her arms in front of her chest.

"No, no—I mean, your letter is amazing too. It's just that . . . Beth Ann doesn't have a reason to write, you know? Not that you have a reason, but I mean, you love me. Beth Ann could just stay out of the whole thing."

It was this ability of Deirdre's to ignore what was right in front of her, to go looking for some sort of approval from people she didn't even know or have reason to care about instead of focusing on the love she did have, that drove SJ crazy. "Right," she said to Deirdre now. "I love you." *And somehow,* she thought, *that makes me about as good as chopped liver.*

For the three days she was in jail, Deirdre hadn't really thought much about Mark and Sophie, about what to tell them, how to make the story sound . . . kid-friendly. But there was nothing about sex that was kid-friendly. She didn't know what she'd say when the time came. In jail, Deirdre had spent her time thinking about Frances Worthington, about how cruel she was and how much power she had, about Anna and the other girls. Deirdre wondered if all the other girls believed what they had heard. She wondered, too, about Forest. She wondered if the neighbors had decided that she was really a child molester or whether they felt sorry for her. She wondered if she and SJ would make it as a couple, and if they would have to move. She thought about how your life really *can* change in an instant, as crazy and clichéd as that was, and about how little control anyone had in spite of all the things everyone did in order to pretend they did. All the steps you took in order to ensure your future. *If I go to this school, if I get this job, if I live in this neighborhood . . .* What a farce.

Now, it was almost Sophie's birthday, and Deirdre hadn't heard from Paul since the bond hearing. Normally, she would go and help out with the party, but she didn't know whether or not she was welcome this year.

"Call Kris." SJ handed her the portable phone.

Deirdre shook her head. "I don't know. I don't think I can." She swallowed. "Can . . . Could you call?"

"What, and ask if it's okay for you to come help with the birthday party? C'mon, Deird."

"I know," she sighed. "I just don't want to talk to Kris."

"You'll have to face her sometime though, yeah? Why not get it over with? Might be easier on the phone first—that's what I'd do."

Deirdre didn't want to talk to Kris. She didn't want to talk to anyone. She wanted her life back. She wanted it with an ache so strong it threatened to burst within her. She couldn't keep it inside. She paced. She flopped. She slept. She zoned out in front of the TV. Nothing helped. She didn't want to go outside because she didn't want to see anybody. By now she was certain the entire town knew about her arrest, and she couldn't face the stares, the looks, the whisperings she was certain would be directed at her. *How did Hester Prynne do it?* she wondered. How did she face that town with her quiet pride and go on living her life, raising Pearl, not minding what anyone said or did? Deirdre didn't think she had the strength in her.

"You can't stay in here forever," SJ said the next morning when Deirdre refused to get out of bed. "Why give them," she motioned to the windows and beyond, "why give them that power over you?"

Deirdre let SJ talk her into a walk through town. They bundled up in turtlenecks and sweatshirts, but Deirdre wished they had grabbed mittens too.

"It's freezing out," she said, shoving her hands in her pockets.

Deirdre and SJ walked the streets of their neighborhood. They walked past the graffiti, duller now but still visible. Deirdre tried to avoid looking at it outright but glanced down and saw just enough of the lettering to make her stomach clench. They walked past Susan and Murray's house. Deirdre didn't look over. They walked through the park and Deirdre realized it had been a good long while since she had been for a run. She imagined herself out on one of her regular routes—feet hitting the pavement, her legs in long, even strides, feeling strong.

"So, Paul hasn't even called me yet and he knows I'm home," Deirdre said.

SJ pulled her sweatshirt sleeves over her hands. "He's probably not sure what to say, you know?"

Deirdre nodded. "It's just . . ."

"I know."

There were still bursts of flaming orange and piercing red on the trees, oaks and a few glorious maples, but more leaves lay scattered on the ground, covering the grass and parts of the walkways. The tremendous beauty of fall was so short-lived.

"You need to call them," SJ said.

"And why haven't my parents called? Jeez, you'd think *they'd* call me." She kicked at some leaves. *And Forest*. It had to be all over school that she'd been in jail. "Did . . . did anyone call while I was . . . away?"

SJ looked over to the basketball hoops. "I had a visitor while you were gone."

Deirdre stopped. "A visitor?"

"Mrs. Gilberto." SJ swallowed. "Mickey's mother?"

Deirdre's heart thudded against her chest and her mouth went dry. She couldn't even ask a question. They both stopped walking.

"She wanted to know if I could help Mickey." SJ turned to face Deirdre. "She wants me to visit him, at least. He has no one." She shrugged.

Deirdre felt an urge to scream. And run. She heard again the detective's voice: *You knew your partner was tutoring Mickey Gilberto*? "SJ, some police detectives came by to interview me about Mickey Gilberto." She waited for a reaction. "I didn't mention it because . . . well, because then I . . ." She hesitated and took a deep breath. "I went to P-town and then . . . everything happened so I haven't had a chance." The truth was, she hadn't thought about it much since then—at least not until she saw Mickey Gilberto that day in court.

SJ looked flushed. And flustered.

"I went looking for you at the library—did Florence mention it? We chatted for a bit. And I ran into Anna Worthington." Deirdre took another breath, realizing she was talking quickly, running her words together. "So that's when I got in the car and drove all the way to the Cape. I don't know why. Driving calmed me down. I didn't know what to think," she said, trying to make SJ understand that she had been thrown off by the police visit, by not finding SJ at the library. "The cops wanted to know why you were hanging around Most Precious Blood Elementary and I didn't know what to tell them. I said you were probably at work, taking a break, but then I found out you'd called in sick and, I don't know, I got worried. I mean, the cops practically suggested you were *involved* with Mickey Gilberto!"

SJ stood silently, stony faced.

"You're not though, right?" Deirdre asked quietly.

Leaves whirled around them in the wind.

Before SJ could say anything, Deirdre continued, "I know you were tutoring him. I mean, that's okay, and I get why you didn't want to tell me you hadn't stopped. Though you really could've, SJ. I mean, jeez. I just . . . I don't know . . . I had this awful gut feeling that somehow there was more going on there. I mean, when I mentioned it to Florence and she pointed out how stupid and silly it sounded, I had to agree. But you'd been so strange and I didn't know what to think . . . Say something!"

SJ turned and started to walk toward the park gate.

"We need to talk about this stuff!"

SJ spun around. "Then what happened in P-town, huh? Tell me about that!"

Deirdre felt the tears building but willed them to stay put. "I know, I know. I need to tell you about that. But for God's sake, SJ, you rented an apartment!"

SJ stood and planted herself. She faced Deirdre squarely. "I'm here, aren't I? I didn't leave."

"But did you want to? Are you here and you wish you weren't?" The tears had a life of their own now and Deirdre couldn't help it. She wiped them away. "Crap, SJ. If you want to be gone . . ." she couldn't believe she was about to say this," it's okay. You should leave. If that's what you want. Not that I'm not grateful you stayed until now. I couldn't have made it through this without you." She dug in her jeans pocket for a Kleenex. "Crap," she said and looked at SJ, expression hardened, cold and distant. "I'm serious. And . . . I hope you don't leave. I really want to be with you. But if you're staying because you feel sorry for me, you should go." Deirdre said these last words softly, but she felt their trueness. It would be okay. If SJ wanted out, Deirdre could let her go.

PART THREE

NOVEMBER

CHAPTER ONE

NOVEMBER LOOMED OUTSIDE the window, gray and overcast. This was the depressing part of autumn that even in New England made you think about Paul Verlaine and his long sobs on the violin. SJ almost knew the poem "Autumn Song" by heart; Deirdre taught it to her ninth-graders every year and so ended up reciting it at home. Every year she said, "Did anyone ever really feel like that? How could Verlaine be so pessimistic about fall?" And every year SJ reminded her that Verlaine was clearly talking about November and not September or October.

This year, November stretched particularly long and cold and drab. Not much to look forward to—and SJ hadn't yet been to visit Mickey as she had promised. She couldn't put it off any longer, so she pulled on a thick turtleneck sweater and gathered her hair into a ponytail.

"Hey, hon?" she yelled from the bedroom.

No answer.

SJ peered into the dining room. Beyond the archway, in the living room, Deirdre slept curled on the couch. SJ stuck her wallet in her back jeans pocket and grabbed her keys from the top of the bureau. She threw on a down vest and unlocked the front door.

Deirdre rubbed her eyes. "SJ?"

"Be right back. Just got to run this errand." And SJ slipped out.

The jail parking lot was almost full. With holidays approaching, visitors became more frequent. SJ stood in line before the metal detector. She put her wallet and the down vest on the conveyor belt.

"Name?" the guard with the clipboard asked her. He searched on the visitors list and checked her off.

"We're full up right now. Next group," the guard told her and pointed to an empty hard plastic chair in the hallway, the last one in a row of people. SJ was aware of how few white people there were. She pulled the chair out from the wall.

"Excuse me," she said to the older African American man in the next chair. He stared straight ahead and said nothing.

SJ hadn't thought about Mickey much in the last couple weeks, not since Deirdre had been arrested. Promising his mother she would come had been a mistake. It seemed years had passed between September and now. She had been another person then, and today she felt like a newer, smarter version of herself. She wanted to get up and leave, bolt without saying anything. She glanced at the man next to her, noticed his white eyebrows, thick and unruly. He clutched a cap in his hands. She wanted to ask him whom he was here to visit. So many people. Could it be that all of them were visiting someone who had committed a crime? Were there that many criminals?

Two guards accompanied Mickey and led him to the chair opposite SJ behind the glass. This was a different visiting room than the one where she had met Deirdre. He picked up the phone. "Hey," he said. He slouched in the chair, all knees and arms and torso, ankles shackled.

"You look tired," SJ said. The jumpsuit was baggy; his face looked more angular, sharper. She thought about Detective Mahoney's words, how they had *strong evidence* against him. "Your mother said you wanted to see me?"

Mickey shifted in his chair. "This hellhole," he said. He sounded like a little kid, plaintive and suddenly earnest.

"I'm . . . I don't think we're supposed to discuss anything."

Mickey leaned forward, his jaw tensed. "You gotta help me."

A guard peered over from across the room.

"Mickey . . ." She couldn't bring herself to ask the question, half afraid of the answer, half certain suddenly that she already knew, certain in any case that they couldn't discuss it here. She just looked at him. What could she say?

Mickey's eyes clouded over, and for a second SJ thought he might cry. "Jesus," he said. "You gotta talk to my lawyer. He'll listen. You're . . ." He looked SJ up and down. "Christ, you gotta talk with him."

"What did your lawyer say?"

Mickey, standing there in his garage: "*What if he wanted it?*"

"It shouldn't matter if he believes me, right? Lawyers, that's their job, to defend you no matter what," Mickey said.

The visiting room was overheated. SJ pushed up the sleeves of her sweater. The room buzzed with conversations, an occasional laugh. She noticed the man with the white eyebrows talking to a young man who might be his son. The man looked so defeated; the son, his dark eyes hard, mouth set. SJ thought of Mrs. Gilberto, the way hope alternated with despair, so you could see it in her eyes, hear the hope slip into her voice then cut out. She saw again the way she had clasped her purse, keeping the hope bottled up, the pride too, but wanting, wanting more than she ever wanted anything before to release them and so convince SJ that her son was someone worth saving, still worth loving.

"You gotta believe me. I . . . didn't . . ."

"Mickey, not here." She put up her hand. "Stop. It's okay."

"You'll talk to him then?" He leaned forward. Cuffs clinked.

SJ felt the damp hair at the nape of her neck. She couldn't promise more than she was able to do. "Listen. I—I just don't think there's anything I can do . . . I'm not sure I'm the one . . ." Her voice drifted off. It was so strange, this speaking on a phone to someone just in front of you.

"Just talk to him. Just—that's it. " He rubbed his hands on his thighs. "I need you to do this." His voice, carefully monitored, calibrated. SJ heard it then, the insincerity, the tone a subtle shift, a deliberate ploy to get SJ to do what he wanted. *What if he wanted it?* Mickey shook his head. "This is some crazy shit," he muttered, the tone gone now, his own voice back.

SJ saw herself then, showing up at Mickey's garage, remembered the drive that night, the horrible kiss.

Mr. Freeman.

"Your mother," SJ said, one arm folded in front, "she's pretty worried about you."

Mickey's gaze shifted again. She couldn't detect whether there was any honesty or sincerity there. He shrugged. "She's a tough lady. She's been through worse."

Worse. What could be worse than your son in prison for rape and murder? SJ tried to swallow. She had been so certain of his innocence. And she had promised his mother. But what could she do, really? How had she let things go this far?

He smiled crookedly. A smirk. "You should ask your girlfriend what it's like in this hellhole. Ask her how they treat people like us."

People like us. SJ had to fight the urge to leap and say, *She's not like you! She's nothing like you!* She blinked. It was so hot. She wiped at her brow.

Mickey laughed a mean little laugh. "Even me, stuck in solitary, I heard about her. She tell you I saw her? Talked with her?"

SJ felt the heat rise to her face. Deirdre hadn't said much about her time in jail—a few comments about the other women, several prostitutes and others, caught dealing or using drugs. She hadn't said anything about Mickey. And SJ had asked few questions. They both seemed to think that the less they talked about it, the less real it might seem. She stammered, "Look, I'm sorry. I've got to go."

It was a fatal mistake to bring Deirdre into the discussion. Mickey gestured with his cuffed hands. "Yeah you know, what the fuck?" he said. "And thanks for nothing."

"I'm sorry," SJ said again. "I . . . I'm sorry." She hung up and hurried out of the room.

In the car, SJ fumbled with her keys and let the tears fall. How could she have thought him innocent? She felt dirty suddenly, the kiss a sordid memory, a terrible mistake that would forever tie her to Mickey Gilberto, child molester and murderer. She started the car, the tears a torrent now. She rubbed the snot from her nose on her sweater sleeve and turned off the radio so she could focus on the drive. What had Deirdre said—*If you're staying but you want to leave, you can*? Was that it? It should be clear, shouldn't it, whether or not she wanted to stay or leave, but it seemed the murkiest thing to her. Her brain was like a mud puddle. She thought she had genuinely cared about Mickey. She thought she had wanted to help him. And now her muddled brain seemed to be telling her something else; it seemed to be saying that maybe—she hated to admit it—but maybe her initial impulse to help Mickey had been about something else altogether. She remembered him walking into the library, looking for literacy classes, and the way she eagerly agreed to teach him. She remembered feeling him next to her, the faint smell of his cologne and watching the way he concentrated on forming each word. In those moments, she had felt sure that she understood him. She'd felt committed to helping him learn to read.

SJ realized with a kind of sickening thud in her gut that maybe helping Mickey had been really about her. Maybe, she was starting to realize, she had been more jealous of Deirdre than she had been willing to admit. She had scoffed at Deirdre's need and desire to be wanted, but wasn't she guilty of the very same thing?

It was a terrible realization. You see yourself as one kind of person, the kind of person who would never use someone, who would never hurt someone willingly, and then you do it. How do you become the kind of person you profess not to like? It wasn't as though SJ saw herself as someone with hard-core fixed ideals about what she would and wouldn't do, but to admit to yourself that your motivations aren't pure and that in fact you might do things you never thought you would do—that was tough. To say it out loud would be a whole different ball game. SJ put her car in drive.

CHAPTER TWO

DEIRDRE SAT CURLED ON THE COUCH and sipped her coffee, watching the sky darken into a steely shade of gray. Snow in November was not a long shot; Bradley had endured an occasional pre-December storms and even enjoyed occasional white Christmases, a phenomenon Deirdre remembered as being more frequent during her childhood in Gloucester. How she and Paul had loved snow days, those gifts of pressure-free time—nothing to prepare for the next morning, a clean slate of a day. When she was younger, Deirdre loved most to spend a snow day outside with Paul, sledding on the hill next to the library, each of them pulling a Flexible Flyer first down the block to the park and then up to the hill's summit where they would lie on their stomachs and careen down, the snow sticking to their eyelashes and cheeks. How many times would they fly to the bottom and trudge back up? They lost track, spent entire days like that outside, their wool mittens soggy and heavy with ice by evening, toes frozen in their boots so when they finally returned home and walked inside, hot chocolate with marshmallow fluff waiting for them, and they removed their damp socks, their reddened toes would ache in the warmth and their cheeks would flush a happy crimson. As she got older, though, Deirdre preferred spending a snow day inside, reading a book that wasn't required for anything. Or baking. Even as an adult, on those rare occasions that Brandywine cancelled school, Deirdre still had the urge to make chocolate chip cookies. A simple reflex: snow day equals chocolate chip cookies.

But today she didn't feel like any of that. She sat in her flannel pajamas and sipped lukewarm coffee and stared into the terror of empty hours to fill. Several voice messages clogged the answering machine—a few from her mother, two from Paul though those sounded perfunctory, as if he had been cajoled into calling, even one from Evelyn Moore—but Deirdre couldn't bring herself to call back. She wanted their love and concern and then couldn't bear their sympathy. It was all too weird. Nothing yet from Forest. A few days earlier, SJ and Deirdre had driven by Brandywine and the building had seemed sad, broken, maybe even a bit bedraggled, a place with its own secrets and not the lovely, elegant private school everyone thought it was.

"It looks kind of ugly, doesn't it?" Deirdre had said. She'd been surprised to see Brandywine in that light. She had been so excited when she was hired, loved being thought of as a "Brandywine teacher." She had felt chosen, one of the select few, as if she had joined a sorority or an exclusive country club, forgetting of course that she was an employee and not a member. Still. Working at Brandywine had its privileges, among them knowledge of certain events about town, face recognition by many of the movers and shakers. And now, certainly, she was known by everyone, but not for the reasons she would have liked.

Deirdre was startled by the phone ringing. Caller ID revealed a number she didn't recognize. She let it go to the answering machine.

"Hello? Ms. Murphy?" Deirdre didn't recognize the voice. It hesitated. A throat clearing. "Yvette Delambre calling."

Instinctively, Deirdre straightened up, sat with her feet

firmly on the floor, and picked up the phone. *"Bonjour, madame,"* she said. "I'm sorry, I was just—I was in the other room." She tightened her grip on the phone.

"I'm calling," Madame Delambre said, "about the students. I hope it's okay. I don't want to bother you, but I'm having quite a struggle and I'm hoping you can help."

Deirdre felt tongue-tied, stuck, as if she were face-to-face with a movie star and suddenly struck dumb.

"Ms. Murphy? You are still there?"

"Yes." Deirdre swallowed.

"I thought, if it might be amenable to you, we might meet to discuss this? Would it work for you to meet me?"

"Um . . . sure. Yes, I can meet."

"Wonderful. Are you free today? How about the library at one o'clock? The main branch. Does that suit you?"

Deirdre glanced at the clock. "Sure, I'll meet you then."

Madame Delambre. All French teachers knew of her; she had written the very textbooks Deirdre had been teaching from. Deirdre had first heard of Madame Delambre when she was a graduate student, learning grammar from the woman's legendary tome. Deirdre had been embarrassed when she took the placement test and was required to take French Grammar I. How was it that she had spent time in France, had become, according to Agnès, "a beautiful French speaker," but still needed French Grammar I? Still, the class had been helpful—fun even—and Deirdre recounted the story to her students who struggled and thought themselves further behind than everyone else. "I had to take Grammar I when I was in graduate school," she would tell the girls. "And here I am now, your teacher." She would see the girls' faces change a little, hope in their expressions.

Deirdre had even met Madame Delambre once, though she was certain the woman would not remember it. At one of the national foreign language teaching conferences, Deirdre had been selected along with a half dozen other teachers to meet with a publishing company that was interested in hearing directly from teachers what they would most like in a textbook. It was, as it turned out, Madame Delambre's company and she, the celebrated author, was present at the meeting. It had all felt very luxurious and important. The teachers had been given a complimentary breakfast, rich, buttery croissants, cappuccinos, delicious fruit, jams, and *pains au chocolat*. Deirdre had not offered many tangible ideas—she wasn't big on textbooks to begin with—though she did say that what she wanted most in a French textbook were simple, clear instructions. Half the time, she had said, her students couldn't understand what was being asked of them. But when she offered this piece of advice, the others around the table either looked at her as if they didn't know what she was talking about, or they glanced away, embarrassed that she had been included in the group and had offered such a silly suggestion. Madame Delambre had not reacted at all. She had continued sipping her cappuccino, her steely gaze unflinching. Deirdre had left that meeting wondering why she'd been invited.

On another occasion, a local conference, Deirdre had the opportunity to hear Madame Delambre speak about foreign language education. The largest conference room had been secured for what was a sellout crowd, teachers arriving early to save seats for their colleagues, all the best chairs taken a good thirty minutes before the talk was scheduled to begin. Deirdre had managed to get herself a decent place, on the aisle, not too far from the front. She had sat ready to absorb every word from this acclaimed author and teacher, the *doyenne* of French language education. All around the room, everyone sat poised with pens and empty legal pads and notebooks. And when she was introduced and walked out onto the stage, all flowing and graceful in her gauzy skirt and scarf, a kind of hush came over the room. The entire conference room held its breath. Here, at last, the magic words they all needed, the recipe they could follow to make them better French teachers. They felt certain that they were about to hear the secrets of the master herself, She Who Writes the Venerated Textbooks. Madame Delambre would tell them what they needed to know. They were giddy with expectation, hardly able to wait, thrilled to be able to return to each of their schools as new and better teachers, able at last to turn their students on to the beauty of French—but more than that: able to help each student speak French fluently, communicate flawlessly, finally get that accent, use the subjunctive.

Except, of course, that didn't happen.

Madame Delambre had been, Deirdre admitted to herself, rather ordinary. She had nothing to say, not to Deirdre at least, who had sat stunned as the students around her scribbled things on their legal pads and in their notebooks. But Madame Delambre wasn't saying anything new at all, nothing revolutionary, nothing that was going to change much of anything. Deirdre had wondered if she hadn't been listening carefully enough, if she hadn't truly understood the words coming out of Madame Delambre's mouth. There must be some deep, complicated meaning Deirdre was missing. She glanced at the man sitting next to her. He was writing furiously, and Deirdre peeked at his notes. No, she understood—or at least she and this man understood the same things. Then why was he writing them down? Wasn't it obvious how to engage your students?

Still, after leaving the conference, Deirdre had thought Madame Delambre must have had an off day. Clearly, as someone so sought after, an expert in the field, she must have been ill prepared for that particular presentation. But now, here she was calling Deirdre for advice about working with the students.

Deirdre arrived early. She hadn't thought quickly enough to suggest a different meeting place. She parked along the side and entered the main door, checking the smaller meeting rooms to see if Madame Delambre had arrived first. She hadn't. Deirdre settled herself into one of the three small rooms, glad at least that Madame Delambre had suggested the main library and not SJ's branch, though she was more likely to run into patrons she knew here. She pulled her chair to the side of the table so she could see Madame Delambre when she arrived and shield herself from the view of others. She hoped she looked professional enough, black turtleneck sweater, black-and-white pants, black shoes. Professional and conservative—after all, what must Madame Delambre think of her? What kind of stories had she been hearing?

"Oh, Ms. Murphy, I do hope I haven't been keeping you!" Madame Delambre flew into the room, a burst of color. She unwrapped a purple cape to reveal a thick lavender scarf draped over a floral sweater. "I am so grateful that you agreed to meet me." Her cheeks were flushed, her eyelashes dark with thick mascara.

"Of course. Absolutely. But please, call me Deirdre. It's disconcerting enough to have the students call me Ms. Murphy. I still wonder sometimes who that is!" She gave a nervous laugh.

Madame Delambre squinted and gave Deirdre a puzzled look. "Well," she said after a few seconds, then pulled out a chair and settled into it, straightening her long blue woolen skirt and crossing her ankles. Deirdre noted the tie-up leather boots. Madame Delambre was, if nothing else, the picture of elegance. She had to be in her sixties at least. Or more, it was hard to tell.

"It is so nice to finally meet you," Deirdre said.

"Well," Madame Delambre said again with a sweeping motion. "We have met before, haven't we? At the big conference," she added when Deirdre hesitated. "That awfully dreadful publishing session." She smiled.

"I . . . I didn't know if you'd remember."

"You were the only sensible one there, weren't you?" Madame Delambre spoke in that British way of making everything into a rhetorical question.

Deirdre laughed. "I think you're flattering me; I was the one who said nothing of any value!"

Madame Delambre spread her hands on the table. A topaz on one finger, chunky gold bands on two others. Her nails were manicured and bright pink. "On the contrary. What I recall is that the others were merely trying to impress my simpleminded editors or *me*, either of which was silly judgment on their part." She waved her hands as if to say, *Let's be done with this.* "Anyway, doesn't matter. Here we are with a problem to solve."

Deirdre couldn't quite believe what she was hearing. Madame Delambre remembered her? She had come across as *sensible*?

"Morgan Abernathy . . ."

"I'm sorry. What did you say?"

"You are not listening. You know," Madame Delambre removed the lavender-rimmed glasses she had put on while Deirdre wasn't paying attention, "I took this job because of you. I thought, *If that sensible woman taught these students, it will be easy.* I was sure they would be good students . . ."

Here it comes, Deirdre thought. *The inevitable slam.* She prepared herself.

Madame Delambre looked straight at Deirdre, her blue eyes alert and focused. "I was right," she said. "They *are* good students. And I can tell you have taught them well. They are disciplined and they think well. But . . ."

Deirdre tensed. Beneath the table, she folded her hands, fingers pressed, thumbs locked, knuckles whitening.

"I can tell there is something I am missing. There is no liveliness. I think they miss you too much." She smiled again. "You obviously know them. I thought perhaps you might give me insight that could help me reach them better?"

Deirdre felt herself blushing. She had not expected praise from this woman. "Does Martin Loring know you are meeting with me?" She unclasped her hands and stretched her fingers.

"Oh, that man!" Madame Delambre made a dismissive gesture. Her bangle bracelets jingled.

"Well, it's just . . . I hope we're not breaking any laws or anything."

"Laws?" Madame Delambre raised her eyebrows.

"I mean, I'm not sure if I'm supposed to be speaking to anyone at school." Deirdre fidgeted.

"Oh for heaven's sake, why not? Who better to help me with the girls?"

Deirdre gave a half laugh. "I'm sure some people would think anyone but me! Anyway, as you said, we're here now, and I'd love to help if I can. Tell me more."

Madame Delambre launched into a detailed description of Deirdre's classes, the older girls in particular. "That Morgan Abernathy is just terribly belligerent." And the way that the others, dutiful though they were, seemed to merely go through the motions, answering by rote, not displaying any enthusiasm at all. "But," Madame Delambre continued, "I don't think this has been your experience with them, am I right?"

Deirdre had to admit that no, it hadn't been her experience at all. The girls were normally very engaged and interested, eager to participate and to demonstrate their ability. "Morgan can be tough," Deirdre admitted. "I wouldn't say belligerent, but she does have her moments." She wanted to ask about Anna Worthington but she didn't dare, too afraid of how such a question might be taken.

They talked for close to two hours. Madame Delambre asked Deirdre for her ideas about how to teach various structures—the *si* clauses and compound tenses. "But what sort of exercises do you give them?" she asked at one point. "What makes the girls respond?"

Deirdre shifted uncomfortably on the wooden chair. "Exercises are good," she said, "but I try to make everything into a scenario, you know, as if it's happening in real life . . . I mean, as much as I can," she added when she noticed Madame Delambre frown a bit. "Well, I mean with *si* clauses it's obvious, right? *If it rains this weekend, what will you do? If you miss the bus, how will you get to school?* Stuff like that. And I give them pair exercises . . ." Deirdre realized she had so much to say and had missed talking about her students, her classes. She could go on and on, coming up with ideas, various scenarios, especially once she realized that maybe it *wasn't* obvious. But isn't that what all French teachers did? Had Madame Delambre retired so long ago from teaching that she couldn't remember how to bring language alive for her students?

As they were gathering their things to leave, Madame Delambre stopped wrapping her scarf for a moment. "I appreciate everything you have told me," she said, "but I am not certain I will be able to do as you suggest. Your success is because of *you*. Even listening to your ideas, I could feel your energy and excitement. That is what makes you such a successful teacher for these girls. I am not certain I have the same enthusiasm."

"I find that hard to believe." Deirdre stopped buttoning her jacket. "You're . . . you're legendary!"

Madame Delambre scoffed. "I'm old. You have a gift." She pointed her finger at Deirdre. "We need to find a way to ensure you can use it." She finished wrapping her scarf and fastened her cape. "To teach is your calling. You must not stop."

"I'm not sure I have much choice." They hadn't talked at all about Deirdre's legal troubles. Madame Delambre had not once mentioned Anna Worthington or referenced the allegations. "Clearly you know what I'm going through right now. I don't think any school is about to hire me."

Madame Delambre nodded somberly. "I suppose this is true. Yes, of course."

"I appreciate your kind words, though." Deirdre smiled and started to walk out.

But Madame Delambre grabbed her arm. "Forgive me, it might not be my place, but I do not understand. You are a great teacher. Is it not a waste for this school to let you go? You are not a risk. What a ridiculous notion. Americans," she muttered and shook her head. "Such talent, it is a shame." She patted Deirdre's arm and let go.

Deirdre didn't say anything. She wanted to hug this woman. Here was a formidable French woman, a teaching legend, saying the very words she had longed to hear.

"If I can be of help," Madame Delambre said as they exited the library, "please, do not hesitate to call. You have my number. And, if I may, might I contact you again for other ideas?"

Deirdre nodded, but her eye caught a flier on the community bulletin board. *SPECIAL TOWN MEETING*. Her knees grew weak. *SAVE OUR CHILDREN*. Then she read her own name. The meeting was because of her. And it was about to start.

CHAPTER THREE

CARS PARKED EVERYWHERE, in spaces that weren't really spaces. Here at an angle. There alongside the curve. A crowd pulsing at the door, trying to push its way in. Deirdre imagined a lynch mob, what one might have been like, the anger a living, unstoppable creature. She hesitated and considered hopping back in the car, pulling out, and heading home. Instead, from the backseat of her car, she grabbed a hoodie and put it on, yanked the hood up over her head.

A chilly wind blew through the gray November sky. It was dark, those late-fall afternoons that already felt like evening. The crowd at the door moved and shifted. Deirdre hurried along the curb, quick steps toward the building. She had to get inside. She wanted to hear everything, see who was running the show, though she had a pretty good idea. She spotted Forest's car. What was he doing here? And there was Beth Ann's car too. Deirdre's face burned. Was everyone in town at this meeting?

Deirdre froze on the fringe of the group and strained to hear. On the lamppost two fliers, their corners flapping in the wind—Leo Rivera's face, even now, after he'd been found, after he'd been buried; and another, with big red letters, announcing this very meeting. The truth rose up in Deirdre, a sharp stinging pain. That's why she was here, that's why the meeting had been called in the first place.

This was all because of Leo Rivera and what had happened to him. Bile burned at the back of her throat. She stuffed her hands in her pockets to keep them from shaking. Mickey Gilberto was still casting a dark shadow over her life. She pushed her way inside.

The place was packed. It was hard to imagine that so many people cared whether or not Deirdre kept her teaching job, hard to imagine that this many people thought gay teachers should be fired. Here in Bradley, Massachusetts, where people were supposed to be tolerant. Liberal even. Deirdre looked around. The man next to her wore a thick corduroy jacket and jeans. She wouldn't have guessed he was a hateful person. The women behind her were older, gray-haired, and housewife-looking. Where the hell was Forest? And what was he thinking about all this?

A gavel on the podium. Deirdre stood on her tiptoes, craned to see the stage. There was no mistaking the voice.

"I'm so grateful to you all for showing up," Frances Worthington crooned. "This is an important time for our town and we need to take control. We need to get things back to the way they should be. Like many of you, I've spent my whole life in Bradley. I'm proud to live in this town and call it my home."

She sounded like a politician making a stump speech. People clapped wildly.

"You and I both know that there are gay people in our town—we all have gay neighbors, some of us have gay friends . . ."

No beating around the bush, Deirdre would give her that. She was admitting outright what this was all about.

"And this isn't about someone's right to be gay. And this is most certainly not about being homophobic. But we have to draw the line somewhere." Heads nodding. Susan and Murray stood near the front of the crowd, looking up at

Frances Worthington, their faces unreadable. Deirdre pulled her hood closer over her face. "And when children's lives are at risk, it is our responsibility to take action." Applause. "Our community has been hit with an unspeakable tragedy . . ." Frances Worthington paused, acting as if she were gaining her composure. Deirdre felt the heat rising, her throat constricting. Frances Worthington could not have cared less about Leo Rivera until now when it suited her cause. She turned from the microphone. From behind the podium, Mr. and Mrs. Rivera stepped forward. Leo Rivera had his father's eyes, you could see that immediately. Mr. Rivera had that brave face you see on television when people are making appeals for their children's safe return. Mrs. Rivera looked empty and defeated, ravaged. Mr. Rivera approached the microphone and faced the crowd.

"My wife and I appreciate your concern." He put his arm around Mrs. Rivera. "We . . . we are wanting to help make sure no one else suffers like our little Leo." At the mention of his name, Mrs. Rivera covered her mouth with her hand. Her husband pulled her tighter. "These . . . these . . ." He seemed to be searching for words. Frances Worthington took a step closer to him and placed a hand on his shoulder. "Homosexuals are not safe for our children." His thick Brazilian accent made him seem all the more sincere. Mrs. Rivera nodded and wiped her eyes. Some more nods from people in the crowd. Polite applause.

"Thank you," Frances Worthington said, smiling at Mr. Rivera. She patted his shoulder and looked to the crowd. "None of us can know what these good people are going through. We are all so sorry for your loss." She took Mrs. Rivera's hand in her own. The room fell silent, respectful. She peered at them both with sincerity and turned back to the mic. "Let's thank the Riveras for coming tonight and making this difficult public appearance." More applause. A few women wiped away tears. "I don't know about you, but I want my children to grow up in a safe neighborhood, just like it was when I was growing up."

A man near Deirdre pumped his fist. "Yeah!" he yelled.

"I want them to be able to play outside and not worry. But I know," she continued, sensing the crowd's nervousness, "we can't always control the world outside our homes. And yet . . ." She paused and scanned the crowd. "And yet, don't we all expect to send our children to school and have them be safe?"

Deirdre's mouth went dry.

Frances Worthington's voice gained strength. "Schools are no place for homosexuals. When something as horrible as what happened to Leo Rivera can happen in . . . our streets . . ." Deirdre heard the hesitation before she said *our*; there was no way that Frances Worthington thought of her street as the same street the Riveras lived on. "We all take pause. And certainly we like to think our schools are safe places for our children, don't we?"

The fist-pumper shouted, "Right on!" Much applause in the room. Deirdre was getting hot under the hoodie. She hesitated to take it off. Out of the corner of her eye, she spotted Forest, arms folded, in the middle of the crowd. About fifty people blocked her way to him, and she wasn't at all sure she wanted to push by so many potential enemies.

"So I'd like to propose a referendum. We must tell our politicians that we won't take it anymore. We won't stand for it!" Frances Worthington was yelling into the microphone, eyes wild. She looked possessed.

Deirdre tried to catch Forest's attention. She stood on tiptoes and waved her hand. But he wasn't looking her way. He kept his focus on Frances Worthington. The rest of the crowd stood watching too, a thrum of energy waiting to be released. Were any of them supporters? Deirdre couldn't tell.

Now Frances Worthington was saying something about Brandywine Academy, about its superior education, and Deirdre could feel uneasiness grow in the crowd. Murmurs and shifting feet, scuffing. *She isn't reading her audience. She'll think they all agree with her.* Even from this distance, Deirdre could see Forest's face flush red.

"Hey, we got kids in public school!" the fist-pumper said.

"Yeah," another man chimed in. "We can't just fire our teachers."

Frances Worthington held up her hands. "Now wait a minute—" that charming smile, gracious, "of course I know it's different in public school. That's why we need to make this a law. We need this thing settled once and for all. We need to be sure that our children are safe—don't we? Isn't that why we're all here?" She surveyed the crowd, arms spread wide, and that smile. "If we're not careful, our children will end up like poor little Leo Rivera."

At the sound of the boy's name, the crowd murmuring grew to a loud swell. Deirdre saw Forest shaking his head, arms still folded. "My own daughter—" and Frances Worthington's face grew flushed, her voice shook. "My own daughter was molested by a teacher she professed to care for, a well-respected teacher, but unbeknownst to us, this teacher was a lesbian . . ."

Deirdre held her breath, felt her heart pound in her chest and throat.

"And this teacher . . . this predator . . ." Frances Worthington practically spit out the words, "she took advantage of my daughter. She preyed on my daughter."

"Her daughter was molested? How horrible," Deirdre heard one woman whisper to another.

"Can you imagine? A lesbian teaching in an all-girls school? That's sick," the woman's friend said.

Deirdre felt her face blaze, her hands trembling. But something pushed her forward. "Excuse me," she said, elbowing through the crowd. "I'm sorry. I need to get through."

Frances Worthington went on: "Homosexuals should not be allowed around children. If they want to be gay, that's their right. But we cannot let them around children. It just isn't safe. I can't undo the damage done to my daughter—"

"Your daughter," Deirdre interrupted, close to the stage now. Her hands were balled into fists in the pocket of her hoodie.

"Excuse me?" Frances Worthington peered into the crowd.

"Your daughter," Deirdre repeated, more loudly, "your daughter wasn't molested!" She turned and faced the crowd, hands and legs shaking. "None of what she is saying is true." She pointed at Frances Worthington. Everyone stood still, watching, a few slack-jawed, some frowning. Deirdre saw Forest shaking his head. *Don't say it*, he seemed to be telling her, but she couldn't help herself. "That woman is what's wrong with Brandywine. Anyone can tell you that." She looked at Susan and Murray, who watched her, stony faced. She scanned the crowd. "Do you all believe the nonsense she is telling you?" There, in the back of the crowd, SJ, her expression one of surprise. Madame Delambre, nodding, a smile forming. Deirdre took the mic, gripped it firmly. "What happened to Leo Rivera had nothing to do with . . . Mickey Gilberto isn't gay. He's a pedophile . . ."

"Exactly!" a man yelled from the crowd. "A perv!"

Deirdre felt her knees shake. She swallowed.

Frances Worthington tried to grab the mic. Deirdre yanked it away. "You need to leave," Frances said, her voice steely.

"So you can spread more lies?" Deirdre didn't care who

was watching. She didn't care that there was a roomful of people. She turned back to the mic. "She is lying to you . . ." From the corner of her eye, she caught sight of the Riveras. She turned, held the mic away. "I'm sorry about Leo," Deirdre said. "But it wasn't a gay person who killed him."

Behind Deirdre the crowd was no longer silent. People shouted at her to leave; they yelled at each other—"She has the right" or "She doesn't have the right" or "Perv" or "Crazy." The volume rose, filled the room with the people's anger. Deirdre was half-conscious of it all, half-conscious that she had caused a scene, that everything was out of control. She glanced about—SJ trying to make her way through the crowd; and Forest, still standing, not moving. She waved her arms at him. "Forest!" she yelled. "Hey!" He looked as if he might say something or move, but he did neither. Around him, people jostled and gestured and pointed at Deirdre. In the back of the room, a real fight broke out, shoves and then fists. People scrambled to get out of the way, pushed against the others, blocking them in. "Hey!" "Move!" It was a barroom brawl.

Deirdre started to speak into the mic again, but stopped.

"Deird!" SJ was trying to get her attention. "Deird, c'mon! We need to get out of here!"

Deirdre blinked. She put down the mic—where was Frances Worthington? The Riveras still stood clutching each other. But when Deirdre turned to join SJ, there was Frances and the security guard.

THE GIRLS: PART III

The girls missed their favorite teacher. When she was at school, they had vied for her attention, longed for her words, her input. They feigned disinterest sometimes, but they always knew whether or not she was paying attention.

In class, they had craved being near her. It was an addiction like any other. They couldn't get enough, couldn't go one day without being near. On the days they didn't have French, they used to find reasons to stop by. They would ask questions about upcoming assignments, or an assembly. Mondays provided the most excuses, when they could ask about movies she might have seen over the weekend. In the spring, they all became Red Sox fans, learned enough names to throw them out casually.

The girls wouldn't have acknowledged this need to be around Ms. Murphy. In all innocence, they would have said that she made them feel important, made them feel heard. They saw in her a way to be a woman, someone other than their mothers, with whom they had complicated relationships. Ms. Murphy, they might say, was so smart. She was so interesting. She expanded their world tenfold. And when they went home, they brought her with them, filled the dinner conversation with things they had learned from her. *Did you know . . . ?* they would say to their mothers and fathers. *Have you ever heard . . . ?*

Their relationship with their French teacher was just short of all-out adoration. Some of them might even admit to a crush. It was common, they had heard, to fall in love with your teachers. *Even another girl?* Well, yes, they would say. It happens at all-girls schools. It wasn't as if some of them weren't equally in love with Mr. Macomber. They dreamed about him at night, and on sleepovers; the younger ones would sometimes prank call his house—his number was listed—and hang up when he answered. Almost every teacher had his or her fans and the girls all imagined that the admiration worked both ways. They knew each teacher's favorites—the girls who were asked to take attendance, to run errands to the office, or to fetch something the teacher had left in her car. They knew who was likely to get the extra-detailed letter of recommendation or who might be asked to run the literary magazine or head up the chess club. None of these things came as a surprise to any of the girls.

It is a little-discussed fact of high school life that both students and teachers have favorites and are often quite open about their preferences. These girls hated that their favorite had suddenly become an un-favorite of the administration, but what did the administration know about teaching anyway? Not much, the girls were convinced. The girls were surrounded by bad teachers; even at Brandywine, they had their fair share—teachers who did little more than offer worksheets to complete or homework in the book to be graded the next day in class. It was unimaginative, the girls complained to each other. And why didn't they just get fired? Now, here was Ms. Murphy, the best teacher they had, and she was gone. Now, here was Anna Worthington getting all the attention. They knew Anna had been a favorite. And truthfully, while they could tolerate it when Ms. Murphy was still their teacher, they had a harder time accepting it now.

C HAPTER FOUR

AND THEN CAME THE REST of the accusations. Hilary first, followed by Lydia. What were they trying to do? It didn't make any sense. Even Martin Loring seemed to think there was something odd about the newest accusations, something trumped-up and false.

Beth Ann stopped by a few days after the town meeting. "I heard about the meeting," she said when Deirdre let her in. "Sounds like you made quite an impression."

"Yeah?" Deirdre said, pleased. "She was going to let them all think that I molested Anna. I just couldn't let that go." They sat in the living room sipping Blue Moon lattes.

Beth Ann took a deep breath. "There's no way to say this . . ." And she blurted it out, about how Hilary and then Lydia came forward, each with a story of how Deirdre had kissed them, and how, in Lydia's case, Deirdre had in fact kissed her multiple times. "But," Beth Ann added, "Martin Loring is suspicious. Sounds like too much, even to him."

"Oh God." Deirdre sat on the edge of the couch. "But that's still crazy. What are they thinking? God." She shook her head.

Beth Ann removed the cover on her latte. "Ellie says, *Mom, they're attention whores.*" She sipped her latte.

Deirdre shook her head again. "I don't know. Not those girls."

"Ellie says they're all like that."

"I know what she means, but they're attention whores in a different way. This . . . this lying and making stuff up, that's not them." She stuck her paper cup on the coffee table. "That's not the Hilary and Lydia I know." She thought of how the girls behaved in class, how they wanted to please and impress her. "They like to show off what they know—they definitely want me to notice their hard work—but this . . . this just seems so unlike them."

Beth Ann didn't seem too fazed. "Mmm." She swallowed a gulp of coffee.

"It's too mean-spirited. They would know what it would mean for me, how dangerous it could be."

"Maybe they're doing it for you." Beth Ann walked to the kitchen. She tossed her cup in the trash.

Deirdre twisted the cardboard sleeve around her paper cup. "But still. It's my life they're fooling around with."

"Maybe that's the point. Maybe they're trying to get Martin Loring to see how ridiculous this whole thing is—see that if their accusations are ludicrous, then why couldn't Anna's be ludicrous?"

"You think?"

Beth Ann smiled. "Honestly, I don't know. But it sounds good, doesn't it?"

Deirdre wanted to believe it. She wanted to think that Hilary and Lydia were coming to her aide, that all the girls were secretly behind her, and that these new accusations were their form of protest, a modern-day *Lysistrata*, girls banding together to achieve a common goal. She might truly believe it if she could trust her instincts again, if she could remember how the real world functioned and not this crazy fake world she had been thrown into.

The door opened and shut. "Hey, hon!" The smell of outside wafted in, fresh and bright.

"We're in here," Deirdre called.

SJ stepped into the living room, cheeks pink from the cold. She kissed Deirdre on the cheek.

"You're home early," Deirdre said. She felt herself blushing, as if she had been caught doing something wrong. "I don't think you've met Beth Ann yet, Ellie's mom? You've heard me talk about Ellie."

"Of course." SJ and Beth Ann shook hands.

"So Beth Ann had some news—"

SJ stopped.

"She was telling me there are more accusations." Deirdre twisted around from where she sat on the couch.

"What?" SJ turned pale.

Beth Ann strode across the room and picked up her purse. "No one is taking them seriously. Not even Martin." She wrapped a black scarf around her neck. "Listen, I've got to go." To Deirdre she said, "Keep me posted, will you? And I'll do the same."

As Beth Ann left the house, SJ took off her jacket and walked to the bedroom. "Tell me about these accusations. Shouldn't we be worried?"

"I *am* worried. A little. But Beth Ann says that seriously, Martin thinks they're ridiculous—"

"But why make them in the first place? What's that about?" SJ interrupted as she emerged from the bedroom.

"I thought the same thing."

"What if they get on the stand and say that you've . . . What are they saying exactly?"

"I don't know—that I kissed them, I think? Multiple times, even! It's ridiculous when I think about it."

"Well, let's hope a jury or a judge thinks so too."

"The thing is, don't those girls know they're playing with my life here?"

"Oh good. I'm glad to see you are taking this seriously!" SJ flopped onto the couch.

"Of course I am, but . . . I just don't even know what to think anymore. Or what to do." She snuggled up against SJ. "For now, let's just not think about it, okay? Maybe it'll all go away."

"A questionable defense strategy, but for now . . ." SJ kissed Deirdre on the top of her head.

Beth Ann's visit, unexpected, had jolted Deirdre, not altogether unwelcome but not altogether pleasant, either. Her days had become small, just her and SJ and what little routine they had together. In the weeks since her arrest, her old life—and that's how Deirdre thought of it—her old life already seemed remote. Three months into the school year, the seniors would be freaking out about college applications, panicked about essays, and looking for reassurance, hounding their favorite teachers for recommendation letters. Deirdre normally had upward of fifteen or twenty to write and she wondered who would take up the slack. The new students would be settled in by now, feeling at home, no longer awkward about participating in school traditions, singing the alma mater as if they'd known it all their lives; no longer having to peek at the cheat sheet they kept jammed in their pockets for the Friday assemblies; calling the teachers by the inevitable nicknames passed down from class to class; teachers would be excited about the upcoming Thanksgiving break, eager for the first real vacation from the franticness that is back-to-school. Though truthfully, the beginning of the holidays didn't really give anyone much rest, not until Christmas—and there would be the knowing looks from one teacher to another. *Hang on,* they would say. *It won't be too long now.* Even Beth Ann seemed no longer new to town, to the school. She had talked about Brandywine as if she'd been part of it for years.

Just thinking about it all exhausted Deirdre. Part of

her wanted to see the girls, or at least let them know she was thinking about them, wondering how they were doing without her. Part of her envied Madame Delambre, forging relationships with the students, becoming their new connection to French and the French-speaking world. And some part of her wanted to forget that she had taught at Brandywine, or that she'd ever taught at all. Just seeing Beth Ann had brought the girls' neediness right into the house, and where once Deirdre might have been exhilarated by it, now she felt a mixture of anxiety, fatigue, and still, yes, a jolt of adrenaline. It was tricky, this business of being needed. Deirdre had been unaware of it in such an intense way until now, and she wondered how much being needed had fueled SJ's desire to help Mickey Gilberto. She wanted to talk with SJ about all that, but at the same time, she couldn't. She couldn't bring herself to even mention Mickey Gilberto's name. They still had not talked about Deirdre's adventure in Provincetown, either, and both of those topics hovered in the air, a palpable heaviness. Maybe they might not ever talk about them. Couldn't she and SJ forge ahead and create a new, longer-lasting relationship? Couldn't they make this thing work together? At the moment, it felt like they could, and that was enough for Deirdre.

CHAPTER FIVE

AND SUDDENLY, IN EARLY NOVEMBER, Anna Worthington recanted.

She came downstairs and announced that no, Ms. Murphy hadn't "gone after her," hadn't made her feel uncomfortable, groped or touched her, hadn't been inappropriate with her in any way.

"But I saw the two of you kissing," her mother said.

"You thought you saw," Anna insisted. She was tired of being left out at school, of the other girls insisting that they, too, had kissed—or had been kissed by—Ms. Murphy. They were saying it, Anna was sure, to make fun of her, to show the school how silly it was to believe her story, how it couldn't be true if all of them were saying it.

"I know what I saw." Her mother wouldn't back down.

"What you saw—" Anna spun around to face her mother at the kitchen island, "was me kissing her, okay? I kissed her. That's the way it went."

Her mother sputtered, "It . . . it's inappropriate . . . it's her fault . . ."

"Oh for God's sake, Mother! Stop it. Just stop it. This whole thing is out of control. *I* did it. Have me kicked out of Brandywine, why don't you?" And she stormed off to her room.

For a long while, Anna had believed her mother when

she said that everything that happened was Ms. Murphy's fault. She believed it when her mother said that Ms. Murphy had crossed the line with all the girls. "I'm not surprised," her mother had said when they heard about the other, more recent accusations. "There will be more, mark my words."

"You think she was after us?" Anna had asked back when they were first discussing the "incident in the van."

"Homosexuals are known predators," her mother had said. "They have to convert children. I know it sounds silly, but that's what they do."

"So you think she deliberately set out to . . . to brainwash us? Get us to . . ." and Anna had paused for a second, felt herself blush, "fall in love with her?"

"In a manner of speaking, yes. I think that's exactly what she did."

At first, Anna wanted to believe it. She wanted to think she had no control over how she felt, that it was a spell that made her feel crush-y and lightheaded and like she never wanted to leave Ms. Murphy's room. She didn't want to acknowledge that it might be *her*. So she found herself thinking about her mother's words and wondered if it might really be a good idea to prevent gay people from teaching. Hadn't life been easier when Hilary, Lydia, and she spent their time looking for dresses for the sophomore semiformal, wondering who to ask from among the St. Michael's boys they knew?

When the girls first approached her about getting Ms. Murphy in trouble, she stood her ground. "It's not my fault," she told them. "She doesn't belong here. She's affecting all of us."

Lydia had spoken up immediately: "Oh my God, you're ridiculous!"

Hilary had grabbed Lydia's arm. "See? I told you. Forget it." She pulled Lydia to leave.

Only Morgan Abernathy had listened with any real interest.

And Morgan was the only one still by her side.

Now, here it was, close to Thanksgiving break, and Anna had never felt lonelier. She'd spent hours and hours going over it, trying to remember if Ms. Murphy had ever, even slightly, encouraged her, had ever let Anna think that she had thought of her as something other than one of her French students. Anna replayed those early weeks of school, all the minutes that led up to the final one, when she found herself alone in the van with her favorite teacher, a woman who took up much of her imagination, and Anna had some-how found the courage to kiss her.

When the charges were dropped, the *Boston Globe* featured the story on page one of the Metro section and the *Register* had it right there on the front page.

One day later, Lydia called Anna. "Hey," she said. "Saw the news. That's cool. But what happened?"

Anna blinked back tears. "I guess it wasn't really her fault, you know?"

"Too bad she got fired though, huh?"

Anna couldn't hear any particular tone in Lydia's voice, just a kind of tiredness or sadness. "Yeah. I think what's done is done though. That's what my mother says."

At that, Anna was certain she heard Lydia hesitate. "You know she's moving? Hilary heard she's moving to P-town. Guess she'll be happier."

"Do you think she'll teach there?" Anna asked in a quiet voice.

"Dunno," Lydia said. "I doubt it."

"Yeah." Anna took a deep breath and sighed. She couldn't help it. The tears fell. "I'm really sorry."

"I know," Lydia said.

They made tentative plans to hang out over Thanksgiving.

"Maybe a movie or something?" Lydia suggested.

"I didn't mean to ruin everything," Anna said, blowing her nose. "But I did, didn't I?"

"The others will come around. Hilary will come around. It'll be okay."

CHAPTER SIX

FEAR STILL PERMEATED THE AIR IN BRADLEY. Worse now that the bright sunshine seemed to be permanently gone, replaced with gray skies and that cold, piercing wind. Mickey Gilberto still had not been brought to trial, but he had been formally charged. The *Globe* reported another man too, someone the article alleged had done the actual killing, an older man, someone Mickey had met in a chat room. The *Register* reported accusations back and forth, each man insisting the other was mainly responsible. The fact that both men had been apprehended might have been enough to put people's minds at ease but still somehow an uneasy tension lingered. You could feel it woven through conversations, an invisible string linking everyone together. SJ thought of it like an old house, a stately Victorian, nicely painted and detailed, but, on closer inspection, in desperate need of updating, with its peeling ceilings and drafty windows, hidden pipes leaky with terrible plumbing. It was hard to tell whether folks felt scared for their children—it wasn't as if fewer children appeared out of doors, or the after-school kids stopped coming to the library, though SJ did feel a kind of distance from a few of the parents who picked them up—real or imagined, she couldn't say. There was no way to determine what they knew; if, for example, they knew that SJ had been teaching Mickey Gilberto to read, and so therefore was contaminated by close proximity, or whether they knew that Deirdre-Murphy-the-child-molester-teacher was her partner.

SJ felt branded with an expiration date, past due. "I think we need to move," she had said to Deirdre, and then realized what that meant, what she was suggesting.

She watched the hope on Deirdre's face, heard the careful monitoring of that hope in her voice when she answered: "But I love this house, don't you?" And then, "I'm open to it. Let's see."

Gone, at least, the leaden weight of the arrest and looming trial. Those days had gaped with uncertainty, great yawning crevasses that made you want to leap off the edge. The town meeting over which everyone was still arguing; the endless letters to the editor, some even now still appearing like out-of-season Christmas cards, the sentiments sincere-sounding but so long after the fact that you wondered, *Why bother?* What was the sense in doing it now, except to jump on the bandwagon? The conversation had changed; the charges had been dropped.

Of course, for SJ and Deirdre, things were far from settled. Deirdre still didn't have a job. And SJ still had the apartment; she had to make a definitive decision—break the lease, sublet, or something else. Deirdre had not yet divulged details about her little escape to Provincetown. And for her part, SJ certainly had said nothing about seeing Mickey at his garage, and nothing about the kiss. So there were definitely things to be worked out. If they could be worked out.

A fog had settled over Bradley, a brooding gray that was the result of the weather, yes, but also of this other constant element—fear, nervousness, distrust. SJ likened it to Puritan times, the way she had felt as a kid reading about them. She remembered now the glum feeling she had experienced, curled on the couch in the Marblehead house or in bed with the comforter pulled up to her chin, reading those books for her English classes. She remembered the unshakable feeling of doom and sadness; she had wondered then how the Puritans could be the precursors for so much that Americans, or at least New Englanders, took for granted—the work ethic, town meetings, and education. She remembered how gray everything had been in her imagination, how the characters seemed to move through their lives in a slow shuffle. Funny that now, walking around Bradley, SJ saw the town through the same pallor and she could swear her legs felt weighted down, however bright her daydreams.

In the East End, things were a bit different. There, the feeling was one mostly of sadness, palpable and with its own particular weight, but less gray, less accusatory. This part of town had endured so much loss, though still the kids played outside at recess at Most Precious Blood, and still the boys shot hoops in the park, and still girls strolled to the corner store and giggled with their girlfriends. There was still Bingo on Wednesday nights in the church hall, still buyers for lottery tickets, still boys careening on their BMX bikes and skateboards. But to SJ at least, all of this went on as if under a veil, thinly layered and ever present.

At work, the other librarians and staff gave SJ a wide berth. Elliot chatted with her less frequently or went out of his way to find Florence when normally he would come to SJ with questions. Florence remained her steadfast self, but even she seemed less inclined to hang out with SJ during lunch break or linger over morning coffee as they used to.

On this day, SJ cornered her. "Florence . . ."

She looked startled, surprised to hear SJ's voice, see her standing so close to the photocopy machine. "Sara Jane . . . hello." Florence adjusted her scrimshaw. She was wearing a new silk blouse, one that SJ hadn't seen before.

"You're avoiding me." SJ crossed her arms.

Florence flipped through the papers she held in one hand. "I've been busy. You know that."

"Busy," SJ nodded. "But that's just an excuse, isn't it?"

Florence blushed. "I thought you might need your space, a little time. I didn't want to intrude." She shifted the pile of papers. "I'm glad—it's good that the charges have been dropped, isn't it? That must be a huge relief. I'm happy. For you both." She started to walk away.

SJ wanted to grab her; she half-wished Florence would give her a hug. "You were right about Mickey Gilbero," she blurted.

Florence turned and gave a little smile. "I'm just glad things are settled." She walked back toward her office, heels clicking on the floor.

Sometime that afternoon, after Florence and Elliot and the others had left the library, after the streetlights had come on and the dark had overtaken everything, SJ found herself sitting in her office, at her desk, looking again at the picture of Deirdre taken on the Cape. She saw again someone she would hardly recognize now, a version of Deirdre she hadn't seen in years. And somehow, in that beach memory that was preserved in the way that photographs have of turning the past into a kind of lie, SJ was catapulted back to Marblehead, to the landscape of her youth, a place she visited rarely now and viewed only through a grainy and safe distance.

Early in their relationship, Deirdre had insisted that they were both boat people and therefore destined to be together. And while it was true that Gloucester and Marblehead share a coastline and that thick New England air, Gloucester's harbor is full of fishing vessels and lobster boats, while Marblehead's is panoramic, a distinguished collection of leisure crafts—lovely wooden and fiberglass sailboats, several yachts, a schooner or two.

SJ had laughed. "I've never been on a boat."

"From Marblehead and you've never been on a boat?"

"Nope. Didn't own one. Didn't know anyone who owned one."

"How is that even possible?" Deirdre had said. "Isn't that like living in Maine but never eating lobster?"

But SJ had just smiled. "I'm sure there are Mainers who are allergic."

"Okay, but boats . . . you can't be allergic to boats."

"We just didn't know anyone who had one. It's not that strange."

Still, Deirdre maintained that boats were their common denominator. "There's something about growing up around them. I don't know. It's silly maybe. I just think there are things we'll immediately get about each other."

But growing up around boats had meant for Deirdre a rough-soled existence, all salty sand and mist. Not so for SJ. Her growing up had been the country club and polo shirts. She didn't have that same feeling about the coastline as Deirdre, no matter how much Deirdre insisted she did.

"I'm sorry to disappoint you," SJ had insisted, "I simply don't have that love of the ocean that you do."

Deirdre couldn't be dissuaded. "It's there. You've just buried it deep."

At first, SJ found Deirdre's certainty amusing. She would laugh. "Whatever you say. I've buried it deep." But after some time together, SJ didn't understand why Deirdre couldn't see that she had been wrong. Even after knowing SJ, hearing about her childhood, meeting her parents and visiting their home, experiencing its austerity and lack of warmth—still, she had insisted they shared a common culture and love.

"Look," SJ said during one of their Cape Cod trips, maybe the very one from the photograph, "I enjoy the

beach. But I don't have this love affair with it like you do."
She could see the way Deirdre lit up immediately whenever
they spent time at the beach. Or whenever they went to Boston, even—the harbor there a far cry from either Gloucester
or Marblehead, but still, Deirdre seemed to revel in the at-
mosphere. She seemed to come alive, walk with more skip
and confidence. SJ wondered why Deirdre hadn't wanted to
live on the water then. But Deirdre had insisted that she'd
left that life behind.

"I get nostalgic for it, I guess. But live there? No way."

SJ couldn't point out what a contradiction she was, the
way Deirdre moved through the world of fish and seaweed,
salt water and air—even the replicas they visited, even if it
wasn't Gloucester—those worlds she navigated with a confidence and ease. She was completely herself. And this one
they lived in—the private school world of Brandywine, of
Bradley, their neighborhood—in this world, Deirdre's ca-
dence shifted, her gait was less jaunty.

And it was in this moment, the photograph on the desk
in front of her, that SJ knew with a clear certainty that she
wouldn't move with Deirdre.

CHAPTER SEVEN

DEIRDRE STUCK TWO MORE PHOTOS in the cardboard box, their plastic frames scratched and old and needing to be replaced. She was following the realtor's advice, trying to declutter and remove enough pictures to make the house seem like it could be anybody's and not uniquely, specifically theirs. The realtor said that when people were looking at houses to buy, they liked to imagine themselves in the house and not feel as if they were peeking in on someone else's life.

Deirdre hated the thought of people traipsing through their house. It was one thing to show off your house to friends—even to interested acquaintances; it was another to have people you didn't know walking about, looking with a critical eye, appraising your home. Deirdre herself wasn't like that. She was, she knew, a realtor's dream. She had fallen in love with each house she and SJ had looked at. She could always see the possibilities—the potential—even if there wasn't much to go on. She liked the fenced-in courtyard in one, the nonworking fireplaces in another. She liked the large pantry in that expensive blue Victorian they had looked at early on, the bay window in the white one.

Deirdre lifted the box of photos, grabbed one from the bookshelf, and shoved it beneath the flap. She stuck her feet back into her slippers and scuffed into the dining room, plunked the box on the floor in front of the china cabinet.

In this house, Deirdre had loved the idea of the couple she and SJ might become. She thought she loved the built-in china cabinet, the unfinished upstairs, the shiny black-and-chrome appliances in the kitchen, sunlight in the living room. But of course they had been fooling themselves. The nostalgia tugged at her, threatened to spill into sadness, but mostly she felt relief. As soon as she and SJ had made the decision to split, after the tears and the apologies, Deirdre felt a release, an instant lifting of tension.

She looked around the dining room again and sighed. It was nearly twelve thirty and the open house would start at two. She needed to take a shower and pick up the balloons she'd promised to bring to Sophie's birthday party. Deirdre was still surprised that Kris had reached out. The other day, she had called to ask for help with face painting and to see if Deirdre could pick up balloons. Deirdre had promised to be there by one thirty and now she was going to be late.

Deirdre pulled up in front of Paul and Kris's house, a large stucco Tudor-style with a lush green manicured lawn. She always felt like a kid when she visited them. They lived in a house that was more than twice the square footage of Deirdre and SJ's house. They had furniture *sets*—not the kind of eclectic, garage-sale style that Deirdre and SJ lived with. *Postdorm*, Forest had called it the one time he drove home with Deirdre. Their lawn—Kris referred to it as the *grounds*—needed the work of a part-time gardener. Kris "required" a house cleaner even though she herself didn't work outside the home. What she did all day, Deirdre couldn't imagine. And why there wasn't time for her to clean the house, Deirdre didn't understand. Kris hardly let the kids get the house dirty to begin with.

Deirdre stood at the front door, balloons in one hand, the other poised to ring the bell. She heard high-pitched squeals coming from around back. She glanced at her watch: 2:10.

"You're late." Kris opened the front door before Deirdre had a chance to ring the bell. "I was getting worried." Kris was wearing brown linen pants, a brown shell, and a cream-colored cardigan with brown and golden leaves. The gold buttons were leaf-shaped too. She took the bouquet of balloons, her nails perfectly manicured and painted a deep mauve. "Come in," she said. "The girls are all here. They're out back." She turned, her blond hair bobbed and styled just so. She wore brown leather sandals that clacked on the tiled floor.

Deirdre glanced down at her own khakis and long-sleeved T. "I thought we were going to play games," she said. She'd pulled her hair back with a rubber band and opted for sneakers at the last minute. "I thought we'd be running around." She followed Kris to the kitchen in the back of the house.

Kris pointed to the table. "I've got all the makeup for face painting. The girls want manicures as well. Can you do those too?"

Deirdre laughed.

"It's okay," Kris said, grabbing a bottle of Perrier from the refrigerator, "they'll be happy if you just paint their nails. And I bought some decals for you to stick on too, if they want."

"Isn't that more up your alley? I'm good with the running games—you know, organize some kickball or relay races or . . ." She looked around. "Where's Paul? And Mark?"

Kris unscrewed the top from her Perrier. "They're out on their mountain bikes." She rolled her eyes. "Guy-bonding while we're having some girl-bonding. It's the first sunny day in weeks."

"They're missing Sophie's birthday party?"

The glass door slid open. "Dee Dee! Dee Dee!" Sophie ran in and threw her arms around Deirdre's waist.

"Aunt Deirdre," Kris corrected. She walked over to pull the door shut.

"Hey, Sophe! How's the birthday girl?" Deirdre ran her hand through Sophie's long blond hair. She looked like a miniature version of her mother—that perfect hair, sharp blue eyes. "I like your outfit. Did you get it new?" Sophie was wearing navy cargo pants and a navy-and-white-striped pullover. Deirdre took Sophie's hand and stepped back. "Very cool."

"See, Mom?" Sophie spun toward Kris. "Told you it would be better than a dress." She turned back to Deirdre. "Mom wanted me to wear a dress." She made a face.

"You like dresses," Deirdre said. "I've seen you wear lots of them—pretty ones too, I might add."

"Thank you," Kris said to Deirdre. "Anyway, she wanted to wear these, so why not? It's her birthday, right?" Kris pushed her hair behind her ears.

Sophie looked up at Deirdre and rolled her eyes again. "Mom says you're going to do the makeup? Cool." She pulled Deirdre outside by the hand.

"Face paint." She twisted to look over her shoulder at Kris.

"Hey, sweetie," Kris knelt next to Sophie, "can you let Aunt Deirdre and Mommy talk for a minute? We'll be right there. Take these out back." She handed Sophie the balloons and turned to Deirdre. Once Sophie was out of earshot, she pulled the sliding door shut and said, "Listen, I know you've been going through an awful lot. And I'm really sorry." Deirdre felt herself tense, felt the heat rise to her neck and face. "I'm sorry that Paul isn't here."

"So, it isn't really bonding time with Mark . . ."

Kris put down the Perrier. "Bit of both, truth be told.

But it was my suggestion. I wanted to talk with you alone because, well, sometimes Paul just doesn't get things. We've been following the news of course. And reading the paper, all those horrible editorials, the letters and all. And we're so glad that girl came to her senses and dropped the charges." Kris laughed. "Paul says you're moving."

"Yeah. To Provincetown . . ."

"What'll you do there?" She crossed her legs.

"Mom? Dee Dee?" Sophie pulled open the door again. "C'mon!" Cool autumn air blew in, bright with November sunshine.

"I don't know," Deirdre said to Kris. She followed Kris to the backyard. The picnic table was covered with an orange tablecloth patterned with black cats. Bowls of chips and Doritos and popcorn sat on top.

Sophie and her friends careened around.

"There's an opening at the arts center there that I'm going to look into. And I have a lead on an apartment."

Kris smiled. "Well, it will be terrific to know someone we can visit in Provincetown! Sophie won't let us go too long without coming to see you, that's for sure." She rubbed her arms. "It's chillier out here than I thought."

Deirdre looked at her niece, standing now in the middle of a group of girls, all ten-year-old confidence and swagger. She hoped Sophie might stay that way, feisty and sure of herself. She had a hard time picturing her turning into one of those needy high school girls, but you never knew.

"I'm sorry about you and SJ." Kris took a chip from the bowl.

"It's okay—thanks. But you know, it really is for the best. For both of us. She's actually going to help me move."

Kris laughed again. "You . . . girls!" She shook her head. "It's just that breaking up—it's a lot to go through right now, isn't it?"

Deirdre nodded. "It is—but it's fine. I think we both realized something going through this whole ordeal." She didn't mention SJ's apartment or how hurt she had been to find out she had kept it the whole time. Nor did she mention her own fling that SJ certainly had suspected but hadn't known about until they both disclosed everything. She didn't tell Kris about the night SJ came home from the library after working late, how she had sat down next to Deirdre on the couch and said that she wasn't going to move to Provincetown and didn't think being together was right anymore, how once the words were spoken, Deirdre felt as though she had been holding her breath and could finally exhale. Yes, she had agreed, it would be better for both of them if she moved on by herself.

"Hey, who wants face paint?" she said now. She grabbed Sophie's hand and led the troupe of girls inside.

THE BOGEYMAN

The *Register* named the accomplice: Gerald McPhee. Convicted felon. Child molester. He wasn't from Bradley, a fact that made people relax a little bit, relish the feeling that at least someone "like that" hadn't grown up in their very midst. If Gerald McPhee wasn't actually from Bradley, didn't actually live in the town, then people could go back to thinking that Bradley was a good place where unspeakable things did not happen to children. People could think they had chosen well, that they were living where they were meant to—or any other such notion people tend to develop about their lives. Bradley hometown pride was again justified.

Of course, there was still Mickey Gilberto, but the stories made you think that if Mickey hadn't met Gerald McPhee, then, well, who knows? Gerald McPhee was a bad man, and somehow, someway, he convinced Mickey Gilberto to kidnap his next-door neighbor, and together they did awful things to the boy.

According to the papers, it was Gerald McPhee who had actually killed Leo Rivera, so in truth, Mickey Gilberto himself was the accomplice. This fact, too, made people breathe easier. They understood how someone could be vulnerable, how it was unfortunate but still understandable. *There but for the grace of God*, they thought when they read the journalist's explanation of how the two men met, how Mickey Gilberto had come under the other man's sway, how the holes in his own life left him wanting to please this man, how in spite of everything, Mickey Gilberto was ready to convince little Leo Rivera to get in the car that day back in August.

This story made sense to people. Vulnerability, they understood. Weren't we all susceptible? Couldn't we all point to people that we might do just about anything for? People could see how an older, more experienced person might have power over someone younger and more needy. None of this excused what Mickey Gilberto did. The editorials still called for the death penalty—most of them anyhow.

SJ wondered what Mrs. Gilberto made of this news. Did she, too, feel a bit relieved that at least her son wasn't solely culpable, wasn't the bogeyman people made him out to be? She might wonder how her son met this terrible man. She might regret that there had been any need for her son to connect with Gerald McPhee, might even replay Mickey's entire life in her mind, try to locate the moment when things went most awry, but of course it was too late for any of that. Leo Rivera was gone and there was no bringing him back.

Still, SJ found herself thinking that Mickey hadn't intended to murder Leo Rivera, and that fact alone gave her some solace. She felt sorry for him. What a terrible mess he had made. What a terrible, horrible mess.

CHAPTER EIGHT

DEIRDRE STOOD ON HER DECK, the forwarded letter from Anna Worthington in her hand. *I'm sorry*, Anna had written. *I wish I could take it back. And I hope you love your new place in Provincetown. Brandywine just isn't the same without you. P.S. You will always be my favorite teacher.*

Deirdre was grateful for the apology, small as it was. She was grateful as well that the newspaper had printed an article when the charges had been formally dropped. Beth Ann had come by with a bottle of champagne. Susan and Murray had called. And yet, the damage had been done. She put the floral note card back in its envelope and stuck it in her jean pocket. Here, she felt worlds away from Brandywine and the girls. The afternoon sun warmed her face. The wind was sharp and damp.

Though SJ had applauded her return to the ocean, she had worried that Deirdre might be too far from civilization and get lonely.

"There's the ferry to Boston," Deirdre had reminded her. "More and more people live here year round too."

"Yeah, and they're alcoholics," SJ said. "You sure it's the right move?"

"It suits me. Besides, if I don't like it, I can come back, but I want to try."

SJ had helped her move into the apartment, a lovely

condo that the owner was happy to rent during winter. Deirdre hoped she might convince him to let her stay on, but she was fairly certain she'd have to look for a more permanent place to live come summer. Their house in Bradley was on the market. SJ promised to take care of things on that end and would be in touch once they had buyers.

Deirdre pulled on a heavy sweatshirt and headed out. She walked down Commercial Street, empty now, many of its stores closed for the season, to MacMillan Pier. Fishing boats still bobbed in the water. Scallopers. Lobstermen. Deep-sea boats. An optimistic whale watch company.

The wharf was quiet in the late afternoon; no tourists, not many fishermen either. Boats were either still out, if they were working, or moored if they weren't. The tide was low. Seaweed clung to the wharf posts in thick, dark ribbons. One seagull picked at a crab shell. Two others flew in graceful swoops overhead. The air smelled of fuel and fish, a slick smell, not unpleasant but one that for Deirdre was redolent of an earlier life. She thought of Maria Da Silva, her parents, all those memorial services at Our Lady of Good Voyage. A life she vowed never to be part of. And yet here she was.

She had been drawn to this remote tip of land that curled into the Atlantic as countless others had before her—fishermen, yes, but also artists and writers and all kinds of people who lived on the fringes of society. At the west end of Provincetown, dunes stretched like endless hills of sand and sea grass, not exactly what the Pilgrims had hoped for when they made land and rowed ashore. To them, the Province Lands looked formidable, inhospitable, and they turned their ship the other way, crossed the bay to Plymouth. But sitting on MacMillan Pier, Deirdre felt the rightness of this place in her bones, in her lungs, the deep breaths of cold November air.

She fingered Anna's note in her pocket. It was hard not

to regret things—harder still to let go of the life you thought you wanted, the love you imagined was what you deserved. She had hoped to hear from Forest before she moved, but she hadn't.

"Give him a call," SJ had urged.

"I will," Deirdre had said. And she'd meant it.

She rose, stretched, and headed back down Commercial Street.

In the distance, approaching, a cyclist, wire basket loaded with groceries. Deirdre recognized the hair, the shape of her face.

"I heard you were in town," Jamie said, and skidded to a stop.

"What? Oh my God. You heard?" Deirdre said.

Jamie laughed. "P-town is a village. Everyone knows everything. Besides, you're not exactly anonymous. Apparently, you've been spotted at the A&P."

Deirdre blushed. Her face had been on television and in the papers so many times that she was recognized with some regularity, even here.

"But you've come to the right place," Jamie said. "All kinds of people have sought refuge in P-town and we know how to give them space." She cocked her head. "So, is that what you're after? Or . . . you want to come over for dinner tonight?"

Deirdre smiled and accepted the invitation.

"See you at six!" Jamie called over her shoulder, pedaling away.

A dinner invitation. Salt air and lapping waves. Tomorrow, a job interview. And not a needy girl in sight.

End

Acknowledgments

The Year of Needy Girls has been a long time in the making and there are many people to thank. These words barely convey my gratitude.

First and foremost, I'd like to thank Kaylie Jones for her belief in this book, and Johnny Temple, Susannah Lawrence, and everyone at Akashic for their hard work and support. This is truly a dream come true.

Thank you to my teachers: Marita Golden, Tom De Haven, and Bill Tester. And to Richard McCann for his early encouragement and guidance.

Thank you to everyone in Tom De Haven's novel workshop at Virginia Commonwealth University, where the seeds of this novel began oh so many years ago.

For their invaluable help with research and for taking the time out of their busy lives to explain legal ins and outs, thanks to Detective Sherrie Kendall, Kim O'Donnell, and Irene Good. For showing me around the city jail and spending time to answer all my questions, a big thanks to Sheriff C.T. Woody Jr. and Michael Whitt.

For being patient and honest readers—in addition to dear friends—I'd like to thank Connie Biewald, Ginny Pye, Julianna Nielsen, Mary Langer, Michele Young-Stone, Susann Cokal, and Nathan Long. For encouragement in the early days of this book, I'd like to thank Brenda Giannini and Maribeth Fischer.

I'm grateful for time away to write and I'd like to acknowledge and thank Trudy Hale and the Porches writing retreat as well as Mary Langer and Carrie Grady for generously offering time and space at their own getaway haven in Wallingford, Vermont, and Kim O'Donnell for sharing her little bit of heaven in Floyd, Virginia.

And finally, thanks to Cindy, for everything. My life would not be complete without you.